KATE DOUGHTY

THE FOLLOWER

AMULET BOOKS
NEW YORK

Cataloging-in-Publication Data has been applied for and may be obtained from the Library of Congress.

ISBN 978-1-4197-4801-1

Text copyright © 2021 Abrams
Book design by Hana Anouk Nakamura

Printed and bound in U.S.A.
10 9 8 7 6 5 4 3 2 1

Amulet Books are available at special discounts when purchased in quantity for premiums and promotions as well as fundraising or educational use. Special editions can also be created to specification. For details, contact specialsales@abramsbooks.com or the address below.

Amulet Books® is a registered trademark of Harry N. Abrams, Inc.

ABRAMS The Art of Books
195 Broadway, New York, NY 10007
abramsbooks.com

*To my parents, whose warnings about the dangers
of social media have clearly been taken to heart*

XXXXXXXXXXXXXXXXXXXXXXXXXXXXXX
PROLOGUE

The cassette slips out of Alex's trembling hands and clatters to the floor. She dives for it, and when she picks it up, her hands are still shaking. She whips around, half-convinced that she's being watched, but the third-floor hallway is empty. She reaches back into the house's ancient dumbwaiter—a favorite hiding spot—and pulls out a tape recorder.

Below her, she can hear the soft noise of the radio and the occasional clatter as her mother makes dinner for Frank. Normal sounds. Homey sounds. Sounds that don't fit with how off she feels. The stairs behind her go down, down, down all the way to the first floor, where her mother is blissfully unaware of Alex's terror, humming and making pasta and waiting for Alex's father to get home from work. She doesn't believe Alex. No one does.

The hallway is empty but Alex still feels too exposed. So she climbs the staircase up to the fourth floor of the mansion. The turret room.

A small bed is tucked into a nook, overhung with a pink tulle awning. The walls are covered in paintings of the flora and fauna of upstate New York; the bay window looks out onto a beautiful view ending in the faint silhouettes of far-off mountains.

Alex sees none of this. Instead she crouches down and fumbles with the tape player, ready to listen. Listen for—something she can't quite place. Some kind of proof of what she suspects. Of the danger that she is in.

She stands up and goes to the door. Locks it.

Alex sits on the floor, inserts a blank white tape into the recorder with a familiar *snick*, and presses *Play*.

A loud *thump* echoes from below. The hair on Alex's arms prickles. "Mom?" she asks, her voice quiet and shaky. Something feels strange; something is wrong.

"Dad?" It's not until her voice comes out that Alex realizes how close she is to crying. *Maybe he is home. Maybe*... She rushes to the open window, leaning out and scanning for his car in the driveway below.

Alex chokes off a scream.

Her mother is in the driveway. But it isn't her mother, because Mom's eyes aren't glassy like that; Mom's limbs don't bend in that way, jointless and broken, like a rag doll's. Mom isn't bleeding from a gash in her chest— she can't be, because Mom is in the kitchen, making lasagna and singing to herself...

Except the house is quiet. Quiet except for one soft noise behind Alex. A soft noise that Alex can't hear over her panicked breathing, over the terror of seeing Mom like that, so far down below, so still that she can't possibly be real.

The soft *click* of the dead bolt unlocking.

Alex is still staring down at her mother when something *slams* into her from behind. She lurches forward and the cassette player falls to the floor. Buttons mash; *Record* pops up in place of *Play*.

For one long second, Alex is in the air. Weightless.

And then she is not.

The sound of Alex's impact fades into a still, thick silence. Inside the turret room, the door is locked once more. The sound of footsteps—normal now, not the catlike quiet it had once been—slowly fades as they descend toward the two bodies on the pavement. In the space before the sirens, the screams, a father's cries of anguish, there is only one noise. One noise, so soft that it would be impossible to catch unless someone knew it was there. Unless someone was listening, very closely, for it.

The *click-a click-a* of a cassette reaching the end of its tape.

Midsized home renovation/family vlog channel. Instagram, Twitter, YouTube. Content specializes in renovation, DIY, and slice-of-life entries from teenage triplets and house-flipper parents. Most-viewed posts: Our New MANSION (For 3 months) (NOT CLICKBAIT)│Get ready with Cecily Cole (MUST-SEE MAKEUP)│PRANKING MY SISTERS: Paint Edition (SHE CRIES) (NOT CLICKBAIT)│

XXXXXXXXXXXXXXXXXXXXXXXXXXXXXXX
CHAPTER 1

Amber

CECILY'S LAUGH ECHOES ACROSS THE LAWN.

"No, not like that," says Rudy. "Laugh *prettier.*"

Cecily stops laughing and glares at Rudy.

"Just a few more," Amber coaxes from behind the camera. She needs just one more good picture of her sister. "Leg out, back arched, label to camera—"

Cecily repositions herself and smiles warmly up at Amber's phone. Amber can't stop herself from thinking how gorgeous Cecily is. Tanned skin, waves of blond hair, tiny waist. Crystal glass raised in celebration. Behind her, party lights twinkle on the patio. The suits and bright cocktail dresses of far-off guests fade into the background as she extends one pointed foot—a trick to make her legs look even longer—and pops a hip to maximize the effect of her skintight dress.

"Perfect," Rudy says. "And . . . laugh. But pretty this time!"

"Ignore him. And don't laugh; cough," Amber instructs. It's one of her tricks; the secret to a "candid" laughter pic. Amber knows all the tricks to a good Instagram picture by now. After all, it's been the Cole family's livelihood for years. She's already contemplating the best filter to use: probably Evanscene or Nightglow. Party lights surround Cecily like a halo. It's perfect for a lavish party, for the mansion-studded life of the infamous Cole Family Realty.

She'll barely even have to edit it. Cecily looks *that* good.

Cecily coughs. Amber snaps pictures. Cecily continues to cough. It sounds like she's dying.

"Done," Amber says finally, exiting the camera app and opening her editing software. This will have to be a low-key edit on one of the half-dozen photography apps she has installed on her phone; they do have a party to get back to, after all. Even though her mother probably would consider Amber's disappearance to edit photos for the rest of the night a worthy sacrifice, she thinks, suppressing an eye roll. She can hear her mother's voice in her head: *Your sister's on the rise! We have to help her all we can!* But does that really mean that Amber has to go from being in every other photo, to every fifth photo, to a rare group shot? Or does her mother really think that the best use of Amber's time is editing Cecily into perfection?

Faster than Amber can blink, Cecily slumps out of photo posture and dumps today's sponsored product—some kind of energy tea—into a nearby shrub. A flask appears in her hand as if by magic, and she refills her cup with a generous splash of gin. Rudy gets the flask next. He takes a pull and passes it to Amber, who waves him off. She's hunched over her phone, busy applying filters, facetune, and color correction to fix Cecily. Bring out the green tones in her blue eyes, erase her almost-nonexistent pores, accentuate the curves of her cocktail dress. When she finishes, she's staring at a perfect version of her sister. And if Cecily is already the perfect version of Amber, then that makes this facetuned stunner double perfect. "Caption," she says, holding her phone screen out for her brother and sister to see.

"You know what they say about Instagram captions," Cecily quips, wiggling the flask in front of her sister's face. "Write drunk, edit sober."

"Oh," Rudy says. "I thought they said to use as many emojis as possible."

"Guys, this is *serious*," Amber says. Rudy snorts.

Her sister swipes the phone from Amber's hand and starts typing. "Here: how about, *Never sorry to soiree—Happy 20th, Mom and Dad. Here's to our newest project.*"

"Don't forget to—"

"I'm going to add the sponsors. *Sheesh*, you're starting to sound like Mom," Cecily mutters, leaning back to hold the phone out of her sister's reach. Amber is annoyed, but the feeling passes quickly. It's hard to stay mad at Cecily. Cecily, the up-and-coming beauty guru. Perfect Cecily, who genuinely believes that makeup is about confidence, about *feeling* beautiful, not just beauty itself. Of course, that's easy for her to say.

Amber supposes that, in another world, she would be in front of the camera 24/7 with her sister, not behind it—if, of course, she were about twelve sizes smaller. Even though she shares Cecily's dimples, perfect teeth, and loose, wavy hair, on Instagram it seems like the only thing that matters is her size. Online, size eighteen doesn't exactly pull followers—or at least, that's what Mom had hinted as she slowly edged Amber out of their posts. So Amber has been using her once-vlog-worthy knowledge of the latest fashion trends to help dress the family in between shooting and editing photos of her siblings. Lately, she appears in the occasional group shot. A quick acknowledgment of the camera girl.

Not for the first time, Amber wonders how she went from being one of a trio to being behind the scenes. Of course, she knows why: engagement. But just because her mother thinks that their Cecily- and Rudy-centric posts perform better doesn't mean that Amber *likes* being pushed to the background. Or that it doesn't hurt.

Amber is jolted out of her thoughts by Cecily shaking the flask in front of her face. "Come on, loosen up." She hands the phone back to Amber, who adds one more line before posting the photo with a caption: *Staying fit this summer with @BoostEnergy. #mansion #renovation #soiree #summer #coletriplets #tripletsofinstagram.*

"There, you posted it," Cecily says, looping her arm through Amber's. "Can we just have fun now?"

"Hey, I was always having fun," Rudy cuts in. Amber rolls her eyes and finally takes the flask, filling her glass halfway to the top.

"To the move," Rudy says.

"To being done with work for the rest of this stupid party," Amber adds.

"To our careers," Cecily says. "One million followers, here we come." She shoots her siblings a playful wink. "Don't worry, I won't forget you when I'm a famous beauty guru."

On Instagram, Cecily's perfect laugh and evening makeup are broadcasted to the hundreds of thousands of users following the Cole triplets under their account name @ColeTripsHouseFlips. The post includes three other pictures to please the algorithm: one of the three siblings an hour ago, taken by Mom; another of Rudy, flexing next to a pyramid of hors d'oeuvres; and another of the house they're partying at—the one they're about to leave.

The three-million-dollar McMansion is the latest in a long line of opulent houses that Cole Family Realty has bought, remodeled, and resold for double the price. The downstairs is decked out in splendor for Mr. and Mrs. Cole's twentieth-anniversary party, all string lights, pricey decor, and fragile tchotchkes. Upstairs, the rooms are bare. All of Amber's electronics and clothes are packed away. Tomorrow, they will move on to the next fixer-upper. Amber can't complain; sure, moving all the time sucks, but it means a new mansion to play in every few months, and that means a fresh stream of the content that makes the triplets famous. Before and after pictures. Luxury estates. Designer clothes. A window into the life of the rich and richer. Their followers eat it up.

Amber massages her temples with one hand; she'd spent all afternoon editing posts and her head is buzzing from the screen time. But it'll all be worth it when the likes and comments start coming in. The Cole Patrol— their fanbase—is always super vocal at going-away parties. Speculating on the next place, wishing them well—Amber watches the number of likes on their last post soar and feels the familiar rush that comes with being *popular*, with being *liked.* Successful. Even if she is the least visible member of the trio, she could still share some of their glory, right?

She knows that the moment Rudy and Cecily hit their beds tonight, they'll be scrolling through comments and DMs, responding to fans. Cecily, of course, will give supportive comments about her fans' makeup looks and take suggestions for products or looks to try in her future videos. Rudy, as always, will report on the latest internet drama when he isn't acting as the "host" of the trio, leading livestreams, vlogs, and progress posts about the renovations. The renovation focus had moved to the forefront of his content once their mom took a larger role in managing their account. Amber knows her brother isn't a fan of the content itself, but she often catches

Rudy up late at night, chatting with fans and taking suggestions for his next video.

Amber also doesn't mind responding to the occasional DM. She loves seeing people react to Cecily's makeup looks or give feedback on their renovations. It feels surreal to be a part of so many people's lives like that. To have so many people know her—or, at least, her and her siblings. It gives her more than a small thrill. The irony that Cecily is the one who probably enjoys the attention—and all that comes with it—the *least* is not lost on Amber.

Rudy groans and nods his head in the direction of their parents. "You'd better drink up. Mom's waving us over to mingle."

Cecily takes another sip. "How do I look?" she asks.

Compared to the facetune? A little shiny. "You look great," Amber says.

Cecily eyes her sister up and down before giving her a friendly elbow. "I don't care if the algorithm favors it," she says, half-laughing. "We have to stop matching. This green totally makes your eyes pop, mine look like . . . dirt or something. And having to stand next to those curves in a bodycon dress is just *not* fair."

Amber can't resist a small smile, but she's still in work mode. "Matching increases our engagement by—"

"Okay, you two," Rudy mutters, grabbing his sisters and steering them through the garden and toward the terrace, where fairy lights shimmer over a sea of guests. Their parents are surrounded by a cloud of lawyers, businessmen, realtors, and other adults trying to show off their wealth. The usual suspects, here to ogle carpeting and crown molding and the latest in ostentatious interior design. They look exactly how anyone would expect: overdrawn lipstick, tight sport jackets, smiles that are just a bit too wide. Amber can't help but notice several god-awful fashion choices. They've clearly dressed up in an attempt to impress the Coles and are failing miserably if you ask Amber, whose top rule of fashion is to wear what makes *you* feel gorgeous, not what someone else might think is "cool" or "in." But judging from the way so many of the guests are fiddling with the buttons of their blazers or tugging at the seams of their dresses, most of them likely dressed up for the Coles first and themselves second.

But Amber almost doesn't fault them for trying. Almost.

It is, after all, the social event of the summer. The Coles spared no expense for their twentieth-anniversary soiree: tuxedoed waiters, top-shelf liquor, roving platters of oysters. The patio is buzzing with what Rudy calls "sneaky small talk" and Cecily calls "being fake" as the adults try to assess one another. Amber likes to sit in the background and play a game with herself, translating the conversations into their real meanings.

"I love that dress. Where's it from?" *What brands are you wearing?*

"How's your commute? Where do you work?" *How prestigious is your neighborhood? What's your salary?*

"How do you know the Coles?" *How big is your house? How expensive, how old, how state-of-the-art renovated?*

"Got any weekend plans?" *Do you have a summer home? What, you don't have a lake house? My god, are you even* worth *talking to?*

Mr. and Mrs. Cole are making said small talk with Ms. Lonetti, a financial advisor and recurring guest at their ridiculous parties. She spots the triplets and beckons them over with a jeweled hand, flashing teeth too white to be real. "Oh, aren't you three a-*dor*-able!" she says. "Matching outfits! Did you do that, Marie?"

Mrs. Cole's laugh is sweet and bubbly like champagne. "No," she says. "They do that all on their own."

Amber and Cecily exchange a glance. As *if* Amber or Cecily would even *consider* dressing matchy-matchy if their mother hadn't meticulously planned their outfits for the highest degree of follower engagement. Amber shoots Cecily a half-apologetic look, and her sister responds with a half smile and an eye roll, as if to say, *Remember when our Instagram account used to be just for fun?*

But the costume is effective. Their outfits—dark green bodycon dresses that Amber had chosen for the occasion—match in everything except size, which Amber is all too aware of. Of course, dressing identically increases more than their follower engagement—it also increases the number of lewd comments about threesomes. Even though they thrive on positive fan engagement, Amber dreads reading through the account's creepier DMs.

Rudy completes the Cole sibling look in khakis and a navy blue sport jacket with green accents. If Cecily's and Amber's looks reel in the men, he's the reason that half their demographic is girls between the ages of eleven and eighteen. Amber can't help but think that the three of them look exactly on-brand with their Instagram content: like the kind of people who use the word "summer" as a verb, not a noun.

"Well, you look lovely," Ms. Lonetti says.

Mrs. Cole smiles blandly at the financial advisor and steers the triplets across the patio. "Tell me the posts are up," she says. Amber nods. "Excellent—thank you, sweetheart. Now, you three know your places, yes?" she asks. Before they can answer, she inspects them one by one. She un-smudges Cecily's mascara, and Amber watches Cecily's hand twitch in annoyance as she thumbs her clutch. It's one of the few things that Cecily is never without—a basic touch-up kit for moments like these. Because Cecily can't bear to be less than perfect. Rudy and Amber exchange an amused look as their mom fusses over Cecily. Mrs. Cole turns to Rudy next, straightening his tie and artfully mussing his hair. She barely glances over Amber before smiling and saying, "Now, smile and play nice while I go get your father."

Amber scans the party for avenues of escape, but it's too late—their mother has already steered them into the fray. Mom squeezes Cecily's and Rudy's shoulders before vanishing into the crowd. The Cole triplets are officially on display.

Other adults surround them, all pretty, prying, and eager to shape their own multimillionaire children into the next generation of social media stars.

Amber watches as Cecily and Rudy turn "on," plastering on the wide, bright smiles that they reserve for adults at these kinds of gatherings. She puts on her own smile. After so long online, it comes easily. The show starts now.

Ms. Lonetti is replaced by a businessman with a hideous tie. "How are you kids? How's school? How are those posts doing?"

Cecily speaks first. "It's great," she says, beaming. "Sure, we don't get football, but being homeschooled does have its benefits. More time with these two," she says, giving Rudy and Amber a playful shove. "Summer break is still exciting, though!" Amber starts to play the translation game with her siblings, too: *If I have to sit through one more "school day" dedicated to best vlog practices or Instagram stories, I am going to jump off a building.*

The revolving door of party guests continues, and once the booze kicks in it's a whole lot easier to smile through the small talk. The triplets alternate sips of gin with their lines.

"Yes, I'm looking at colleges in California." *No, I'm looking for agents in LA.*

"No, no boys—focusing on school for now." *Eww, you are old enough to be my father.*

"No, we're only seventeen—not eighteen for almost a whole year!" *Creep, creep, CREEP.* Amber can't tell if it's the gin or the lawyer asking the question about when she'll be legal that makes her want to puke.

"Oh, your son has an Instagram? How nice!" *What's his engagement? How many followers does he have? Is he sponsored?*

Just as the smile plastered on Amber's face starts to hurt, a loud clinking sound saves her. Everyone looks toward the stage, and the flood of adults trying to get a piece of the triplets is temporarily distracted. Amber uses the lull in action to whip out her phone and check on the last post. It's doing well; she opens her Instagram and takes in the abundance of internet validation. It feels good, warm, even if the followers are here for Cecily and Rudy, not her.

She combs through the comments. Even though their fanbase is largely supportive—*Cecily, you look amazing! Oh my god, GORGEOUS!*—there are always a few bad ones.

> ➡ Haha, is that a PIMPLE on Cecily's face?

> ➡ Wow, I've never seen a green whale before.

> ➡ Wish I could get you girls together. I'd do some drilling with you two, if you know what I mean 😉

Amber makes a face and deletes the comments. Sure, Mom says that any kind of comment is good for engagement, but even she is okay with cutting the ones that affect their "image."

The gin makes deleting comments easier.

The glass *clinks* again, and a quick elbow from Cecily has Amber stuffing her phone into a matching green clutch and looking up into the eyes of her mother. Mrs. Cole stands next to their father; the couple looks as immaculate as their children. Emerald dress and jewels for Mom, black suit for Dad. Wide smiles, teeth whitened into oblivion. Mrs. Cole strikes the champagne glass one last time.

"Thank you all for coming to our 'little' party," she says, chuckling at her own joke as black-tie waiters filter through the crowd to hand out glasses of champagne. Rudy, who Amber is pretty sure is now tipsy, mimes retching. Their mother gestures at the McMansion looming over the party guests. "Celebrating our sale of this *ah*-mazing refurbished colonial mansion for three-point-one million dollars."

"And, of course, our twentieth-wedding anniversary," Dad cuts in with his trademark grin, eliciting a playful—and choreographed—slap on the shoulder from Mom. The crowd laughs and applauds. They're so cute. So in love.

Amber would believe it a lot more if they hadn't rehearsed it all afternoon. Or if they hadn't spent the last few weeks huddled together, trying their best to fix the family finances.

"Of course, dear," Mom says.

"We are also excited to announce our newest project," Mr. Cole continues, wrapping his arm around his wife. "The Cole family is setting off for gorgeous upstate New York to start on our biggest, most extreme, most expensive project yet: a beautiful eight-thousand-square-foot home that dates back to the eighteen hundreds!" A few gasps from the crowd. *Unnecessary*, Amber thinks. But then again, adults are weirdly dramatic about these things.

"We hit the road tomorrow," Mrs. Cole says. "We're so pleased to be able to bring this historic home back to its former glory and prepare it for another long-term family." After inflating the value by several million dollars, of course.

The crowd lets out another round of applause.

"He's going to say it, isn't he?" Rudy asks, taking a swig of his drink.

"Someone definitely will," Cecily agrees. "My money's on Mom, though."

"Loser finishes their drink."

They clink glasses of spiked seltzer. Amber decides not to ruin their bet by mentioning that Mom delivers the line seventy percent of the time. Mr. Cole continues. "You know, to us, renovating old masterpieces like this one—and our new project, 976 Tremont—is more than just a job."

"We fall in love with each of these houses—" Mrs. Cole starts.

"And watching her fall in love with these homes makes me fall for her all over again," Mr. Cole finishes. The crowd lets out an *aw*. Rudy rolls his eyes. "Many of you know this, but when we started flipping homes, our marriage was in a very . . . rocky place. I'm not proud of it. But I am proud of how these homes have helped us find each other again."

"In fact," Mom says, "you could say that we started out renovating these homes, but managed to renovate our marriage instead." She finishes with a love-struck look at her husband that makes Amber almost feel sick. Rudy lets out a "Ha!" and Cecily dutifully downs the rest of her drink, tottering on her wedge heels.

"If you're curious about seeing the Tremont house—for its beautiful architecture, the progress on its renovation, or, maybe, as a future residency," Mrs. Cole says with a wink, "be sure to follow our lovely, talented children on Instagram! It is Instagram, right darlings? I do so lose track of what you kids are on these days." Amber rolls her eyes. As if the family isn't kept afloat by their sponsorship money. As if Mom doesn't know their follower count off the top of her head.

"Cole triplets!" Rudy calls out on cue, grinning at the crowd. "@Cole TripsHouseFlips!"

"Yes, dear," Mrs. Cole simpers. "They post great before and after pictures, and some snapshots from our daily life as well! They're quite the celebrities—"

"Not real celebrities," Mr. Cole jokes. Rudy glowers.

"*Our* celebrities," corrects Mrs. Cole.

"*Our* celebrities," Rudy mocks, rolling his eyes. Amber watches as Mom finishes up the speech with a few well-placed humblebrags about the selling price of the current mansions, their clientele, how house flipping is really "such a dream."

"More like a nightmare," mutters Rudy. Mrs. Cole finishes the speech, and small talk begins all over again.

After the lights have faded and the catering team finishes clearing the patio, Amber posts one last picture of the McMansion. *So long! Here's to bigger and better things—new house on Friday!* 💯 *#moving #project #renovation #real-estate #triplets.*

Then she braces herself to head inside, where Mom and Dad have doubtlessly already turned on her siblings. It's the one and only perk to being the least popular triplet.

"You really do have to look the part, champ," their father is saying to Rudy. "You could use a little more muscle definition. You do know you're named after a football player, don't you?"

"Rudy was named after a football player?" Cecily asks in mock disbelief. "No way!"

Mrs. Cole hones in on her. "What happened to your dress?" she asks, plucking the spaghetti strap from her daughter's shoulder. "How did this get so wrinkled? You need to be mindful of these things. Editing can only go so far, dear. We'll have to check on how that last post performed," she adds, spotting Amber in the entryway. "Or is that what you were doing on your phone during the party, Amber?"

"I was checking on the sponsored post," Amber mutters. It's her secret weapon: the one thing guaranteed to get Mom to pivot from any conversation topic.

"About that," Mrs. Cole says. "Your father and I were talking and . . . we think we need to up your sponsorship count. This new project is going to take a lot to pull off, but I promise it will be worth it."

Amber and her siblings exchange a look. From what she's heard their parents talking about, it has to be. Mrs. Cole looks at Amber, pleading, and Amber caves for the three of them. "Sure, Mom. However we can help."

Mrs. Cole smiles and puts an arm around her. "That's the attitude! Great job tonight, sweethearts." The tone of her voice almost makes Amber relax a little. Almost. "Now, you three need to get to bed and rest up. Big day tomorrow. New house, new us! Oh, one more thing," she adds, and just like *that* her voice is ice. "You do *not* want to find out what happens if I catch you three drinking at one of our parties again. Understand?"

Amber and her siblings nod.

"Night, darlings." Mom's voice has done another one-eighty, back to chipper. It's a clear dismissal.

As soon as the three turn and head down the hallway, Rudy is mocking their dad underneath his breath. "*Need more muscle definition. As if.*"

"It's just the money stressing them out," Amber says. Her siblings don't respond.

They head upstairs to their rooms for one last time. "Are you guys sad about leaving?" Cecily asks.

"Hell no," Rudy scoffs. He slings an arm around both his sisters' shoulders. "Hey—don't let the parents get to you. The 'gram loves ya, the rest of the summer is going to be amazing, and this house? We've already taken all the photos we can here. It was running out of content anyway."

"Do you think this next house will be . . . it?" asks Cecily, her voice quiet. Amber knows what she means by "it": the house that will finally get the Cole family out of debt. Once they don't have to maximize their sponsorship count to keep the family above water, maybe they can focus on their content and finally breaking one million followers. With that kind of following, it feels like they can do anything—if, of course, they're able to get the family out of debt first. And if their mom agrees to relinquish her control of their account once they do.

"Sure," Rudy says, and Amber thinks that all the small-talk practice must be working. Her brother is getting much better at lying.

➡ **@DaniLovesCats:** Oh my god, you're so gorgeous, I want to die.

217 Likes   Reply

XXXXXXXXXXXXXXXXXXXXXXXXXXXXXXXX

CHAPTER 2

Rudy

"WHAT IS *UP*, COLE PATROL? RUDY ASKS, BEAMING INTO THE CAMera at the followers tuned in to their livestream. Being "on" for the camera comes more naturally to him than it does to Amber and Cecily, so he takes on the role of video "host." He feels his jaw lock up and knows that it's time to turn the camera on his sisters, if only to give himself a break from smiling. He continues. "I hope you people are having a lovely day. I'm here with my sister Cecily..." he says, yanking her into frame. She grins, flips her hair over her shoulder, and gives the camera a thumbs-up. "... my sister Amber..." Amber turns the camera on herself for a split second and gives it a shaky smile before flipping it back on her siblings. "... our parents..." A shot of the Coles, standing on the front steps of their newest mansion. "... and last but not least, Mrs. Armstrong of Herbert and Armstrong Realty, here to give us, and all you guys, the grand tour."

Mrs. Armstrong gives the camera a small, unsure smile. "Excited for it," Mrs. Armstrong says, her voice wavering. The realtor's being camera-shy is fine by Rudy; it'll only make the Coles seem better by comparison.

"But before we go in," Rudy continues, "here is the amazing outside of the new mansion!"

Amber dutifully pans over the exterior of the house. To Rudy, the neighborhood around Tremont Street looks like the kind of place with a homeowner's association that monitors lawn height to the centimeter and gets vicious over Christmas decorations. Of course, the Cole family won't be here long enough to find out. Their timeline is short: six quick weeks to renovate the house, furnishings included, and document it for the 'gram before moving on to the next project—and, as their mother constantly reminds them, the more they shave off that timeline, the better.

All four floors of the house reek of old money and spoiled finery; now, it's speckled with broken windows, peeling paint, and sagging shutters. For some reason, Rudy finds himself thinking of rotten fruit, or a dissonant minor chord. Behind the Coles, a long driveway stretches into the woods toward town. Tremont Street is a few hundred feet behind them, obscured by the trees. The lot is very secluded, but Rudy imagines it will feel a little less isolated once they've finished some much-needed yard work. He tries to picture the mansion when their parents are done with it: repainted exterior; weatherized windows; sleek, open-concept kitchen. Modern, with welcoming castlelike vibes.

"Now, isn't she a beauty?" Mr. Cole asks.

"By the time we're finished, she'd better be," Mrs. Cole mutters, so quietly that only Rudy and his father can hear. Mrs. Cole turns to the camera, and just like that she is on again. It's no secret where Rudy gets his acting talent from. "I'm ready to get started!" she chirps.

Rudy moves behind Amber and watches her phone as she crouches down and maneuvers the camera, catching the house at its worst angles— a.k.a., the best angles for the Coles. On the livestream, comments are already flooding in. Rudy watches their viewer numbers skyrocket into the tens, the hundreds, the thousands of thousands. It makes him dizzy to think about that many people tuning in to them, in to him. He feels flushed with excitement. He bends down and starts to read over Amber's shoulder.

➡ Ungh! Cecily is Soooo Hot.

➡ You've got your work cut out for you! That's the worst mansion I've never seen.

➡ Morticia Addams called.

➡ I want a tour! Especially of the showers ☺

➡ It's mine.

Something about that last comment is . . . strange. He points it out to Amber. She clicks on the avatar.

It is, unmistakably, a picture of their new house. The Tremont house. That's weird.

His eyes scan over the username of the last comment. @Alex_Grable. Amber clicks on the account: no likes, no followers, no posts. Only the one photograph of the house. Created just hours ago. As if it was made for them.

Something about it feels wrong. Wrong and . . . intriguing.

Amber clearly shares his confusion, but she gives him a look that says, *Don't even start speculating.* It's too late; Rudy is already wondering why on earth this account would have a photo of their new house, but there's not much he can do about it right now. He has a livestream to host. Maybe they are just a superfan.

As Rudy turns back to the camera view of the Tremont house, he realizes that the woods around them have gone quiet. All the small animals are silent. A thought comes to him: *This is the kind of silence that means danger.*

Rudy shakes it off; he's just being paranoid.

Amber stops panning and gives him a thumbs-up. Rudy takes a deep breath to brace himself before popping back on camera. "Come on in!" With a sweep of his arm, he leads them through the wide double doors.

Mrs. Armstrong launches right into a description of the foyer. It is vast and empty, complete with a wide, sweeping staircase and worn hardwood floor. There are white squares on the walls where paintings used to hang, back when this place was a home. She mentions proudly that the realty company did a quick cleaning themselves before the Coles arrived. Rudy catches his mother's stern glare and mimes zipping his lips; he knows better than to mention on the livestream that the Coles had been warned that the once-abandoned home is a popular spot with squatters.

It's quiet here, too. Rudy's unease returns.

"The woodwork in here dates back to the eighteen hundreds," Mrs. Armstrong says, beaming at the Cole parents. She seems unclear whether she should be looking at Mr. and Mrs. Cole or at the camera, and her resulting swivel makes Rudy's neck hurt just looking at it. "I do hope you'll retain as much of the original house as possible—there are some lovely features, and it's just so nice to have these historic places preserved, especially in a town like Norton, where they're few and far between . . ."

She trails off as she leads them into the kitchen, eyes drifting to the small cage that had been set up in the corner.

"And, of course, here is Speckles, everyone's favorite rabbit and a reminder to support cruelty-free cosmetics," Cecily chimes in, sweeping open the cage and cradling the dwarf rabbit in her arms. "Who's the cutest little pet?"

Rudy rolls his eyes and chimes in. "Nuisance, more like," he says to the camera, winking. "Should have named him Houdini, the way he keeps escaping and getting into my stuff." The kitchen is now home to the Cole family pet: Speckles the rabbit. A ridiculous name, if you ask Rudy. The Coles moved around too often to have a real pet, but his sister had begged and begged and begged until their parents finally relented—and of all animals, she chose Speckles, a runt-of-the-littler dwarf rabbit that's always managing to escape from his cage and get into Rudy's things. In their last house, Speckles had made one of his great escapes and had been found, along with a smelly pile of rabbit droppings, in Rudy's guitar case. Cecily said that it was his fault for leaving it open on the floor, but still. Rudy gives Speckles a look. It's cute and fuzzy, sure, but it's no dog.

"Aw, you're just jealous that he loves me more," Cecily coos.

"Kids!" Mrs. Cole cuts them off with a gale of fake laughter. "We have a tour to finish!"

"Uh, as I was saying, it would be lovely to preserve the character of this place," Mrs. Armstrong continues. From the look on her face, that does not involve rabbits.

Mrs. Cole gives Mrs. Armstrong the fakest smile that Rudy has ever seen, and that says a lot because he's seen more than his fair share of fake. He knows that the entire downstairs is going to be completely redone. The realtor leads them through the rest of the cramped kitchen that Rudy just *knows* is going to be made open-concept, as well as a study that he can picture their dad sanding bookshelves in. But despite his parents' mention of these—and other—potential upgrades, Mrs. Armstrong keeps talking about the original wood paneling, the hand-carved stair railing . . .

Rudy leans in closer to the camera as she leads them down a particularly decrepit hallway and toward the upstairs. "I smell demolition," Rudy croons. "Lots and lots of demolition. Hey—leave a comment and a like if you want that livestreamed." The second step on the stairs lets out a high-pitched creak as he puts his weight on it, and he makes a face for the camera. Amber smiles; Cecily gives him a loving eye roll. Rudy tries to keep up the energy; sometimes he feels like he's performing as much for his family as for his internet audience.

The grand staircase leads to a landing. Rudy can already picture Mom glossing over the cracked paint and decorating it with expensive, delicate vases. A hallway off the landing contains four bedrooms, two on either side, which the triplets have already laid claim to. Rudy's free weights and guitar are in the largest one, and Cecily has set up a mirror and started unpacking her closet in the room with the best lighting. *For my makeup tutorials.*

Amber's things are in the room across from Cecily's.

"I see you've already found the bedrooms," Mrs. Armstrong simpers as the camera pans over various belongings. "We can head up to the third floor, then, since you kids have already made yourself so . . . at home . . . on the second." Her smile is too wide. Rudy begins to wonder if the realtor is the reason he feels uneasy.

The third floor is an even bigger disaster. It's a creepy maze of paint tarps and broken furniture that makes Rudy hesitate. Several of the windows have been boarded up, doubtlessly broken by teenagers tossing rocks, if the few stones on the hall floor are any indication. Mrs. Cole eyes her children and makes a cranking camera motion with her hands. Rudy drags Cecily back on camera to crack jokes, plug Cecily's upcoming makeup video, and debate the best kind of varnish for the floor. From behind Amber, Mrs. Cole nods with approval.

"Are those *cobwebs*?" Cecily asks, making her mock-scared face.

"Sis is afraid of spiders," Rudy says, giving the camera a wink. "But you'd know that from our earlier vlogs!"

"And here's the master east bedroom," Mrs. Armstrong says, motioning the family into a giant, derelict room. "As you can see, it needs some . . . work."

Understatement. The wallpaper is peeling, the floors are water stained, the ceiling is cracked. Rudy catches his parents exchanging a look.

"It'll be a challenge!" Mrs. Cole says with an impressive amount of fake bravado. It may fool their followers, but Rudy isn't buying it. Rudy catches her glaring at their father and knows that Mrs. Cole is beyond angry. This renovation is in much worse shape than Mr. Cole had led the family to believe. On the drive here, his dad had described the house as a fixer-upper with character. A little work, sure, but a lot of promise. Mr. Cole was so clearly trying to be optimistic, to believe that this home could fix things. Rudy and his siblings had smiled and nodded along. Even Mom had seemed hopeful.

But this house is a mess. It's going to be a difficult renovation—and that's without the financial troubles that led them here in the first place. But what choice did they have? After all, the more "fixer" there is in your "fixer-upper," the cheaper it is, and the bigger the profit.

At least, that's what his dad had told them as they drove down the driveway and set eyes on the house for the first time. It didn't exactly fill Rudy with confidence.

"When did someone last live here?" Rudy asks. "Let's have some house history!"

"Well, uh, the last family to live in this house did so around ten years ago." Is it just Rudy, or does the realtor falter? "Uh, it's about due for a new family."

"I'm sure it is," Mrs. Cole says.

"Check out the state of these walls, though!" Rudy exclaims. "We're going to have to tear 'em down—Cole Patrol, don't you think that these walls would look *great* with a graffiti-style paintjob? A little pre-renovation

renovation? Drop a like, make a comment if you think we should do 'em up Cole style, a whole mural—"

"All right, sweetie." Mrs. Cole cuts him off, effortlessly shooting down another one of Rudy's ideas. Ever since money had gotten tight, it had been *post this, post that*—but Rudy and his mother have very different ideas of what makes good internet content. A video of them painting the walls beige, for example, isn't on Rudy's list of ideal posts.

But he is the one with the fans. Rudy turns back to the camera and shoots it a wink followed by one of his trademark smirks. The minute the camera pans off him, he gives his mother a look. Another idea, shot down. And he *knows* that it would bring views . . .

"Come on, Mom. Don't you want to test how a coat of EverBright paint will hold up against some artwork?" Rudy whispers, taking a page from Amber's book of parental persuasion. If there is a way to his mom's heart, it's through one of their sponsors.

She makes a noise that's not entirely disapproval. Progress.

"Gucci did do a graffiti shoot earlier this season," Amber chimes in.

"Yeah," says Cecily. "It would be *so* on-brand. And I could use some more clothes."

"You wish," Rudy says.

"All right, kids," Mr. Cole says, cutting in. He turns his attention to Mrs. Armstrong and nods for her to continue. She leads them back into the hall and opens up a small door in the center of the hallway.

"And here we have a truly unique installation: dumbwaiters," she says. "They're still fully functional, although I'm sure they could use some . . . touching up."

Everything in this house could use some touching up, Rudy thinks. Still, he peers into the dumbwaiter. That's pretty cool. Behind him, Amber captures it on camera.

Mrs. Armstrong turns the family down the hallway again, but before she can open her mouth, Rudy interrupts her. "What's that?" he asks, gesturing at a rectangular cut in the ceiling.

Mrs. Armstrong glances upward. "Oh, just attic access. Of course, it's unfinished." She reaches up for the panel, but the string sticks. She turns back to the family, grimacing. "I'm sorry—I think the previous owners must have sealed it off, for insulation purposes. It is nothing more than an unfinished crawl space—the master key and a good toolbox should open it, if you want to look around later."

Creepy, Rudy thinks. *Definitely on-brand with this strange mansion.*

The realtor brings them farther down the hallway. "All right, well, there is one more room up here," she says, leading them toward a small door nestled between two decrepit bedrooms.

"Oh, is this the turret?" Cecily asks.

Mrs. Armstrong gives her a strange, pained smile and reaches for the door handle.

It sticks.

Mrs. Armstrong's smile falters. She shoots the camera a hesitant glance and tries once more. Again, the door is stuck. No, not stuck. Locked. "That's strange, it was unlocked this morning . . . at least I thought it was . . . ," she murmurs.

"Spooky," Rudy remarks, winking at the camera. Cecily rolls her eyes.

Mrs. Armstrong pulls two keys out of her suit jacket pocket. "No matter. These are the keys to the house—your keys once this tour is over. They unlock every door in the place." The keys look more like movie props than anything—thick metal skeleton keys that probably weigh a ton.

"When you said the house dated back to the eighteen hundreds, you weren't kidding, huh?" Mr. Cole says.

"Of course not," Mrs. Armstrong says. "This is a very . . . historical house." The door opens with a *snick*. She lets out a relieved sigh and shoots a forced smile at the camera. "Right this way!"

She leads them up a rickety flight of stairs to another small door. This one, too, is locked. She opens it with the skeleton key. The room that's revealed is hexagonal in shape and full of light, offering gorgeous views of the surrounding wooded hills. Rudy takes everything in. The room feels strange, somehow. As if it's holding its breath.

Cecily follows them in. "The lighting in here is amazing!" she exclaims. "I should totally set up my makeup studio in here!"

Mr. Cole's not looking at the lighting. He's staring at the trim of the big bay window. Rudy's eyes follow his father's gaze. Mr. Cole is staring out the window, and he's gnawing on his lower lip. Rudy recognizes one of his father's obvious tells—the reason that he never made it as a gambler. He's gone quiet. Too quiet.

Mrs. Armstrong sees him staring. "Yes," she says in a low voice. "I'm afraid this is where it happened."

"Robert?" Mrs. Cole asks. "Where what happened?"

Rudy sees the panicked look cross his father's face and wonders what the hell is going on.

"What happened?" Amber echoes.

It's too serious in here, Rudy thinks, so he steps in with a joke. "What, someone jump out the window?" But his joke falls so, so flat. Mrs. Cole turns to Rudy and makes a slashing motion over her throat.

Mrs. Armstrong looks confused. "I was under the impression that your family knew about the house history."

"What history?" Rudy asks before his mom can shush him.

"That there was a . . . suicide in this room."

"Turn off the camera. Now," Mrs. Cole snaps. Rudy and his sisters stare at their father, dumbfounded. He knew that Dad was desperate to make this renovation work, but this? The house's being in bad shape is one thing, but hiding a *death* on the property? Mrs. Cole glares at her husband. *If looks could kill,* Rudy thinks, *Dad wouldn't have a chance.*

Amber cuts the footage. On Rudy's phone, notifications ping as viewers comment on their livestream, asking why it ended, if the realtor had really said that someone had committed suicide.

Mrs. Cole turns on her heels. "What do you mean, a suicide?"

Mrs. Armstrong gestures at the window. "I'm sorry, I thought your husband had informed the family . . ."

Mrs. Cole looks at her husband. "*You knew about this and didn't tell me?*"

He rocks back and forth ever so slightly, still gnawing on his lower lip. "I—I did know. But it's such a good opportunity, and don't you think that houses like this *deserve* another chance? I knew that if anyone could do it, we could, and—" He falters. "It was the only property we could afford, Marie."

"Later," is all Mrs. Cole says. Rudy has never seen his mother's jaw clenched so tightly before. She turns to the realtor. "What happened?"

Mrs. Armstrong starts slowly. "The . . . victim was a seventeen-year-old girl. From what I've heard, she was going through a lot of . . . pressure . . . with school. She jumped. Poor, poor thing. It was a horrible time for this house. It deserves so much better." Rudy eyes her. He has the distinct feeling that Mrs. Armstrong isn't telling them everything.

Rudy exchanges a look with his sisters. *Someone had died in this house.* Why would he want to do paint swatches and talk about crown molding when he could be telling a spooky story about the house's history? Judging by his phone notifications, their followers are already excited about this break in normal renovation content. Rudy catches Amber's eye and mouths a word to her: *Viral.* After a second, she glances at her own phone and nods back.

"That's why it's so lovely to have another family living here," Mrs. Armstrong tries to start again, but Mrs. Cole ignores her.

She turns to her Amber. "I don't suppose you cut before she mentioned the suicide." Amber shakes her head. "Great." Mrs. Cole sighs and runs a hand through her hair. "We'll have to discuss what we're going to tell everyone."

"E—everyone?" the realtor asks.

"Their followers!" Mrs. Cole snaps. "On the livestream we've been doing this entire time—they have almost a million followers on Instagram—"

"Uh . . ."

"Of course we're going to tell them, Mom," Rudy says, trying to keep the pleading tone from his voice. "This could go viral."

Mrs. Cole presses her lips together and looks to Amber, who nods. Cecily is silent. Mrs. Cole turns back to the realtor. "Will this decrease the value of the house?"

"Honey," Mr. Cole says, finding his voice for the first time since Mrs. Armstrong broke the news. "You don't get houses this big this cheap without a few . . . drawbacks."

Mrs. Cole doesn't look at her husband. "I said. We'll talk. Later." Rudy winces.

The realtor plasters on a smile. "It's time to write this house a new history," she says. "Besides, if your lovely children think that this could go viral . . ." Mrs. Cole gives Rudy and Cecily a look. They'll discuss this later, after they finish editing and posting the video version of their livestream. "Why don't we . . . head downstairs?" Mrs. Armstrong asks, ushering them out of the turret room and toward the main level. As the realtor goes on and on about mahogany wood and paneling, Rudy motions at Amber to turn the livestream back on. This is better than he could have believed. After a few seconds of pleading looks, she finally does. Mrs. Cole might want to be cautious, but he has other plans. This is his chance to create content that is *actually* interesting. And besides, Mrs. Armstrong had already exposed the death to the livestream, right?

Amber points the camera at him.

"So, what do you think?" Rudy whispers, grinning at the camera. "Did someone die here? Is our new house haunted?" He makes an exaggerated screaming face, holding it just long enough to be captured as a potential thumbnail. Amber gives him a thumbs-up; Cecily rolls her eyes. "Come on, Cece," he says. "Think of all the supercool dead girl makeup looks you can do!"

Cecily doesn't laugh. Rudy continues. "Leave a like, a comment, let us know—should we try to contact her ghost? Is there one?" He casts a glance toward Mrs. Cole at the front of the group. She hasn't noticed that they're filming. Rudy decides to quit while he's ahead. "And, on that huge news, I think it is time for us to sign off—from a spookier house tour than we expected! Guys, we're so excited about this new project—and we're excited to show you everything, every step of the way. Thanks, Cole Patrol. And don't forget to follow us! And, as always, have a great day! Bye!"

The second the camera is off he feels his face react, and experiences the usual wave of exhaustion that comes with being *on*. But instead of just being fatigued, this time he's also excited. As soon as the realtor leaves, he's going straight to the account to check the comments. He's *sure* that the Cole Patrol is going to be as enthusiastic about the ghost as he is. He's ready to stop with the renovation and start shooting something *fun*.

But once Mrs. Armstrong leaves, Rudy finds himself cornered by his mother. She's seen his impromptu livestream part two. Rudy gets an earful, but he's not listening to her going on about engagement or brand management. Instead, he's thinking about the suicide. About what this could mean for the account.

"Don't forget to take 'before' shots of all the rooms." Rudy tunes back in as Mrs. Cole rounds out her lecture with advice on how to pivot back on-brand. Rudy nods absently. It's a small price for staving off his mom's irritation. And besides, Amber and Cecily will make it fun.

When Rudy and his sisters finish their mom's photo assignment an hour later, Rudy grabs his guitar from its case and joins Amber in her room, where she's editing the livestream footage. He sits against her bed and jams softly on "Blue Ghost Blues" while she edits photos. It feels appropriate.

After a while, he wanders back to his room, where his phone is charging. He puts away the guitar and picks up his phone, scrolling through the internet, making search after search. Across the hallway, he can hear Cecily cooing at Speckles. A quick glance confirms that she's let the dwarf bunny out of his cage and brought him upstairs to explore her room. This house really *does* have good acoustics. But all Rudy finds online are vague details; searching for "*Norton suicide 90s*" yields too many obituaries, and "*976 Tremont Street suicide*" doesn't result in any direct matches. He does find one promising lead: the archive website for the county paper. If he had a name, he's sure that he could find more, but when he calls the realtor's office to ask about the house's last owners, it goes straight to voicemail. He leaves a message; hopefully they'll get back to him tomorrow.

"Rudy," Amber calls from her room. "Come here for a second."

She has their livestream pulled up on her computer. It already has a ton of views, likes, and comments—and most of them are about the suicide revelation. The spooky aspect is definitely good for engagement.

"Great, right?" Rudy asks. "I'm so excited to respond to comments later—this is such a cool twist from our usual content."

"No, it's that same account," Amber says. She gestures at the comments, and Rudy starts to read.

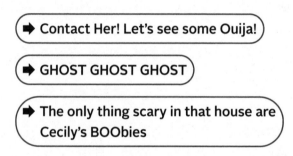

➡ **Contact Her! Let's see some Ouija!**

➡ **GHOST GHOST GHOST**

➡ **The only thing scary in that house are Cecily's BOObies**

Finally, he sees what Amber is referring to.

➡ **It's mine.**

Another weird message from the same account that they had noticed earlier, the one with the avatar of the Tremont house. @Alex_Grable. Amber goes to delete it then frowns back up at Rudy. "What do you think?"

He shrugs. "We've gotten weirder comments, I guess. It's probably just some high school kid messing with us."

Amber frowns and checks the account's activity. "Weirder than this?" she asks.

Whoever Alex Grable is, they've been all over the Cole family's Instagram. While Rudy was jamming out on his guitar, Amber had managed to post several previews from their "before" photo shoot. There was even a photo of the turret room with a "scary" filter. On every post, Alex Grable had left a comment.

The living room: *Mine.*

The kitchen: *It's mine.*

And then, on the turret room: *This is mine. It belongs to me. That's why I locked it.*

➡ **@SteveD123:** tell us about the ghosts!

252 Likes   Reply

➡ **@GodlyMomma3:** No! That's DANGEROUS. Do NOT attempt to contact the dead, do NOT invite them in . . .

196 Likes   Reply

XXXXXXXXXXXXXXXXXXXXXXXXXXXXXXXXXX

CHAPTER 3

Cecily

CECILY WISHES THE RANGE ROVER WERE LOUDER. BUT THE OVER-priced behemoth is surprisingly soft-sounding from the inside, so there is no roar of the engine to cover the awkward silence between Cecily and her father. The car itself is less of a vehicle and more of a prop, something Mrs. Cole had justified buying so that they could "keep up their image." It had made its fair share of appearances in posts and vlogs, but Cecily wasn't sure if that made up for the ridiculous car payments. Of course, those wouldn't be a problem, either, if it weren't for her dad.

Cecily cannot believe that her dad had failed to mention to any of them that the house they were moving into was the location of a suicide. It's creepy beyond belief. She doesn't blame her mom for being crazy pissed at him.

She absently reaches into her handbag to make sure her go bag of makeup is inside. It is. She doesn't carry much in it, just a palette with creams that can be used on her cheeks, eyes, or lips, a mini eyeliner, concealer, and of course, her holy grail product: a travel-size bottle of Luxe makeup remover. She'd been so excited when they agreed to sponsor her last year after a couple of her posts featuring the product—and one about her go bag—had performed ridiculously well.

But even the prospect of touching up her makeup wasn't enough to distract Cecily from the house. She replays the afternoon over and over in her head. Someone had *died* in the Tremont house. *Died.* Finally, Cecily can't stand the silence anymore. "I can't believe you knew and you didn't tell Mom."

Mr. Cole sighs and shoots her a pained look. He has no poker face. He's not as good at acting as the triplets are. "I just . . . thought it needed some love. I know you're worried about the house, but I also know this family. And I know that we can take care of it."

Cecily softens. He sounds so . . . hopeful. She gives him a small smile.

But then he continues. "Besides, the money we save can go in your, uh, college fund."

Cecily's expression sours. "You mean the empty one?" she mutters.

"What did you say?"

"The empty one," Cecily repeats, louder this time.

Her father's hands tighten on the wheel. Cecily watches him swallow, hard, his Adam's apple bobbing up and down in his throat. "Cecily, honey, I know that things haven't been easy, but . . . rehab really helped me. And I'm thankful for you kids for sticking by me, through everything." He starts to gnaw on his lower lip. His tell. Rudy pointed it out to her and now she sees it all the time.

"You didn't just lose *your* money, dad," Cecily says, finally. But her words are more sullen and bitter than angry. This had been their lifestyle for more than a year now, ever since a check bounced and they realized the extent of her father's problems. "Most influencers with our following are rich, you know. We could have a house in the hills; I could have started a makeup line—"

"*Cecily Jane.*" She'd pushed too far. "That's *enough.*"

"What are you doing to do? Ground me?" Cecily asks. "Take my phone away? Happy to do it. Would *love* to have you tell me you don't need the money."

Her father doesn't answer. The snappy retort didn't feel as good as Cecily thought it would. In fact, she doesn't feel good at all. She used to enjoy spending time with her dad. Before he started gambling. Before he started losing. It's not about the money or the mansions, not really. It's about the fact that she hasn't been allowed to be anything less than perfect since.

They need maximum engagement, Mrs. Cole says. Maximum sponsorships. They need the money. And Cecily's makeup videos get the most sponsors and engagement out of all her siblings', so that's what gets on the schedule—censored by Mom, of course. Mrs. Cole does research, curates the trendiest looks, and sometimes primes Cecily on internet gossip so she can give talking points while she does up her face. That means more celebrity news and less talk about formulas, ingredients, price points, and what makes makeup, well, makeup. But that is what it takes to keep the sponsors coming. Or, it is the least risky option.

She sighs, trying to calm down. At least Mr. Cole is making an effort. He did go to rehab. She knows that he feels the financial pressure, too, but *he's* not the one who's been put on an aggressive posting schedule to compensate for his terrible, terrible taste in sports teams.

She closes her eyes and tries to think of what she will do once her family is out of debt. While she's not entirely sure what exact direction she'll choose, she knows it will have to do with makeup. Either doing makeup professionally, or starting her own line . . . Her mind wanders and she imagines herself in an ad for her own makeup line, made over to perfection. Entirely flawless.

Social media isn't all bad.

Sure, the money is nice, but what's even better are the DMs she receives from people trying out her makeup looks. The best part of makeup is giving people confidence. That ready-to-take-on-the-world feeling that comes with a bold lip or the perfectly winged cat eye. She always reads her comments, and she especially savors the feedback on the videos where she gets really detailed on more advanced techniques, like intricate contouring, or offers tutorials on concealing more than just blemishes—stuff like birthmarks or small scars. Just last week, a fourteen-year-old girl from Iowa had sent her a message about how much more confident she felt after watching one of Cecily's videos on covering up acne scars. She said it gave her the confidence to try out for the cheerleading team and that she'd made the squad. Cecily had read the DM over and over again. Feedback like that makes it all worth it.

But she wants to do more. Maybe one day, when finances are a little less tight, she'll be able to make other kinds of makeup videos, too—the kind her mom deems "too risky" for their audience. As if she doesn't know her own audience or what they care about. She longs to make videos about the processes behind makeup—the formulas, testing, what it means for a brand to be truly vegan or cruelty-free—but for now, seasonal looks and challenges are what get views. At least according to her mom. So that's what Cecily does.

They pull up to Pete's-a-Pizza, the only take-out game in the entire suburb. They're a little over two hours from New York City, yet the place markets itself as having the best pie outside the city. Not exactly a ringing endorsement. Cecily can't believe they had to drive fifteen whole *minutes* to get to this second-rate restaurant. There probably aren't even any good makeup outlets in Norton.

She's double-checking her makeup in the lighted mirror in the visor when her dad breaks the silence. Her mascara is smudged. She thinks of the makeup remover inside her go bag.

"Make sure to double-check about nuts—"

"Dad, it's *pizza*," she replies, getting out and slamming the door. Smudged mascara be damned. No one in the pizza place will notice. The sound echoes through the empty parking lot, interrupting the subtle hum from the neon sign above her, where the *a* in "Pizza" is slowly beginning to flicker in and out. Not that Cecily is dismissive of Rudy's nut allergy; it's just that, well, it's pizza, and any excuse to slam the door on her father feels like a good one right now.

A single bell above the door rings as she walks up to the counter. The place is a little on the grimy side and empty except for a lone teenage boy slurping soda and browsing his phone at an end table.

The cashier is staring at her. She's about Cecily's age, with wavy hair and wide brown eyes that straddle the line between pretty and off-putting. Cecily sweeps her hair over one shoulder and stands up straighter. Encountering kids her own age makes her nervous, though she does everything she can not to show it. She finds herself wishing Rudy and Amber were with her. "Uh, order for the Coles, please," she says finally. "One pepperoni, one Hawaiian? Called ahead about a nut allergy?"

"I knew it!" the girl says, and Cecily tenses. She knew *what?* "You're Cecily Cole!"

Oh. A fan. Cecily relaxes a little. She conjures up a smile and gives a little wave. "That's me! Hi. I'm here for pizza? I mean, I'm new in town. But pizza, too."

The girl's face explodes into a huge grin; Cecily half expects her to sprint out from behind the register and hug her, she looks so excited. "Oh my god, can we take a picture? You are like, *so* famous. I can't wait to tell my friends that I met Cecily Cole! I'm Bella, by the way."

She sweeps her platinum-blond hair—clearly a dye job, judging by her tanned skin and black eyebrows—over her shoulder and makes a quick check for a manager before darting around the counter to pose with Cecily. When she extends her hand to take the picture, she reveals perfectly done nails and a phone case covered in stickers from various clubs at Norton High. She must definitely be close to Cecily's age, then. She's shorter than Cecily, closer to Amber's height, but her bubbly energy more than makes up for it.

Cecily suddenly feels shy. And nervous. There's a part of her that worries her fans will be disappointed when they meet her in person and see that she's just a normal teenager. One with perfect makeup, but still, just a regular girl. "Uh, yeah," she murmurs. She imagines what Rudy would do and plasters a smile on her face as Bella adjusts the phone above their heads, searching for the perfect angle. Bella snaps the picture, and Cecily remembers her smudged mascara. *Maybe the lighting will be bad, and it won't be obvious*, she tells herself. *Maybe Mom won't notice.*

Bella definitely doesn't seem to. "Oh my god, thanks a ton!" she squeals. "So you said you're new in town?"

Cecily forces herself to maintain the smile. "Yeah. We just moved into a house on—"

"You're fixing up the Tremont house!" Bella interrupts. "Of course! I just watched your video. I *thought* the thumbnail looked familiar, but it seemed too good to be true—you know, having the Cole triplets here. I watch every one of your videos. I mean, your makeup is *fantastic*—" She pauses to take a breath. Cecily likes this girl. "Okay, wait, was it fake? Did you really not know about her until the tour?"

"Her?" Cecily asks.

"The murder-suicide girl," Bella says, lowering her voice a notch. "Alex Grable? Track star, went psycho and stabbed her mom?"

"Her *mom*?" Cecily asks with a gasp. "I thought she just . . . jumped out of the window . . ." Her palms suddenly feel clammy, her throat dry. She pictures the view out of the turret, the ground so far below.

"Nope, she stabbed her mom first and then jumped," Bella continues with a shudder. "Like, twenty years ago. Shit. I guess you guys really didn't know."

Cecily feels her hands start to shake. A suicide is one thing, but a murder? How on earth are they going to sell this house? How can she film makeup videos in a house where someone killed their *mother*?

"Are you okay?" Bella looks directly at her, eyes wide with concern. Cecily nods, aware she needs to not overreact in public but reeling internally from this new bit of information about the house. An awkward moment passes, and then thankfully Bella charges on. "Uh, I can't wait to see it fixed up, though! I just know you guys will make it amazing. But it'll be *so* weird to see the local haunted house all fancy."

Cecily's chest flutters. "Uh . . . haunted?" She's trying to sound casual but doesn't think she's pulling it off.

"Oh, you know, ghost stories, kids trying to scare each other, that kind of thing." Bella waves a hand as if to dismiss her words, and Cecily knows she's definitely not pulling off the casual act. She needs to pull herself together. "Oh my god, I can't believe you're here," Bella says a moment later. Now the conversation seems to have really stalled. "Oh—oh yeah. Pizza. Gimmie a sec."

She disappears behind the counter. Cecily turns to survey the rest of the restaurant and realizes that the boy is staring at her. A weird stare.

"Hey," he says.

She gives him a quick, strained smile and looks away, praying that he'll take the hint. But of course he doesn't. She hears the scraping of his chair as he gets up, walks over, and leans on the counter next to her. She prays he won't ask for a picture. Taking pictures with random fanboys always feels a little creepy, even more so when her brother and sister aren't there with her.

"I'm Steve," the boy says, sweeping his hand through his hair in a way that's clearly choreographed to be sultry. It isn't. "What's a girl like you doing in a place like this?"

"I have a boyfriend," Cecily lies.

He takes a step back. She's said the wrong thing. "Hey, I'm just trying to be friendly." He's tall, dark haired, not bad looking. Of course, every single positive thing about his appearance is negated by the way his face soured when she indicated she wasn't interested. He crosses his arms as he looks her up and down. "I heard you talking about Instagram. Is your boyfriend one of those influencer types, too? I bet he's a douche, whoever he is."

"Leave her alone, Steve," Bella says. She gives Cecily an exaggerated eye roll as she reappears with the pizza, and the tension is instantly gone. "Don't you know who Cecily Cole is? She's *famous*. You don't have a snowball's chance in hell." She rings Cecily up. "Twenty-six even. And I promise all the kids in this town aren't like this loser. Hey—we should hang out sometime."

The chip reader beeps and Cecily grabs her card, giving Bella a quick smile. "Sure."

"I can grab your number, or . . . ," Bella says hopefully.

"Uh, oh, I forgot my phone," Cecily lies. She shoots a half look at Steve and sees understanding flash across Bella's face. "Why don't you just DM me on Instagram or something. You know, we're—"

"I know your account," Bella says with a laugh. "Definitely."

Cecily grabs the pizza and shoots Bella a genuine smile as she turns to leave. She tries to think less about the murder-suicide news and more on the potential hangouts. Sure, they're here for only a month and a half, but that doesn't mean she has to be cooped up inside the whole time. Suburb kids have to have fun, too, right?

"Hey, I'll DM you, too!" Steve calls as she leaves. "In case you get scared, all alone in that big, creepy murder house. In case you need someone to protect you from all those ghosts."

Excerpt from *Tube Talk*, a popular YouTube commentary channel in which social media influencers discuss other social media influencers. Hosted by internet personalities Ron Nguyen & Vincent Sanchez.

8 million subscribers

Ron: And the next item on our viral hits of the week is a house-flipping channel—the Coles'—that claims their new renovation is, get this, haunted. Their followers think they might have to move! Thoughts?

Vin: The Coles? Ghost hunters? Please. From their feed, it looks like their only talents are screwing in lightbulbs and being hot!

Ron: Well, my dude, welcome to Instagram.

XXXXXXXXXXXXXXXXXXXXXXXXXXXXXXXX

CHAPTER 4

Amber

BY THE TIME CECILY AND MR. COLE RETURN, AMBER AND RUDY have dug an ancient, warped table out of one of the downstairs rooms and set it up in the kitchen. Amber has no doubts that it will be one of the first things to hit the curb once the renovation starts. Cecily and Mr. Cole set the box down, and the smell of melting cheese fills the room.

"Thank god," Rudy says, reaching for a slice straight from the box. But as he leans forward, he trips and pinwheels in the air before he catches himself. "Ahh!"

"What are you doing here?" Cecily asks, bending over to pick up Speckles as he darts out from in between Rudy's feet. "Did you escape again? You're so smart!"

"He's not smart; you just keep forgetting to lock his cage!" Rudy grumbles. Amber can't help but giggle at his expense, even if he is right. Rudy rolls his eyes and goes for the pizza again, only to be interrupted a second time.

"Hey, you're sure there's—" their mother starts.

"No nuts," all three triplets say in unison.

Rudy takes an exaggerated bite. "See, Mom? The mess of *cheese* and *pizza sauce* didn't kill me. Besides, my EpiPen's already unpacked and in my nightstand. C'mon."

All the same, Mrs. Cole watches Rudy carefully as he chews and swallows. Then, satisfied that he's fine, she turns to examine the spreadsheet on Amber's computer.

Amber grabs a slice of pizza and a paper plate. "I thought we might not have working dinner this week, you know, since we just got here," she says, hardly daring to hope.

Sure enough, her mother gives her a tight smile. "I'm sorry, sweetheart. I know it's not ideal, and I know you guys work hard, but . . . we can't afford to take a break right now. Not yet." She turns the laptop to face the rest of the family. "Now, this is very important. This is a big week for us on social media, what with the livestream and the renovation before pictures and those posts from EverBright."

"I'm telling you, graffiti would be so fun—our followers would love it," Rudy says.

"But do the sponsors want their paint to be associated with—"

"We'll use other paint, then," Rudy says. He tries to keep his tone light, but Amber can hear how annoyed he is. "Come on, I really want to give the fans something cool."

Mrs. Cole shakes her head. "Image, dear. We're a renovation channel, not an art showcase. We can't take any risks right now—we need these sponsors."

"But—"

"I said *no,*" Mrs. Cole says. "Maybe you'll think about this the next time that you post something without authorization." Of course she's still angry about Rudy rebooting the livestream to shoot the ending of the home tour. Amber shifts, uncomfortable. Maybe she shouldn't have enabled him.

Rudy gives their mom a massive eye roll. "Mom, it's my account—"

"It's the *family's* account."

"Well, it used to be—"

Mrs. Cole turns to the girls. "Either of you have any good ideas? Don't forget the three *A*s: attractive, aspirational, and, above all, authentic."

Rudy catches Amber's eye and makes a face that definitely isn't in line with the first *A*. Amber knows how he feels—he hasn't had any kind of influence on the content they post since their mom took over. Neither had she. Sometimes she misses doing fashion segments on their channel, but unlike Rudy, she's never had the courage—or the confidence—to argue with their mom about it. Amber doesn't think that she can handle having her mother look her in the eyes again and tell her that "her kind of content" just isn't getting the best engagement, isn't the best look for their channel. Of course, "her kind of content" doesn't really mean fashion, does it? At least, not straight-size fashion. So, Amber serves as the camera girl. And the photo girl. And the data girl.

"Amber, I need you to do an analytics check after dinner, make sure our performance is lit, as you kids say," Mrs. Cole says. Amber cringes. Her mom continues. "Now, as I'm sure you've noticed, this house is going to be . . . a lot of work." *Translation: way more work than they'd intended.* "Your father and I are going to be contracting out some local help, just to make sure we can finish in time for the big open house. And this means that you—Amber, you especially—need to be very, *very* careful of your shots. No workers. To our internet followers, this is just going to be *us*, okay? I don't care if you film while a crew is here, just so long as that crew is—"

"Off camera," Amber says. "We know the drill." Privately, she wonders if any of their followers are dumb enough to believe that the Coles actually flip houses at light speed with just the help of three seventeen-year-old kids.

"But, as always, we need content," Mrs. Cole says. "Any ideas?"

"We could do some nice unpacking shots," Amber says. "And the turret room offers some great views."

Mrs. Cole nods. "Cecily will be doing more makeup videos, of course. Summer looks, in honor of the month of July—gold and green are really in this year. Oh, and Cecily, your sponsored post did come through—they're sending some makeup and dye products for some kind of rose-gold mermaid look—"

"What's that, buzzword vomit?" Rudy jokes. Mom ignores him.

"—so be on the lookout for those," she continues. "Otherwise, we have the paint, the varnish, some cabinets that I think would look *darling* in the pantry . . . but, of course, we have to be smart, kids. Au-*then*-ticity, that's what the sponsors are paying for."

Mrs. Cole looks around the table, and Amber realizes that Cecily hasn't spoken for the entire meal. She's made herself busy playing with Speckles, clearly trying to avoid the conversation. She sighs and returns to the table, grabbing a piece of pizza and making an exaggerated *I'm chewing* face before Mom can ask her to contribute.

"Ideas? Earth to Amber," Mrs. Cole says, half-joking. "I can't think of all these myself!"

"Maybe we can, like, do a poll on colors or something," Amber suggests.

"And leave the house to the internet?" she asks in mock horror. "No. Maybe we can do some paint-coordinated makeup looks; I have some pastels in mind that would look lovely on Cecily. And you'll be editing, of course."

Amber nods and shuts her mouth.

For a second, no one says anything. The house creaks above them through the silence, and Amber's thoughts stray to the dead girl. She isn't the only one, because Rudy pipes up.

"That's it?"

"That's it," Mrs. Cole says.

"We're seriously not going to talk about the dead girl right now?" Rudy asks.

Their mother shifts uncomfortably. Like Cecily, Mr. Cole has also been silent for this entire meal. "There isn't anything to talk about," Mrs. Cole says finally.

"Nothing to talk about!" Rudy says. "Have you *seen* the livestream's engagement?"

Mrs. Cole hesitates. "It's not on-brand—"

"I'll pull it up," Amber says, surprising herself with her own impulsiveness. "It's definitely driving traffic."

"What do you think, Cece?" Rudy asks. Across the table, Cecily is still silent.

"That's right, dear," Mrs. Cole says. "Are you feeling all right? You've been quiet." Mrs. Cole's brows furrow in concern. *Can't have the breadwinner get sick*, Amber thinks, bitterness tinging the thought. But Cecily shakes her head.

"I met some local kids at the pizza place," Cecily says. "They told me something. That before the girl upstairs . . . killed herself, she stabbed her mom. Then she jumped. They both died."

There is pin-drop silence at the table. A suicide is one thing, but a *murder?* Rudy's eyes light up.

Mrs. Cole turns to her husband with a look that is all ice.

"What else is there?" asks Rudy. "Who did you talk to?"

"Just the cashier—I didn't have much time," Cecily admits.

"We *have* to investigate, or ghost hunt, or something—figure out what happened!" Rudy says, as if their mom hadn't nixed the ghost idea just moments before. He takes a huge bite of his second slice of pizza and keeps talking, mouth full, before Mrs. Cole can interrupt him. "And before you shut me down, check out the engagement for the livestream. It's ridiculous. This stuff gets *views.* Ghost hunters would make a great video. We could get some night filming gear, walk around in the dark, work on our fake screams—or maybe there *is* a ghost—"

"We are *not* ghost hunting," Mrs. Cole says, getting up and walking behind Amber to check out the comments. "And don't you start making up conspiracy theories or investigating this house. It's not part of our brand."

"Don't I get *any* say in what this account posts?" Rudy asks.

"Mom." Amber pulls up the analytics and shows them to her. Rudy is right. The house tour is already one of the most popular videos on both their Instagram and YouTube accounts. It already has more than two million views and thousands of comments.

The top one? *Definitely haunted.* With more than five thousand likes.

It's followed by:

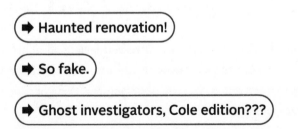

➡ Haunted renovation!

➡ So fake.

➡ Ghost investigators, Cole edition???

And then, there it is again. The @Alex_Grable account.

> ➡ Don't you DARE put graffiti on those walls, don't you dare deface that house! It was there before you and will be after! Don't you DARE!

Amber hovers over the reply for too long, which catches her mom's attention. "What are you looking at?" Mrs. Cole asks.

"It's nothing," Amber says. "Just a weird account, some kid named Alex. The profile picture is this house, which is super weird, and Rudy and I noticed them commenting earlier but figured it was just . . . some prank."

"Alex?" Cecily asks. Amber feels her sister's breath on her cheek as she peers over her shoulder at the computer screen. "Alex what?"

"Grable?" Amber says, turning to face Cecily. "Why—what's wrong?"

Amber watches the color drain from her sister's face. "Alex Grable," Cecily whispers. "That was her name. The girl who died."

Amber stares blankly at Cecily as she digests what she just said. "It's a . . . a messed-up prank, then," she says finally, wanting to reassure Cecily, who spooks easily. But she knows she doesn't sound convincing. Amber looks to Rudy, hoping he will have something funny to say to lighten to moment, but even he is at a loss for words.

Amber turns her attention back to the post. The comment has tons of replies, mostly users trying to bait Alex Grable or asking about the profile picture. Alex hasn't responded.

The silence in the room is thick, uncomfortable. Amber can feel the nervousness radiating off her sister. She shoots Rudy an imploring look. He catches her eye and nods. "Someone's a little too invested in off-white for the bedrooms," he says finally, but the joke falls flat.

"How did they even get a photo of the house?" their mother asks, a little frown creasing her forehead.

"The livestream," Rudy replies.

And then a comment pings in underneath a graffiti art photo Rudy posted as renovation "inspiration"—in part to get under his mom's skin, Amber suspected.

"It's Alex Grable." Cecily's breath hitches as she taps the screen.

> ➡ I already told you not to paint the walls.
> I told you, I told you, I told you.

Mrs. Cole stares at the screen, her frown deepening. "No," she says finally. "It's not Alex Grable. It's some troll trying to freak you out; probably some local kid. See why we needed to be told about this ahead of time?"

Amber glances at her dad, wondering what he's going to have to say about all this, but he simply nods.

"Ignore the account," Mrs. Cole continues. "We can always block them if this escalates. Hopefully whoever it is will just get bored." Her voice trails off as she watches the views spike higher and higher. "Of course, any attention is good attention . . ."

Amber doesn't even have to look at her brother to know what he's thinking. This is the opening he's been looking for. The invitation to explore some more interesting content.

"It's not on-brand . . . ," her mom mumbles. "But it is getting good engagement."

"Good engagement?" Rudy finally jumps in. "This is going to be our most-viewed livestream, ever. Wouldn't the sponsors like that?"

Mrs. Cole presses her lips together, and Amber silently congratulates her brother for using the S word: "sponsors." If there's a time when they need to please the sponsors with numbers, it is definitely now.

"Fine," Mrs. Cole says. "We can do . . . some . . . ghost stuff. But nothing too insensitive. I want to screen every idea—and I mean *every* idea—before it goes on the account. And don't tie it into the renovation—we'll be telling potential buyers that it's just a story for internet fun. Which it is. Understood?"

Rudy nods, a grin splitting his face. Next to him, Cecily has inched even closer to the screen, scrolling up and down. Amber realizes her sister is reading and rereading the comments from Alex Grable. It's going to be harder for Cecily to shrug off the trolling, Amber knows. Almost as hard as it will be for her to admit that it bothers her.

Amber isn't sure how she feels about it. Sure, new content could be fun, but if someone around town is already mad enough about their renovation to make this account . . .

Mr. Cole silently places his crust on his plate and gets up to leave the table. *Rookie mistake*, Amber thinks. Like a T. rex's, Mom's vision is based on movement.

"You're not going anywhere," she says. Mr. Cole freezes. "We need to talk."

The triplets stand up in unison. This is their cue to leave. "We're, uh, going to unpack," Amber says.

They're on the second landing when the fighting starts. Even with a floor beneath them, they can still hear the strained sound of their parents' discussion.

"How did you think it was okay to make a decision like this without talking to me?"

"Just what we needed," Cecily mumbles as Amber strains to hear her dad's response. "A house with good acoustics."

"Let's go to the third floor!" Rudy says, steering his sisters away from their rooms and down the hallway. "To investigate. Guys, we get to post about the *ghost*. We need to find out everything that happened here."

He leads them upstairs. Another floor almost muffles the sound of the argument happening below, but not entirely. Amber knows this one could go on for a while.

The third floor is unfinished, punctuated by empty bedrooms and hanging tarps. In the half-light of a mostly burned-out lamp, it's creepy enough to be distracting. Rudy walks down the hallway.

"I think I'm going to sleep in the suicide room tonight," he says. "Maybe take some nighttime footage, like in those TV shows."

"Didn't Mom say we needed approval—"

"Oh, come on, Cecily," Rudy cuts her off, getting right to the heart of the matter. Amber knows that her brother knows as well as she does that Cecily is actually scared. "It's not *real*."

Cecily doesn't answer.

"Rudy Cole, ghost hunter," Amber snorts, giving him a friendly shove on the shoulder. She winks at Cecily.

"Come on!" Rudy says, walking out onto the landing. "It'll generate great traffic. Our fans are going to eat this up!"

"You're not wrong about that," Amber muses, setting off down the creepy hallway after her brother. It takes her a few steps to realize that she's not being followed. "Cece?" she asks.

"You're not *that* scared, are you?" Rudy asks, pausing before the stairwell. "I mean, sure, it's kind of creepy, but just think of the traffic we're gonna get . . ."

Cecily wraps her arms around herself. "What do you guys think about the . . . account?" she asks. She doesn't say its name. *Her* name.

Amber answers slowly. "I mean, it's not really Alex Grable, right? Like Mom said, it's just some kid messing with us. Someone local who stopped by before we moved in and took the profile picture."

"Or maybe it is her," Rudy teases, wiggling his fingers for emphasis. "Rising from the dead to make an Instagram account. That's what I would do if I were a ghost. Maybe she's haunting the house right now." He reaches for the turret room door and turns the handle.

It sticks.

"Didn't that realtor lady unlock it?" he asks. He tries it again. The noise of the dead bolt against the doorframe seems to echo just a little too much. It's locked.

"Come on, let's go downstairs," Amber says. Her sister's fear must be rubbing off on her because she feels a shiver go down her spine.

"Yeah, that's where the key is," Rudy says, leading them back to the first level. But as soon as they reach level two, Amber knows they won't make it to where the key hangs in the kitchen hall.

Muffled voices sound off below. At first, Amber can't make out any words, but then Rudy opens the door to the dumbwaiter and the sound echoes up to them. "I know things have been hard, but I believe in this family—" Their dad's voice is tinged with desperation.

"On second thought," Rudy says, closing the dumbwaiter door. "I can get the key and sleep there some other night. Don't want to walk into that hurricane."

Cecily nods.

"Hey, cheer up!" Rudy says. "Let's watch a movie or something."

Amber shoots him a relieved glance. She knows Rudy is eager to ghost hunt, but Cecily seems really freaked out; ghost research can come later. Amber is following them into Cecily's room when she remembers all the work she has to do. "Got photos to edit," she says, her face falling. "You're not going to facetune yourselves."

"Can't you do it later?" Cecily asks. She's perked up for the first time since dinner. "Come on. I want to watch some sci-fi."

Amber gives Cecily a look. Easy for her to say—all she has to do to pull her weight on the account is sit there and be perfect, photogenic Cecily. But Amber? This won't be the first time she stays up half the night editing photos.

"You're coming," Rudy says, grabbing her arm and steering her into the room. In spite of herself, Amber gives them a small smile. "Cecily's right. You're not going to die if you post an unedited photo."

Cecily feigns a melodramatic heart attack, and Amber actually giggles. She follows the two into Cecily's room and sinks into her air mattress, smiling as she listens to her siblings fight over whether to watch sci-fi or action. Cecily finally lets Rudy pick and runs back downstairs to get Speckles.

Amber takes out her phone to check the 'gram one last time. She freezes.

"I wish Mom had let me put your cage in my room," Cecily coos at the rabbit as she walks back into the room. "The kitchen is so far! And you're just so fluffy—" She catches sight of Amber and pauses. "Amber? You okay?"

"It's Alex Grable again."

"Don't call it that." Cecily shudders. "She's dead. I hate it. It's creepy."

"We're talking about the account, not her—" Rudy starts, but Amber cuts him off.

"It's our new follower," Amber says. She holds up her phone and shows them the latest comment:

➡ **You mess with that house, I mess with you.**

➡ **@xoxogirlieK:** UGH, Rudy is such a DREAM. So big and strong from lifting all those boxes. And the construction? He can drill me anytime . . .

308 Likes   Reply

XXXXXXXXXXXXXXXXXXXXXXXXXXXXXX

CHAPTER 5

Rudy

RUDY IS AWAKE LONG BEFORE THE REST OF HIS FAMILY. HE SPENDS
the early-morning hours talking to fans online. They're all super enthusiastic
about the ghost, and so is he. Spurred by their interest, he starts googling
the Tremont house and Alex Grable. Now that he has a name, his searches
yield *results*: a couple old newspaper articles about the murder-suicide and
a small story about the dedication of a memorial bench in the local park.
Since Alex Grable was a minor at the time—only seventeen—details are
slim. Aside from discovering the exact year of the incident—1997—Rudy
only manages to confirm what Cecily has already told them: that Alex Grable, a senior in high school, had snapped. They found her mother in the
driveway with multiple stab wounds. Alex's crumped body was discovered
beneath the open window of the turret. From what he gathers, the case is
considered closed. A murder-suicide.

There are pictures attached to the article: The first is a photo of the
Tremont house. Their house, covered in crime-scene tape and surrounded
by police. But the worst picture is the school photo of Alex. Teenaged gan-
gly limbs, braces. She was seventeen. Exactly Rudy's age. She looks so . . .
normal. What could have made her want to kill her mom?

Mrs. Cole comes downstairs and Rudy snaps his computer shut. He knows
that she won't like him looking further into Alex Grable, even though she'd
okayed some of the ghost content. Thankfully, his mom is almost instantly
distracted by Amber's arrival as she comes down to make coffee. She gives
Rudy's sister a once-over. "What *are* these bags under your eyes? Didn't I
tell you to moisturize? You might have to sit out the next shoot, honey."

Amber's face falls, and Rudy winces. It's no secret that she's been in
fewer and fewer posts in recent years. Which isn't fair, he thinks, since

Amber's old content—mostly fashion and thrifting hauls—didn't exactly require her to be stick-thin, did it? Of course, he knows a lot of people wouldn't see it that way. Maybe Mom is just trying to protect her.

But, that being said, Amber does look awful. "I couldn't sleep," she mumbles. "Bad dreams."

"Nightmares?" Rudy asks before his mom can answer. He fixes himself his usual protein shake and shoots Amber a look. "About . . . ghosts?"

Amber shrugs, trying to act casual. "I thought I heard someone walking around upstairs," she admits. "But it was probably just some dream."

"Or a ghost," Rudy says, taking a seat at the kitchen table. Amber giggles. On the bar, Speckles shuffles around in his cage. Rudy can't believe that Mom let Cecily keep him there, but apparently it is okay since they'll be installing new countertops anyway.

"Not funny." Cecily cuts in, walking into the kitchen. She gives Speckles a pat before she opens the fridge and makes a face at its contents.

"Hey Amber, isn't your room right underneath the—"

"I said it's not funny," Cecily says, interrupting her brother.

Before Rudy can reply, his dad walks into the room.

"I got up to go to the bathroom, hun. That's probably what you heard," he says. "Man, this house doesn't keep secrets! Can hear anything anywhere." He gives the family a shaky smile. "Hey, you kids notice anything different about the kitchen? I set it up yesterday."

Rudy looks around and spots it. There, above the sink, is the small slate plaque that has followed them through every single renovation: *The Cole Family: Est. July 6th, 1991.* Underneath their parents' wedding anniversary are the triplets' names.

Usually, a gesture like that would have made his mom blush happily, or at least smile at his dad. Today, though, she gives no reaction.

Mr. Cole soldiers onward. "I thought that . . . now that the plaque is up, we're officially home." Crickets. "And, uh, Marie, speaking of the house. I've been meaning to talk to you."

Mrs. Cole shoots him a withering look. "Oh?" Rudy is impressed by how much disdain she can convey in a single word.

Mr. Cole continues. "The realtor recommended some local people for the construction; I'm having them over today. I'm going to hire a long-term handyman—and don't worry, we'll have him sign an NDA, stay off camera, the whole nine yards. I know how much you care about our image—"

"I care? You think I'm the only one that cares? What about our sponsors? Our fans? Do you think they care—"

Rudy exchanges a look with Amber and Cecily.

Slowly, Amber slips her plate off the table, like she's trying her best to make minimal noise. The lip of the china clinks. Mrs. Cole's head snaps toward the noise. She visibly tries to calm herself.

"Ah, kids—since there are no photo shoots on the schedule today, why don't you three help clean out the upstairs rooms?"

"Why can't you get your junk movers to do that?" Rudy huffs. He has better things to do—like discover more about Alex Grable's death.

"Because they charge by the floor," she says. "The attic and the turret room are on you three. Besides, the realtor said there is a lot of junk up there; maybe you can hunt around for valuables." She lets out a frustrated breath. "Or, since it's getting a lot of engagement, maybe something that can make the story about the ghost really *pop*. An old diary, or a music box . . ."

Cecily looks green. Rudy feels bad for her, even though he's excited that Mom has finally gotten on team ghost. Not that she had any other choice, what with that kind of engagement and where their money comes from.

"Come on, Mom. She died twenty years ago, not in the eighteen hundreds," Cecily says, but her voice sounds shaky.

Mrs. Cole gives her a look. "Don't back-talk me, Cecily Jane. Besides, that should give you something to do while you're unpacking your rooms—I'll look them over, of course, before we post anything. Oh, and set up your makeup studio. We'll want before and after pictures of it, too." She pauses. "Amber, of course," she adds.

Amber nods.

Rudy aims carefully and throws his napkin into the trash can with an NBA-worthy follow-through. It clinks off the rim.

"Talent," Cecily says in a monotone.

He shoots her a look and walks over to the napkin, dunking it into the trash. Of course Cece's content gets prioritized. Of course everything is all about her makeup. "Hey, why doesn't Cece just do her makeup in the turret room?"

"Rudy—" Cecily starts.

"Amazing views, great lighting," he continues.

"*Rudy*—"

"You're not *scared*—"

"You know, that might not be a bad idea," their mom says. "Best to keep the ghost thing front and center; piques interest. Maybe you can shoot some Halloween-themed things there, Cecily. Great idea, Rudy. It's settled."

Rudy sticks his tongue out at his sister.

"I hate you," she mutters, and her voice quakes enough to make him regret pushing it.

"Love you too, sis," he says, standing. "Come on, let's go." He leads his sisters upstairs, giving the squeaky step a glare. "So, Cece. You going to come or ditch us to set up your makeup studio?"

Cecily shakes her head. "Last thing I want to do right now is unpack. I can't *believe* that you volunteered me to do makeup in that horrible turret room." She shudders. "I hate how much you're enjoying this."

"Cecily, there's nothing in there," he says. "But we can start with the attic, if you want." Cecily doesn't answer. They pause underneath the attic door. Rudy yanks the string, but nothing happens.

"Want me to get the key?" Amber asks.

Rudy shakes his head. "Nah. The realtor said it must have been sealed, right? Sounds like a lot of effort to open. Let's do the turret first. We can help Cecily set it up, do a minirenovation, just for her. Make it look really good."

Cecily's expression softens. "All right."

The triplets hear the sound of the front door open and junk movers filing in beneath them.

"I don't get the big deal about keeping them off camera," Cecily says. "Do you really think anyone believes that we do it all ourselves?"

Amber shrugs. "Viewers just want the illusion. I dunno; it's nice to pretend, I guess."

"Why?" Cecily asks.

"Because if we can do it, they can do it, too?" Amber asks.

"I think Mom just wants another thing to be mad about," Rudy says, opening the turret door. Someone must have been in it this morning, because it's unlocked. "She'll probably be on the warpath for a while."

"I don't blame her," Cecily mutters.

For a second, they all stare up.

"It's dark in there," Rudy says.

Amber shoots him a look. "Chicken," she says, flicking on the light and climbing the stairs. Cecily doesn't move until Amber calls down: "There's some really cool furniture up here!" she calls. "Come on!"

Rudy eyes his other sister. "After you," he says, and then follows her.

The turret room is actually not bad—beams of light enter through skylights and the bay window, cutting through the room and sending motes of dust dancing around them. Piles of junk line the walls, punctuated by the odd piece of furniture. Rudy stares at the turret window, trying to imagine Alex Grable standing there, her mother lying dead far below. That girl, with the brown hair and braces . . .

Rudy shakes his head to clear the thoughts and heads over to one of the cardboard boxes lining the walls. He peers inside. "Hey, Cece, you might like this one!"

She looks over. "If it's a dead rat or something . . ."

"Nah, it's all these old clothes. Don't you do, like, vintage makeovers ever?"

Cecily comes over, intrigued. "Yeah, actually."

"We could upcycle some of the stuff, too," Amber says. "Ooo, we could have a turret haul, like a thrifting haul, and show it all off."

"Not a terrible idea," Cecily says grudgingly as she pushes aside some old cans of paint and reaches for a cardboard box. It contains mostly clothes—

dresses, blouses, sweaters, and even what looks like an old track uniform complete with a sweet varsity jacket. Then her face sours. "Not funny."

"What?" Rudy asks.

She pulls an old, broken doll from the bottom of the box. "Ha. Ha."

"Wasn't us," Amber says.

Rudy reaches for it. "Creepy," he says with a grimace. "Guys, we should do a haunted doll video. It would be *so* cool—Cece, you could do some cool doll makeup or something. We can make it a themed week!" He examines the doll, turning it over. "Hey, there's something sewn on the dress—*R-e-e-n-a*."

"Reena?" Amber asks. "Or Ray-na?"

"The second one?" Rudy says, but it comes out like a question. The doll is really not that creepy—just an old princess doll, wearing a pink dress with long, braided hair. Maybe something Alex owned when she was younger. Before everything went wrong.

"Who cares?" Cecily grumbles. She folds a couple of the prettier blouses and dumps the rest back in the box, beginning the junk pile. Rudy shrugs and explores the rest of the room. He removes a drop sheet in the corner to unveil an antique desk, stacked high with cardboard boxes. The desk itself is made of old, sturdy wood with tons of little drawers. It's covered in carvings and embellishments.

"Cece, c'mere," he says. "This thing has, like, seven million compartments. Need a makeup chest?"

Cecily walks over to examine the desk. In the background, Rudy can hear the click of a phone shutter sound as Amber snaps pictures. Can't he just have one morning where no one is shoving a camera in his face? Can't he clean out a room without it being documented for Insta, without having to worry if he looks attractive or buff enough in his ratty cleaning clothes? He shoots Amber a look and almost instantly regrets it. After all, it's not her fault that they need to post so often.

Rudy goes to move one of the boxes stacked on top of the desk. It's full of paint; maybe they can use that for some kind of shoot later. He opens the second box. "Jackpot!" he cries. "Look at these."

The box is full of cassette tapes. "Simon and Garfunkel—oh, awesome, Miles Davis. Good taste, whoever owned these."

"Cassettes?" Cecily asks, opening and closing desk drawers. "Aren't those, like, ancient?"

"Absolutely," Rudy says, digging through them.

"How are you even going to listen to those?" Cecily asks.

"There might be a player in the box," Rudy says, rummaging around. He digs one out from underneath the mound of tapes. "Yes! And it records, too—I could make my own mixtape, or . . ." His voice trails off. He's never recorded himself playing guitar before. It definitely wouldn't be content for Insta, but it could be fun.

"Sounds like a lot of effort to me," Cecily says, ruining his train of thought. "Why not just record on your phone? I do like the desk, though. Can we move it?"

"Sure," Rudy says. He doesn't answer her first question. There's something about recording his music on his phone that just seems too . . . permanent. Too easy for someone like Amber or Mom to find and post on the account. "Where to?"

Cecily sighs. "By the window. Now that you've put the idea in Mom's head, I'll never hear the end of it if I don't set up in this room. Whatever. It'll be fine."

"Because there are no ghosts here and you are definitely not afraid of them?" Rudy asks.

"Yeah," Cecily mutters, turning back to survey the rest of the room. "That's exactly why."

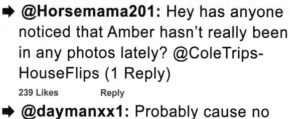

→ @Horsemama201: Hey has anyone noticed that Amber hasn't really been in any photos lately? @ColeTrips-HouseFlips (1 Reply)

239 Likes   Reply

→ @daymanxx1: Probably cause no one wants to see that. Hot girls only. Team Cecily forever.

14 Likes   Reply

Cecily

EVEN WHEN ALL THE JUNK IS CLEARED OUT OF THE TURRET room, it's still not ready to be a makeup studio if you ask Cecily. She puts her hands on her hips and examines the layout of the space. She'll have to move the desk across the room to better take advantage of the lighting, and maybe install some ring lights. She sighs and leans back onto the desk, trying to collect herself. Amber and Rudy had left to unpack their rooms long before the turret was entirely clean, leaving Cecily to finish sweeping up the space. It really is a nice room—or it would be if she could stop staring at the window, imagining Alex standing there, silhouetted against the light.

Suddenly she is hyperaware of how alone she is.

There's no way she can move the desk on her own, so she follows Rudy and Amber's lead and heads downstairs to unpack her own bags. Cecily listens to them joking around as she procrastinates, redirecting to the kitchen to find Speckles. She takes him out of his cage and back to her bedroom, where she cradles him in her lap, stroking his light, spotted fur. She sighs, feeling the tension ease out of her. Rudy might roll his eyes and call Speckles a gerbil under his breath, but Cecily loves him. She stares into his soft, brown eyes and smiles. No matter what she posts or what she looks like online, he will always look at her just like that. She smiles and holds him close, breathing in the musk of his fur.

But she does have to unpack.

She lets Speckles hop around her room while she hangs her outfits up in the closet. Across the hall, she can hear Rudy giving Amber a rundown on some newspaper articles that he found about the murder-suicide. Cecily doesn't join them.

She arranges her outfits in the closet, one by one. Some of them are gifts from sponsors, but most of the more expensive items she'd owned were resold on ThriftMark after they'd appeared in a photo or two—after all, the family has to give the illusion that Cecily Cole has an endless wardrobe. In reality, Cecily travels light, with a few base pieces augmented by whatever strange stuff her sponsors sent her to wear. She runs her fingers through a strappy number that any mom who didn't double as a social media manager would have been scandalized by. It's hard to police your daughter's clothing choices when her image is the vast majority of your income.

Cecily takes a deep breath in and tries to calm the ever-present feeling of *pressure*. She listens to Amber and Rudy speculate and goof off as they clean, and she tries not to feel bitter. Bitter that they're not being pressured to make posts *all the time*, bitter that the focus on her content means that Rudy and Amber are in fewer and fewer posts. Rudy hadn't reported on internet drama in a while; he really only hosts the vlogs and livestreams now, and Amber—well, she spends most of her time behind the camera instead of in front of it.

Cecily knows that she should be happy, that she should feel lucky and popular and special to have such a huge internet following—and there are moments when she truly does. But those moments have been fewer and farther between as her family has sunk deeper and deeper into debt. She promises herself that when she's done unpacking she'll take a break to look at fan posts and videos to cheer herself up. That is the best part of social media right now.

For the first few years, Rudy, Cecily, and Amber managed the account themselves, slowly amassing followers by filming behind-the-scenes renovation things and other one-off videos like Rudy's drama reporting, Cecily's makeup, and Amber's fashion segments. Then a house underperformed on the market, their mom caught their dad gambling away their children's college funds, and suddenly the checks coming in from tiny sponsors became a critical part of their income.

Their mom dived in. From then on, Mrs. Cole made sure that it was "audience engagement this" and "post performance that" until their sponsors weren't so tiny anymore. She cut Amber's features, moved Rudy to a hosting role, and shined a spotlight on Cecily. *Her little makeup guru,* Cecily thinks sarcastically.

She misses those early days. Back when Amber was posting fashion videos weekly and Rudy was gleefully digging up and investigating all the influencer drama he could find. But now that Amber worked behind the scenes and Rudy's commentary content had been cut—her mom didn't want them becoming a drama channel, she'd said—Cecily is the only triplet who still has her niche. Of course, they all post about the renovation content, but that isn't the same. Things between her and her siblings feel . . . distant.

Downstairs, a *thunk* and several curses jolt Cecily out of her reverie. It sounds like the junk movers are almost done clearing out the first floor.

Cecily hangs her favorite Gucci top in the closet and glances toward her bedroom window. It looks out onto a wide lawn that's in serious need of some landscaping, striped with afternoon shadows from the looming woods. The lighting in here really isn't that bad; maybe she should just set up in her room and invest in a couple extra ring lights. But no—Rudy had already gotten Mom to agree that she should be in the turret room; she had to. Especially after how much "viral potential" her mother said the haunting angle had. Cecily swallows her unease.

She gives up on clothes and unpacks her bookshelf—among the romance and sci-fi novels are old chemistry textbooks and some lesser-known titles on makeup manufacturing. Sometimes, when she's sitting down for a homeschooling session between renovating a house and making social media posts, she wishes she were at a real school—one without lessons on the best practices for shooting a vlog. Maybe even one with a chemistry lab and actual advanced science classes.

She's been meaning to update her book collection for quite some time; she reads every book on the science behind makeup that she can get her hands on. But Mom isn't exactly . . . excited to switch up Cecily's makeup videos from simple tutorials to in-depth talks about emulsification agents, pigments, and what makes a formula vegan. And god forbid she alienate a potential sponsor by expressing a distaste for makeup that isn't cruelty-free.

She closes her closet and turns to her makeup stash: shears, brushes, palettes galore. Not for the first time, Cecily finds herself thinking about how nice things had been before Mom started managing her and her siblings. Not for the first time, she finds herself wondering if maybe, just maybe, her makeup videos are getting popular enough for her to make it on her own. Not as a Cole triplet, but as . . . Cecily. Who doesn't have to be perfect, who could post the videos *she* wants—strange looks that aren't guaranteed to succeed, deep dives into the chemical elements of a successful formula . . .

Of course, her family would have to get out of debt first.

The hallway has gone quiet. She slips downstairs with Speckles and returns him to his cage in the kitchen, locking it before she climbs the stairs to check on her siblings. She finds Rudy sitting on his bed with the second-hand acoustic guitar their dad got him for his sixteenth birthday, listening to the tapes from the turret room.

"Whatcha doing?" she asks.

"Trying to figure out these chords by ear," he responds.

"Aren't there websites with chords?"

Rudy makes a face at his sister. "I know. I just like doing it this way—it's more challenging. Besides, you hear that crackle on the tape, you know it's got character."

"Or that it's broken."

"No, they still work! I mean, I've only gotten through one so far, and it's been pretty good. Odd background noise, though, but nothing to complain about. Everything is *so* nineties, it's great."

"I'm guessing you don't want to help me set up the desk in the turret room," Cecily says.

"In a minute," he replies. "I just want to figure out this chord progression . . ."

Sure. One minute in Rudy guitar time is about a thousand years.

Cecily wonders if she can convince Amber to help her. But when she walks over to her sister's room, she finds Amber still fully packed except for her MacBook, tablet, and stylus. She's set them up on the floor and is lying on her stomach, glaring at the screen. Amber is in work mode, like always.

"What are you doing?"

"I'm trying to clone part of one turret room picture to cover up some of the weird boxes in the corner," she says, but her voice is flat. Like she's annoyed. Or distracted. "I'm working. Still not sure what I'll do about the doll—and then I need to go back and track our post engagements from earlier; Mom wants a report of how we're doing . . ."

Cecily isn't sure how to answer. When they were little—and when they first started the account—she and Amber had been so close. But ever since their mom's micromanaging about "engagement" and "successful posting practices" had pushed Amber behind the camera, things have been . . . different. She is different. Distant in a way that Cecily isn't sure how to fix. "I'm guessing you can't help me finish moving the desk, then," Cecily says quietly.

"When I'm done," Amber says in a monotone, turning back to the screen. "Don't worry, these photos are going to be sick, wait and see. You look gorgeous." She sounds so exhausted.

"Thanks, Ambs, " Cecily says. Amber doesn't even look up as she leaves the room to search for her dad. Maybe he will help her out.

Downstairs, the junk movers have really transformed the place. Without the odd pieces of furniture or boxes covered in painting tarp, the whole house seems massive. Her voice echoes through the first floor.

"Dad, I need you to—" When she turns a corner into the kitchen, her father is deep in conversation with a short Hispanic man. "Sorry," she says, flushing. "Is this a bad time?"

"Cecily!" Mr. Cole says. "I would like to introduce you to Mr. LaRosa. He's our secret weapon on this project—his team will be doing a lot of the installation and landscaping that your mother and I can't get to."

"Nice to meet you, Mr. LaRosa," she says. His handshake is firm, his smile kind.

"Please, call me Joseph," he says. "Mr. LaRosa makes me feel old, and I'm too much in denial for that." Cecily smiles, genuine this time.

"What's up, sweetheart?" Mr. Cole asks.

"Oh, I just wanted to move a desk upstairs," she says. "But you're busy, so I'll just get Amber and Rudy to do it sometime later."

"You kids were cleaning out the turret and the attic, right?"

Cecily nods. "Turret, actually. We couldn't get in the attic—isn't it sealed?"

Her dad sighs and gives Joseph a look; this is clearly only one of many problems on their to-do list. He offers Joseph a brief explanation of the house tour and what the realtor had said about the attic. Joseph instantly suggests a fix, and Mr. Cole loses himself in a list of potential solutions, and then yet another, longer list of other problems they would have to deal with first. Cecily coughs, trying to regain his attention.

"I'm sorry, what did you need?"

"A desk moved. But I can ask later . . ."

"Well, I think I'm on the clock," Joseph says, giving her a friendly smile. "I can help you out, since we're waiting on Mrs. Cole to begin the tour, anyway."

"Is this for your makeup studio?" Mr. Cole asks.

"Yeah," Cecily says. "If that's okay."

"Sure! One thing first, though." Joseph walks over to Speckles's cage and smiles through the bars. "Who's your furry friend here?" he asks, clearly charmed. Cecily is instantly won over.

"His name is Speckles," she starts, but she doesn't have time to get any additional words in before Rudy and Amber appear in the hallway. They introduce themselves to Joseph, and the first thing out of Rudy's mouth is, "Know anything about the dead girl?"

Cecily winces. Joseph shakes his head. "That was before I moved here. I've only been in town for the last ten years or so, but I've really liked my time in Norton. Lovely place."

Cecily can't tell if Rudy is oblivious or if he's deliberately ignoring the attempt to change the topic as he continues. "Do you know where we can find out? Our followers are dying to learn more."

"Followers?"

Cecily lets out a mental groan as her dad launches into an explanation of social media and the logistics of being paid for posting photos of their renovations online. Mr. LaRosa seems confused, but perhaps a little impressed. "You remind me of my own kids—got two in college always trying to get me to video-chat this and text that. I just can't keep up."

"Neither can I," Mr. Cole jokes. "That's why I leave it to them. And they leave the construction to us."

Joseph laughs. "Now that, I can handle," he says. "I'm glad that you're fixing the place up. I think it's always a shame when homes go unlived in. And I know the rest of the town will see that, when you're done with the place."

"The rest of the town?"

"Robert?" Rudy is cut off by the sound of their mom rounding the corner. "Robert, where's the master key?" She sees Joseph and stops short.

"Er, please," Mr. Cole says. "Allow me to introduce you to my lovely wife."

Mrs. Cole wipes the scowl off her face and greets Joseph before turning to her husband. "I thought I told you to leave the key on the kitchen island."

"I did, honey."

"Well, it's not *there*—"

"Er, there was a key on the bannister when I came in," Joseph says, almost shyly.

Cecily's mom vanishes back toward the entry and returns a few seconds later with the key. "Thank you," she says to Joseph. Then to Mr. Cole, "You're hiring him, right?"

"Absolutely," Mr. Cole says.

Mrs. Cole gives Joseph's hand a warm shake. "Thanks again. I'm looking forward to working with you."

"Likewise," Joseph says, before turning back to Cecily. "Now, what was it you needed moved?"

Between her dad, Rudy, and Joseph, it takes about twenty seconds to move Cecily's desk into the prime position for turret makeup, lighting-wise. As they place the desk down, Cecily spots a stray cassette tumbling out of a drawer. Her dad grabs it.

"You know what these are?" he asks, incredulous. He turns it over in his hands. "See, kids, this is a *cassette*—"

Rudy rolls his eyes but smiles as he takes the cassette from his dad. "Weird. This one's not labeled," he says.

"Ah," Mr. Cole continues. "That could be a *mixtape*, because, you see, back when kids didn't have iPhones or iMusic or Apple everything, we actually had to record songs from the *radio*."

Rudy snorts. "I know what a mixtape is, Dad," he says. "And yeah, sure, teenage boomers were the OG music pirates. Got it." He gingerly picks up the tape, trailing a tangled mess of ribbon behind it. "Looks like it needs a little love."

"You're really going to go through all the effort to untangle and rewind it?" Cecily asks.

"Of course," Rudy says.

"Well, I'll leave you kids to it," Mr. Cole says. "Me and Mr. LaRosa— Joseph—have some planning to do. And then, if you kids want to help, we'll start ripping up the floor."

Cecily doesn't respond enthusiastically, but Rudy mutters some vague promise as they leave.

As soon as they're gone, Amber sits up on the desk and turns to Cecily. "Hey, Cece, some girl named Bella messaged the account while I was unpacking—she says she met you? Invited you to hang out?"

"Oh, yeah," Cecily says. "She works at the pizza place. I thought it might be fun for us to hang with the townies. What do you think?"

Rudy raises an eyebrow. "We'll only be here for, like, a month. And did you hear what Joseph was saying about the town? I hadn't thought about it before, but—"

"—they might not be happy that we're here," Amber finishes.

Cecily flushes. She hadn't thought that the town's . . . lukewarm reception toward the Coles would extend to Bella and her friends. "Hey, you don't know that," she says. What she doesn't say is how eager she is to get out of this house and have *something* besides social media to do. She watches her siblings hesitate and decides to pull out her trump card. "I'll bet that Bella knows more about your girl ghost," she adds. That gets him.

Rudy smiles at his sister. "You know, I think that messaging your friend might not be a bad idea after all."

DMs. To: @ColeTripsHouseFlips From: @Dad Brad

➡ Hey Cecily

➡ Hey Beautiful

➡ Hey sexy

➡ Hey

➡ Hey

➡ ANSWER ME YOU BITCH.

Amber

AMBER STARES OUT THE WINDOW AND COUNTS THE NUMBER OF streets they pass as the Range Rover heads into town. There aren't many. She stifles a yawn; again, strange noises had kept her up all night. This house "settles" more loudly than any one she's ever been in. Of course, the real reason for her exhaustion is probably that she's been awake since early morning, lying in bed and thinking with equal dread about both the impending posting schedule and all the photos she has to edit.

Now, she's squished in the backseat with Rudy and Cecily while their parents listen to soft rock on Sirius XM. They're heading into town to check out some flooring at the local hardware store. The Range Rover rounds a corner, and Amber gets a view of the town center in the light for the first time.

It's larger than she expected; the widely spaced lots and wooded backdrop of the Tremont Street neighborhood make it easy to forget that they *did* actually move into suburbia. There are a few busy restaurants, some shops, and crowds of high school kids on coffee shop patios, sipping lattes and soaking up the summer sun. On summer vacation. For a second, Amber finds herself wondering what it must be like to be a normal teenager. To go to real school, not their mom's homeschool, where all the electives are social-media based. To not have, say, a small infinity of photographs to take and edit when they get home.

Mr. Cole pulls up to the hardware store and Amber files out behind Rudy. She looks around, but no one seems to recognize them. No, that's not right. No one seems to recognize them the way that they usually do— by looking starstruck, or running up to them and asking for selfies. But the townspeople aren't totally oblivious, either. Their gazes linger too long to be passing over irrelevant strangers. It's less the feeling of being admired by fans and more the feeling of . . . being watched. Scrutinized.

Amber shakes off her feelings of unease. It's all right; the majority of the town is probably just too far out of their age demographic to be anything but skeptical of any social media stars, not just the Coles. Most of them probably don't know what an influencer even is.

She follows her siblings into the hardware store.

Mr. Cole wanders off to find the manager, while Mrs. Cole instantly heads for the accent section, excitedly asking for Cecily's opinion about what kind of fixtures they should use for the upstairs bathrooms. Amber distances herself from her mom and sister and snaps a picture—a true candid. Of course, once the camera is out, nothing is the same; Mrs. Cole catches Amber photographing and poses Cecily and Rudy among the lighting fixtures, the windows, and the carpeting. Cecily, of course, has to take a break between pictures to touch up her makeup with products from her ever-present go bag. *Because she can't handle a split second of not looking perfect*, Amber thinks. She rolls her eyes when no one's looking and continues taking pictures.

Finally, her mom directs her to be in some shots with her siblings. They pose near some cool-looking doors. After snapping just a few pictures, her mom hands the camera back to Amber and tells her to choose something to post.

Amber hesitates. She knows which one her mom would like best—the one of Cecily beside a chandelier, the light dancing across her face. But Amber doesn't want to post that one. She scrolls back in their account history. She can't find the last time she had a solo photograph. She hesitates, then posts the group picture of the three of them. At least she's in this one.

"You went with the door pic?" Mrs. Cole asks, glancing at the phone. Amber waits for her to argue, but her mom is distracted by the manager's arrival. "Plan to use the Rudy and Cecily ones all week—maybe schedule those in advance when we get home."

Amber fights the urge to roll her eyes as she agrees. Her mother turns to Mr. Cole and a graying man in a blue apron who introduces himself as

Mr. Brendan O'Donnell, the owner of the store. Mr. Cole instantly launches into talk about dark wood flooring, and the conversation goes smoothly until Mrs. Cole chimes in about their social media following. She'd been unable to get a sponsor for the flooring, but she is still trying to cut costs wherever possible. "We have a large following, you know. I wonder if we can help each other—what if we posted about your store for a discount? We'd expose you to all our followers—"

Mr. O'Donnell's face hardens. "No partnerships. Sorry."

Amber watches as her mom gapes like a fish and Mr. Cole cuts in, going back to conversation about varying kinds of dark hardwood. Mr. O'Donnell is polite, but his answers to her parents' questions are curt. Not exactly fantastic customer service. There is absolutely no material worth vlogging here.

That is, until Mr. O'Donnell says, "Now, for historical authenticity—"

"Oh, we don't mind about that," Mr. Cole interjects. "We just want to make a nice home."

Mr. O'Donnell lets out a small laugh. "Well, I am a high school history teacher, so it's kind of my area of expertise."

"Really?" Mr. Cole asks, ever the dad.

Mr. O'Donnell nods. "In fact, I'm a member of the local historical society. We don't have protections on the Tremont house yet, obviously"—he shoots them a look—"but it is a property that we're interested in acquiring, since it dates so far back. We're trying to preserve the roots of the town. I know that to some people, houses like Tremont might just seem like old, out-of-date buildings—or worse, buildings that should be torn down for new developments or weekend homes—but a lot of these buildings have been around since the eighteen hundreds. I think it would mean a lot if the Tremont home, one of the oldest in the town, could be preserved as closely as possible."

Amber's parents falter. She wonders how on earth they're going to field this one—historical preservation definitely isn't on their list of renovation goals. In fact, there is only one: sell, no matter what.

Mrs. Cole speaks softly. "Well, I'm afraid that's just not what buyers want."

"It is a town landmark. We want to make sure it's taken care of. Not defiled."

Mr. Cole lets out the world's fakest laugh. "Oh, we won't be defiling anything! Now, about that flooring . . ."

Amber is distracted from the rest of the conversation by a shout from down the aisle. "See? I *told* you that they were here!" It's a short girl with platinum hair, around high school age, flanked by two other kids.

Amber tenses, but Cecily clearly recognizes the girl. "Oh, hey—Bella, right?" she asks. Mrs. Cole shoots her a look that clearly says to deal with fans elsewhere; Mr. O'Donnell is acting weird as it is. So Amber and Cecily lead Bella and her friends into the next aisle, where Cecily introduces Amber and Rudy. "Amber and Rudy, this is Bella. Bella, Amber and Rudy. Who are your friends?"

"This is Miles and Jada," Bella says, gesturing to the kids behind her. Miles is tall, with light brown skin and a clear lax-bro vibe. Jada, on the other hand, is darker skinned with a build that appears both slight and strong. Amber wouldn't be surprised if she were a dancer. Jada turns and catches her staring. Amber feels her own face heat up and quickly averts her gaze. Is it just her, or is a small smile tugging at Jada's lips? By the time she risks another glance, Cecily and Bella have started talking again.

"How did you find us?" Cecily asks.

Bella flushes. "Don't be mad, but I recognized your car from the vlogs. We were across the street, at the Cityside Coffee—you should come sometime."

"She's kind of a superfan," Miles chimes in. "Just *had* to know what you guys were picking up in here."

Rudy rolls his eyes and leans against a shelf showcasing different metallic finishes for varieties of lighting. "Only the most basic flooring options possible."

Amber laughs and chimes in. "If it were up to Rudy, he'd renovate the house using the weirdest stuff he could find." She can feel Jada's eyes on her as she speaks.

"You mean like that one?" Bella asks, pointing out a lighting fixture that's built to look like a tangle of glowing wires.

"Absolutely," Rudy says. Amber can still hear her parents and the hardware store owner talking about wood in the next aisle over. Rudy must be distracted by them as well, because he continues with a question. "Speaking of weird . . . do you know the guy that runs this place?"

"O'Donnell?" Miles asks, peeking through the shelving to look at him talking to the Cole parents. "Steve's dad, right? Nah, not really. He donated a bunch of wood a couple years ago so the Cub Scouts could build catapults, though, so he can't be that bad."

Clearly, the frosty temper is reserved for them. The out-of-towners.

Jada mimics Miles, peering through the shelves at Amber's parents. "You're forgetting about the house, though."

Miles nods. "Ah. Makes sense."

"About what?" Rudy asks. He never could stop asking questions. Amber isn't sure if she wants to learn any more about the Tremont house than they already know, but Rudy? Rudy always has to figure out *everything*.

He turns back toward them. "Oh, he's just all about preserving the town's history and stuff. I dunno, something about 'keeping Norton unique,' or whatever. I think he kinda sees the whole mansion-renovation thing as another sign that the area's being taken over by rich NYC weekenders. And, well, he's not wrong."

"Some people think it's a historical property that shouldn't be messed with," Bella admits. "They want to get it on some kind of list to protect it, but they haven't had any luck, with the whole murder thing."

"It's been empty for twenty years!" Amber protests. "They should be glad that at least someone is doing *something* with it!"

Bella shrugs. "They want it 'restored,' not renovated so some millionaire family can move in."

Jada nods. Amber can't help but notice the way her hair falls in her face, how her voice is low and musical when she speaks. Is it just in her head, or are Jada's eyes lingering on her, too? Amber bites her lower lip and tells herself not to get her hopes up. Sure, she's out to most of the internet, but that doesn't mean that Jada knows she's a lesbian. Or that Jada herself would be at all interested. Still, she can't help but think that Jada is holding her gaze for just a second longer than normal.

Bella jerks Amber out of her thoughts with a laugh. "I still can't believe that someone's living in the haunted house."

"Haunted?" asks Rudy, his eyes lighting up. "Do tell—I, for one, think that this is the coolest house we've been in. I almost want to set up night cameras and see if I can record anything. I bet the internet would love it."

"The town might not," Jada says.

"Well, some people definitely think it's haunted," Miles says. "Between the Grables, and that other kid—"

Amber feels her face pale, but Rudy beats her to the question. "'Other kid'?"

Bella looks at him, surprised. "The Grables weren't the last family to live there. You knew that, right?"

Not another kid. Not another—

"You have to tell me," Rudy says.

Bella seems all too eager to comply. "Well, there was that Andrews kid, about, I dunno, ten years ago? Evan? I was in, like, first grade when it happened. He fell while they were painting; everyone said it was a freak accident, but . . ."

"But?" Rudy asks. Amber almost rolls her eyes. He's practically drooling. Next to him, Cecily is quiet. She looks a little sick.

Bella is cut off by the sound of Mrs. Cole's voice calling for the triplets. Rudy doesn't take his eyes off her. "Can we—"

"Here," Bella says, handing him her phone. "There's a bonfire happening this weekend—you guys should definitely come. We'll fill you in then." Bella swaps numbers with Rudy and Cecily. Amber's debating asking Jada for *her* number when Cecily, Bella, and Miles break to take a quick selfie. She tries to work up the courage, but before she can make a move toward Jada, her parents are there, greeting the other kids and steering them toward checkout. Of course.

Mom hadn't been able to get any kind of discount on the wood. Amber watches Mr. O'Donnell as he rings them up, wondering what he really thinks about the renovation, what he's not saying. If he knows anything about this Evan kid.

As her family continues their afternoon errands, Amber realizes that Mr. O'Donnell isn't the only townie to be . . . frosty toward them. Their day around town results in a strange flip-flop between fans who gush over them and ask for selfies, and townies who either approach them with guarded, cautious greetings or practically ice them out of conversations. There is a pretty strict age divide between the former and the latter. Word had clearly gotten around by the time they stop for coffee later that afternoon. The barista takes one look at their fancy shoes, expensive jeans, and stylish haircuts before he forms his face into a stoic wall and asks them if they are new in town.

Which, of course, they are.

No matter where the go, it's always the same. The ask. And then, when Mr. Cole reveals that they are fixing up the Tremont house, the feigned surprise. About half the town is aware of them—or what a social media influencer even *is*—and the other half is oblivious. Teenage cashiers stare at designer goods with thinly veiled jealousy; the man at the post office goes on a tirade about how wealthy New Yorkers keep ruining small towns by buying vacation homes in "scenic upstate," inflating property values. Opening them up to the kind of people who would *want* a renovated McMansion. *People like you*, he implies.

But no matter their reaction to the Coles, no one offers any information about the deaths. Not that Amber or any of the Coles ask, of course. But that doesn't stop Amber from listening more closely to her parents' conversations with other adults than she normally would, or from feeling uneasy. *Just new-house jitters*, Amber tells herself. *These people are just small-towners suspicious of the social media folk, not vindictive townies actively harboring a secret.* But as the Range Rover nears the Tremont house, she finds that harder and harder to believe. After all, they'd already uncovered one more secret about the "death house": that Alex Grable wasn't the only

78

one. There had been another. A boy. And Amber has a strange gut feeling that he isn't the only thing the Tremont house is hiding.

They round the corner and the house comes into view.

Cecily screams.

Mr. Cole slams on the breaks. Amber feels her mouth drop open.

A side of the turret is streaked with blood. No—not blood. Paint; it is paint. It has to be. A deep red trickles down the side of the window and over the porch awning before dripping onto the driveway right in front of the Range Rover. And in the middle of the dark circle of red is—something. A bent, broken shape. Rudy's already out of the car, and Amber leaps up to follow him. She sprints toward the turret, years and years of interval running finally paying off. Above her, it looks as if the house is bleeding, as if Alex Grable has committed suicide and bled all the way down.

For a terrible second, Amber catches sight of the twisted shape underneath the turret and thinks that it is going to be a body.

But as Amber nears, rationality catches up with her panic. It's not blood; it's paint. A dark red paint that could only have been thrown from the turret window. Which means that someone had been inside their house.

She stops, barely winded, next to an exhausted Rudy. Up close, she finally recognizes the twisted, broken lump that lies in the center of the pool of red paint.

There, drenched in what looks like blood, is the wrecked remains of her computer.

Comment on the latest Cole post:

➡️ **@ExoticRuby:** Rudy's so hot. Too bad Instagram boys are dumber than a bag of bricks.

265 Likes   **Reply**

Rudy

CECILY HAD SCREAMED. AND RUDY? HE'D PLOTTED. THE MOMENT he saw Amber's computer in the middle of a faux blood stain, his mind started going a mile a minute. And it kept going, even while his mother had called the police. Even after the Coles had gone to bed. Of course, Rudy had spent half the night thinking about the Tremont house and the other half on their account, answering DMs. A lot of them were about the house, and more are about Alex Grable—the account, not the person. A lot of people had noticed the messages, and Rudy wasn't sure how to respond.

Mrs. Cole had called immediately to report the break-in—it had to be a break-in; there was no way that blood paint came from anywhere but the turret—and, after confirming that they were safe and that there was no one in the house, gave a full report to the police. By the time she'd finished giving the report, it was already late in the evening, so Mrs. Cole had agreed to wait until the next morning for a full inspection from the officers. *Of course she would*, Rudy thought. His mom never wanted to make a scene.

At least, not to the public. At home, Rudy knows all too well how dramatic she can be. The previous evening had been one long cry of *How is she going to* edit? from his mom, who had insisted that the situation be remedied as soon as possible. Unfortunately, Amber's computer had more high-end graphics processing than all of the other Coles' combined—she couldn't exactly borrow Rudy's. So, early the following morning, Amber and his dad had headed out, first thing, to buy another laptop. Sure, it is another expense that the Coles can't really afford—much like the cost of repainting the exterior of the turret—but what does another few thousand dollars matter when they are so far in the hole already? And Mom has a point: They can't afford to delay a sponsored post because of Amber's computer mishap.

Mishap. That's what she is calling it. Not a break-in, not vandalism; a mishap. As if someone accidentally dropped a bucket of paint out their window. *No*, Rudy thinks. There is more to it. There were three deaths in the Tremont house, plus the Alex Grable account, and now this. Someone had been *here*.

Rudy can't stop thinking about it. Even his morning workout feels off—he's too preoccupied with, well, everything Tremont.

The hardwood arrives around nine, while Rudy and his family are still waiting for the police.

They've barely begun unloading when something *else* goes wrong. "Robert! Where did you put the key?" Mrs. Cole's voice echoes through the house. Mr. Cole looks at Rudy over the wood they're carrying and shakes his head.

Mrs. Cole steps onto the porch in time to see the headshake. She gives a very exaggerated eye roll. "Great. Who did it, then? Did a ghost do it? Rudy, if this is a prank—"

Amber calls from the kitchen. "It's by the sink, Mom!"

Mrs. Cole grabs the key and returns once Rudy has set the wood down, giving him a brief side hug. "Sorry—I'm sorry. We just really don't have the time to waste on this renovation." She's right. This house is larger than any other project they'd taken on. Aside from the grand foyer and kitchen, the first floor of the house also has a formal dining room, a parlor, a study, and a den. All of which are now bare, thanks to yesterday's "hunks moving junk."

Rudy notices that his mom's eyes keep straying to the driveway. There is no police car to be seen. Cecily and Amber join them on the porch. A gray blur darts about between Rudy's feet and he pounces on Speckles himself.

"Cecily!" he says, but he's only half upset. He might smack-talk Speckles, but now that he's cupped in Rudy's hands he just seems so *tiny.* And those big brown eyes . . . Rudy feels the chaos of the past day calm, just a little bit. He smiles.

"See! I knew you loved him!" Cecily says. "I'll put him back—there's my little escape artist!"

"Good catch, Rudy," Amber says. "I don't think Speckles would last long in these woods."

"Nope. Basically hawk takeout," Rudy jokes, and Cecily admonishes her rabbit as she carries him back inside.

Rudy is about to retreat back inside to do some more googling about the history of the house when his mom starts talking about *work*. "Now, you've all seen the weekly spreadsheet, right? We've got a couple posts going out today and a few more we're scheduled to shoot. Let's do a few while the light's good out front, then maybe some in-progress ones in the kitchen."

Rudy rolls his eyes. "Do we have to?" He'd so much rather play investigator than livestream host. But his mom just ruffles his hair. Oh, no—she is *not* going to get him to shoot another boring renovation post. He speaks up before she can continue. "I'd rather brainstorm ghost content for the livestream. You said I could."

Mrs. Cole thinks about it. Her eyes stray toward the red-stained tower, and the rest of the family's follow. "You can brainstorm," she says slowly. "But you have to come to me with a script before the livestream. If—and only if—I approve, you can mention it. We don't want to be offensive. So don't mention the ghost by name, don't connect it to any real history here—no specifics about this house that might dissuade potential buyers, you understand? When buyers ask, it's all a story for social media. We made it all up. Bring me the script when you have it."

Rudy fights the urge to scowl. A script? He has to write a script? Can't she just trust his judgment?

"What about the Alex Grable account then?" Rudy asks. "What if people ask about it on the livestream? We got so many DMs about it yesterday."

"Don't call it that," Cecily says. Rudy makes a mental note to check himself; Cecily has seemed really freaked lately.

"Our follower, then, whatever," Rudy says.

"Don't worry about what you're calling them, because you're going to ignore the account," his mom orders. "Don't mention them in the DMs, don't mention them on the posts. Final." She holds Rudy's gaze until he nods. Fine. Then she continues. "So, where were we? Today's posts. Yes. A couple of those are for some sunglasses sponsorship; we need the money if we're going to keep fixing up this house. Ooh—you three should go outside while it's still overgrown, do some sunbathing shots. Amber?"

Amber nods. Rudy opens his mouth to argue but shuts it; Amber already looks so exhausted. He wonders how much of her computer hard drive had been recovered and how much work on their posts she'll have to make up. So he doesn't argue as they get ready. A few minutes later he and his sisters are outside in swimsuits and beach towels, stretched out on the weedy lawn.

Rudy gives Cecily a look. Her level of enthusiasm is about where his is: nonexistent. Rudy is itching to get back to work, to learn more about the house—and he's here, stuck playing pretty boy.

"This is perfect," Amber says, obviously trying to lighten the mood. "Something like . . . suburban wilderness or whatever. We can think of something catchy, play up on the fact that everything is, well . . ."

"Creepy and overgrown?" Cecily asks.

Rudy can't take it anymore. He *has* to ask his sisters what their thoughts are on what the kids at the hardware store told them.

"What do you think about the other kid?" Rudy asks as Amber paces around them, searching for the optimal angle. "Another boy died—that's what Cece's friends said, right? Do you think they could be connected? I mean, one family tragedy is coincidence, but two? And now—"

"Not funny," Cecily says. "Look, I know you like playing investigator, but if you stir anything up Mom's going to murder you. That is *so* not what we need right now." She turns back to Amber. "Let's just get this post over with—I need to practice makeup for the sponsored stuff."

Amber shrugs and positions herself slightly above Rudy and Cecily. "Hey, it's what Mom wants. Okay, now, point your toes, long legs, yes—sunglasses down, I've got to make sure the label is in—"

Rudy stretches out for optimal ab definition. He tries to get into the headspace to smolder, but somehow he can't. He just feels so . . . tired of this. He can't stop thinking about Mom shooting down his posts, how she'd rather have him posing for sex appeal than doing what *he* wants. *Okay*, he thinks. *That's not entirely fair.* But still. Sometimes, it feels like all Mom—and some of their followers—thinks his only role on the account is to be a hot guy who occasionally investigates weird drama or builds things. And, if he is being honest with himself, that feeling had turned from a slight misgiving in the back of his mind to something that, well, bothers him. Something that keeps him from concentrating during photo shoots like these.

Sometimes, he just wants to be more.

Besides, this is such a boring shoot. Another stupid sunbathing shoot that says nothing except that he and Cecily work out to keep their image right for Insta. And then he spots a dilapidated door that has already been kicked to the curb by their dad. He gets up and yanks it over to them. "Here! This will make things more interesting. We can do *Titanic* style."

"Ew, no. I don't want tetanus," Cecily says.

"Amber, you get in the picture then."

Amber hesitates. She's about to open her mouth when a car rolls into the driveway. A police car.

The three jolt upward.

The car crunches over the uneven dirt driveway and comes to a stop before the triplets. Two officers step out: a lanky Asian man with thick glasses and a short Caucasian woman with dark, curly hair. The man tips his hat at them and smiles. Lines crease his face; he has to be at least as old as their parents. "Hello there. I'm Sheriff Kevin Yang, and this is my deputy, Maureen Perry. Are your parents home?" The officers take in the *Titanic* photo shoot and sunbathing setup with stoic expressions, although Rudy thinks he can spot a flicker of confusion on the woman's face.

Amber stows her phone in a pocket and introduces the three of them. "Our parents are right inside," Rudy says, leading the officers onto the porch. None of them elaborate on the photo shoot. The moment Rudy and the officers enter the foyer, he regrets it, but it's too late for the officers to unhear his parents' argument.

"Blood, Robert!"

"You know how it would look if people—"

"Mom!" Rudy shouts, drowning them out. "The police are here."

His parents go pin-drop silent. Rudy imagines his mom sweeping her messy hair into an elegant French twist and putting on her "nice family" face.

"Don't judge too hard; we're only just getting started," Mr. Cole jokes, rounding the corner and shaking hands with the sheriff and his deputy. Mrs. Cole emerges from behind him. They look like the picture of domestic bliss, dressed in matching overalls still smudged with dove gray paint from their last home renovation. Mrs. Cole smiles, all bright and welcoming. If they hadn't been shouting just moments before, the illusion would have been perfect.

They make quick introductions, and Mr. and Mrs. Cole launch right into an explanation of the break-in and vandalism. They'd left the paint up for the officers to see, and they hand over the remnants of Amber's old laptop as evidence. The two officers take detailed photographs of the remnants of the turret's paint and inspect the first floor. They find no signs of forced entry, despite Mrs. Cole's constant reassurance that they definitely locked up. "Well," Perry says, "with so much going on, perhaps you forgot to lock up after all." Rudy watches a muscle in his mother's jaw twitch at the suggestion of her negligence, but she doesn't say anything. He takes note of the officers' process—how scrupulous they are while gathering evidence, the way Perry is constantly photographing and Yang is always writing on his notepad, so no detail escapes. Calm. Collected. Meticulous. Assuring. Rudy takes mental notes. When he gathers clues about the Tremont deaths, he wants to be just as thorough.

Once they're finally finished, Yang and Perry gather the Cole family in the kitchen. Officer Perry speaks first. "Mr. and Mrs. Cole, kids, we want you to know that we are taking your complaint very seriously. We will be taking the computer in as evidence and filing an official report. Vandalism, destruction of property, potential breaking and entering, and trespassing at the very least. That being said, I feel the need to inform you of a bit of history of this residence."

Rudy sits up straighter. This is exactly what he's been waiting for.

Yang coughs. His eyes shift from the parents to the kids, clearly uncomfortable. "Of course you're aware of the house's . . . history and all, but what you might not have thought too much about is how this house has been abandoned for the last ten years. It's become a bit of a local legend, and a popular spot for squatters or teenagers looking to trespass. I'm sure you've seen what the local teens have done to some of the upstairs windows."

Mrs. Cole nods. "Don't worry, we're replacing all the broken panes," she says. "Does this mean you think that the vandalism . . ."

"Is likely just local teens seeing how far they can push your residence," Perry says. "The dark paint, the destruction of property—it's not out of character. Many trespass in this house; wouldn't surprise me if they had ways to sneak in and out. That being said, I do not believe them to be a physical threat to your family's safety. While we pursue leads, I want to recommend a security system. Advertise it heavily outside your home; it should help locals get used to the fact that someone is living here."

"Yes, of course," Mrs. Cole says. "We already have a system—it just hasn't been installed yet; it's only our third day here. Do you have any . . . usual suspects?" she asks.

The officers exchange a look. "We'll do what we can, but with no camera and no witnesses . . . it may be difficult. Such petty vandalism charges always are."

Mrs. Cole gives them a curt nod. Mr. Cole puts an arm around his wife. "Really appreciate it. Thank you Sheriff, Officer."

"No problem," the sheriff says. "We'll call you, should anything turn up. You have a nice day now." He turns toward the door, but his partner hesitates.

"Er, did you know that your kids were playing outside? On a door?" she asks Mrs. Cole. Then she turns to the kids. "You all should be careful; there can be nails in those things."

Mrs. Cole turns to her children and raises an eyebrow.

"We were doing a *Titanic*-themed wreckage photo shoot," Rudy says.

"Photo shoot?" the deputy asks. "Playing models?"

Mrs. Cole lets out a surprised cough. *Oh no*, Rudy thinks. *Here we go.* "Oh. I thought you knew. The triplets aren't playing models. They *are* models. On Instagram."

"Oh."

Rudy is hoping that Officer Perry—who can't be older than in her late thirties—is just going to say that she knows about Instagram and end the conversation, but to his disappointment she's clearly clueless. Before Officer Perry can do more than make a confused facial expression, his mother is already pulling out her phone and thrusting their feed in the deputy's face. "Here's their account—we post about the renovation, too. You should follow us; we can help keep you up to date on things happening around your hometown!"

The deputy takes a small step back and glances at the sheriff. "Er, I will, thanks," she says. "Just, uh, be safe out there! And call us, should anything else happen."

"We know how to handle ourselves. Don't we, kids?" Mrs. Cole says.

Rudy swallows. "Of course." His mind strays back to the Alex Grable account. *The follower*, he can almost hear Cecily correcting. Then again, it hasn't posted in a while. He gets an idea. "Hey, Officer," he says, leaning against the bannister of the grand stairway. "What . . . happened in the house?" He leans too far; a loose wooden dowel pops out of the railing, clattering to the floor. Rudy gives a shaky grin and sticks it back on. "I mean, can you tell us anything about the deaths?"

Cecily shakes her head, letting out the word "no" in an almost inaudible whisper.

"Rudy," Mrs. Cole cautions, but from the expression on Officer Perry's face, Rudy can tell she knows something.

"The realtor told us that some girl killed herself," Rudy powers on before his parents can stop him. "And then Cece heard something in town about how she killed her mom first, and then something about the last owners also having an, uh, accident? We'd just like to straighten things out. Sir and ma'am," he adds, an afterthought.

Sheriff Yang shakes his head. "We can't discuss case details. I'm sure you understand."

"That's all you know?" Rudy presses.

Sheriff Yang and Officer Perry exchange a weighted look. He nods, ever so slightly, and Officer Perry turns to the family. "Evan Andrews fell from a ladder while painting the fourth floor," she says. "Ruled an accidental death. I can assure you that, despite what some citizens might like to tell stories about, there is no relation."

Mrs. Cole looks at Rudy in horror. "Of course. I'm sorry, sometimes Rudy speaks before he thinks."

Sheriff Yang claps a hand on Rudy's shoulder. "Natural curiosity; no offense taken."

"Well, uh, don't worry," Mrs. Cole starts. "About the house—I'm sure that the top-notch luxury renovations are going to really up the value of this neighborhood."

It's clear that the remark falls flat. Sheriff Yang gives her a slow nod. "I hope so," he says. He tips his hat one last time. "Nice to meet you sir, ma'am, kids. Give us a call if you have any trouble, and have a nice day, now."

They walk the police officers outside and watch as the car pulls away.

"They seem nice," Mr. Cole says. "Lots of small-town charm."

"We are in the suburbs," Cecily deadpans.

"They seemed like nice officers," Mrs. Cole reprimands, giving Cecily a look. "And good advice about the alarms. Shoot! We forgot to get a picture of you three in front of the cop car. That could have made for a nice thumbnail. I wonder if they'll let you do any jail-themed photos; that could be great clickbait for when numbers are low." Inside the house, a cell phone starts to ring. "That's the paint—Robert, come *on*. I told them we're going full sponsorship or nothing, and you have to back me on this."

Rudy's mom follows his dad inside.

Amber elbows Rudy. "I can't believe that you asked them about the murders! What are you thinking? That we can work a second one into our ghost post?"

"Uh, come on, guys," Cecily says. "Don't you think that's a little . . . insensitive? I mean, they did actually die here, didn't they?"

"It's got viral potential, Cecily," Amber says. "Besides, they're dead. Who cares?"

Rudy wiggles his hands at Cecily and cackles. "Well, maybe they care—if they're ghosts. Oooooo." He heads back inside. "Come on, I need a snack— then I want to reach out to the fans again, see what kind of ghost content would be best to post!"

"For real, though," Amber says, following him. "We're definitely talking about this on our next livestream—maybe we can get some supplies, do something creepy, like a séance."

"But we have to *keep it generic*," Rudy mocks. "I can't believe Mom's not letting us get into specifics. That's the *good* part."

Cecily rolls her eyes. "You two are awful." She turns her head upward and shouts, voice echoing across the house: "If there are any ghosts lurking around here—go after these two, not me! Leave the makeup girl alone!"

Comment on the latest Cole post:

➡ **@randum44:** Nothing's hotter than a girl who can do construction.
174 Likes   Reply

XXXXXXXXXXXXXXXXXXXXXXXXXXXXXXXX

CHAPTER 9

Cecily

THE CAMERA FLASHES. THE TRIPLETS SMILE SO WIDE THAT CECILY feels the sides of her mouth begin to wobble.

"Is that the last one?" she asks, stepping down from a stool and tossing a screwdriver onto the kitchen floor. Today, they're playing renovation. Perfect and fake. Right on-brand. "These overalls are killing me. *So* not flattering. Don't even pretend that Mom didn't pick out this outfit," she says.

"That obvious?" Amber asks, but she looks pleased.

"You're the fashion guru! Are you sure you can't convince Mom that this look is just not working?"

"What do they think we do, renovate dressed like farmers?" Rudy's tone is wry.

Amber laughs. "Hey, if one of you wants to pick a fight with Mom about overalls, be my guest," she says, checking the readout and giving them a thumbs-up. "But that will mean retaking all these photos in new outfits," she adds with an evil grin.

Rudy makes a face. Amber checks the readout and mimes a high-five.

"Next time, then," Cecily says, unbuttoning the overalls and letting them fall to the floor. She straightens the gym shorts and designer T-shirt she was wearing underneath and steps out of the overalls, reaching into the fridge for a Diet Coke. "How much longer are Mom and Dad going to make us pretend to renovate houses with them?"

"That's what we do," Amber says.

"That's what our *parents* do," Cecily replies. She watches Amber's face, hoping for a reaction. Even just a little smile like the one she got before. Anything to let her know she's not the only one who's pretty much had it today.

Amber switches the camera off. Cecily sighs as she looks at her brother and sister, still decked out in spotless "paint clothes" their mom chose for them, which cost more than an average seventeen-year-old's entire wardrobe. They'd spent the past several hours posing with various power tools, "concentrating" on renovation-related content.

Cecily glances at the clock and realizes the end is in sight. They're supposed to be done with this photo shoot and gone within the next fifteen minutes, when Joseph and the real crew will arrive to demo the rotting kitchen cabinets and knock down a wall or two to make it a true open-concept, per Mrs. Cole's vision.

Just then Mrs. Cole appears in the kitchen hall and asks to see the fruits of their labor. She frowns a bit as she looks through the photos. "Cecily— try to smile as much with your eyes as your mouth. Otherwise, gorgeous. We need more of you—we're going to try and reel in some more sponsors; maybe we can do some concept shoots later today."

Cecily stiffens. Of course. She doesn't know if she can handle any more sponsors, any more *perfect*. Her mom continues. "The real crew will be here in ten. Amber, want to give me some of the best stats from this week? Did you all make it on trending?"

"I'll check." Amber whips out her phone. As Cecily watches, Amber scowls. But only for a moment. Then Amber rattles off the usual report about engagement and increased follower count in a stiff, far-off voice, throwing in a few words about how the deaths and Rudy's brief livestream mention of ghosts have dominated the comments. Mrs. Cole nods, seemingly placated. Amber shoots her siblings a look. "I forgot something," she says. "In my bedroom."

That's all she has to say. Rudy and Cecily follow her upstairs and into her room, where she locks the door after they all settle in. She's only just begun to unpack; clothes and various electronics are spread throughout the room. Rudy sits on her bed next to a couple of their external hard drives, which contain archives of old content. "What's wrong?" he asks.

"That account is back," Amber says solemnly. Cecily feels her stomach twist. "The . . . follower." Cecily lets out a slow, shaky breath. She hasn't been able to get the image of the turret out of her head. Streaked with blood. So far, every time she's sat at her desk to work on makeup in the turret room, all she's been able to think about is the dead girl—the dead girl who Rudy likes to pretend is a ghost, whose name someone is using as an account handle to mess with them. And it's working.

Amber slides her phone toward her siblings.

Rudy lets out a low whistle. "Man, Alex is not happy."

Cecily's mind flashes back to the turret room, the window, the girl. She feels sick. "Rudy—"

Her brother rolls his eyes. "Fine. This follower, then. They've commented on all our posts now. At least, all the ones about the house."

Cecily scrolls through the account history. After the *Titanic* photos yesterday, they had added updated shots of every room affected by the renovation. The knot in her stomach tightens.

Even as Cecily scrolls through the pictures, her phone lights up with a flood of notifications. She'd had her phone on silent, so she hadn't seen the sheer volume of notifications that clued Amber into the account until now. People are sending her messages, tagging her—because the follower is leaving more comments. Some on every photo.

➡ Leave This House Alone.

➡ You touch those walls, I touch you.

➡ Get out.

➡ Get out.

➡ Getoutgetoutgetout.

➡ GET OUT OF MY HOUSE.

Cecily shivers. Rudy laughs, but it sounds forced. "Can ghosts even make Instagram accounts?"

Cecily gapes at her brother, trying to figure out if his bravado is real or not. Why isn't he stressed out? How can he be so . . . cavalier about this? "This is creepy. We need to talk to Mom."

"As if she'll do anything about it," Amber mumbles.

"I think we still need to try," Cecily says, more firmly this time.

But Amber just rolls her eyes. "It's generating a ton of engagement." Before Cecily can protest, she adds, "Mom would probably murder me on camera if she thought it would make us hit one million."

For Cecily, it seems like all the air is sucked out of the room. "I . . ." Cecily opens and closes her mouth, unsure of what to say. She knows Amber is being sarcastic, but she also knows she needs to say something. She's just not sure what.

"Have you read the replies?" Amber continues. The moment is gone. She clicks a comment.

➡ That's my house. Get out of my house.

➡ Replies (11)

➡ Your house?

➡ Hey, @ColeTripsHouseFlips, you've got a psycho fan

➡ Can it, creep

➡ This is so fake lmao

➡ Creepy! Stop!

Cecily's brow furrows. She navigates to the newest comment and reads the replies—there are already three more. This stuff *is* really generating engagement.

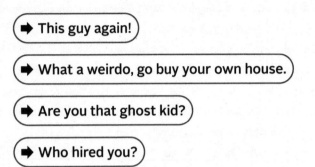

➡ This guy again!

➡ What a weirdo, go buy your own house.

➡ Are you that ghost kid?

➡ Who hired you?

Rudy catches on to her concern. "Don't worry, it's just some internet weirdo." When Cecily's face doesn't change, her brother flops onto Amber's bed and shoots her a smile. "Think positive! This is great, they're going to make us famous."

"Doesn't this bother you? Even a little?" Cecily asks, hating the fear that tinges her voice.

Rudy shrugs. "We've had weird comments before."

Cecily shakes her head. "The username. It's *Alex Grable.*"

Rudy swallows and nods. "I didn't say that they aren't . . . messed up to be doing it," he says in agreement with a shrug. "But I guess you're right that Mom should probably know. Even if we're not going to do anything about it."

"Still want to do your ghost livestream now?" Cecily asks, hoping against hope that the answer will be no.

But of course not. "Oh, absolutely," Rudy says. "I've already started writing the script. No way I'm stopping now—and no way I'm letting some follower with the ability to google the history of a small town scare me off of it."

Cecily sighs. At least she got him to agree with her about telling their mom about the follower ramping up his posts.

The triplets head downstairs, and Amber asks their parents to come into the library for a moment. Judging from their faces, Cecily can tell her parents aren't thrilled to have been pulled away from supervising the kitchen demo and cabinet installation.

Rudy acts as spokesperson for the triplets and fills his parents in on the latest posts from the follower. Mrs. Cole cuts him off midway through and asks to see his phone so she can read the comments herself.

And then she responds exactly how Cecily was afraid she would. She scrolls through the comments and takes note of the number of replies. "It *is* generating engagement," she says.

"It's weird though, right?" Cecily asks, trying to keep a pleading note out of her voice. "The username . . ."

Mrs. Cole nods. "I know, sweetheart. But there's nothing . . . illegal . . . about having that username, and they haven't posted any . . . direct threats. It's nothing you kids can't handle." She smiles up at Cecily, who is trying hard to keep her expression even. To not show how upset she is. After all, perfect people don't get upset. Mrs. Cole continues. "As long as people keep responding, it generates engagement. And that gets us closer and closer to trending."

"On that note," Rudy says, winking at his sisters. "Just check out the threads about my graffiti art in the master bedroom. It's got this follower really riled up. Talk about generating engagement! I think we should—"

"Rudy, no." Mrs. Cole holds up a hand. Rudy frowns.

"I'm just saying, I think it's a good idea—"

"I said *no*." She snaps. Then she sighs as her face softens just a bit. "Listen, it wasn't a bad idea at first, but now that the graffiti idea got this follower's interest, I think it's best if we don't proceed with it."

Amber takes a breath and starts to speak. "But—"

Cecily is surprised. It's unlike Amber to disagree with their mom. At least not openly.

Mr. Cole cuts her off. "Your mother is right. Don't engage with this guy. If he wants to comment and drive up engagement, he can do so all he wants. But we're not going to interact with him."

Rudy scowls. "Are you serious? It's one-third *my* account—I should be able to do what I want on it."

"Rudy, this is *our* account," their mother says with a patronizing smile. "We all help. This is a family account—and we have all outvoted you."

Cecily stares at her feet. She feels Rudy looking at her but she doesn't say anything. Without her, they have definitely outvoted Rudy and Amber. Cecily wants Rudy to do his posts, but why can't those posts be things that *don't* rile up their internet follower?

"Seems like you only cared about the account when we started earning money, Mom," Rudy mutters.

"Rudy," their father says. The warning tone in his voice is loud and clear.

But if Rudy hears it, he chooses to ignore it. "Speaking of that money, where do you think it's gone, huh? Why are we living in this dump when—"

"That's enough!" Mrs. Cole says. "Amber, go into the account and take away Rudy's admin privileges. Rudy, that means you won't be able to post or respond to DMs from your phone. And I'm considering canceling your ghost livestream—which I didn't want to let you do to begin with, remember? Rudy, you need to sit down and have some serious thoughts about how *your* actions affect *this* family—"

Rudy takes a step back. His face is bright red, and Cecily can see that he's furious. "What? You're seriously not letting me talk to fans anymore? And the livestream? Come on, this is ridiculous." His voice cracks.

Cecily winces. She knows how much of a blow this punishment is to her brother. Responding to fans is one of his favorite parts about the account—especially in the last couple years, as Mom took more and more control of their content.

"What I say goes," Mrs. Cole says. "And I think you need to have some punishment until you learn that. I'm serious here, Rudy. You are to have no interaction with fans—no DMs, no chats, no Twitter polls," she says firmly. "If you start taking me seriously, I'll restore your privileges to the livestream." She pauses, and Cecily holds her breath, wondering if Rudy will fight back. He doesn't. Instead he just glares at their mother, who pretends not to notice.

"Amber?" she says finally.

Cecily cringes. She doesn't envy Amber right now. If she agrees to do what their mother is asking, Rudy will see it as a betrayal; Cecily is certain of it. But what else can her sister really do, except exactly what their mom asks?

"Okay," Amber says, her voice small.

Cecily looks at Rudy. The hurt and anger are coming off him in waves.

"Seriously?" Rudy shouts. He shakes his head as he turns to storm upstairs. "If anyone needs me, I'll by in my room. *Thinking about how my actions affect this family.*"

After a second of awful silence left behind in Rudy's wake, Mrs. Cole turns back to her daughters. She plasters a chipper smile on her face. "Now, why don't you finish up that sunbathing shoot? And when you're done, Cecily, start planning a new makeup look. I'm thinking summer, gold, sunshine . . . and less formula and industry talk, this time. I'm worried that you're getting too technical, that viewers will start to drop off."

Cecily feels herself nodding. Another perfect makeup look, coming right up. Minus the science, minus the industry talk. Tailored for maximum engagement. She fights the urge to let her shoulders slump.

Ms. Cole continues. "Amber, get the camera for your sister. Oh, and set up an alert for when this follower posts. Just because we're not interacting doesn't mean we can't keep tabs on them. The moment he's bad for engagement, we're blocking."

Cecily runs upstairs to change into a bathing suit. She looks at herself in the mirror for a long moment. Does she look good enough? She turns her head to the side to get a better view of her eye makeup. Is her highlighter hitting the right spots to accentuate her cheekbones? Has she completely disguised her undereye bags? Are her eyebrows perfect? Her eyeshadow properly blended?

As she heads back downstairs, she pauses in front of Rudy's door, unsure of whether or not she should check on him. She decides to wait and let him cool off a little on his own first. She feels bad for him, but she also knows that he made his own bed by mouthing off to their parents so harshly.

It's not that she disagrees with Rudy—she's often daydreamed about having more control over their content, or even breaking off on her own to focus on her more scientific content, but she knows a losing battle when she sees one. Now is not the time to try and convince their mom to give them some freedom—not when the family finances are so precarious and their careers are their best shot at clawing their way out of debt. Cecily sympathizes with Rudy but feels that he needs to learn how to pick his battles. As she passes by his room, she can hear her brother stomping around and a clash as he knocks over something that sounds like buckets.

Amber is waiting for her in the now-empty kitchen. She shuts her computer. "Alert's up. We'll get a ping whenever they post." Cecily shudders. "I know," Amber says. "I'm not looking forward to reading more of their comments, either—but I'd rather know what they're up to."

"Yeah," Cecily says as Amber follows her down the hallway. They grab towels and sunhats from the closet. Finally, Cecily can't take it anymore. "I can't believe you took away Rudy's admin privileges," Cecily mutters.

"Well, what do you want me to do?" Amber asks, swiping a towel from the lower racks. "Stage a coup? I don't exactly have the pull that you do."

"What's that supposed to mean?" Cecily pulls open the door and they head outside.

"Oh, please. *Amber, take some pictures of Cecily there, there, lying on the ground there, in a bikini there*—I bet if you'd spoken up, she would have listened. Not been so hard on Rudy."

For the second time that day, something her sister says leaves Cecily stunned. Does Amber really feel this way? When was the last time they really talked about stuff? With a jolt, Cecily realizes that she can't remember. She didn't know Amber felt that way. "I—"

Ping.

Their phones vibrate in unison.

> ➡ **ColeTripsHouseFlips has begun a livestream.**

Cecily glances at her sister, who looks as confused as she feels. Would Rudy really risk doing a livesteam after their mom so adamantly forbade it?

Amber has her phone out already, so Cecily peers over her shoulder as she opens the video feed.

The camera jostles and reorients itself. Someone—it has to be Rudy, doesn't it?—is in one of the upstairs bedrooms. The third-floor master bedroom, Cecily realizes. A hand touches the camera again, stabilizing it. Then, Rudy comes into view, wearing gym shorts and a T-shirt.

Cecily and Amber exchange horrified glances. Amber curses. "I was so focused on the alert that I didn't wipe out the admin privileges yet," she gasps. "It's only been, like, fifteen minutes—"

"Leave it to Rudy to do something like this," Cecily says, leaning closer to her sister.

"You can say that again," Amber says with a snort. Rudy disappears, and from off-screen, something metal clangs. "What's he up to?"

Then Rudy reappears, this time lugging a bucket of paint. Cecily freezes.

"No way," Amber whispers.

Cecily only watches as her brother smiles at the camera. "Hey, Cole Patrol," he says. "Who wants to watch me give this room a makeover?"

Amber and Cecily exchange a look of horror. In the kitchen, their parents are supervising the three crew members that Joseph brought in to help out with the demolition. Oblivious to what's happening above them.

As one, the sisters sprint upstairs. What the hell is Rudy thinking? The second step lets out a screech and the other boards protest underneath their feet as they climb to the third floor. For one heart-wrenching second Cecily truly believes that one of the steps is going to give way and send them falling through. They make it to the third-floor landing and burst into the old master bedroom.

"Rudy—"

"Amber! Cecily! Say hi to the Cole Patrol!" He picks up the phone, and just like that, they're on camera. Cecily forces her face to snap into a camera-ready smile; next to her, Amber seems to falter. Rudy is grinning from ear to ear. He props the phone back up, where it faces the blank, white wall of the master bedroom. He takes their hands and drags them into frame. Cecily gives the camera an uneasy smile. What is Rudy playing at here? Mom is going to murder them. Her. But whatever this is, Cecily realizes she's already an accomplice, as is Amber. Just being in the room makes them guilty. Rudy smiles at his sisters, but Cecily knows him well enough to tell that it's not his real smile. He's still mad about before. He confirms her hunch when he speaks: "I'm just doing some impromptu live-streaming to address our little follower friend. You know the one, Cecily—the one whose name you're too scared to say?!"

Cecily shoots him a glare. Seriously? Just because Mom revoked his admin privileges doesn't mean he has to take it out on her. She'll show him scared. She reaches into a bucket and pulls out a paint brush. "Oh, yeah?" she asks.

Rudy shoots her an evil grin. "Now we're talking! Come on, Ambs." Amber hesitates, and Cecily watches her brother go in for the kill. "Get on-screen with us! It's the least you can do." Cecily watches as guilt floods Amber's face. "You can't let the people down!" Rudy says.

There *are* a lot of people watching. Followers are hopping onto their livestream by the thousands. Cecily reaches for another paintbrush and holds it out to her sister. Slowly, Amber takes it.

"Excellent! Rudy says. "Now, I thought I would make our graffiti-themed photo shoot a little more . . . spontaneous," Rudy says, leveling them with a wicked grin. "I wanted to buy some spray paints, but I figured, why wait? Splatter paint will look just as cool."

Cecily watches him dip in a brush of his own. This is all happening so fast, but she feels . . . excited. Good.

"I found these in the turret," he says. "A little better than sea-foam, don't you think?" He turns to his phone. "Hey! Comment which color I should do next—we got, uh, green, blue, yellow, something called ochre—"

"*Rudy!*" Amber says, shooting the camera an uneasy glance.

"Aw, come on," Rudy says, successfully prying the lid off a few cans of paint until he finds the color he wants to start with. He dips his brush in the paint before he looks back at the camera and winks. "Amber's just nervous." He turns back to his sister. "We're going to repaint it anyway, we might as well have some fun, right?" He stands tall and takes a few steps back, shooting the camera one last smile. "Well, guys, here goes nothing! Get ready for my parents to be m-a-d, mad." He laughs and splatters a line of electric-blue paint across the wall with a delighted shriek. "Come on! Cecily, you next!"

So Cecily dips her brush in the next shade of paint—some kind of mustard yellow—and splatters that in streaks next to Rudy's blue. Then she lets out a shriek of half shock, half laughter and dives back in, going for another splatter. This—this feels *good*. And not just the painting—the *doing*. It had been an awful long time since any of the triplets had posted something this big without their mom's approval.

Cecily turns back to Amber, and she can feel that the smile on her face is real. She thinks that she might actually be *beaming* as she holds the paint out to her sister. "Come on," she says. Rudy holds up the phone. She's on camera.

Cecily holds her breath, wondering what Amber will do. Suddenly it feels like she's handing Amber more than just a paint brush. Will she take it?

Amber takes the brush. She flicks a small splatter of paint on the wall.

"Aw, come on! You gotta do better than that!" Rudy says, laughing.

Amber shoots him a wicked grin and grabs an entire pot of paint, chucking it at the wall in a massive wave of green.

"Hell yeah, that's it!" Rudy roars. Cecily lets out a whoop. Their parents definitely must know that something is up by now, but Cecily couldn't care less. Rudy grabs a brush and paints streaks of bright, aggressive neon, a far cry from the "cinnamon oatmeal" shade of beige that their mother had selected for the upstairs bedrooms.

Cecily feels something slimy dripping down her neck and realizes that Amber just splashed her with a blob of paint.

"You did not just get paint in my hair," she says in mock anger.

"I sure did," Amber says with a laugh. "And I hate to break it to you, but your hair is not looking very perfect right now!"

With a cry of mock anger, Cecily stops painting the walls and starts painting Amber, dousing her in orange. Amber gives her a look of mock horror before grinning and throwing a splatter her way. Then, as one, the girls turn on Rudy. Their clothes are ruined, and the brands they're repping might not approve of this kind of casual vandalism—but sponsorship brand integrity be damned. Cecily can hear the pings and pops of comments, likes, and donations coming in through their livestream. Do their followers *like* this side of the Coles?

"How do I look?" Cecily asks, walking up to the camera to show off her paint-splattered face. "Do you guys want a paint-style tutorial anytime soon? Or is painting Amber enough?" she jokes. "I—" She catches sight of a comment and watches the smile slide off her own face in the camera readout as her happiness vanishes. The notifications crescendo to a flood as their followers tell her something she already knows. Her voice is a whisper. "They're back."

In a second, Rudy and Amber are over her shoulder. Rudy films using his front-facing camera so their audience gets to see them react to the follower's comments in real time. The follower's comments have been upvoted, reacted to, and replied to. And there's more than one. Together, they read:

➡ **WHAT ARE YOU DOING TO MY HOUSE?** (1.1K replies)

➡ **I TOLD YOU, I TOLD YOU NOT TO!** (59 replies)

➡ **GET YOUR FILTHY HANDS OFF THOSE WALLS!** (112 replies)

➡ **GET OUT OF MY HOUSE!** (81 replies)

➡ **IT'S MINE! IT'S MINE, IT'S MY HOUSE! IT DOESN'T BEONG TO YOU!** (222 replies)

"Well, this guy just can't take a hint, can they?" Rudy asks. He looks up, straight into the camera. "Here—let's send them a message."

Chills trickle down Cecily's spine. "Don't—" Cecily starts, but it's too late. Rudy is already turning from the livestream and dipping his brush in black paint. He approaches the wall and, without looking back at the livestream, paints a bold message in big, sloppy strokes. Cecily feels herself freeze. She doesn't protest, can't make herself move. She can only watch as he paints.

Rudy lets out a laugh and turns back to the camera, pointing at his words. "What do you think of that? Huh?" He winks at the camera. "And if you guys want more, make sure to tune into our livestream tomorrow. We'll be talking *all* about *our* house." And then, with a last bark of laughter, he strolls over to his phone and shuts the camera off.

The livestream is over. The girls are silent. Cecily hears a plopping noise and realizes it's the sound of paint dripping from their bodies onto the floor.

"What did you do?" Cecily asks.

"I made us go viral, that's what I did," Rudy says.

"He's right—oh my god, we just passed nine hundred thousand views, and counting," Amber says.

"What did you *do*?" Cecily repeats.

"This is really blowing up," Amber continues, wiping her hands on her jeans before scrolling through her phone, switching to analytics. "It's going to generate a ton of traffic for the livestream tomorrow—this is awesome, you guys."

"You *baited* the follower," Cecily gasps. Now that the adrenaline of being on-screen is gone, what they'd done is setting in. Rudy turns on her.

"No," he says. "*We* baited the follower."

"This could get us to a million followers," Amber says. "Here. Wait. Pose. We need to post a picture."

Cecily hangs back. Rudy and Amber look at her, expectantly. "Well?" Rudy asks. "Are you in?"

She'd already been in the livestream. Even if Cecily isn't in the photo, she's still part of this. She looks from Rudy to Amber. "Fine," she says. "But only if Amber is in it, too."

For a second, Amber falters. Then she props up the phone on an ancient nightstand and sets a timer, stepping into frame with her siblings.

Together, they smolder under the message, looking as intimidating as it is possible to look when you're seventeen and covered in rainbow paint. Amber posts the photo, along with a schedule for their next livestream. It doesn't need any caption other than the message above their heads, wet paint still dripping down the cracked, ancient wall of the bedroom:

THIS IS MY HOUSE NOW, BITCH.

Ron: Man, I love this. Absolutely terrifying. Can't wait for them to get picked off one by one, horror-movie style. They got themselves a new follower.

XXXXXXXXXXXXXXXXXXXXXXXXXXXXXXXXX

CHAPTER 10

Amber

IT'S NOT LONG UNTIL HURRICANE MOM HITS.

"I expected better of you three. Especially you, Amber." Amber flinches. The afternoon work is over and the demolition crew is gone; in the aftermath of Rudy's livestream the entire family is assembled in the newly demolished kitchen.

"Mom, that livestream was viewed by nine hundred thousand people," Rudy cuts in. "And now that it's posted, we're on—what? Nine hundred ten thousand followers and counting? C'mon."

"That's not the *point*!" Is it Amber's imagination, or does her mom sound a tiny bit less mad than she did a moment ago? "The *point* is I didn't know. How do you think I felt when I saw that livestream? Your own *mother* . . ."

Amber tunes out the rest of what her mom says. She can't stop thinking about the livestream—but not because of the follower. She's thinking about one of the comments left by a fan.

> ➡ **Go Amber! We need more of her; feels great to see a plus-size queen.**

The comment had been liked more than a hundred times. A *hundred*. Sure, it is just one comment, but Amber keeps going back to it on her phone, just to make sure that she hadn't made it up.

The sound of Mr. Cole breaking his silence brings her back to earth. "It was high engagement," he muses. "And it was one time, right kids? Assuming you'll never pull a stunt like that again . . . how did it do?"

Amber realizes that everyone is looking at her. "We've hit trending," she says softly.

Her mother sighs, her expression unreadable. "I can't deal with this right now, I really can't. You're off the hook—but just this once. I have a big call with West Coast sponsors in—a minute. And in the meantime: No. More. Posts. Remember, my posting strategy is what made you this big, and it's the only thing that can keep you this way."

"Promise," Rudy says, rolling his eyes. "Cross my heart and hope to die."

Mrs. Cole doesn't have time to answer; her Bluetooth headset chirps and she shoots him one last look before stalking into the library, plastering a huge smile on her face. "Quinta! It's *so* great to hear your voice. How can we help promote more of your fabulous shades?"

The triplets are alone with their father. He looks like he's trying to figure out what to say.

"Now," he says finally. "I won't always be around to bail you guys out like that. So I meant what I said about no more stunts, okay?"

Rudy and Cecily get up without responding, but Amber gives him a tight smile. "Thanks, Dad," she says, before following her siblings down the hallway. It's not until they reach the second-floor landing that Cecily turns around. But she's not angry or upset like Amber thought she'd be; instead, she's smirking.

"All right," Cecily says. "We didn't get grounded. You know what that means."

"What?" Rudy asks.

"The bonfire, duh," Cecily says.

Amber had almost forgotten.

"Do you think we should still go?" Amber asks. "After—"

"Of course," Cecily cuts Amber off.

"Let's go," Rudy agrees. "See what there is to do in Nowheres-ville, USA."

"Fine." Amber gives in. When Rudy and Cecily agree on something, it takes a lot more than her to stop it. And Cecily does seem really excited.

"Yes!" Cecily says. "Hey—I can even do your makeup, get you feeling really beautiful and ready to impress those Norton babes. Apparently half the high school 'it' squad is going to be there."

Amber caves. She and Cecily hadn't sat down to do makeup and get ready in, well, forever. It reminds her of old segments they used to do, where Amber would pick out the clothes and Cecily would do some elaborate makeup looks to match.

"Okay. Sounds fun." As if anyone will look at her next to glamorous Cecily. But then she thinks back to the comments on the livestream. Maybe she's wrong. Maybe they will.

Rudy rolls his eyes. "I'm going to go start recording my debut album then, since you two are going to take about five hours."

"You can tell Mom we're leaving," Cecily says. "And then meet us in the car in about thirty minutes. Bella texted me the address."

Forty-five minutes later, Amber is admiring herself in the mirror. Glossy, loose waves cascade over a perfectly made-up face. She looks good. She feels good. Like Photoshop in real life. She wonders if Cecily feels this good all the time.

Cecily is buried in her closet, lost in a maze of designer clothing as Speckles hops around her. Of course she let him out again—but Amber doesn't mind. He is super cute, and she needs some bunny therapy after all the stress of Hurricane Mom. "Amber, what are you wearing?" Cecily asks, reemerging with a small blue dress that Amber *knows* will accentuate her every curve. "What do you think about this?"

Amber makes a face. "I'm sure it'll look great, but it's a bonfire, right? Do you really want to scrape up your shins walking through the woods in that?"

Cecily reevaluates the dress and hangs it back in her closet. "You're totally right. What would I do without you?" She shakes her head and puts her hands on her hips, staring into the closet. "Sorry. I guess I just really wanted to, I don't know, make a good impression? Live up to the hype?"

Amber softens and walks over to the closet and sifts through it. "Don't worry, Cece," she says, shooting her sister a smile. "You could go in your *pajamas* and still live up to the hype. They'll love you. But how about this?" She pulls out an old, flannel top that she knows is one of Cecily's favorites—even if she rarely wears it on camera.

Cecily takes it. "Ooh, I love this one. And it is super soft. But isn't it too . . . laid-back? For an influencer?"

"It'll make you look like an L.L.Bean model," Amber says. "It's perfect for the woods. And if you're comfortable in what you're wearing, you'll be comfortable talking to the new kids, too."

Cecily gives her a side smile and puts on the flannel. "I guess I should have known that I would fall prey to a famous Amber fashion faux pas," she jokes.

"Don't sacrifice comfort for fashion!" the girls say in unison and dissolve into a fit of giggles. Amber is actually surprised that Cecily remembers it—she hasn't recited her fashion rules on camera in *forever*.

Amber eventually settles on a crop top and her blue jeans, still splattered with paint from the livestream. The crop top definitely breaks a couple plus-size fashion rules, but Amber doesn't care, and even Cecily admits that the paint-splattered jeans look cool.

But despite all her persuasion that this bonfire in the woods is going to be casual, Amber can't stop Cecily from stuffing her go bag of makeup and makeup remover inside her purse. "Just in case," she says.

Rudy is waiting for them in the Range Rover, wearing ripped jeans and an "artfully worn" T-shirt from his favorite designer. Amber still isn't sure if the label is worth the price tag, but her brother loves the "shabby-on-purpose" aesthetic. "You two ready?" he asks.

"Oh, hell yes! I need a drink," Cecily says as she slides into the backseat. Amber grins, secretly pleased her sister let her take the passenger seat.

"You sound good, by the way," Rudy says as they pull out of the driveway. "If you ever want accompaniment, let me know."

"What?" asks Amber.

"Wasn't that one of you? Humming? I could have sworn I heard someone . . ."

Cecily shakes her head. "Wasn't me."

Amber makes a face at her brother. "Maybe you're just going insane from listening to all those tapes."

Rudy wiggles his eyebrows at her. "Or maybe it was . . . *the ghost.*" He says, putting on his best spooky voice.

Amber giggles. "Shut up!"

"Seriously," Rudy says. "We *have* to ask around about the legends and start brainstorming all the content we can do—this is going to be *so* cool. Right, Cecily?"

In the backseat, Cecily is silent. "Sure," she finally says, but her voice is flat.

"You okay?"

She crosses her arms and looks out the window. Amber feels a tinge of regret; Cecily is clearly still freaked out from before. "Can we just stop talking about it?" Cecily asks.

"Uh . . ." Even though Amber can feel herself getting excited about the ghost content, she scrounges around for a different topic. "Rudy's only talking about it because he's nervous about meeting the townies, anyway," she teases. Cecily is clearly relieved for the subject change.

Rudy rolls his eyes. "Am *not!* These kids are going to love me. I might even finally try to form that garage band—"

"Please, you say that at every house! I'll believe it when I see it."

The conversation dissolves into banter about Rudy's questionable singing—"Stick to guitar!" Cecily says, laughing—and by the time they pull up to the trailhead, the Tremont ghost story is out of Amber's mind.

Bella is waiting for them at the trailhead, bouncing up and down on the balls of her feet in excitement.

She sweeps her platinum hair over her shoulder and gives Cecily a huge hug. "It's so weird, meeting you guys! Weird but cool, I mean. I've been following you, like, for *ages*. I used to watch all your hair tutorials." She turns to Amber and, before Amber can react, goes in for another hug. Her smile is too genuine for Amber to be annoyed. "You, too! I miss that fashion content. I swear you're going to think that we're all total slobs."

Amber laughs. "What are you talking about? You look fantastic!" Bella gives her a mock curtsy in her outfit—edgy black ripped jeans that she *totally* pulls off and a band tee—before greeting Rudy.

"Everyone's so excited to meet you all!" she says, leading them into the woods. "Be warned, though. Norton has to be *so* much more boring than—where were you last? California?"

"I don't know," Rudy says. "Sure, we were in Cali, but we were staring at paint swatches the entire time! Thanks for the invite."

"Anytime!" Bella says, striding down the trail in front of them with practiced familiarity, even as they leave the streetlights behind and the trees surrounding them begin to cut off the moonlight.

Despite her outward bravado, Amber feels nerves rise in her chest. She reminds herself of how good she looks thanks to Cecily's amazing makeup job. After all, half of a look is confidence. But what if they don't like her? What if this goes terribly? She shakes her head. If they hate her, well, the Coles are moving again soon. It won't matter. They won't matter. She tries to summon some of Cecily's self-assurance. She thinks about the comment—*Go Amber! We need more of her*—and feels herself stand up a little taller.

Up front, Bella is talking a mile a minute. "I swear, none of them *believed* me when I told them I met you—I'm pretty sure some people are going to lose money when you three actually show up to this party. They're going to *flip*."

"Great," Amber deadpans.

Through the trees, Amber starts to see a few stray flickers of light as the bonfire comes into view. It's in the middle of a clearing, surrounded by high school kids drinking and dancing. Amber has the strange realization that although she can see them clearly in the firelight, they have no idea that she is watching, or that Bella and the Coles are even approaching through the woods. Once she enters the firelight, she will be just as exposed to anyone in the woods around them.

She shakes off the feeling. This is a *party*. She's supposed to be having fun, not be paranoid. She reassures herself that there is no one in the woods besides these high school kids.

Bella rounds a large oak, and the four of them step into the firelight. Amber takes in the scene ahead of them. Scores of kids are loitering around a bonfire, talking and laughing in smaller groups. A makeshift bar is set up on one side, far away from the fire, where a group of girls mix cranberry juice and bottom-shelf vodka. Off to another side, a group of boys toss a light-up Frisbee through the darkness. Near the far edge of the woods, a smaller pocket of kids are passing around a joint. The unmistakable scent of pot reaches Amber's nose. Someone is playing pop music, and a few kids are already dancing, pausing to scream lyrics amid gales of laughter. They look so . . . happy. So normal.

Bella leads them into the clearing, and just like that, Amber feels like everything stops. Heads turn, friends grab one another and speak in hushed whispers. A few kids even point.

"Everyone, this is Cecily, Amber, and Rudy *Cole*—but you already know that," Bella says, laughing. Amber gives a self-conscious, shaky wave and hopes she doesn't look as awkward as she feels. Bella leads them over to a cluster of kids to their right, making quick introductions. The boy from the hardware store, Miles, is here along with some jersey-sporting football players and a few other guys that easily fit into the jock stereotype. A group of girls who Amber assumes must be Bella's core group of friends wander over, including Jada and a girl named Alicia who introduces herself as Bella's bestie.

"Of course we all know them!" one of Miles's friends says. He introduces himself as Trent and walks toward Rudy, going for a bro-hug, and Amber's brother is instantly on. He waves off offers of a drink—explaining that he's DDing—and effortlessly strikes up a conversation about the local sports teams. He's always been good at that—at getting people to like him.

Amber can't help but feel just a little jealous.

"Hey, remember me?" someone asks. When Amber turns, it's a boy who she definitely does *not* remember.

Cecily frowns and whispers in her ear: "I met that guy at the pizza place. His name is Steve, I think."

Steve comes in for a hug, too, but Cecily offers a handshake instead. He makes a sour face and takes it. Amber can't tell if it's the firelight, or if her sister is actually . . . nervous. Amber shares the feeling; something about Steve is . . . weird. Creepy.

He sidles up to Cecily and moves to put a hand around her shoulder, but Cecily inches away. Rudy shoots Steve a glare. "Cecily, is this dude bothering you?" Cecily doesn't answer, but Steve backs away all the same.

"C'mon, Steve. Hands off the designer goods," Miles jokes.

Bella leads the triplets around and makes more introductions. Several partygoers cut through the crowd to talk to the them—well, to talk to Amber's siblings. She tries not to let her confidence fade as small crowds form around Cecily and Rudy. Someone turns the music back up, and the drinking and dancing and chatter resumes. Even the kids who haven't come to introduce themselves are clearly intrigued, sending curious—or jealous—glances their way.

Amber looks around. While some people approach them, clearly fans, others make sour faces and whisper what she assumes are snide comments behind red Solo cups. Are they just jealous? Or is it something more sinister?

When Amber's attention returns to her siblings, they're both occupied. Cecily, Bella, Alicia, and a small crowd of girls are deep in conversation about evolving makeup trends, like which brands are going vegan and cruelty-free, and who has the best range of foundation for diverse skin tones.

"I'm so glad that a lot of brands are moving away from animal testing," Cecily says. "I have a rabbit, too, and to think about what all those other bunnies go through—that's why I really encourage my followers to go vegan when it comes to makeup."

The girls crowd around Cecily to gush over pictures of Speckles— Amber catches cries of "Oooh, he's so tiny!" and "I want to meet him!" Then someone asks Cecily which ingredients are vegan and which aren't, and Cecily goes off on a tangent about how Carmine is a common animal-based product used in a lot of red pigments. Amber watches with a small smile. Cecily is in her element, and the girls around her actually seem . . . interested. Someone switches the topic to affordable, drugstore vegan makeup, and Amber notices a few other girls detaching from the crowd, hooked.

On her other side, Rudy is talking workout routines with Miles and a couple of the other boys. Amber figures he's about two minutes away from getting roped into that game of Frisbee. All it will take is for someone to mention jamming, and she'll never see him again.

And then, all of a sudden, Amber is alone.

So she decides to do what she always does when she feels pushed off to the side: She snaps back into picture mode. The fire would make good lighting; they could go with some kind of rustic, camping theme. As she sets the frame, she notices that the girl from the hardware store, Jada—as if Amber would forget her name—has broken off her conversation to stare at Amber from across the fire. Amber locks eyes with her and confirms what she thought the first time she saw her: that this girl is beautiful. She has rich dark skin and hair tied up in bantu knots, and her look—skinny jeans, an oversize T-shirt, black combat boots and a denim jacket—broadcasts complete confidence. The kind of confidence Amber wants to have. When they make eye contact, Jada doesn't look away. She just smiles and nods her head at the log next to her.

Amber takes a deep breath, then walks over and takes a seat.

Jada slides closer. "Hey. Good to see you again. Jada, remember? Jada King. From the hardware store."

"Of course," Amber says. How could she forget? She feels her confidence falter. "But, uh, you probably want to talk to Cecily. She's that one." She points a joking thumb to her sister on her left.

But to her surprise, Jada cocks her head. "What are you talking about? I'm here to talk to you."

Amber blinks. "Oh," she says awkwardly. "Well, then, hi."

Jada laughs and slides closer. "So tell me, how does the life of the rich and famous compare to little ol' Norton? Bored to tears yet?

"It's quiet," Amber admits. "But that's kind of nice. It has pretty good pizza, too, so that doesn't hurt."

"That's the only thing it has. Besides bonfires and football, the only thing to do around here is hunting—if you're into that sort of thing. And drink, I guess," she adds, reaching for the bottle that's made its way over to them. She takes a pull and passes it to Amber. Across the bonfire, one of the boys starts making exaggerated revving noises. Jada rolls her eyes. "Of course it took them about five minutes to start talking about ATVs. Welcome to the sticks." She shoots Amber a bright smile, and Amber realizes that she's been staring. But Jada doesn't seem to notice—or if she does, she doesn't seem to care. Or maybe . . .

Amber returns the smile. Jada laughs and points to the bottle Amber is still holding. Amber hands it over and Jada takes another swig from it.

A few feet away, Miles is talking loudly to Rudy about the best trails. "We should go," Ambers hears him say. "But don't wear your Yeezys. They'll get trashed."

Amber wonders how her brother will respond to that offer; riding ATVs is not exactly his thing. But then something in the woods catches her attention. A movement, just off to the side of the clearing. Miles must see it too, because he raises a hand as he looks out into the woods. "Hold up," Miles calls out. "Hey! We're over here."

"Let's go see who's coming," Jada suggests. Amber gets up and follows her over to the group of boys.

"Whatcha looking at?" Jada asks, peering out into the darkness. "I didn't think anyone else was coming."

Miles shrugs. "Thought I saw someone out there. Guess not."

Amber doesn't add that she thought she saw someone, too.

Cecily and her new group of friends wander over. Cecily loops her arm through Amber's and smiles. She's definitely having fun.

"What's going on over here?" Cecily asks.

"Miles thought he saw someone, but no one seems to be coming. And they're not expecting any more kids to show up," Amber explains. She's suddenly feeling a little nervous.

"Maybe it was Alex Grable's ghost," the boy named Trent says, eyeing the triplets.

"Okay, you *have* to tell me," Alicia says, cutting in. "Did you seriously not know that the house was haunted? On your vlog, I mean. Was that fake?"

Amber decides to let Rudy and Cecily take this one. She and Jada exchange looks as Cecily shakes her head. "I mean, I guess our dad knew, but the rest of us had no idea. Honestly, we're still sketchy on details. She . . . killed her mom, right?"

"Stabbed her, then took a swan dive straight through the window," Trent says, whistling cartoon-style as he draws the flight trajectory in the air with his finger.

"Trent," Jada starts. "Come on."

"Come on, what?"

She shrugs. "I mean, the girl's dead."

"And won't care what anyone says about her anymore," another boy, Brennan, says, laughing. "Besides, I heard she was a psycho. Hey, Trent, remember when you dared Miles to sneak in and spend the night? How was that sleepover?"

Miles laughs. "Dude, it was *terrifying*. I coulda sworn I heard someone walking around all night."

"Sure," Trent says, laughing.

"Wait—" Cecily starts. "You slept in the house? The one we're renovating?"

"Oh, we used to sneak in," Bella explains. "You know, on dares. Haunted house shit. I remember in eighth grade, I bet Tommy McCalister twenty bucks he couldn't spend the night there. Dude lasted about twenty minutes."

"But you guys have been there for almost a week now," Alicia chimes in. "How is it?"

"Honestly, I'm kind of spooked," Cecily admits, and all eyes are on her. Amber watches her sister channel "camera mode." "I am definitely not looking forward to renovating the turret room."

"Do you know anything about her?" Rudy asks

"Dude, I heard she was a Carrie," Trent says. "Super disturbed. Social misfit, picked on at school, all that stuff. Drove her totally batshit crazy. Finally snapped, but the house is so isolated that the only people around to hurt were her mom and then, well, herself."

"Nah, I heard she lost some track scholarship and had a total meltdown," Miles interjects.

"Wasn't she homecoming queen?"

"So was Carrie—"

"I heard that someone put a curse on the house," Miles continues. "Think about it! First the Grables, then that boy—"

Rudy cuts in. "Yeah—there was someone else, right? Police said it was an accident."

Bella nods. "Evan Andrews," she whispers.

"Who was he?" Cecily asks.

Amber is surprised when Jada breaks her silence to answer. "His family moved into the house about . . . a decade or so after the Grables died. In 2009, maybe? They started repainting it, and there was some kind of accident with the scaffolding. Their oldest kid, Evan, fell and died. I think he was sixteen."

"They'd only been living there for, like, a month," Miles adds. "The house has had a pretty . . . bad reputation since then. No one has lived there since."

There's a second of silence as everyone takes the story in. The fire crackles. The other groups of teenagers drinking and smoking and laughing seem strangely far away.

"Honestly, I'm glad we're just flipping it," Cecily admits. "It's got a weird vibe. I definitely wouldn't want to live there, either. Too creepy."

"Hey, Trent, remember that night sophomore year when we pitched baseballs into the third-floor windows?" Miles asks, and just like that the conversation veers away from Alex and Evan and into dares, drinking, sports, and other teenage stuff. Amber and her siblings are caught in a flood of high school gossip, complaints about local law enforcement, and dirt on nosy neighbors. The nervous feeling Amber had earlier has passed, and she starts to relax.

The bottle gets passed around, and Amber takes a long swig. Before she knows it, Rudy's talking music, Cecily is deep in conversation about the chemical formula for some kind of foundation or another. And then Amber finds herself seated by the fire again, next to Jada. They talk about anything and everything. About bad part-time jobs, colleges in California, and the pros and cons of homeschool. Every time Jada laughs, Amber feels her tension ease, her self-consciousness dissolve. Talking to Jada is easy.

Effortless. And it doesn't hurt that Jada is ... cool. When Amber listens to her gush about high school drama or the robotics team, it almost makes her wish that she went to a regular high school. Jada cracks a joke about hicks and social media, and Amber finds herself laughing along. It's been ages since she's bonded so easily with another girl like this. It's got to mean something, she tells herself.

The bottle is finished and a new one appears, as if by magic. Someone turns up the music *again,* and soon half the kids are up and dancing around the fire. Then, three quarters of them. Some of the couples slink off into the woods.

Amber swallows her courage and is about to mention an ex-*girlfriend* when Jada's hand skitters across her upper thigh. Just the lightest touch. That little touch confirms what Amber dared to suspect. To hope. Jada is into her, too.

Amber doesn't realize that Jada has stood up to dance until she's extending her hand.

"Come on," Jada says. If she were sober, Amber would be afraid of getting caught like this, tipsy-drunk and dirt-streaked and dancing close with someone new. Self-conscious. But she isn't. The alcohol has made everything feel warm and fuzzy. And Jada—Jada has made everything warm, too. With a jolt, Amber realizes that she doesn't really care about how any of the other kids at the bonfire see her or think of her. Not as long as she's dancing with Jada.

So Amber takes Jada's hand and stands, and suddenly they are dancing, close—so close that Amber can make out each individual eyelash. There's one on Jada's cheek. She reaches out to brush it away, and then they are kissing. Lightly. Nervously, at first. Then harder.

Her lips are soft and warm. Amber's mind goes blissfully blank.

A song changes. Then another. And another. Rudy and Cecily and the party itself fade into a meaningless blur.

When Jada's eyes stray toward the shadows beyond the tree line, Amber's follow. Her hand puts the smallest bit of pressure on Amber's lower back. Amber feels herself nodding.

The two of them leave the protective circle of light around the bonfire and slip into the woods, just out of sight, and then those hands are on her waist, her hips, and Jada is kissing her again and Amber is kissing her back, *hard.* It feels effortless, weightless. Jada's hands move from the small of her back to her hair to her hips. Amber cups Jada's face and pulls herself toward her as Jada's hand grazes, ever so lightly, across her breast—

Snap.

Amber jerks away. Jada follows her gaze into the forest, confused. The woods are silent. The first thing that pops into Amber's mind is the follower, the person behind the Alex Grable account. She shakes her head to clear it. Why is she thinking about Alex Grable? Probably because of all the kids talking about her before.

"Who's there?" Amber calls out.

"What—" Jada starts, but Amber quiets her, listening.

And then, another sound: the unmistakable crunch of footsteps on leaves. Coming closer.

"Not cool to spy on us," Jada calls, but no one answers. "Miles? Trent? Cut it out!"

Silence. The footsteps stop. Amber shakes herself; she's just been drinking, she's just paranoid, it could just be an animal, it could just be—

The firelight behind them catches the bright glint of something twenty yards ahead of her. Something silver. Something metallic. And around it . . . a shade of darkness blacker than the rest of the night. A faint, almost indistinguishable silhouette.

Someone is there. A jolt of fear spikes through Amber. She grabs Jada's wrist and *runs.*

Amber sprints back toward the bonfire. They'd gone farther than she'd thought; branches snag her jeans and scrape at her exposed midriff as she darts toward the flickering firelight. When she breaks through the clearing, she runs straight to Rudy. He starts, almost spilling his soda. "Are you okay?" he asks. "What's up? Did something happen?"

Amber nods, then shakes her head, then opens her mouth and closes it a few times before answering. Her drunk mood has pivoted on a dime, from warm and fuzzy to terrified. Rudy's eyes comb over her, and Amber becomes all too aware of her smudged lipstick, the twigs in her hair.

"We were . . . in the woods," Amber finally says. "And someone was *watching* us."

"What?"

"Some perv," Jada cuts in. "Well, I didn't see him, but—"

"I swear he was there," Amber says. "I—I saw a shadow, and I heard someone moving around. I really did, Rudy. You have to believe me."

Cecily joins them. Most of their circle has noticed Amber's panic by now, but the party goes on in the background, a constant stream of noise.

"Are you all right?"

"Where's Steve?" Miles asks, scanning the crowd.

Amber looks around and confirms it: Steve is gone. Jada lets out a laugh of relief. "Oh, thank god. That makes so much more sense. I mean, better the creep we know, right?"

"I'm gonna hit him," Bella mutters. "What a jackass."

"Think it could have been Steve, Amber?" Cecily asks.

"I—I don't know," Amber admits. Slowly, her breathing returns to normal. She begins to flush, realizing too late that she's become the center of attention. "I'm sorry, I . . ."

"Let's just all go sit by the fire a bit," Cecily says, concern etched all over her face. Amber allows her sister and the others to lead her and Jada back toward the logs surrounding the firepit.

Bella gestures to an empty log and Amber takes a seat. She's happy when Jada sits down next to her.

"Hey, let's play Never Have I Ever," Bella says. "Here, I'll go first: never have I ever made out with an internet celebrity in the woods."

Everyone laughs at that, and someone starts passing around another bottle. Amber tries to cast off her fear and relax again. It was probably Steve, she reassures herself.

The kids finish the first game of Never Have I Ever and move on to another, stupider game of Truth or Dare. Amber watches her siblings drop more and more of their "social media" personalities as they get comfortable with the crowd, and when Jada slips her hand into Amber's pocket to pull out her cell phone and exchange numbers, Amber realizes with a jolt that she must be fitting in, too.

Jada hands her the phone back, smiling shyly. "That's if the whole night-time stalker thing wasn't an excuse to run away from me."

Amber laughs and immediately texts her. "No," she says. "Absolutely not."

Before too long, the fire is all but embers, and even the kids with the most lenient parents start heading home to get some sleep. When the triplets finally pull back into their driveway, Amber feels buzzed and happy. The moment of intense fear she felt in the woods seems like a distant memory. Cecily stumbles out of the car, giggling. Above them, the mansion is dark. Somehow, it seems to be leaning over them. For a drunk second Amber is seized by the idea that the structure is unsteady, that it's going to collapse, that the turret is going to rot away and fall right on the Range Rover.

Then the smallest flicker of movement catches her eye.

Amber starts. There. The turret. For a moment she swears she sees her—Alex Grable—in the window. Amber sways backward; the trees seem to bend. No, she's drunk and the house is still. No one is standing in the window.

Next to her, Cecily grabs her arm, and Amber knows that she's not the only one thinking about the ghost girl. Cecily sucks in a breath and shouts up at the house: "I'm not scared of you!" She punctuates the cry with a shriek of laughter. Amber joins in, cackling. She and Cecily lean into each other, drunk and laughing hysterically.

Rudy takes Cecily's hand and begins to gently steer her toward the front door.

"All right, Cece. We're getting you inside."

Cecily giggles.

As Rudy guides his sisters across the lawn, Amber pulls out her phone to make sure that Jada's number is still in it, half-convinced that she'd imagined her. She smiles. Then, out of habit, she flicks on Instagram.

"Look," she slurs, stumbling up to her siblings. "We're famous."

"We're already famous," Rudy says.

Amber shows them the phone. "We're still trending. *Still*. We've never trended this long. And all the posts are doing ah-mazing. You're welcome."

"Welcome?" Cecily asks. "You're barely in any of them. Rudy and I are carrying the team."

"I do every single one!" Amber half-slurs, half-shouts. Seriously? Cecily is going to accuse *her* of not pulling her weight when—

"Okay, quiet down," Rudy mutters, flicking the lights on and steering the girls inside. Their parents are definitely asleep by now.

But Amber doesn't want to let it go. "Every. Single. One," Amber repeats as she teeters up the stairs. But she's not an angry drunk. She's veering toward sad instead.

"You're drunk," Cecily says.

"You're perfect," Amber retorts. It's the best insult she can think of.

Together, they stumble up the staircase, Rudy in the middle, looking like entrants in a designer-brand three-legged race.

Rudy steers them toward their rooms. "All right you two," he says. "It's time for bed." At her room, Amber detaches, stumbling for the doorknob. Rudy opens it for her and she collapses, face-first onto her bed.

"Good night, Ambs," he says, then closes the door behind him.

Amber's door creaks as it shuts, and she finds herself looking upward, imagining for a strange second that the noise she'd just heard wasn't her door creaking but had come from somewhere above her. That it was a different sound altogether. It almost sounded like . . . a step.

No. She's just buzzed, that's all. A little buzzed and a little tired and maybe a little . . . happy. She closes her eyes and replays the first kiss, the night, the dancing in her head as she pulls the covers over herself. Then, she switches to a vision of Cecily, screaming at the house that she isn't afraid of it. Well, maybe it's time that Amber stop being afraid, too. Of the house, of Mom, of ruining their precious *engagement*. Because being in Rudy's impromptu livestream had felt . . . good. She'd felt powerful. Seen. And someone *had* seen her.

We need more of her.

If Rudy could splatter paint over the walls, she could at least take a selfie, she could at least stop hiding . . . She smiles to herself, letting the last dregs of alcohol fill her with confidence as she falls asleep. Amber isn't going to be afraid of this house, either.

At first, she's not sure what wakes her.

It's late. Her mouth feels dry, her head heavy. She sits up in bed, listening to the sounds of the house, trying to figure out what woke her up. Trying to tell what is wrong.

Amber slides out of bed and turns on the light, peering into the dark hallway. No one is awake. Then why does she hear the sound of running water? She turns on the hall light then tiptoes downstairs.

The sink, the only functional aspect of the kitchen, is silhouetted by a window against the moonlight, through a desert of broken flooring and naked beams.

And it is running. Water is just beginning to spill over the edge.

Amber walks over and turns it off. The kitchen is so, so quiet without the noise. Too quiet. She reaches into the murky water and pulls the plug, listening to the strained noises of water trying to recede before she realizes that there is something clogging the drainage. Something in the garbage disposal.

She wishes she'd gotten someone else up. Rudy, Cecily . . . but it's just a sink, right? She can take care of it herself.

She flicks the grinder on and is met with the horrible grating noise of something that cannot be processed. She turns it off. The darkness is complete around her as she reaches down into the blades beneath the sink and yanks her hand out with a yelp. There is something in there—something that shouldn't be. And there is something *stuck* to her hand.

She turns the light on and screams.

The water in the sink is a murky and rusty red, and on Amber's hand—on Amber's hand is a piece of red, matted fur. Bloody fur. She stares back down into the water and watches in horror as the disturbance made by her hand swirls some of it down the drain, as the water eddies and flows.

There is a large mass half-crammed into the garbage disposal. A large mass that Amber *knows*, a large mass that used to be soft and warm . . .

Bile collects in Amber's throat as something rises to the water's surface. All that is left of a single long velveteen ear. All that is left of Cecily's rabbit.

She turns and throws up all over the demolished floor.

Comment on the latest Cole post:

➡ **@BradySue:** God, it must be nice to be seventeen-year-old millionaires . . .

359 Likes   Reply

Rudy

AMBER AND CECILY ARE INCONSOLABLE. CECILY HAS LOCKED HER-self in her room, wailing, telling anyone who will listen that she *locked* the cage, she knows she did, she did, she did. Downstairs, Rudy listens to his other sister dry-heave into the garbage can. Even hours after removing the poor creature from the sink, Amber can't stop shivering and whispering, "I *touched* him."

Their parents, while horrified, insist that Cecily's rabbit must have got-ten loose and mistakenly fallen into the water and become stuck, but Rudy can't stop thinking about returning home last night. The sink hadn't been on. Had Amber or Cecily woken up in the middle of the night to get a drink? They swore they hadn't, and Rudy believed them.

Their parents don't know what to think. Eventually, they conclude that, with his cage in the kitchen and a clear pile of renovation tools, debris, and odds and ends all over the floor, Speckles could have hopped his way up onto the counter. Dad had even checked, and there were no signs of a break-in. Besides, Rudy's parents had been home all night and hadn't heard anything.

All the same, the next morning workers arrive to install a security sys-tem just as the sheriff recommended. It's another cost, but they can't afford to take any risks with this renovation.

So their parents expedite the security system installation, just in case any squatters who used to call the place home had wandered in for a drink. Having the house "armed" each night before they fall asleep does make Rudy feel a little safer.

After Amber and Cecily have some time to recover, the triplets docu-ment the security system installation on Instagram and spend the morning taking photos. Cecily doesn't feel like taking portraits today. Instead they post a loving farewell for Speckles—*The best bunny a girl could ask for*—on their account and then move on to the rest of the house. They capture the view from the turret, the study bedroom in the light. Amber takes some photos of Rudy with his workout gear. He smiles through them, but everything feels . . . stale. This is the role he has to play. The charismatic host, the hot weight lifter. He's all too eager to relocate to the third floor.

Rudy gives the attic string another yank before remembering that it's still locked. When he turns to face the rest of the hall, Amber is looking into the dumbwaiter.

"This is crazy," she says. "I can't believe it goes all the way down!"

Cecily shudders. "Be careful. You're going to fall in."

"Am not," Amber says. "Though I wonder what it's like to go down."

Rudy slides over and glances down into the dumbwaiter shaft. It's long and dark, with all kinds of spooky cobwebs. He gets an idea—one that's way better than playing Ken. "What if we could?"

Amber is skeptical. "I mean, I *guess* someone could fit in there, but . . ."

"No, I mean our phones—let's throw one in there and videotape it all the way down. For fun."

"Oooh," Amber says. "Like a long shot of our faces receding into the darkness? That would be really cool. And spooky."

"Maybe . . . ," Cecily concedes, but she seems interested. Rudy will take any chance to distract her from Speckles, so he hauls up the dumbwaiter until its top is just below the third-floor entry. Amber positions her phone, hitting Record. All three triplets look down at it, and Cecily gives a wave as Rudy lets it lower, recording their faces retreating up the shaft.

He yanks it back up. "Let's see how it looks!"

Amber plays it back. "It looks so cool—maybe we can even make it an intro for our livestream." And it does; their faces shrink amid a spooky tunnel of gray-blackness. A great intro to any kind of haunted house video.

"What's that?" Cecily asks. Amber pauses the video. "On the wall, there."

Amber zooms in. She's right, there is something on the wall. A strange, white scratch . . . a word. Writing.

"R?" Rudy asks. "Is that what it says?"

Amber squints. "I think so. I can't tell."

They send the phone down again, pointing at the wall this time. When the video comes back, the letter is clear. "Yeah," Rudy says. "R. What do you think it means?"

Cecily shrugs. "Maybe it's, like, construction or something."

"I don't know . . ." Rudy leans toward the lettering. Somehow, he doesn't believe it. It looks almost . . . handwritten. No. It looks like it has been *scratched* into the inside of the tunnel. "Maybe it's the same person as the doll, right? Wasn't that an R name?"

"Reena," Cecily says, shuddering. "Can we please not talk about that creepy doll?"

Amber shrugs. "Well, the video is pretty good—we can definitely use it if we decide to keep going for the spooky angle."

Rudy feels himself itching to get out his phone and ask his followers about the dumbwaiter writing, but he can't; even after his splatter-paint livestream's success, his mom had revoked his administrative privileges. He feels his mood sour. If he can't post or interact with people, what's the point of being online at all?

They try to capture a few portrait photos around the third floor before heading downstairs for lunch. There's one of Cecily and an ancient tea set from some previous owner, and a couple of Rudy and Cecily sliding down decrepit bannisters.

They make it back to the first floor and head into the kitchen to grab lunch before the flooring crew arrives.

Rudy pops a bagel into the toaster and moves to make a protein shake. He is digging around in the cabinet when his mom finds him. "Rudy? Can I talk to you?"

He turns around. "Sure." Amber puts some afternoon coffee on; Cecily rummages through the fridge. He can tell that both of them are listening.

Mom sighs and leans against the wall. There isn't much kitchen left to talk in, really, besides the sink and a few cabinets that act as a makeshift pantry—and most of those will be gone this afternoon once the crew comes in to start the flooring. "I know that we've been . . . hard on you, lately. That you haven't been happy with the choices this family is making about the account."

That's the understatement of the year, Rudy thinks. He wonders where she's going with this.

"I know you want to do other, wilder things, but . . . it's just not our brand, Rudy. And now isn't the right time to try something new," she says. "Why don't you put your music online, huh? Learn some pop songs or something—you could be our pop star!"

Rudy cringes. "I don't play that kind of music." *And girls don't really swoon over boys that play blues standards*, he almost adds.

"Why not?"

"I just . . . don't want to," he says, giving up trying to explain. Music is something he does for himself, not to get other people to . . . like him on the internet. And if something he posts actually does well, Mom wouldn't let him stop, would she? He isn't Cecily—he doesn't *want* his hobby to become something he has to do for social media. Besides, at this point he's a little more interested in the strange things happening in this house than he is in posting for their account.

Like the rabbit. Could it really have just . . . wandered in there? Swam all the way down into the garbage disposal? Or . . .

When Mom had first removed his admin privileges—immediately after the livestream—it felt like he was going through a physical withdrawal from being cut off. He wanted to post about the house, his theories, everything that was happening—but he couldn't. He'd done investigative content before, of course, but it was usually digging into or commenting on internet drama. And now that he has something real to look into, all the internet drama just seems so . . . inconsequential.

Of course, that's when he is allowed to post things that aren't pre-scribed by his mother.

"Well, then I don't want to do your posts, Rudy," Mrs. Cole says. She sighs and leans on the counter, giving him a small smile. "It's not that I don't think you have good ideas—I really do—it's just that this account is all that's keeping us afloat right now, and I don't want to do anything risky, anything that could . . . jeopardize that. There's a lot riding on this. You understand that, right? We're about to enter the second week of the renovation, and we need all hands on deck here."

Rudy doesn't say anything. He finds his protein powder and takes it out. Eyes the bagel in the toaster, where it's beginning to turn golden-brown. Even when their kitchen is in shambles, his mom always insists on having basic appliances to make daytime meals. The toaster and coffee maker will get stowed away as soon as afternoon work starts.

In the harsh sunlight filtering in through the window, his mom looks . . . deflated. Stressed. Rudy can tell she's got more to say, but he has no idea what it could be. Mrs. Cole shifts her weight, boards creaking in the silence underfoot. "I need you to give it back, Rudy."

"Give what back?"

"Give the plaque back, Rudy. I know you took it."

In the background, Amber and Cecily stop what they were doing.

"The . . . plaque? Like, the family one?" he asks, filling his blender bottle with powder and water and shaking it to make the drink. When he glances to the wall he sees that, sure enough, the plaque is gone.

"Rudy, this is serious. Stop messing around and look at me." Rudy fights the urge to get angry. Of course whenever something goes wrong it's *his* fault. Of course Mom thinks that he did it.

Cecily and Amber are both frozen, watching them. Cecily has a Pop-Tart halfway in her mouth. Rudy's bagel pops out of the toaster.

"I don't know what you're talking about, Mom," Rudy says, meeting her eyes. She looks so, so tired. "I didn't take it." He sips his drink. He's so distracted and trying so hard to not lose his cool that he takes a bite of his bagel without even buttering it.

"We were out last night, remember? And don't we need it in its frame for the livestream tonight?"

"Exactly," Mrs. Cole says. "And it's missing. Now, come on—I'm not mad, I'm really not. But you need to give it back."

"I didn't take it," Rudy repeats, and he feels his frustration rise. "Maybe the crew moved it for the demo. I'm not the only other person in the house, you know—"

"Don't make me cancel your livestream, Rudy. You're the only one desecrating the—oh my god." Mrs. Cole pivots from angry to . . . afraid. Cecily's eyes widen.

"What?" Rudy asks, and then he feels it. Something is wrong. The heat. His face is hot, hot and itchy and—

He raises a hand up to his face and feels the bumps of sharp, bright welts. He rushes to the bathroom mirror, but he knows what's happening before he sees his reflection.

His face is covered in hives. *Itchy,* painful hives.

His mom sprints in behind him. "What did you eat? What did you—"

"Just a bagel! And a sip of my shake!"

From the kitchen, Cecily reads off the bagel label: "Made in a facility that uses and produces tree nuts . . ." Mrs. Cole curses.

Mr. Cole arrives at the sound of shouting. He takes one look at Rudy, sees Cecily holding the bag of bagels, and figures out instantly what happened. "I just bought those! I thought that was the brand we always buy. I—"

Mrs. Cole is hunching over Rudy. "How do you feel? Are you okay? Do you think we should go to the hospital?"

Rudy shakes his head and stares at his face in the mirror, stretching the skin left and right. It only makes the hives puff more. They're exploding all over his face, his neck, his shoulders. Underneath his clothes, he feels the itch of them creeping across his rib cage.

Rudy's dad is beside himself. "Oh my god, Rudy, I am so sorry. I thought it was the brand we always got, I thought—"

Rudy tries to tell his dad it's not his fault, that those are the bagels he always eats, but all he can manage is a grimace. "I—I'm fine, I don't need the hospital—I mean, I can breathe, I'm fine, I just—need some Benadryl."

Mrs. Cole rushes off and returns before Rudy can do anything other than stare at his contorted skin. This has happened before, of course, but not in a long time. He stares at his skin, caught up in the morbid curiosity of his own misshapen face, neck, shoulders.

"Here—take three, no, four—the livestream's not until the evening; maybe the swelling will have gone down by then."

The livestream. His one chance to interact with fans all day, and he is going to miss it. And of course Mom's first thought is the livestream—Rudy has to be hot for the camera, as always. Get that female demographic. Well, it looks like he's not going to be able to do that tonight.

Cecily and Amber appear at the door of the bathroom. Rudy raises an eyebrow at Cecily. Behind her, Amber's mouth is hanging open.

"Ready to be on camera, sis?" Rudy asks her.

"Get some rest," Mrs. Cole says. "Maybe it'll go down by tonight . . ." She doesn't sound very confident.

Rudy swallows the pills and lets his mother's panicked planning fade into the background. He stares at his skin, puffing up as he watches. The last time this had happened, he'd been in second grade. The bullying had been merciless. He can only imagine how much of a field day their followers would have with this. Because, sure, he loves talking to his fans—but that doesn't mean that he doesn't read *all* the comments sometimes. And there are always mean ones, even if they're the minority.

In the background, he can hear his father apologizing endlessly to anyone who will listen, going on and on about how exhausted he already is from the renovation and swearing, promising that he will make things better.

Rudy opens his mouth to say something, but he can already feel himself slowing down, his eyes drooping.

Maybe his mom is right; maybe the swelling will magically vanish before the Ask Us Anything livestream . . .

He can feel the Benadryl kicking in already.

But when Rudy wakes up from his medication-induced slumber, the welts are still very visible. Better, for sure, but unmistakable. He shows off his not-quite-healed face to the family downstairs.

Mrs. Cole looks at him and massages her temples, sighing deeply. Rudy can tell she's trying to work out what to do. Rudy can't be on camera; not like this. Amber and Cecily make sympathetic faces.

Amber lets out a low whistle. "Not your best look."

Rudy shakes his head and chuckles. "Hey Ambs, beauty is in the eye of the beholder."

"At least it should be cleared up by tomorrow, right?" Cecily asks, but she doesn't sound convinced.

"Did you guys ever figure out if that was the usual bagel brand?" Rudy asks. "I thought it was, but I've never had a reaction with them before . . ."

"It was the same kind we always get," Amber confirms.

"They didn't used to have that 'made in a facility that also processes nuts' warning," Mrs. Cole says, clearly distraught. She gives Rudy a tight smile. "I'm sorry, we should have checked again—"

"It's fine, Mom," Rudy says. "Just some hives. Nothing crazy."

Mrs. Cole nods. "Still, don't worry—we checked the labels of everything in the cabinets and did a total purge. I'll go out and buy new bagels tomorrow. I know cross contamination isn't uncommon, but I think that we should switch up brands, just to be safe."

"Thanks, Mom. That must have been so much work . . ." Rudy wants to protest that it really isn't *that* big of a deal, but his mom looks utterly exhausted, so he switches topics instead. "Ready for the livestream?"

Mrs. Cole stops rubbing her temples and begins to drum her fingers on the tabletop. "Amber, go get ready to be on camera," she orders. "Rudy, are you up to switch with Amber and record?"

Rudy nods. "Yeah, sure."

The triplets spend the next few hours in the turret room, pushing furniture around and watching the light fade through the large window. Rudy finds himself wondering about Alex, falling through that window. What time of day it was. If she could see the beautiful view of the mountains when she fell.

"On the bright side, at least you slept through some of the reflooring noise," Cecily says. "I couldn't hear myself think all day." Her eyes are red. Rudy wouldn't be surprised if she had spent the afternoon crying over Speckles.

"It was awful," Amber echoes as she positions key lights. "And you also got to miss Mom freaking out over her Bluetooth headset all afternoon. Apparently she's lost it. Again. If she has to buy *another* one, Dad's going to flip."

Rudy shakes his head. "Maybe someone threw them out the turret window, like your laptop," he jokes, but it falls flat. It's like no one in the family is willing to even joke about the weird things that have been happening since they moved into this house. Uncomfortable, Rudy starts to fidget as he searches for another, better joke to clear the dead air. He finds a stray flap of wallpaper and picks at it as he thinks. And then he spots something strange: a color that doesn't belong.

"Rudy!" Amber scolds, but he's not paying attention. He's caught the edge of the wallpaper, and there's . . . something beneath it. Something colorful. He peels further back, and to his surprise, a large chunk of paper comes away.

"What are you—" But Amber cuts herself off as he finds another loose edge of wallpaper and steps back, bringing an additional segment of paper with him. Almost the entire wall falls bare to reveal a mural.

Underneath the wallpaper, the walls had once been white. Someone had painted over them, rolling hills and sticklike trees and the familiar outline of distant mountains.

Someone had painted the view out the window. The view that Alex Grable had seen as she died. Rudy tries to shake the thought from his head, but he can't—all he can do is stare at the painting, taking it in.

"What the . . . ," Amber whispers.

"Do you think . . . Alex could have painted this?" Cecily asks.

Rudy is about to agree when he spots something at the bottom of the painting. "Maybe not," he says, pointing out a tiny set of initials by a fern: *BG*. "*BG*. Who could that be?"

Cecily shrugs. "It's still creepy."

"Hey!" Amber snaps her fingers to get their attention. "We can look over that later—we're starting soon. Get in position."

Rudy watches Amber fuss with the flowing top that she picked out to wear for the livestream.

"Don't worry," Rudy says. "You're camera-ready." Amber had picked out clothes for Cecily, too. Even Rudy had gotten the Amber fashion treatment, but his pristinely ironed shirt is lying on his bed, unworn. What is the point of getting dressed up when he can't be on camera?

The glow from Cecily's ring light glints off the sheers and clippers sitting next to the mirror on her makeup desk. She checks out her reflection. Her makeup is perfect—taupe eyeshadow, a popping red lipstick, cat eyeliner. Not too little, not too much. Just enough. Rudy can barely tell that she'd spent the day crying about her bunny.

"Now, you get in position," Rudy says, shooing Amber out from behind the camera. Despite the day's events, he's never felt so . . . relaxed before a livestream. It takes him a minute to realize that it's probably because he's not in it, because he's not preparing himself to be "on" for everyone.

He waits for his sisters to get into position and then begins the countdown. "All right! And we're live in five, four, three, two—" Cecily yanks Amber closer to her, into the center of the shot. The camera flicks on. Rudy presses *Live*.

There is a beat of silence.

Of course there is. Rudy is the one who usually says the intro. He gestures at his sisters from behind the camera, and Amber recovers first. "What's up, Cole Patrol!" she says, giving the camera a shaky smile. As she speaks, her voice gets louder, more confident. "As promised, your favorite haunted home renovators are coming to you live from, uh, the very spooky murder room, a.k.a. the turret room."

"A.k.a. my makeup studio," Cecily chimes in, laughing. "But, yeah, makeup video coming soon, lovelies—stay tuned for that! Sorry I haven't been posting—it's just been *so* busy moving in and getting settled in a new place. Oh, and huge shout-out to Bella and her friends for welcoming us to town. I'll link to her account below; definitely show her some love. Today, Rudy is taking a break from the camera, so you're getting a lot more

Amber!" Amber gives a thumbs-up. "But that's enough from us! Let's hear from you! This is a Q and A, after all."

Amber leans toward the computer and begins reading out questions from the chat. There is the usual—sponsor deals, makeup comments for Cecily, questions about their routines and the renovation. Behind the camera, Rudy reads the comments, as well. He notices questions rolling in over and over again from the same account: @S_ODon.

➡ Does Cecily have a boyfriend?

➡ Who's Cecily's boyfriend?

➡ I don't see a boyfriend on your account.

➡ Does she have a boyfriend or is she a liar?

➡ I KNOW YOU CAN SEE THESE DOES SHE HAVE A BOYFRIEND ANSWER ME

Rudy pauses. Could this be that guy from the bonfire who was hitting on Cecily? Steve, right? He ignores the comments and gives Amber a thumbs-up as she reads through the rest, watching his sister's nerves fade away as she and Cecily joke with their audience. It had been way too long since Amber had been featured like this. He feels a pang as he realizes that's something he's never really thought much about until now. *Does it bother Amber to not be featured?* he wonders.

Most of the comments ask about the ghost girl and the story behind the haunted house. What had happened? Do they think the house was haunted? Have they seen anything? The girls explain that they haven't seen a ghost. They don't mention the turret vandalism or the bunny, but Amber goes into excruciating detail about the sounds she's been hearing at night. Cecily looks spooked on camera, and they play up the drama to great effect.

"And that's why," Amber says, drawing out the words, "we've decided to do a séance to contact this ghost!"

The commenters are thrilled. Rudy gives his sisters a double thumbs-up. Amber grins at the camera. "Yeah," she says. "I think that can be arranged." She steps off camera for a few moments, and Cecily recounts for their audience what her sister is doing—fetching the candles she has stashed in her bedroom.

Rudy can tell that Cecily is nervous about doing a séance, but she's being a good sport.

Amber returns standing next to Cecily. She's brought more than just candles. She'd also grabbed the old doll. Cecily feigns surprise at seeing the creepy doll, and Rudy smirks. The viewers are eating it up. Of course, the entire routine had been preplanned and Mom-approved.

➡ I'm already pissing myself.

➡ Oh my god, did it MOVE?

Aside from the stray comment about respecting the ghost, the response they're receiving is overwhelmingly positive.

Amber kills the lights. It's totally dark outside; the only light in the room comes from the blinking of the camera display and the blue light of the laptop, presenting the endless list of comments in front of them and bathing their faces a pallid blue-gray glow.

Amber lights the candles. Rudy watches their flames cast strange shadows across the mural on the wall behind them. It's out of camera frame, but he can see it just fine.

Amber looks to Cecily to start the séance, but she shakes her head.

"All right guys," Amber says. "Are there any ghosts here? Knock once if you're a ghost. We invite you to possess this doll, uh, Clarabell"—she winks at the camera—"and communicate any wishes that you have had from your past life."

There is a second of spooky silence. Rudy imagines that their livestream audience is holding their breath; the comments have slowed. Nothing.

Then, as planned, Rudy makes a bang, off camera. Amber shrieks. "I thought I saw something!" she says. "A shadow—right, right over there." But of course, there's nothing. When they'd huddled that afternoon, they had carefully planned every shriek, jump scare, and "ghost" appearance they were going to do in their livestream. Fake, sure. Entertaining? Absolutely. A few theatrics never hurt anyone.

"Is there anything you want to tell us?" Amber asks. "We invite the ghost to speak! Uh, make a noise if you can hear us! Or touch one of us."

Now it's Cecily's turn. "Did you—did you feel that?" she asks, her voice shaky. Rudy is impressed. He knows that Cecily isn't exactly pro–ghost content, but his sister's still pretty good at acting. "I felt something cold, I know I did . . ."

Rudy checks on the post. Their livestream is blowing up; cash is flowing in. Apparently, they'd been tweeted about by a couple commentary channels, other influencers, and e-news outlets—a whole new wave of viewers had just joined, causing their attendance to skyrocket. Along with one follower in particular. He waves to get Amber's attention, and she glances at the comment readout. She freezes.

> ➡ **DON'T INVITE HER IN. DON'T MESS WITH THE GHOSTS.**

Other followers have found the comment. They're asking them to answer it, to address this strange person who's posted on so many of their Tremont photos. Rudy had expected the follower to comment, but somehow seeing the posts come in, in real time, makes them all the more real.

Amber shoots Rudy a concerned look, and he shrugs. He knows that they're supposed to ignore the follower, but right now that seems impossible. So Amber answers, shaky. "Some people are worried about our safety. Don't worry, we're big and strong—and, we have Rudy to protect us!"

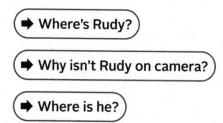

Amber's eyes go wide. Cecily and Rudy are shocked, as well. Alex Grable keeps posting.

➡ **Where's Rudy?**

➡ **Why isn't Rudy on camera?**

➡ **Where is he?**

Cecily is frozen. Amber collects herself and turns to the camera, smiling. "Looks like we've got more than a ghost haunting us, huh?"

➡ **Where's Rudy?**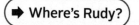

Rudy can't keep quiet anymore. "Hey!" he says, voice clearly audible from behind the camera. "I'm right here—who did you think was filming? How's it going, Mr. Creep? Did you see our latest posts? What did you think about the paint job, huh?"

Cecily gives Rudy a warning look. Laughing emojis appear all over the livestream as their fans taunt the follower and congratulate Rudy on his "epic prank." But then, the emojis and supportive messages are drowned out by something else. The follower is going *insane:*

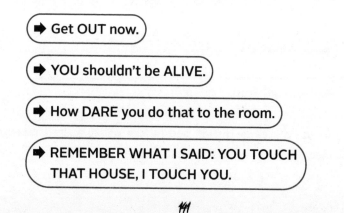

➡ **Get OUT now.**

➡ **YOU shouldn't be ALIVE.**

➡ **How DARE you do that to the room.**

➡ **REMEMBER WHAT I SAID: YOU TOUCH THAT HOUSE, I TOUCH YOU.**

And then one message, on repeat:

➡ I warned you.

➡ I warned you.

➡ I warned you.

➡ I warned you.

➡ I warned you.

➡ I warned you.

➡ I warned you.

➡ I warned you.

➡ I warned you.

➡ I warned you.

➡ I warned you.

➡ I warned you.

➡ I warned you.

➡ I warned you.

Rudy looks back to his sisters, and he can tell they are freaked out. Amber's mouth is slack, and Cecily looks frozen.

Even Rudy is unsettled. This is much more of a response than he'd expected.

"Shut it off," Amber whispers, so only he and Cecily can hear. "He's taking over the livestream. No one else can even get a comment in." And she's right. The follower is commenting so frequently that all other comments get lost in the fray, unnoticed, unanswered. This isn't what was supposed to happen. Rudy watches the warning flicker over and over in the comments, unrelenting.

Amber turns the lights back on. The comments continue. Cecily is still frozen, petrified, eyes frantically scanning the endless array of comments. Rudy gestures at Amber to wrap up.

"Well," Amber says, swallowing hard. "That might be all there is for now, folks. Stay tuned for our next video—we've got a great surprise coming your way, and I know you'll love it." But her voice sounds forced. Canned. "And, uh, don't forget to follow! Bye!"

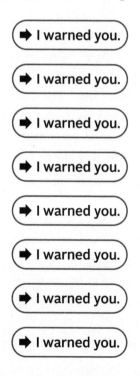

➡ I warned you.

➡ I warned you.

➡ I warned you.

➡ I warned you.

➡ I warned you.

➡ I warned you.

➡ I warned you.

➡ I warned you.

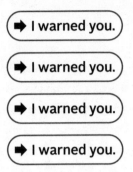

➡ I warned you.

➡ I warned you.

➡ I warned you.

➡ I warned you.

Amber walks forward and shuts the camera off. She turns toward her siblings. For a second, no one says anything. Rudy knows he should say something to reassure his sisters that there's nothing to worry about, but he's worried. He finds himself feeling a little . . . scared. Or maybe a lot scared. He can admit it.

➡ YOU shouldn't be ALIVE.

"That was weird," Rudy says finally. "Super weird."

"Super weird," Amber echoes. The three exchange looks. No one really knows what to say.

There are footsteps on the stairs. All three of them jump, but it's just their mom, here for a debriefing. "Cecily, great promos. Amber, great thinking about ending the livestream when it all started going crazy." Amber flushes. "And Rudy—what did I tell you about feeding the troll? Now look what you've done—we had to cut off our own livestream!"

Amber's phone pings. "The livestream's hit trending," she says.

Rudy smirks. The uneasiness he felt just moments ago has been replaced with the feeling of being annoyed at his mom. "And, uh, once more, the Cole triplets' viral internet success is because of . . ." He mimes a drumroll and points to himself, laughing as he stands up. "I'll see myself out."

For once, Mrs. Cole doesn't have a response. Rudy realizes that she knows he's right. Even if she won't admit it.

Amber opens her mouth as if she's going to say something, then shuts it.

Cecily lets out a shaky breath. "I'm heading to bed," she says.

"Aw, Cece, it's not that bad," Rudy says. "It's just some jerk—and we made a ton of money, so—"

Cecily's face is tight. "I'm just tired, okay?"

She heads downstairs with their mom, leaving Amber and Rudy alone in the room. Rudy shrugs. "Well, whatever that was, you were great," he says, clapping her on the shoulder.

Amber gives him a small smile and starts disassembling the key lights. It's not until they're on their way downstairs that she answers him. "You know? I think so, too."

She heads to her room to edit and post some creepy doll stills.

Rudy collapses onto his bed and picks up the mixtape on his nightstand. He still has a fair bit to go before it's fully untangled and back on its spool, but he's willing to put the work in for some cool nineties tracks. As he begins to work on it, a loud *thunk* rings across the room from above.

"Ha ha," he calls out. "Very funny." But no one answers. It must have been Cecily messing with him, or their dad moving furniture around upstairs.

His mind wanders and replays the messages from the livestream as he slowly, methodically works to unravel the cassette tape. He's too jumpy for this kind of focused work tonight, he decides. He puts the tape down and pops an old Alanis Morissette tape he'd found in the box into the cassette player. He leans back and tries to let the music distract him from the memory of the repeating messages.

➡ I warned you.

➡ I warned you.

➡ I warned you.

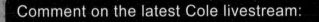

Comment on the latest Cole livestream:

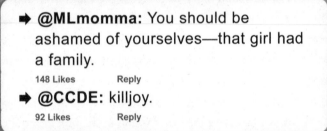

➡ **@MLmomma:** You should be ashamed of yourselves—that girl had a family.

148 Likes   Reply

➡ **@CCDE:** killjoy.

92 Likes   Reply

Cecily

THE LIVESTREAM *DESTROYED* IT. NUMBER THREE ON TRENDING. Fifteen thousand new followers, more than two million views and counting. It's more than Cecily or her siblings had ever hoped for. They review the results over breakfast on the porch: yogurt for Cecily, coffee for Amber, and cereal for Rudy, who'd discovered earlier that his protein powder had been thrown out in the kitchen purge following his allergy attack.

Amber scans their messages, a concerned expression on her face.

"There are a lot of people who are worried," she murmurs as she takes another sip of her coffee. "They think we're going to get murdered by the ghost or the follower or both. I think it's the younger end of our demographic—a bunch of concerned twelve-year-olds."

"And what about the older end?" Rudy asks.

Amber shrugs. "Half of them are just here for the drama; the other half thinks it's totally fake and the ghost story isn't even real."

Cecily shudders. She can't stop thinking of the livestream, of the repeating messages. *I warned you.* How they said that Rudy shouldn't be alive—what had that meant? And Speckles . . . her poor little bunny . . .

The empty cage is still in her room. She hasn't had the heart to throw it out yet.

"Maybe they should be concerned," Cecily says. She sucks in a breath. She'd been up all last night, thinking. *YOU shouldn't be ALIVE.* "The follower . . . do you think they somehow knew what happened to Rudy?"

Rudy and Amber pause.

"They couldn't have," Amber says finally. "They were just messing with us 'cause Rudy wasn't in frame."

"There's no way they could have known," Rudy says, in clear agreement with Amber. "You're being paranoid, sis."

Cecily chews on her lower lip. "What about the ghost?" she whispers. "When Amber said that thing, inviting the ghost in . . . the follower seemed kind of spooked. By Alex Grable, I mean."

"Aw, come on," Rudy says through a mouthful of cereal. "Everything is fine, Cece. My face is back to normal, and look at that engagement! Seriously, even you have to admit that messing with this ghost girl and the creepy follower is the best thing that's ever happened to us. Our account hasn't been this interesting in *years*."

Cecily cringes. She's about to answer when Mrs. Cole appears with a cup of coffee. "And it's going to stop being that interesting," she says. "I know it's fun, kids, but . . . your dad and I talked about it last night, and we're a little concerned about this Alex Grable follower."

"Mom, we haven't pulled views like this, well, *ever!*" Rudy protests.

Mrs. Cole presses her lips together. "We're a house-flipping account, not . . . stalker bait, or whatever is going on with this psycho. That's why our fanbase is here—of course, that and you three—and that's why they'll stay. Last night that troll took things too far. Post all the ghost stuff you want, but block him. Amber, post an announcement later."

"Hey, just because you're mad at me, don't take it out on the account," Rudy cries. "I didn't take that stupid plaque; come on, you can't still be mad—"

"Our minds are made up, Rudy," Mrs. Cole says. Cecily tries to hide her sigh of relief; she can feel the muscles in her back relax as her mom leaves. She knows that Rudy is disappointed, but . . . maybe now things have a chance at going back to normal. Still, she needs to calm down. She knows what will help—a girls' night with her new friend Bella. She's sure Mom won't mind. She dashes off a quick text to Bella.

In desperate need of some fun. Makeovers? A sleepover? Tomorrow night?

The reply comes instantly: *Definitely!*

Their post goes up later that afternoon:

> ➡ Thank you so much for all your support! We're thrilled to have such success with the livestream and to have so many new faces joining the Cole Patrol. And we'd like to announce that we've blocked certain accounts responsible for our online harassment so we can continue giving you the content you love!

Cecily lies on the cold, hard new flooring in the study, wishing Amber would stop staring at their account long enough to take her photo and be done with it. Noise echoes around them; the crew is almost done putting the flooring in the kitchen. Then, it's the rest of the downstairs, followed by an endless list of refurbishing old furniture, buying new pieces, painting walls, designing the bedrooms—it makes Cecily's head hurt just thinking about it.

The crew finished the flooring in the study first, so Cecily is posing to show off the new aesthetic. Or she would be, if Amber weren't so distracted. Cecily arches her back, poses, and Amber snaps a picture.

"Was that good?"

Amber doesn't answer. Something on her phone has her complete and undivided attention.

"You're not seriously thinking about revising the statement again, are you?" Cecily asks.

Then Amber looks up and turns beet red. Cecily reads her expression and grins. She darts across the room and all but pounces on her sister. "You're texting her! Bonfire girl."

"I don't know who you're talking about. And she has a *name*—shit." Amber looks up at Cecily. "Okay, fine. I got Jada's number at the party, and despite the . . . freak-out . . . she seems to still want to hang out with me. I'm just trying not to mess this up, okay?"

Amber tilts her phone toward Cecily, who scans the texts. "Nice use of the winky face. Very strategic."

Amber hits her in the arm with a throw pillow. "Shut *up*." She stares at her phone, then back up at her sister. "It's just . . . I'm no good at this kind of thing. What do I say?"

Cecily furrows her brow in confusion. She's not sure how to step into this role—sure, perfect online Cecily has a ton of admirers, but online romance and romance in real life are two very different things. "You're asking me? I mean, you could just ask her out." Amber's eyes grow wide. "Or, maybe it's too soon," Cecily says quickly. "Hey—I actually invited Bella over tomorrow night; we were planning a sleepover. Why don't you invite Jada? She's cool, it'll be fun to hang out—and that way you're not alone, but if you, oh, I don't know, happen to slip off somewhere into this seven-thousand-square-foot mansion for some private time . . ." She shoots Amber a sly smile.

"Are you serious? That's perfect." Amber texts Jada, then flips to Instagram and makes up a quick post. "And . . . there we are. The sponsored post for the day. You look great."

She does. Against the hardwood, Cecily's hair fans out in a pale golden halo as she smiles up at the camera with a perfect smoky eye. She holds a hand to her collarbone, showing off bright red nails. The caption reads: *New Floor, New Me. And soon—new everything! Fantastic nail color brought to you by RainbowMani.*

It looks good, but does it look good enough? She scans it, looking for flaws in her makeup, her posing, her body. She finds so many. Is her smile big enough? Her teeth white enough? What if she didn't blend her contour well enough? What if this post tanks?

It can't. It has to be perfect. She has to be perfect. She shakes her head and tries not to feel a slow sense of dread as she realizes what that means. "Uh, I've got to go work on some new looks—About Face just sent me their new ice-cream palette, and I still need to do a video on that jelly high-lighter I got last month . . . I don't suppose you want to come and hang out with me in the creepy turret room?" Amber makes a face. "Ah. You're too busy sexting your girlfriend."

"We're not *sexting*—"

But Cecily's already forcing a laugh and heading toward the stairs. "If I see any ghost girls, I'll scream really loud," she promises, but it doesn't come out as jokey as she'd intended. She tries to push down the rising sense of unease.

"I'll come up as soon as I've finished editing this pic," Amber promises. Then, her phone beeps with another message from Jada. Somehow, Cecily doubts she'll be in the turret anytime soon.

Cecily reaches the third-floor landing feeling a lot less confident and a lot more anxious. She can't stop herself from looking at the third-floor bedroom as she walks past Rudy's message scrawled on the wall: *This is my house now, bitch.* She shakes her head and forces herself to continue toward the door to the fourth floor. *Ghosts aren't real*, she tells herself. *There is nothing up here.* She needs to practice her makeup. She needs to be perfect, flawless if she ever wants to succeed in the beauty industry. If fighting off an irrational fear of this house is what it takes, she can do that, right? She's strong enough, right? Right.

She takes a breath and reaches out for the handle. It sticks.

The door is locked. Again.

Cecily shudders and feels a new wave of fear. No way. They'd left it unlocked last night, hadn't they? She could have sworn they had.

She tries the door again. Still locked. Shit. She rolls her eyes. It must be Rudy, right? Playing another stupid prank for some video. She looks around for a camera filming her reaction, but just because she can't find one doesn't mean it's not there. She's going to confront him about it.

She finds Rudy in his room, playing music from the cassette player and doing pull-ups on his Iron Gym. She glares at her brother. "Ha. Ha." She says. "Not funny."

He looks confused.

"Your trick with the door," she says. "Locking it again."

But he shrugs. "Wasn't me."

"Sure," Cecily says, rolling her eyes and trying to shove away her feeling of dread. If it wasn't Rudy, then who locked the door? "Whatever you say. What's that music, anyway?"

"Beastie Boys," Rudy says, transitioning into leg lifts. "I mean, I never thought I'd hear Beastie Boys on cassette, but here we are."

"I never thought I'd hear anything on cassette," Cecily admits. Then, she notices something—or a lack of something. "Why aren't you filming this? You know how mad Amber and Mom would be for you wasting this kind of 'content,'" she says, only half sarcastically.

Rudy shoots his sister a look, letting her know just how much he cares about making content for their mother. "As if you don't waste content every other day. I know half the looks you do don't make it onto the main account."

He's got her. Cecily avoids his eyes. He's right—she *had* been withholding some of her best looks from the Cole triplets' account on purpose. She tells herself that it is because she wants them to be perfect, but really she worries her mom won't like them. No, that's not true. It is because she wants to couple them with more scientific commentary, and her mom definitely won't go for that. And what's more? She kind of wants to post them anyway. But not on the triplets' account.

From the way Rudy is looking at her, Cecily feels like he can read her mind. She shrugs and tries to play off her discomfort. "Well, Mom doesn't always want every one, so . . ." She scans the room, looking for something to help change the subject. Rudy hops off the Iron Gym.

"Sure," Rudy says. "And the key's on the hall table, if you've locked yourself out by accident."

Cecily rolls her eyes. "Thanks."

The key is right where Rudy says it is. Cecily weaves past her father and Joseph with brief hellos, grabs the key, and heads back up. She opens the turret door with a sharp *click*.

And then she hears a soft *thump*.

Cecily freezes. She heard something inside the room, didn't she? *Didn't she?* She hesitates, caught by the idea that when she opens the door there's going to be someone *in* there, in the room, going through her things . . .

Her mind goes back to the séance—god, they'd invited the ghost *in*—and all the fear she'd felt earlier returns, but stronger now, so much stronger.

Calm down, she tells herself. She waits and listens. If what she'd heard was a footstep, there would have to be more, right? But there's no other noise. She eases the door open and tiptoes up the stairs.

The turret room is silent and empty.

Cecily steps in slowly, her senses heightened, listening. But there is nothing. *You're being paranoid*, she tells herself. She walks the short length of the room, over to the antique desk, but even after she's confirmed the room is definitely empty, Cecily still can't shake that strange, jittery feeling.

The antique doll is still sitting on the floor where Amber had left her during the livestream. Its cracked doll face stares up at her. Cecily glares at it. There is no *way* she is going to let herself be freaked out by some stupid horror-movie prop. She takes the doll and opens an old chest in the turret room, shoving it in on top of a bunch of other junk her brother must have found. She closes the lid and locks it, even as she convinces herself that she doesn't need to.

Stupid, stupid nerves.

All right. She clears her head and walks over to the antique desk, sitting down and flicking on her ring light. She reaches for her foundation and . . . it's not there.

She looks down and frowns. No, it is there. Just several inches to the left of where it should have been, of where she always puts it. She glances at her products, trying to assess their arrangement. Wasn't her palette over there? Didn't she leave her go bag on top of the shelf? Wasn't her mirror positioned higher before?

A cold sense of dread creeps over her. Something for which she has nothing to prove, but something she feels like she *knows*. Someone has been sitting here, in this chair. Someone has been in this room. Someone has been going through her things. Touching her products. Moving them around. But why?

She whips around, convinced for a second that there are eyes on her back, that she can *feel* someone watching her.

She runs to the window and looks out, but there is no one. Just the view of the yard and the woods, now a true mirror to the painting Rudy had found underneath the wallpaper. She tries to imagine Alex sitting here, painting the last thing she would see before she died. Cecily shudders. And she still. Feels. Watched.

She turns around to face the room, slowly, half-convinced that someone will be standing behind her, but the room remains empty. The door still hangs open, revealing the stairs below.

Cecily shakes her head. This is dumb. She's only freaking herself out; she is being scared and stupid for no reason. Things had probably just gotten shuffled around when they'd set up the room for their livestream.

Besides, what was it that she had yelled outside after the bonfire? That she wasn't afraid of the house. *And you're not*, she tells herself. She isn't, right? So she forces herself to sit at the desk and start putting a look together. She takes out her phone, but she doesn't turn on Instagram.

Pop music blares across the room, and Cecily begins transforming her face into something pristine, beautiful, perfect. Unafraid. Something that she has to be. Slowly, she forgets about the turret, about the rabbit, about the strange hardware store owner or Amber's scare at the bonfire. By the time she looks into the mirror and sees a beautiful mint-green-and-gold look staring back at her, Cecily feels like herself again. Good. Confident.

And then she heads downstairs to show her mom the look, but along the way everything changes. Because she meets Amber on the stairs and her sister's panicked face tells Cecily something is very wrong. She feels the dread return to her bones, and she knows what Amber is going to show her before she even sees it.

Amber holds up her phone to reveal another comment from the follower beneath the post of Cecily from earlier, lying on the floor and advertising for RainbowMani:

> ➡ I told you not to mess with it. Don't say I didn't warn you.

Comment on the latest Cole post:

➡ **@XXBattlebotx:** Have people been looking at the livestream? There, at 12:54—you can see shadows moving in the background. Someone tell me I'm not the only one seeing this.

246 Likes   Reply

XXXXXXXXXXXXXXXXXXXXXXXXXXXXX

CHAPTER 13

Amber

AMBER BOUNCES ON THE BALLS OF HER FEET, TRYING NOT TO
stare at the door as she waits for Jada and Bella to arrive. She had opted for
an elegant wrap top over a pair of dark jeans, but even though she knows
her outfit is on point, she still feels self-conscious. She'd allowed Cecily to
do her makeup for the night—just the basics: some mascara, tinted mois-
turizer, and a kiss of bronzer on the apples of her cheeks. But is she too
made up? Trying too hard or not trying enough? Too well dressed or too
sloppy to look the part of social media star?

She wonders if Bella and Jada know that she was on the livestream, if
they'd noticed the comments. Not the Alex Grable follower ones—the
other ones.

> ➡ Yes! More Amber! So glad that the Coles
> listened.

> ➡ Wow, Amber looks FRESH.

They make her glow. Amber tries to summon that happy feeling, that
confidence, as she waits for Bella and Jada to arrive.

Meanwhile, Cecily lounges on a folding chair, looking as if she couldn't
care less that their friends are coming over. So effortless.

Rudy is here, too, sitting on the staircase, fiddling with the broken mixtape, trying to coax the film back onto its tracking.

"You do know you can download all those albums, right?" Amber asks.

"Not if I don't know what's on the mixtape," he says. "Besides, I like the
cassettes. They're vintage. And I'm *almost* there."

Cecily raises an eyebrow. "You're becoming an insufferable hipster."

The doorbell rings; Amber catches a glimpse of Bella, outside leaning her bike against the porch rail next to Jada's. Cecily shoots her brother one last glare before opening the door for their friends. Jada immediately gives Amber a tight hug. Amber is enveloped in the smell of her denim jacket—a mixture of evergreen and bonfire smoke over the scent of detergent. She has to fight the urge to hug her for too long.

"Thanks for having me!" Jada says into her ear.

"This is going to be so much fun," Bella adds. "When we were kids, we used to dare each other to sleep over in this house—I never thought I'd actually *do* it."

Jada gives Bella a friendly elbow. "You sure your mom's okay with you staying in a haunted house? All that demonic influence?" she asks, grinning.

"I don't want to get you in trouble—" Cecily starts, but Bella waves her off.

"Don't worry about it; my mom is going to spend all night praying for my soul whatever I do," she says. "If she gets too mad, I'll just tell her that I spent the night trying to bring your hedonistic, social-media-loving souls to Our Lord and Savior." She cackles and slips off her shoes. "Dude, this place is *huge!*"

"Can we get a tour?" asks Jada. Her arms dangle at her sides, and she inches toward Amber. For a split second her fingertips brush Amber's arm. Amber feels her pulse accelerate.

"Of course," Cecily says. "Oh! We can end the tour upstairs and do makeovers or something."

"And, that's my cue to leave and play violent video games," Rudy cuts in. "See ya."

Cecily and Amber lead the girls through the hallway, introducing them to their parents and Joseph as he says his goodbyes. Joseph has made a habit of lingering to discuss renovation logistics long after the rest of the crew had gone home; last night and tonight he'd even stayed for dinner. Amber knows that her parents are grateful for the extra help, and she's grateful for the buffer at mealtimes. Talking about local high school kids and Norton with Joseph is a lot easier than discussing social media analytics with Mom, and Amber will take all the breaks she can get. He's also surprisingly up to date on social media and influencer culture, citing his own kids as the reason. "I have to keep up with them, don't I?" he'd asked the triplets that evening with a wink. "It's how I convince myself that I'm not getting old." He had made a joke about setting up an Instagram account of his own, and Amber had promised to help him take "all the best influencer photos."

Cecily and Amber lead Bella and Jada through all the rooms off the grand foyer, updating them on their progress. Nothing looks too impressive just yet; they're only about a week and a half into the renovation. The most they have to show is the new flooring in the kitchen, study, and half of the hallway. All the rooms are still waiting on paint.

"I love this house," Bella sighs, running her hand over the wall. "But I don't know what's weirder—seeing it totally empty or thinking about it being all fancy. It seems . . . wrong, somehow. Is the upstairs this empty?"

"Nah, we've got furniture in the bedrooms," Cecily says. "But it's pretty sparse. The walk-in could use some shelves."

"Hold up," Bella says. "You have a *walk-in*? I need to see that."

Cecily shoots her a grin. "Absolutely."

To the side, Amber gives Jada a semi–eye roll. "She got to pick her room first," she says. "And, honestly, she's got way more clothes than me."

"Only because sponsors keep sending me things," Cecily says. *Of course*, Amber thinks, *being size two definitely helps with that*. She bites her lip but doesn't say anything as Cecily leads the girls up the stairs and onto the second-floor landing. It's already scattered with a couple pedestals, just waiting for something fragile and expensive.

When Bella walks into Cecily's room and peeks into her closet, her mouth drops. "Is that *Gucci*?"

Jada laughs. "I don't think I've ever even *seen* someone wear Gucci in real life—wait, you said sponsors send you this stuff? You get some of it for *free*?"

Amber can't tell if Jada is impressed or horrified.

Cecily answers. "Uh, well, it's not always great stuff. Sometimes, it's super weird—like this company NastyBabe and, uh, NeoFashion. Once they sent us, like, these *awful* neon-green jumpsuits."

Bella steps farther into the closet. "You know, there's really not as much here as I expected there to be."

Cecily flushes; Amber wonders if Bella is disappointed. "Well," Cecily says. "I sell a bunch of it online, you know. Can't keep everything." *More like can't afford to keep everything*, Amber thinks.

Jada joins Bella in the closet and looks around. Something catches her eye and she reaches for a hanger. "Is this the aforementioned neon-green jumpsuit?" she asks, holding it up. When Cecily nods, she laughs. "I look like a rave threw up on me," she says, handing it off to Bella, who holds it to her chest and strikes a pose. "Seriously," Jada continues, stepping out of the closet. "I think my entire wardrobe is from T.J.Maxx or Old Navy. Are you sure I'm not too basic to hang out with you guys?"

Cecily and Amber shift, responding just a second too late.

"No—" Cecily starts, but Amber cuts her off.

"Er, that would be a great video to do, actually," she says eagerly. "We could do an Old Navy haul, find some cute looks, compare them to other designers—"

Jada laughs. "It sounds like you should be the one getting all the fashion sponsors."

Amber flushes, but she can't keep the smile from breaking on her face. "I actually used to do a lot of fashion content."

"Used to?"

Amber shrugs; isn't it obvious why Cecily gets all the clothes from sponsors? Breaking the silence, Bella sifts through Cecily's closet.

"Here," Bella says. "Screw being normal. Cecily, do you have any other weird clothes? We should do a makeover featuring the weirdest stuff you've got." She scrunches up her face. "Although, now that I think of it, you're *tiny!* I don't think I'll fit into any of it—might have to raid Amber's closet instead," she says with a wink. Amber laughs. She'll gladly lend Bella her clothes anytime.

Cecily perks up. "Or, I could spare you from the hideous green jumpsuits and give you a hideous green makeover instead."

Bella instantly perks up. She grins at Jada. "Her makeup is in—get this—the turret room."

Jada doesn't seem as excited. "*The* turret room? The one where—"

"It had the best lighting," Cecily says apologetically.

"Excellent," Bella says, throwing the green jumpsuit over her shoulder. "Let's go!"

"You'll look ridiculous," Cecily says. Amber is smiling in spite of herself as she leads the girls upstairs. At least Cecily's expensive makeup is a bit less . . . obvious than designer goods.

When Cecily pulls on the turret door, it doesn't open. Nothing. Cecily lets out a panicked half-laugh.

"Uh, good thing you have the key," Amber says, stumbling into recovery mode.

"Is it really locked?" Jada asks. She takes a step toward Amber.

Amber grazes Jada's fingertips with hers, then, on impulse, grabs her hand. She gives Jada a smile. "It's the old house. Mom calls it 'quirky.' A lot of the doors seem to have some kind of auto-lock or something. Cecily has the key though, right?" She gives her sister a pleading look.

"Of course." Cecily pulls out the key and opens the door. "See? Easy. We're in."

The girls walk up the narrow staircase and enter the small, hexagonal room.

Amber watches Jada scan the space, then follows her eyes to the window. "That's where it happened?" Jada asks. Amber nods. Jada's fingers slip out of hers as she walks over and stares at the descent. "That's a long way down."

"Is that painting new?" Bella asks. "Are you an artist, too?"

Amber and Cecily explain about finding the paintings underneath the wallpaper, and the letter *R* carved into the dumbwaiter shaft from their last couple days here. The girls seem suitably spooked and impressed by the "old house secrets," but it doesn't take long for Bella to get distracted from the ghost and start flipping through Cecily's makeup collection.

"I don't think I've ever seen this much makeup in my *life*," Bella says. Amber thinks her laugh sounds a little weird—maybe even a little bitter. Is she jealous? Amber doesn't blame her; she knows the feeling all too well.

Cecily nods. "Yeah. I get a lot of good loot for free to test out, but I don't promote all of it, of course—only the stuff I like."

Jada turns a palette over and yelps. "Ninety bucks?"

"Oh, is it?" Cecily asks, oblivious. "I don't really check the prices when I get 'em. I haven't bought makeup in ages." Amber cringes, but her sister continues. "If you ever want to use any of them, seriously you're always welcome. I have more than I can get through."

"You can say that again," Jada mutters.

Bella sits at the desk and sifts through the eyeshadows until she finds the most neon palette in Cecily's entire collection. "I want the neon ones. Oh—no—wait, I've changed my mind. I want your formal go-to. The Cecily Cole signature look! I want to say that I got the Cecily Cole signature look. You know, so I can brag about it once you're a guru with her own makeup line."

Cecily laughs. "Hey, I don't have a line yet . . . ," she jokes, and she turns around to rummage through her palettes. Amber watches her. Does Cecily want her own makeup line one day? It seems like the logical next step for her, but would she really do it as part of a home renovation channel? Cecily wouldn't leave the channel, would she?

"You can't be far," Bella says. "I mean, isn't that what all the beauty influencers do? Break off and make their own product lines?"

Amber stares at Cecily, trying to read her sister's face as she responds. "I mean, that would be nice, maybe, but we're, uh, a three-person account, and . . ." Cecily falters. With a jolt, Amber realizes that Cecily has to at least be *thinking* about leaving them.

Cecily catches Amber's eye, and without speaking, it's settled. They will talk about this later. Not in front of their friends.

"All right, so this is my favorite palette," Cecily says a moment later, reaching for a square compact. "I absolutely *love* the pearly shimmer of this one. I think it's made of bismuth—and it's vegan, unlike some other palettes that contain things like carmine."

"I *thought* I recognized it from your vlogs!" Bella giggles. "Yes, yes, let's do that one—"

"If you're okay with doing makeup in the suicide room," Rudy says suddenly. He pokes his head through the door. "The parents are asleep. Please tell me you're not doing makeup. I found something."

"What's up?" Amber asks.

"Well, I finally untangled the cassette," Rudy says. He quickly recaps the story for Bella and Jada. "And it's not a mixtape. It's a recording. I think . . . I think it's a recording of Alex Grable."

Comment on the latest Cole post:

➡ **@DareMe:** look at the intro to house livestream. Third floor—does anyone else see the moving shadow behind the camera?

157 Likes   Reply

XXXXXXXXXXXXXXXXXXXXXXXXXXXXXXX

CHAPTER 14

Rudy

THE ROOM IS SO QUIET YOU COULD HEAR A PIN DROP. RUDY waits for the girls to respond. He's not quite sure how he wants them to react. He's not quite sure how to react himself. He had debated going up to the girls, debated even listening to the tape again—but there was too much on it. He had to tell them. And, although he hates to admit it, he doesn't think he can handle being the only one to have heard the tape. Have heard her. He waits with bated breath.

Amber is the first to speak. "Alex Grable? Absolutely no way."

"Are you sure?" Bella asks.

"I mean, well, no," Rudy admits. "That's why I brought it up here, I wanted to get your takes on it. It's, uh, hard to explain."

"Well, what's on the tape?" Amber asks.

"It's better if you just listen," Rudy says.

"Well, you can't just *say* that and not play it," Bella says. "Come on."

Of the four girls, Rudy can see that Jada looks the most uncomfortable, with Cecily a close second. Amber looks a little apprehensive, and Bella looks positively excited.

Amber takes a seat on the floor next to Rudy and motions for Jada to sit next to her. The other two girls join them in a circle.

Rudy places the tape recorder in the middle of the floor, along with a bottle of vodka he'd swiped from his parents' stash. "I'm warning you, though, it's super weird. Kind of disturbing. So, I also brought drinks."

"Maybe we shouldn't . . . ," Jada whispers.

"Well, I definitely want to," Bella says.

Rudy looks to his sisters. Amber gives him a nod, but Cecily . . .

she's clearly freaked out already. "I think you need to hear this," he tells her.

Cecily takes a deep breath. "All right," she says with a nod.

Jada scoots a little closer to Amber. Amber grabs her hand. Rudy cringes. He hates that he's about to ruin his sister's date, but this . . . can't wait.

"Yeah," Bella says, leaning forward. "Let's hear it."

Rudy turns the recorder on and puts the tape in. The room goes quiet. In the recorder, the tape makes an empty clicking noise. He feels himself tense, waiting for what he knows is about to come.

"It's broken," Cecily says, and it sounds like she's trying not to sigh with relief. "Maybe we should—"

"That's the first part," Rudy says, shaking his head. "Some of it was really damaged from being tangled; I couldn't get much of it to work. Only a few words, here and there. The end is clearer, though. Listen."

Segments of syllables start to emerge. He watches Cecily and Amber freeze up as they listen.

Click. Click. "Gra—" *Click. Click.* "Com—" *Click. Click.* "Following—" *Click. Click.*

"It gets better from here on out," Rudy says, as the tape descends back into wordless clicking.

Then, as Rudy knew it would, the clicking stops. But what follows is not the kind of silence that's devoid of any noise. It's the silence that comes with a room—birds chirping, AC humming. When he was listening to the tape in his room, Rudy hadn't thought much about where the silence was from, but now that he's up here, Rudy realizes that it is the silence that comes from *this* room. The turret.

And then the noise starts. The sound of something . . . moving. Something grinding.

Rudy braces himself for the words.

When they come, Bella yelps. He understands; he hadn't expected to hear the voice that came out of the tape, either. It's a small voice, the voice of a young girl, and it's singing, ever so softly, as if someone had recorded themselves singing under their breath. The song is a nonsense rhyme, probably a nursey rhyme—but unlike any rhyme he has ever heard before.

> *Once there was a shooting star,*
> *That shot across the sky*
> *But I don't want to see it there;*
> *So that star had to die.*

When Rudy had first heard this in the darkness of his room, he had immediately froze. The voice seemed so . . . young. Too innocent to be the voice of a murderer. But it had to be Alex Grable, didn't it?

The song breaks off into dissonant humming, keeping the soft, lilting melody. There are soft noises in the background, as if someone is singing while doing housework, or preparing something.

The singer starts to mumble more words, but he can't catch them, only snippets:

> *One floor, two floor, three floor, four—*
> *[. . .] listening at the door—*

And Rudy realizes something that he missed before. The singer isn't being obstructed by background noise; she's trying to make up another verse, recording her ideas. She stumbles around the rhyme scheme for a few more moments of muffled clutter before continuing on in a clearer voice, as if she's finally settled on the right verse:

> *Once there was a shooting star*
> *But she won't be here for long—*
> *Too bad, so sad, no mom, not mad,*
> *Flying and falling and gone.*

There are a few more seconds of dissonant humming, and then a *click* as the blank tape turns over and flips to silence.

"There's more," Rudy says.

Silence.

Click.

Clatter.

The tape hums with the sound of the turret once more. Then, the sound of footsteps, rushed, frantic. Silence. And, over the silence, a panicked keening. Someone is breathing, hard and erratic.

Then, a word: "Mom?"

Rudy closes his eyes and braces himself. This is the worst part, the one that he knows will keep him awake late into the night. The tape begins to play scattered noises of someone stepping, slowly at first, then quickly. Something slams into something else, and then there's a louder scuffle, the sound of something or someone heavy losing their balance—and then silence. At first, he'd thought that this was where Alex jumped, where Alex fell, but that can't be true, because the girl's voice starts again. It's not a rhyme this time, just one phrase repeated:

> *Flying and falling and gone. Flying and falling*
> *and gone. Falling and gone, falling and gone,*
> *falling and gone, falling and—*

Then, an uneven noise, like feet scuffling across the floor, like the sound of someone falling.

Then silence.

Rudy turns the recording off. "That's it," he says. None of the girls answer. They're still staring at the tape, shell-shocked. Rudy can't blame them; that's exactly how he'd reacted when he heard it. He coughs. "Uh, at least, that's what I've been able to salvage so far, between detangling the tape and the deterioration and the mold and stuff."

Still, no one answers. He reaches for the fifth of vodka. Mr. Cole won't miss it; as part of his gambling reformation he's also majorly cut back on drinking. "I thought we might need a drink after that."

"Rudy," Cecily whispers. "What *is* that?"

Rudy doesn't know how to answer. He can only say what he suspects it is. "I think . . . I think it might have been Alex Grable."

Bella reaches for the bottle. "She sounds *insane,*" she says. She takes a drink and passes. "Do you think—it sounds like she just killed her mom."

It takes a long moment for Rudy to answer. "Yeah," he finally says, taking a pull himself. "That's what I thought, too."

"Can you turn up the volume any?" Bella asks. She nudges Amber. "Hey, you're good with recording software, right? Maybe you can, I dunno, do something."

Amber presses her lips together. The bottle comes around and she takes it. "Uh, I don't know," she says. The hesitation in her voice makes it crystal clear how much she doesn't want to touch the murder tape. "It seems like, well, shouldn't we take this to the police? If it is her?"

Rudy had been wondering the same thing. Is it evidence? Can they even prove that it was Alex Grable? But even if they can . . . the tape feels important, like a critical part of the house's mystery. He doesn't want to give it up just yet. "I mean, we can't prove it's her, can we?" Rudy says. "Besides, it's an open-and-shut case. I don't think we're exactly withholding evidence or anything."

"I don't think it would look super good if we started finding evidence for a murder case in our renovation," Amber whispers. Her voice is so quiet, almost inaudible. "Mom wouldn't like it." Rudy nods. Amber is right. Their mom might totally lose it if she were to find out about this. "Besides, there's no real evidence, is there? Just a creepy song thing."

Jada nods in agreement with Amber and scoots a little closer to her. Rudy watches his sister lean on Jada with a look that can only be relief. "The cops here are real sticklers," Jada adds. "Won't even let you off with a warning for going, like, three over. It'd probably go over the wrong way if you turned up with a murder tape. Jailbird doesn't seem to go with your triplet image."

"You okay, Cece?" Rudy asks, glancing at other sister, realizing she's been quiet for a while. "You know what?" He answers his own question by handing her the bottle. "Take a pull. This will help."

Cecily hesitates, then does just that. "Let's talk about something else," she says when she's finished. "Anything else."

There's a moment of silence before Bella pipes up. "I saw your live-stream! And the paint room, Rudy. I just think it's so brave, what you guys did. Directly calling out that creepy dude like that. Weren't you scared?"

Rudy gives her a shaky smile, grateful that she jumped on the topic change. "Nah," he says. "And it's not like they were bothering us. It's more like . . . I dunno, rude of them to impersonate a dead girl, you know? And it was a great excuse to redecorate the master bedroom," he jokes.

"Do you do a lot of painting?" she asks.

He shakes his head. "Nah, but I'd like to do more. When I have time."

"I'd think you'd have a lot of time—I know you're homeschooled, but don't you get summer break?" Jada asks.

"Yeah, we do," Cecily cuts in. "But don't even start him on—"

"Working out, mostly," Rudy says, grinning. "Gotta look good for the 'gram." It's what he would have said online, but it doesn't feel right here. Is that really all he does? Look good for the internet? Well, that and spend way too long googling old ghost stories. He massages his temples. After realizing that the Alex Grable murders had left her father as the sole survivor of the family, Rudy had spent hours trying to find him online with no luck. But he's not about to tell Bella and Jada that.

"And music," Amber chirps up. "Rudy has a—"

Rudy passes her the bottle. "Round two, Ambs?" Sure, he'd talked jamming with the guys at the bonfire, but this is different. Bella seems nice, but the last thing he needs is some fangirl telling their online fan base that he's into music—then his mom would make him post pop covers for sure.

"What do you mean, music?"

"Do you hear that?" Jada's voice is a whisper. Rudy is thankful for the distraction. "Are you sure your parents are asleep? I thought I heard someone."

"Yeah, they're always out cold by eleven," Amber says.

"I'm probably paranoid because I would get in so much trouble if my parents knew I was drinking . . . ," Jada admits. "But I thought I heard someone walking around, or something."

"Or maybe," Bella says, "you're hearing the ghost." It shouldn't be funny, but the alcohol makes Rudy laugh.

"Shut up!" Cecily says, but even she can't keep her voice steady.

"It's okay," Bella says. "We have Rudy here to keep us safe. Right, Rudy?"

Rudy laughs and flexes, even though this business with the tapes has rattled him more than he cares to admit. Listening to them all alone had been anxiety-inducing, and even now he still finds himself hyperaware of all the house's strange noises. "You know it—" He cuts himself off. Was that footsteps, below? Or is he just being paranoid?

"Man," Jada says, "the acoustics in this house sure are great." She laughs, but she seems nervous. She leans into Amber.

Rudy gets an idea. This is the perfect opportunity to learn more about Norton. "All right, so," Rudy starts. "Those first pulls were free. The rest of the liquor I will share with the class if—and only if—you girls give me all the creepy hometown legends."

"He's thinking of starting a ghost-chasing channel," Amber says, rolling her eyes. But Bella is game.

"Fine," Bella says. "We'll spill the town lore as long as we get something in return—the inside scoop about the Coles. And I mean the *real* Coles."

Rudy picks up the bottle and hands it across the circle to Amber. "All right. We're all game? Then you kids know the rules—pass and pull. And, uh, one true fact per drink. Or, if you don't want to answer, you have to do a dare. Ambs, you're up."

Jada looks at her imploringly. "Dish."

"Okay, uh . . . ," Amber says, thinking.

"A true fact. Ideally embarrassing."

"Cecily has a birthmark on her shoulder that I've been editing out of pictures since we started getting popular," Amber blurts out. Rudy feels his eyebrows raise in surprise. Even he hadn't known that.

"What?" asks Cecily, turning toward Amber. She thumbs the mark, small, blotchy, and wine-colored. "You really have been editing this out?"

Amber laughs. "You didn't even notice! Tell me I'm not a Photoshop master." Cecily doesn't answer. "Your turn," Amber slurs, handing the bottle to Jada. "True facts or spooky stories."

Jada swallows the drink. "Okay, uh, spooky stories . . . uh . . . All right, so, uh . . . freshman year, Trent dared Miles to climb up to the turret room one night, and the kid actually did it. We were stupid impressed—he was telling us this whole story about climbing up the trellis—but it turns out he just snuck into the basement and went up the back steps. Oh! But he says that he saw someone else, in here, on his way down. But that he ran before he could see who it was."

Amber shudders. Rudy leans closer to Jada. "Who?"

"Probably just some squatter." Jada shrugs. "Here's a better one—we used to throw rocks at the windows and make wishes if we broke one."

"What did you wish for?" Amber asks.

Jada looks at her sideways. "A hot girlfriend."

Amber flushes to the roots of her hair.

Jada passes the bottle to Bella. "Here's a story about the house," Bella says, with a look at Rudy. "People at school used to say that this house was built by some of the very first people to settle this town. That they had the house foreclosed on them and put a curse on it so that no one else could live here . . . and *live*," she finishes, so melodramatically that Cecily actually snorts. The alcohol is working on everyone, Rudy realizes. He can feel the terror of the tapes fading away and being replaced by something light, bubbly. So bubbly that he can even joke about it.

"Are you sure it's not on an American Indian burial ground or anything?" he teases. "Or that it wasn't previously owned by an evil witch?" He lets out a fake cackle that makes everyone laugh.

Rudy grabs the bottle. This is fun. He feels emboldened. He decides what secret he's going to reveal. "Okay, uh, secret, uh . . . I can play three musical instruments." Cecily had already all but spoiled that one anyway; he might as well come out with it.

"No way," Bella says. "Why don't you post about that? You should, like, totally start a music account. You would have so many thirsty fangirls."

Rudy cringes. "Uh, no way. I don't want music to be work. Besides, thirsty fangirls are only in it for . . . you know."

"Oh, what's wrong with being attractive? Having everyone drool over you? Must be *so* hard."

Rudy opens his mouth then shuts it, trying to find a way to articulate his hazy thoughts. That, no, it isn't so terrible, but at the same time, he's more than a set of abs. At least people like Cecily because she can actually *do* makeup. All he does is crack jokes and look hot, and lately that hasn't felt like . . . enough.

He's about to try and say this when Bella hands the bottle to Cecily. "Next!"

Cecily drinks and takes a deep breath before answering. "I want to start a makeup account. Of my own. By myself."

Amber's mouth drops. "You don't—"

"I mean it," Cecily says. "Where there's no Mom scheduling posts, no stupid paint sponsorships, no houses, no one *photoshopping* birthmarks off of my arms—"

"Oooh," Bella says, somehow managing to slightly slur the vowel. She's tipsy and oblivious. "We forgot about makeovers! You have to do one. I want to see the first drunk Cecily Cole makeup tutorial."

Rudy watches his sisters exchange cold looks, marveling at the tension. Is Amber really that surprised? Cecily's confession doesn't faze him—of course she wants to take her makeup skills and start a career with it. And then something hits him: Cecily carries this account—Cecily and their renovation content. What would he and Amber do if Cecily left? He imagines a future without her, walking through countless empty, worn-down mansions and giving the same canned speech about crown molding and construction while Cecily escapes the endless revolving doors of renovations and actually gets to do something that she *likes* . . .

Before Rudy can collect his thoughts, Amber pipes up, slurring her words. "Hey, Cecily, when were you planning on telling us, huh? That you are gonna ditch?"

Cecily whips around. "We're not talking about this right now," she says, giving Amber the fakest of her fake smiles before turning back to Bella. "Sure, let's do a makeover! What do you want?" With one more cold look at Amber, a tipsy Cecily gets up and heads over to her desk. "Something super colorful and crazy? Or dark and smokey? Or—"

"The Cecily Cole signature look," Bella says, leaning back and taking another sip of vodka. "I wanna see you do it tipsy! Chop-chop!"

Cecily grins at her friends and opens one of the antique desk drawers, pulling out a palette. She takes out a fresh brush. "Okay, folks, so our first choice is to be lazy and totally skip primer altogether."

Bella mocks outrage, and Jada laughs as Cecily feathers the brush over her lid, applying a transition shade, then filling in some midtones in her crease. "Any color suggestions?" she asks.

"Purple!" Bella shouts, and Cecily obliges, dipping the brush into a deep maroon eyeshadow. She's applying it to the outer corner of her lid when she slips and drags the makeup brush halfway across her face. Rudy doesn't know much about makeup, but even he knows that his sister looks ridiculous. Bella bursts out laughing, and Cecily catches sight of herself in the mirror and laughs, too. "Oops! I didn't know I was *that* gone—" She scans the desktop and frowns. "Wait—I must have left my remover in the bathroom." Then her eyes alight on her ever-present go bag and perks up. "Here, I can fix it! Just give me a second."

Rudy and Bella are still chuckling as she reaches into her omnipresent carrying case and pulls out the makeup remover, saturating a cotton ball and then swiping it over her eye.

Cecily is laughing with all of them. Then she is not.

She screams.

She covers her left eye with her hand and then pulls it away, and Bella starts to scream, too.

Rudy chokes on his own breath. He jolts upward, stepping toward Cecily, and when she looks up at him her face is *melting*. He staggers back then lunges forward and grabs her, picks her up, and stumbles downstairs, shuddering under her burden of her weight as he carries her into the bathroom. He has only one thought, and it's to get her to the sink.

Cecily's shrieks become sobs, and then she's hyperventilating, keening and panicked, as he throws her head under the faucet and turns on the water.

Upstairs, Amber screams for their parents. He hears rushed footsteps, and then the only sound is water and Cecily's desperate gasps for air.

She comes out of the water and faces him. For a split second, she seems normal. She is his Cecily, just how she used to be. Then she moves soaked hair out from in front of her eyes.

A wet, oozing chemical burn creeps over Cecily's brow bone. Rudy knows right away that it is not something that water can fix, that they need the hospital, that they need it *bad*—because Cecily's face is *melted*. The remaining skin oozes over her face in a lunar landscape of craterlike burns. Her face is bright and waxy and *wrong*. Rudy feels his stomach turn; the floor lurches, and all at once he is aware of just how much he's had to drink. Too much. Too much for this, too much to help her—

He feels his vision blur as he starts to panic. The alcohol heightens the horror of Cecily's deformed skin, distorts the sound of her screams as she catches a glimpse of her face. The room spins as Rudy whirls around, and his nose is clogged with the smell of something sweet and rotten all at once. Amber is suddenly there, screaming and crying. The hallway is spinning. Rudy tries to focus his vision, but his eyes won't obey; everything is muddled. Amber and Cecily wash and wash and wash, and the screams don't stop. Dimly, he's aware that Jada and Bella have vanished as his parents appear in the hallway.

And then, the world is nothing but noise: a 911 call, Mom's sobs, the sound of sirens shrieking their way toward the house. And one more. One other sound, much louder than the others, one that threatens to drown them out entirely: Cecily's high-pitched, anguished keens as she clutches what remains of her face.

Comment on the Cole triplets' video: Messing with My Sisters: Allergy Prank

➡ **@xxgentlaas3:** God, this was terrible. Why don't you eat some real nuts and actually die next time?

204 Likes   Reply

Amber

AMBER DOESN'T REALIZE HOW LONG SHE'S BEEN SITTING UNTIL she tries to move. Her muscles had frozen up while she sat, hunched over in a plastic white hospital chair next to Rudy as both of them listened to their parents shout at emergency room staff, cry, and then, eventually, fall silent.

That was the worst of it. Amber would take an incredulous *"Do you know who I am?"* over her mother's strained silence any day of the week. She has several texts from Jada on her phone, all frantic apologies for fleeing the scene with Bella in fear of being caught drinking. She'll answer them eventually. She doesn't blame her, it's just . . . she's too numb right now.

The night has stretched on forever, and Amber and Rudy have long since sobered up. And now they sit, dazed, as the ER crowds flow by them.

When their parents finally reemerge, Cecily isn't with them. Amber lurches to her feet, muscles seizing, but she doesn't get a word out of her mouth before Mrs. Cole begins to speak. Her mother's voice doesn't have its usual peppy tone or commanding snap. In a quiet, lifeless voice, Mrs. Cole explains that Cecily has received chemical burns. Hospital staff are still trying to save her left eye. After that, it's likely that she'll need plastic surgery and intense care from an optometrist. "They're moving her into a burn unit," Mrs. Cole explains. "We're . . . not sure if she'll keep her sight, yet, at least in that eye. We will have to . . ." Her voice breaks. "Wait and hope for the best."

"Can you think of anything that it could have been?" Mr. Cole asks. Between their parents and the on-call staff, it feels like they've been over this a thousand times.

Amber and Rudy shake their heads. "She was just . . . putting on her makeup," Amber says. "And then she went to remove it, and the makeup remover, it—" She chokes.

"Do you think it could have . . . I don't know, gotten tainted with cleaning chemicals, or something else for the renovation?" Mrs. Cole asks.

Rudy shakes his head. "I don't know."

Mrs. Cole's jaw tightens. "I can't believe—Cecily—and you were *drunk*, no less!" She cuts herself off and brings a hand to her mouth with a strangled sob. "I'm sorry. I—" She swallows, unable to finish the thought. Amber feels a wave of shame wash over her. Her mother is right. If she had just—done something, told Bella that there would be no makeover, called their parents a minute sooner, maybe . . .

Her mother continues. "Cecily is . . . stable. You can go see her. But . . ." Before she can finish talking, Rudy is standing next to Amber. Their parents lead them down a tiled white hallway and into Cecily's room.

And there she is.

Cecily looks up at them from underneath a bandage covering the entire left half of her face. "Hey." Her voice is cracked; her visible eye is still stained from crying.

"Pirates are in this year," Amber says, and Cecily chokes out a laugh.

Amber feels her knees buckle, and she collapses into a chair beside Cecily's bed. She hears someone saying her name, but she doesn't want to look up, doesn't want to see Cecily and her ruined, burned face, can't . . . She doesn't realize that she's hyperventilating until someone is squeezing her shoulder, hard. She looks up. It's her dad. And even though she feels like a hypocrite, like she doesn't deserve comfort after what happened to Cecily, she leans into him. He is steady. For a minute, she lets him support her.

The family forms a tight, protective circle around Cecily's bed. Cecily answers questions in a confused monotone, clearly a little hazy from everything she's been through. When Mrs. Cole indicates that it's time to leave, Amber stands, Cecily grabs her arm, surprising Amber with her strength. She leans in.

"I saw something," Cecily whispers.

"What?"

"Before the makeup. I saw something. Or, I thought I saw someone."

"Some*one*?"

"A shadow. At the bottom of the stairs, like they were standing in the third-floor hallway." What? Amber wants to tell Cecily that she's making it up, that everything had been a blur of shock and panic for her, and that she can't imagine how Cecily could have possibly been thinking straight . . . But Cecily's eye, the one that's not covered, is wide. Wide and terrified. "Please say you believe me."

"Cecily . . . are you sure you were—"

"Please say you believe me," Cecily repeats.

Amber swallows, hard, and gives a slow nod, thinking of all the footsteps she's heard lately. The missing sign. The turret paint, her computer, Speckles. The mysteriously locked doors. The key that's never where they left it. Is it enough for her to believe that there could have been someone in the house earlier that night? She's not sure, but that's not what Cecily needs to hear right now. "Yes," she says. She's not entirely certain if she's lying or not.

Cecily nods, and her parents pull Amber away.

And then, just like that, they are home. There's a basket on their doorstep—a stack of muffins, still warm from the oven, along with a note:

Just heard. So sorry. Let me know when you'd like to resume work. —Joseph

Mrs. Cole picks it up, numb. "How nice." Her voice sounds far away. She unlocks the door and they enter.

The Tremont house seems so much larger without Cecily.

Mrs. Cole looks around the house. "What are we going to do?" she says, voice breaking. "What are we going to *post*?"

Amber stiffens. She knows her mom is right to ask, but still. Amber shakes her head, as if to clear it. No, her mom is just being practical. They have so many sponsors coming up, sponsors whose money they *need* . . . and all their sponsors want Cecily. *Maybe Cecily will be better by the time she has to post the sponsored videos,* Amber tells herself. *Maybe everything will be fine.* She repeats that thought over and over to herself. Even though she knows that she's lying.

It doesn't take long for Amber to craft the message she wants to share with their followers about what happened. It takes even less time for her to go through the pictures on her phone to find the perfect one to accompany the post.

It's simple: a photo of the three of them from the soiree, laughing. An actual candid.

> ➡ It breaks our hearts to announce that Cecily was rushed to the hospital last night after a severe reaction to a tainted makeup product. We appreciate your support during this time, as posts may not come on their regular schedule. Thank you so much for understanding. We love you guys and we know you're out there with us, pulling for Cecily. <3

The brand that made Cecily's makeup remover was a sponsor, so Amber couldn't mention the suspected product by name. Amber doesn't even bother to check the comments or engagement after she posts it. Instead, she heads right to her room and tries to sleep. She can't. All she can do is listen to her mother on speaker phone with her father, who is still with Cecily at the hospital, talking about how to balance spending time with Cecily and time on the renovation. Then the conversation pivots to the remover.

"Luxe makeup is a huge sponsor, we can't post about the remover—"

"But if something is wrong with this batch, we need to—"

"—call them in the morning—"

Amber tries to shut out her parents and focus on something, anything, other than Cecily. But she can't. Was it really just hours ago that they were all in the turret room, laughing over dumb stories and giving makeovers?

And listening to the tape. She had almost forgotten about it in the horror of the last several hours. Amber shivers. Had it really been Alex Grable?

Could it really be the sound of her killing her mother? The rhymes, the singing . . . it is all too much. Too real.

She had sounded so young.

Then, footsteps on the stairs. Mrs. Cole appears. "I'm heading back to sit with Cecily. You two, stay here and help your father, Mr. LaRosa, and the crew with whatever you can. Amber, take some good photos of Rudy. We can't stop working."

Across the hall, Rudy pokes his head out of his door and waves at their mom, nodding and indicating that he'll help however he can. Mrs. Cole acknowledges him then turns back to Amber. "Amber, the inbox is full of messages from sponsors—reply and confirm them all. Don't let any of them back out. I'm going back to the hospital for a few hours." She hesitates— glances out the window. The sun is only now beginning to rise, and none of them have gotten much rest. "I'll send you photos to post."

And just like that, she's gone.

Amber walks across the hallway to Rudy. He looks up at her, and his gaze is hard. "I saw Cecily pull you aside. Before we left. What did she say?"

Amber nods. She can't not tell Rudy. Not after last night. She swallows. "She thinks someone did this to her. She thinks she saw someone." Amber has been thinking about this ever since they left the hospital. Trying to convince herself that Cecily was hallucinating through the pain, because there couldn't have been someone in their house. Not a person, anyway.

"Someone?"

"Or . . . something," Amber admits. She waits for Rudy to laugh, but he doesn't. Her eyes meet his, and she wonders if Rudy is thinking the same thing that she is: Could it have been real? And if Cecily had seen something . . . could it have been . . . inhuman? It feels insane to even think it.

Amber's phone pings. It's a text from Cecily: *Check the account.*

She knows what she's going to find before she opens Instagram. The announcement post is live, and comments are already rolling in from followers and fans. And one more, from a new account. A new account with a username that's achingly familiar: @Alex_Grable2 instead of @Alex_Grable, clearly renamed to circumvent their block. The account history is the same as the follower's last account: Its only activity is on their posts of the Tremont house. The profile picture is the same.

The follower's comment on their post repeats over and over, obliterating the reassurance and words of love and support from the rest of the Cole Patrol. One message, on repeat:

➡ **@Blondbb123:** Hey, Rudy, Amber, Cecily, I know you don't see this, but I'm worried for u! Do you think he's working for the ghost? I don't want you to get hurt!

264 Likes   231 Replies

➡ **@layla:** Found the 12 year old

101 Likes   Reply

➡ **@topCarsey:** Who wants to tell her that it's fake?

87 Likes   Reply

Rudy

THE COMMENTS COME IN AN ENDLESS FLOOD, CHOKING THE AC-count. Posting and reposting themselves. Rudy doesn't know how the follower is doing it; he pictures them, manic, sitting at a keyboard, typing out the message over and over again.

The follower's comments are getting attention; likes and replies boost them to the top of the feed, along with other messages from confused members of the Cole Patrol:

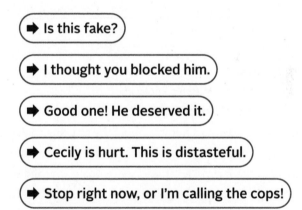

The last comment had already started to rack up likes, along with a cutting response chain about how stupid that user is, and don't they know that you can't call the police on someone being mean on the internet? And the Cole followers are *laughing*. They're entertained. Are these really the same followers that Rudy spends hours talking to? Responding to messages from? Connecting with?

He feels sick.

When he and Amber call their dad down to the kitchen to show him what's happening, he spends a long, long time studying the phone. When he looks up, his face is tight. But he doesn't say what Rudy expects him to. He doesn't say that they should stop posting, or that they need to be careful, or any of that online-safety stuff. Instead, he gestures to the other chairs around the table for the kids to sit.

This is a first. Rudy scrutinizes his father's face for the first time in a long time. Like their mother, he, too, looks haggard and exhausted. He takes a long breath before he speaks. "I know last night was hard for everyone," he starts, "and I want to tell you that . . . that things are going to be okay, that Cecily is going to be okay, and that we can make it through this. As a family." He hands them back the phone. Next to him, Rudy realizes that Amber is on the verge of tears. This should not have happened.

"Cecily . . . ," Amber chokes out, "Cecily said she thought that someone did this to her. On purpose. And the account said . . . he said he warned us . . ."

Mr. Cole sits up straighter. "Why? Has she been exchanging any messages with this follower that we don't know about?"

Amber shakes her head. "No, but what if he—"

"Hey, Amber." Mr. Cole wraps her in a hug. "We're going to get to the bottom of this, okay? Your mom and I think that the remover could have been contaminated at the factory level, and we're going to make our own inquiries into it, all right? I know the police are doing it, too, but since the brand sponsors us, it's really important that we handle this the right way. Especially since we need the money for Cecily, and we need to make sure that, if it was some factory error, this doesn't happen to anyone else."

"But—"

"We're taking this very seriously," Mr. Cole cuts in. "And I want you to know that—both of you. So we're going to look into the possibility of a factory error, but I'm also going to call the police and ask them to come over later this morning, all right? And I'll talk to Cecily about it."

Amber nods, numb. Rudy watches his father stand up and envelop his sister in a hug, rocking her ever so slowly like he used to when they were kids, before they were famous. He almost believes his dad when he says that everything is going to be all right.

After everyone is done crying, they all agree to attempt to get a few hours of early-morning sleep, but Rudy can't manage it. He tosses and turns, alternating between thinking of ghosts and Cecily's warped skin, puffy and inflamed, shiny like wax . . .

And then, of course, thoughts of the follower. Of the house. Of Alex Grable and the rabbit and the turret, streaked red with paint. He stares at the ceiling of his room as the house comes to life beneath him.

He can't stop thinking about the follower. About the messages. *I warned you.*

Joseph arrives around ten a.m., followed by the sound of bookshelf installation in the study below.

"Rudy."

His sister's voice is soft, but he jolts up instantly. Amber is in the doorway, looking as exhausted as Rudy feels.

"Did Cecily . . . ?"

"No," Amber says. "At least, I haven't heard anything. But I need to show you something. I wasn't able to fall asleep this morning. First, I put another notification alert on the follower's new username. But there's something else . . ." She walks over to his bed and sits down beside him, pulling out her phone. "I was thinking, about the posts we've done, and about how dad said that no one would know how to target Cecily through her makeup, and I . . ." Her voice trails off as she scrolls through their channel on her phone. Rudy knows what she's going to show him before it comes up. After all, the video is one of their top posts. It shows a younger Cecily, showing off her go bag. Listing all the things that were in it: Eyeliner. Concealer. The same makeup remover that burned her skin. He watches as his sister holds up the makeup remover to the camera, talking about how it's one of her "tried-and-true, ride-or-die," products. How she's never without it.

Rudy feels his eyes go wide as everything clicks into place. "I mean—"

She cuts him off. "There's more." He looks at Amber. Her face is tight, determined. He hasn't seen her like this before. She scrolls back, way back, and pulls up another video.

➡ **Messing with My Sisters: Allergy Prank. 673,112 views. 9,778 comments.**

And there he is: Rudy, barely thirteen, pretending to gag in front of Amber and Cecily, acting all chokey and melodramatic as he gives a peanut candy an exaggerated chomp. He watches little Amber and little Cecily scream and go into all kinds of theatrics, sprinting for the EpiPen as Rudy writhes on the floor. Screaming about his allergy. About how he is dying.

This is one of the first videos they'd ever made together.

Rudy stares at the video for a long moment. "Are you saying that . . . someone tried to kill me? That they contaminated something on purpose?"

Amber swallows. "I mean, I know it could be cross contamination with the bagels from the factory or whatever, but . . ."

"But you think someone hurt Cecily," Rudy says. "And . . ."

"If they wanted to hurt you based on things they gleaned from our profile, that would be the way to do it."

The words hang in the air.

"How?" Rudy asks. Amber flips to another video:

➡ **Get Swole: My morning routine**

And there is Rudy, explaining about how he makes a protein shake every morning. Holding up the canister of protein powder, explaining why this one tastes best and provides the most nutrients to fuel his workouts.

Rudy thinks back to that breakfast. Of how easy it was to just blame it on the bagels because of the damn warning on the bag. But the more he thinks about it, the more obvious it seems. "I had never had an allergic reaction from those bagels before . . ."

"But putting ground nuts into protein would be easy enough," Amber says softly.

"There's no way we can know for sure, because Mom threw everything out . . ." Rudy shakes his head, thinking. Could someone have really tried to hurt him? To kill him? And then, when that didn't work, could they have gone after Cecily instead?

"You believe the follower. You think they did these things to us," he says finally.

"Yes," Amber nods. She steps forward, sitting on the other end of the bed. "Don't say I'm crazy. Think about it—"

Rudy's mind is racing. "The comments," he says, trying to piece things together. "Those were the first things that were strange, weren't they?"

Amber nods.

"And then there was the paint on the turret. Then Speckles. Then my allergic reaction, and now Cecily . . ." Rudy trails off.

"It can't be a coincidence. Tell me I'm not crazy," Amber pleads.

"I mean, what do we know so far?" Rudy asks. "That Alex Grable killed her mother here, that Evan Andrews died in some kind of freak accident—"

"The messages," Amber says.

Rudy nods. "*Get out of my house,*" he whispers, remembering. "Why? Why does whoever want us out so badly?"

Amber's eyes stray across the room, to Rudy's nightstand. Rudy follows her gaze as it lands on the cassette recorder and the tape inside it.

Alex Grable. The name the follower chose for their account. The name their follower chose to use while stalking them.

Alex Grable is the key to finding the follower, Rudy realizes.

He's about to vocalize this when the sounds of tires crunching up the driveway draw his attention to the window. The police are here, trailed by Mrs. Cole, home from the hospital just in time.

Rudy and his sister dart downstairs. This time, their father is ready and waiting to rush the police into the foyer. Rudy watches Sheriff Yang's gaze hover on the less Instagram-worthy aspects of the Cole household, as Mrs. Cole follows him inside: the dust from the recent flooring, the dishes in the sink, the paint swatches littering every wall. He and Officer Perry take a seat at the table that their parents had set up in the demo'd kitchen for their meeting. With shaky breaths, Mrs. Cole gives an abbreviated version of recent events. She ends by turning to Amber and Rudy. In a slow, halting voice, Amber tells her story of the night. She leaves out the drinking and the cassette tape.

Sheriff Yang nods, his expression grave. Next to him, Perry makes detailed notes. "We've spoken with the hospital staff," Yang finally says. "They haven't been able to confirm the exact chemical compound of whatever burned Cecily from her wounds alone. We aren't yet ruling out foul play. I've been told that you suspect something in her makeup or makeup remover?"

"Yes, officer, we do," Mrs. Cole says, trembling slightly. "At least, the kids say that was all she touched, before . . ." She cuts herself off in a strangled sob. "You said foul play. You really think someone might have done this on purpose?"

"We can't yet rule out the possibility," Yang says.

Rudy exchanges a look with his sister.

"Can we see the room where all of this happened?" the sheriff asks.

The Coles lead the officers upstairs. They proceed without comment, though Rudy can't help but notice lingering eyes on the paint-splattered room. If the follower really did this to Cecily . . . Rudy'd *baited* them. What had he done? Had he been the reason why . . . ?

Next to him, Amber is silent.

The turret room is small and unassuming. Officer Perry takes several close-up photographs of the desk containing Cecily's makeup, capturing it from different angles, then snaps on latex gloves. "Can one of you identify the materials she used?"

Rudy nods and points out the makeup remover, lying on the floor where it had been knocked during the horror of last night. He can't stop thinking about her face, how the skin had *melted,* how he'd been able to see the red, raw flesh beneath.

Carefully, Perry deposits them in a sealed evidence bag. "We'll be running them for prints and chemical analyses," she says. "We'll be in contact with the supplier; if this is an error at the manufacturing level, you may want to look into a class action lawsuit."

Yang turns to the Cole family. "Who had access to Cecily's makeup products aside from you and your family? Is there any circumstance where someone else could have gotten hold of them?"

Mr. and Mrs. Cole look at each other. "Uh, the movers," Mr. Cole begins. "And we also have a long-term crew that's been working on the renovation, headed by Joseph LaRosa, our local handyman. And the kids had some friends over last night."

"How large is this crew?"

"It varies, depending on the day." Mr. Cole is pressing his lips together so tightly that they've gone white.

"And do they ever do work unsupervised by you? Not in the same room, perhaps? Would they have been able to sneak upstairs?"

There's a long beat of silence. "It's possible," Mr. Cole finally answers. "It's possible, yes."

Sheriff Yang nods. Officer Perry makes another note on the pad. "Anything else?"

"It was in her go bag," Amber speaks up. "She takes it with her everywhere."

Their parents curse. She's right. Rudy had forgotten about it—Cecily takes her small makeup go bag with her wherever she goes. If someone wanted to poison her, they wouldn't have had to break into the house. They would have had a ton of chances . . .

"Everywhere?" the sheriff asks.

Amber lists out the locations they'd been to in the last few days: the hardware store, the pizza place, the bonfire, the coffee shops around town . . .

Perry nods and makes note of them all.

When Amber finally finishes, Yang continues. "Last time we were here, we came to warn you about local teenagers and squatters in the premises. Have you had any problems with them since?"

Rudy almost mentions the rabbit again, but decides better of it. He knows it wasn't teenage squatters who did that.

"No," Mrs. Cole says. "We haven't. And we did install that security system . . ."

"Has it gone off?"

"No," Mrs. Cole says, her voice soft.

After a few more questions about the limits of their alarm system, Yang turns to Rudy and Amber. "I'll need the names of the friends you had over last night. We may have to question them." Rudy watches Amber flush as she stammers about Jada and Bella. He doesn't envy her. Last night had been about as awful a date as any he could imagine.

"And do you think they would have wanted to hurt Cecily?"

"No!" Amber says. "They love her. Everyone loves her."

Yang's gaze rests on Amber as if challenging her.

"They were horrified," Rudy finally says, backing up his sister. "They . . . couldn't have faked that." He can still hear Bella screaming. "They're our friends."

Yang nods. "Of course. You understand, we have to follow up on every lead." He takes one look around the turret room, shaking his head. It's too sunny outside; the sky is too blue for everything that has happened. Officer Perry snaps various photographs of the crime scene.

"Is there anyone you can think of who would have wanted to do this to your daughter?" Yang finally asks.

The Coles look to their children.

Amber swallows. "We have this follower," she says. "Under the username Alex_Grable. They've been posting threatening things on every photo of the house. At first, we just thought that it was someone being awful on the internet, but when we posted about Cecily being hurt . . . they said that it was them."

Yang exchanges a look with his deputy. "He said that he did it?"

"Not . . . not exactly. He said, 'I warned you,'" Rudy clarifies.

The officers exchange a look. Rudy can't quite read it, but he thinks it means they don't believe them.

"We deal with trolls all the time, and I *know* this is different," Amber says. "I know that people . . . do these things . . . for clickbait or something, but we're not. We would never hurt Cecily."

Rudy decides to go for it. He tells the police everything that he and Amber had talked about: their suspicions that the follower could connect with the vandalism. He even talks about the rabbit, about his allergy attack—but he doesn't mention the tape. Not yet. It's on the tip of his tongue, but his mother just looks so . . . fragile. So ready to lose it.

Time and time again, he opens his mouth to tell his parents about the tape only to close it. What is he going to say? That he found something that *might* have belonged to Alex Grable, which *might* have something to do with Cecily? What would happen if the police find out that he he has it— would they not care? Or worse, would they think that he is withholding evidence? Could he get his whole family in trouble? Everything is already so bad, Rudy can't bear the thought of making things worse by sharing another one of his insane theories. And then there's one more reason he's not telling anyone, one worse than the others: If he tells them, his mom and dad would know why they were drinking, would know why their reaction to Cecily's disfigurement wasn't as swift as it should have been, would know why this had happened. They would know that Rudy brought up the alcohol. They would know that this was all his fault. And he can't handle that.

Perry's pen flies over her notebook as Rudy speaks. When he finishes, she gives him an approving nod. "That's a lot of connections," she says. "We'll be sure to take that into account. But tell me, do you have any further proof to connect the rabbit and the allergy attack to what happened to your sister? Other than a hunch?"

Rudy feels his face redden. He doesn't. Perry smiles sympathetically. "We'll take note," she promises. "You're quite the . . . investigator, aren't you?" Rudy isn't sure whether or not she means that as a compliment.

Yang nods. His poker face is amazing; Rudy can't tell if he has been swayed by anything he or Amber said. Yang simply blinks twice, nods to Perry, and tells the Coles they may want to start saving screenshots of the follower's comments. "Just in case the situation escalates." Rudy and Amber agree to document their past interactions and drop off the files at the police station the following day.

Afterward, the Coles lead the officers back downstairs and out toward the porch. "Thank you for your cooperation," Sheriff Yang says. "We'll be looking into it."

Officer Perry nods and turns to Mrs. Cole. "We'll do some research into your follower. I don't know how much your family relies on social media from a financial standpoint, but from here on we would advise that, should you continue to post, you do so with caution. Again, we can't say for certain that this follower is behind anything, but we want you to take all necessary precautions."

Mrs. Cole nods.

Yang gives her a tight smile. "Our hearts go out to you and your family. We'll be speaking with Cecily as soon as we're able, and while we're waiting on results from the lab. Have a good day, sir, ma'am, kids."

He touches his hat and leads the deputy to their car. The minute the police cruiser turns the corner, Mrs. Cole crumples into her husband and shakes with great, heaving sobs. Something about the police leaving makes everything feel so real. The family stands and watches the cops drive away, and Rudy feels Cecily's absence like a blow. He wants to crumple just like his mom. Instead, Rudy finds Amber's hand and grabs it. She squeezes back.

Mrs. Cole leads them back inside. "Kids, could you . . . give us a minute? Then we can talk . . . we can talk posts."

Rudy and Amber exchange a wordless glance and head upstairs as their parents retire into the kitchen. As soon as they're out of earshot, he starts talking. "Amber, what did you think about the police?" he asks slowly, trying to gauge her reaction.

Amber shifts. "They seemed thorough, about Cecily, but I don't think they believed us about the follower being behind all of this . . ."

Perry's words echo in Rudy's mind: *You're quite the investigator, aren't you?*

"I think it has something to do with Alex's death," Rudy blurts out. "I think we need to find out what, why they want us out so badly, and how it all ties back to Alex Grable. Because it does, I know it does—"

"Rudy, you *don't* know that—this isn't like internet drama, you can't just play detective and dig up emails—"

Just then, a shout echoes from below. Their parents' conversation has escalated into a fight. A nasty one from the sounds of it. Rudy runs over to the dumbwaiter and opens it so they can better hear what their parents are shouting about. The first thing he hears is something about a private investigator.

He perks up. So maybe his parents don't think that the cops are taking this seriously enough?

"We don't have the money—" That's Rudy's dad.

"This is our *daughter*! We'll find the money!" That's Rudy's mom.

"After the medical bills? You heard them, Marie, even if they save the eye she's going to need plastic surgery, and optometrists, and therapy—"

Money. Of course. They were in a tight spot before this house, and now . . . now, Rudy can't even imagine how bleak the outlook must be.

"We can't stop posting now, can we?" Amber asks. "We need the money."

Rudy shakes his head. "We're barely staying afloat as it is."

From downstairs: "If we had the money—if you hadn't—"

Their father's voice breaks. "Marie, please."

Mrs. Cole's voice dissolves into sobs. For a moment, it grows quiet downstairs, and Rudy imagines his parents huddled together, his dad patting his mom's back to try and comfort her.

Then the conversation starts up again, but they are no longer yelling, so Rudy and Amber have to move closer to the dumbwaiter just to catch snippets of what their parents are saying. They talk about whether or not they should move. Eventually, they seem to decide that, since the makeup remover that hurt Cecily was in her go bag, it could have been tainted anywhere around town. And just like that, the conversation turns back to leaving town and how they just don't have the money . . .

"So many sponsors want Cecily," Rudy says, shaking his head. "I wish I could take her place, but . . ."

"I could do it." Amber's voice is a whisper.

"What?"

"I could do it," she whispers again. "I—I'm not Cecily, but I did the livestream. I can do posts, I could see if her sponsors would take . . . me."

Amber won't meet his eyes. She seems nervous, hesitant. "Amber, you don't have to. What if they comment on stuff? What if . . . ?" The words hang unsaid: *What if it's dangerous?*

"Cecily needs us," Amber says. And that's all it takes.

Rudy takes Amber's hand and they head downstairs. As they approach the kitchen, it's clear their parents are no longer arguing.

"I know. I know you've been trying so hard," Rudy hears his mom say. "I'm sorry, I just . . ."

"It's going to be all right," Mr. Cole says. "It'll be okay."

They walk in on their parents huddled by the counter, their mom wrapped up in their dad's arms. Looking completely and utterly shattered.

"We're going to keep doing the posts," Rudy says. His parents jolt up; they hadn't even noticed the two coming down.

"Absolutely not—"

"We need the money," Rudy says firmly. Then his voice softens. "For Cecily."

"I'm not risking my other two children." Mrs. Cole looks at her husband. "I can't do it, I'm sorry. I—"

Amber approaches her. "We don't have to post about the house, or the renovation," she says softly. She takes a deep breath. "We—we can see if the beauty sponsors will swap out me for Cecily. We can block the follower if he comes back. We can be smart and safe about it."

Rudy stands next to his sister. "Please. We need to do this. Cecily needs us."

Their parents don't answer. Finally, Mr. Cole turns to his wife. "We do need the money, Marie," he says, softly. "Cecily's hospital bills alone . . ."

Mrs. Cole closes her eyes for a long second. When she speaks, her voice is a whisper. "I . . . I think that would work, Amber. It's a good idea." Rudy hears his sister's breath hitch as their mother thinks. Even though Amber is clearly distraught, part of her looks . . . surprised and touched by their mother's faith in her.

"You think the sponsors will take me?" Amber asks.

Mrs. Cole nods. "Yes. Some. But, Amber—you don't have to do this. You know that, right?"

Amber gives her a stiff nod. "I know. But I want to. For Cecily."

Mrs. Cole reaches out and puts a hand on Amber's shoulder. "All right, but only the sponsored ones. For Cecily. And the minute this follower responds or says anything, you need to let me know. Understand?"

Amber and Rudy nod, but their mother turns her eyes to Rudy. "I need to hear you say it, sweetheart."

Rudy swallows and answers. "Yes. I understand."

Comment on the latest Cole post:

➡️ **@cxbswimmer:** Anyone hear the rumors? Apparently they're going to sell the house. Scared off!

128 Likes   11 Replies

➡️ **@asesimmons:** Not true, dipshit.

➡️ **@bobbybb:** Clickbait sites got this one!

XXXXXXXXXXXXXXXXXXXXXXXXXXXXXXXXX

CHAPTER 17

Amber

CECILY'S FACE IS MELTING. HER SKIN IS WAXY, RED. AMBER CAN SEE
the white, pale *bone* beneath her sister's face, and Cecily is screaming. Bella
and Jada are screaming, and when Jada turns around, she is melting, too,
skin peeling off and dripping onto the turret floor like runny wax—

And then Amber is in the hospital, waiting for Cecily. Her parents walk
toward her, in a horrible kind of slow motion. She stands to follow them,
like she's in a trance, and there's Cecily—lying on the hospital bed, face in
bandages.

She looks up at Amber and her remaining eye is cold. Dead. In a voice
that's not Cecily's, she opens her mouth and says, "There. Now you're the
pretty one."

Her sister reaches up to unwrap the bandages around her head, and
when they fall away, Cecily's face is gone.

In the dream, Amber screams.

And when she jolts awake, someone is *there*.

Her eyes snap open, and for a second she thinks that she's still dreaming
because in the darkness of her room, here, in the doorway, is the outline of
a figure, a place of darkness that's blacker that the rest. Her hands fly to her
nightstand light, and she flicks it on, preparing herself to scream—

But there is no one there.

Not anymore.

But there *was*—wasn't there? Or was it just some horrible residual terror from her nightmare?

Amber flies out of bed and into the corridor, glancing left and right, but
there is no one in the hallway. She darts across to Rudy's room, throwing
his door open. Her brother bolts up in bed.

In quiet, shallow breaths, Amber explains what happened. About the dream, about waking, about how she thought someone was *there*. She waits for him to tell her that it was just a dream, but he doesn't. He just moves over in bed, and she joins him under the covers. He pulls her close, but she can't get the dream out of her head. Before long, all the tears she'd held in during the hospital visit and the police investigation are spilling out of her, all over his shirt. He strokes her back with his free hand and whispers that things are going to be all right. Things are going to be all right.

And somehow, despite her fear, she falls asleep like that.

It is still dark when she jolts awake. Rudy is still up. She imagines him alert as she slept. Staring at the door, watching for the shadow that she'd seen. For a few minutes, she just lies there, trying to process everything. And even through the visceral horror of seeing *something* in her room, she can't stop thinking about dream Cecily.

Now you're the pretty one.

It makes her feel bad, feel sick. Because it's wrong.

At least, it is for Amber. Amber knows that Cecily is more traditionally attractive—*translation: skinny*—than her, but all the same, she's never truly thought of herself as, well, ugly. In fact, there are times when she thinks that she's really, truly beautiful, especially when she nails her outfit or wears a look with confidence. If she's the pretty one now, it isn't because Cecily's injury had changed anything about Amber's perspective.

Before she can say anything, Rudy asks her about last night. She retells the story. Awake, in the daylight, it seems so much less believable.

"And you're sure it wasn't a dream?" he asks.

"I—yes. No. Maybe," Amber says. Then she swallows and chooses an answer. "I think—I think it was real." She swallows. "Cecily said that she saw someone. What if it's real? What if there is . . . something here?"

"A ghost?" Rudy asks, and he's not joking.

Amber feels herself tremble as she nods.

"It could have been a dream," Rudy says, but he doesn't sound like he believes it.

Amber fights to calm her heartbeat. "It . . . it could have," she admits.

As the crew begins their last day of flooring, Amber and Rudy pile into the Range Rover and head to the hospital. The drive feels eternal. Amber's phone keeps lighting up with DMs from Bella and Jada. She's been ignoring them since . . . it . . . happened, but she knows she can't ignore them both forever. Besides, Jada's last message was about a pending visit from the police, which Amber realizes is probably a little nerve-racking.

She sends Jada a quick reply confirming that they hadn't told the cops about the drinking or the tapes. She thanks Jada for her earlier messages, but tells her that she's not ready to talk about Cecily just yet. She doesn't even know if she's ready to talk to Cecily just yet. But she has to.

And then they arrive. They find Cecily awake, in a hospital room with sterile lighting.

Her head is in bandages, just like in Amber's dream.

But unlike the dream, Cecily doesn't unveil a monstrous face. Instead, she smiles up at her siblings.

"How—how are you?" Amber asks.

"All right," Cecily says, but Amber can hear the tremor in her voice. "They're still not sure . . . if it's a second- or third-degree burn," she admits. When she sees their confusion, she continues. "They said—they can save my eye, but they're not sure about the level of scarring. They think I'll need some kind of surgery or skin grafts, but they don't know . . . how bad . . . it will be yet." The one blue eye that remains visible is wide, frightened, brimming with tears. Amber wonders how much they should tell her about their discoveries from the past twenty-four hours, if it will scare her to hear their theory about the follower and all the other things that happened leading up to her being hurt.

Or maybe it will make her mad that no one put the pieces together sooner.

Before Amber can decide, Rudy starts to fill Cecily in, explaining everything from the police visit to what Amber thought she saw last night in her doorway.

As Cecily listens, her eyes go wide. "That's like what I saw—they said that it was a hallucination, but I thought I saw—I thought—"

"It could have been a dream," Amber admits. "We have a security system. The alarms didn't go off."

Rudy shoots her a look. "You were convinced it was real this morning."

Cecily reaches out a hand and grabs Amber's forearm. Her grip steady. "Someone did this to me, Amber. This wasn't an accident."

Amber swallows and nods.

"So, what's the plan now?" Cecily asks. "How are the sponsors reacting to me not being able to fulfill any of my contracts?"

"About that . . ." Amber pauses.

Once again, Rudy jumps in and explains their decision to remain on social media. For Amber to do the sponsored posts.

"You can't," Cecily says, her voice rising. "This follower did this to me."

"The police went over a list of people who could have had contact with the makeup," Rudy says. "Us, Bella, Jada, Joseph, the crew . . ."

Cecily shakes her head. "I took that go bag everywhere. I've been trying to think about where it could have happened—the bonfire, the hardware store . . . I can't even remember the last time I used it. Maybe at the bonfire? But I don't think I did, I think I just had it on me . . . but I always have it on me," she says, shaking her head. "Do you think Bella or Jada could have . . . done this?" Cecily asks.

Amber shakes her head. "Cecily, they were so horrified."

She's glad when Rudy agrees with her. "You didn't hear them scream," he says softly. "They couldn't have. That wasn't fake."

"Bella's been messaging nonstop; she wants to visit when she can," Amber says, hoping that it will cheer Cecily up. "Jada, too."

Cecily's face twists. "I don't know . . ." She swallows. "I don't know if I want them to see me like this."

"What about Joseph?" Rudy asks. "Do you think he's a suspect?"

"He seems nice, but that proves nothing," Amber says. "I hate to say it, but someone on the crew makes a lot of sense. They'd have access to everything in the house."

Cecily nods. "Who else?"

"What about the kids at the bonfire?" asks Rudy. "Weren't they talking about sneaking in? If they've been sneaking in and out of the house for years now, they probably have ways of getting in. Miles, Alicia, Steve, Trent . . . and who knows how many others."

"There's also squatters," Amber says. "The police mentioned them. What if one of them got too attached to the house?"

Rudy nods. "But why masquerade as the murdered girl online?"

Cecily shivers. "To scare us. It's working."

Rudy shakes his head. "I think it's more than that. Think about it—the last two families to live in that house have had some kind of death, and now someone's after us, too? This had to start with Alex Grable."

"Or it's someone taking advantage of the house's reputation," Amber argues. She knows that Rudy is convinced that Alex Grable's death has something to do with everything, but . . . right now she doesn't care about a twenty-year-old murder.

"I'm going to listen to the tape again," Rudy says. "Maybe there's something else on there. Something we missed."

Amber shudders. She doesn't want to think about the recording, doesn't want to listen to Alex humming, singing softly about killing her mother . . .

"What do I say when the cops show up?" Cecily asks.

"The truth," Amber says after a long beat of silence. "After all, they should find something. It's their job."

"We didn't mention the tapes, though," Rudy adds. "We figured that, given everything else going on with the house, it wouldn't be good for anyone. It would just stress Mom and Dad out, and the case is already closed. But if you want to tell them, we won't ask you not to . . ."

Cecily is silent for a long second. Then she shakes her head. "You're right. Bring me the tapes when you're done," she says finally. "I want to listen. I want to help." She lets out a strangled laugh. "I'm going out of my mind in here, and it's only been a day."

Amber and Rudy nod and promise to bring the tapes. Rudy wants to start questioning people straightaway, to do some sleuthing of his own, but Amber convinces him to delay his investigative streak for an hour to be with Cecily. They pile around their sister and watch cartoons until the doctors enter.

But when Rudy and Amber drive home, Amber can't stand to be in the house a moment longer. She leaves Rudy to jam out and grabs her sneakers to go for a run.

The neighborhood around Tremont is full of quiet, leafy streets. For a long while, Amber can't hear anything but the pounding of music through her headphones and her feet against the pavement.

Miles later, she returns home and collapses on the porch, drenched in sweat. She glances back at the house and decides that she is finally ready to properly respond to Bella and Jada.

Bella is understanding and promises to visit Cecily once she's ready for more visitors. Amber knows that she should maybe be more suspicious, but Bella just seems so sincere. And when it comes to Jada, she knows that she is more than a little biased.

But that doesn't stop her heart rate from accelerating when Jada suggests meeting downtown that evening for coffee. Jada wants to see her, even after . . . all the horrors of that awful night. Amber is grateful; she doesn't want to spend a second longer in this house than she has to. She leaves for the evening as the workers put the finishing touches on the downstairs foyer. The Range Rover is gone, so Amber decides to bike downtown. The soreness in her legs is a welcome distraction from the revolving thoughts in her head: Alex Grable, the follower, Cecily.

When Amber pulls up to the coffee shop, she's not only sweating from exertion. She's actually . . . nervous. And for once, it's not because of the follower. It's because Amber can't stop thinking about Jada. Or wanting to be around her, like, all the time. As Amber opens the door, she finds herself wondering if Jada thinks about her in the same way. What if she doesn't?

She swallows her nerves. When Jada greets her with a tight hug, Amber almost collapses in relief. They join the line, and Amber is immediately on edge again. Is the cashier being hostile? Are people staring at her out of pity or animosity?

Jada reads the tension in her face. "You sit. I'll order."

She returns with the coffee, and Amber lasts about thirty seconds into their conversation before she breaks. She tells Jada everything, from the police visit to Rudy's suspicions to the figure she'd thought she'd seen.

Jada nods and confirms that she and Bella had been interviewed by the police. "Do you think it could be that guy online? Your follower?"

Amber shrugs. "Honestly? I don't know. It could be anyone . . . but it can't be unrelated, can it?"

Jada nods and takes a long drink of coffee. When she looks back up at Amber, her gaze is intense, piercing. She reaches out and puts her hand on top of Amber's. "How are you doing?" she asks.

"Cecily is healing," Amber starts.

Jada gives her a look that is all pity. "I know. I know Cecily is healing. But how are *you?*"

The question strikes her. Amber can't stop herself from thinking of the dream she had, of faceless Cecily staring up at her. Amber shrugs and tries to say something along the lines of "fine," but her face just scrunches up instead. She takes a long, shaky breath that turns into a half sob. "It's bad, Jada. Real bad."

The tears begin to fall. "It's just—I never thought—" Amber swallows. "We need her sponsors and I said that I'd do the posts, but I don't want to take anything away from her and I—" She swipes at her eyes. "I'm sorry, I . . . it's not just her face. She's changed, terrified, and I don't know what to do. I don't know how I can fix . . ."

"You can't fix anything," Jada says softly, squeezing her hand. "Only the doctors and Cecily can do that, Amber. And you're taking on the sponsors to *help* her, right?"

"Yeah," she says. "It's only that . . . I don't know how to feel. I feel awful about taking posts from Cecily but, at the same time, I'm kind of excited, I kind of want to *do* things with them—content that's more for, well, people like me, but—" She cuts herself off. Her stomach twists. She feels like she's going to be sick.

But Jada runs her thumb over the back of her hand. "You're not a bad person for wanting to make the best of an awful situation, Amber," she says kindly. "If you can take over Cecily's posts in a way that is true to you, I think you should do it. You're not supposed to be a carbon copy of Cecily."

"But what if our followers don't like it? What if the sponsors hate the new direction and—back out or—" Amber's voice falters. She waits for Jada to agree, to tell her that it's better to stick to Cecily's kind of posts and not take any risks, but she doesn't.

If anything, Jada grabs her hand tighter. "Please. They're fools if they don't see how gorgeous you are. Besides, if they don't want to sponsor you because you're not a size two, they're probably not the kind of company you want to be sponsored by anyway."

Amber nods, and to her surprise, the next time she speaks she's blinking back tears. "Thank you. I—I think you're right. Sorry," she adds, swiping at her eyes. "It's just—with everything—it's been hard."

Jada nods and squeezes her had. "I know. And that picture, after everything—"

"What picture?"

Jada's face pales. "I thought you knew."

"Knew what?" Amber asks, a feeling of dread rising up in her throat.

Jada pulls out her phone and flips to the Cole account. There, in their tagged posts, is a photograph of Cecily in the hospital, head wrapped in bandages. It's dark, and obviously taken through the half-open blinds that cover the interior window of Cecily's hospital room. Cecily clearly has no idea she's being photographed. She's watching TV with a dead-eyed, expressionless stare.

Amber freezes. The handle that posted the photo isn't the follower. It's just some fan; their post history has them all over the Cole forums, among other internet celebrities. She tries to imagine whoever took this photo entering the hospital, finding Cecily's room, taking the photo from the busy hallway as nurses and doctors and patients pass by. Posting that shot of her sister at one of her most vulnerable moments for *likes*.

"I'm so sorry." Jada tries to pull the phone back, but Amber reaches out for it.

Amber scans the comments for the follower, but there's nothing—this must have been someone local, someone who recognized them in the ER and snapped a photograph, turning Cecily's pain into their thirty seconds of internet fame. She swallows hard and fights the sadness rapidly turning to anger in her chest.

Jada must see this, because she squeezes Amber's free hand, drawing her attention back. "Are you sure you want to do the sponsored posts? I'm—I'm worried about you. Have you thought about going dark online?"

Amber shakes her head. "We can't. The follower stuff is scary, but Cecily . . . she's going to need serious medical treatment. They're trying to save her eye, Jada. We earn most of our money through sponsors—I don't know how we'll pay for anything otherwise."

"What about the house?"

Amber bites her lip. The house, which was already more work than they could handle before the murder-suicide and Cecily. "We have to sell it before we make anything, and even then we have to pay Joseph, the crew, cover what we've already spent . . ."

Jada nods and reaches her other hand across the table to trace a thumb across Amber's face. "Hey, Amber, it's going to be okay. I'm here for you."

Amber leans into the touch. "Thank you."

"Do your posts," Jada says with a small smile. "Maybe you can make something good come out of this."

"Maybe," Amber says. "Maybe you're right."

"Of course I'm right."

And when Jada leans across the table to kiss her, Amber almost forgets that anything is wrong at all.

Comment on the latest Cole post:

➡ Great to see more of Amber! Bigger Girls represent!

312 Likes   1 Reply

➡ **@xxdonttouch:** Found the whale.

Rudy

SEVERAL DAYS LATER, RUDY SCROLLS THROUGH INTERNET forums, sites, and archives until it feels like his eyes are going to bleed. He's been at this for hours, sifting through the digitized archives of the *Norton Community Star*. At first, he was looking for contact information for Alex's dad—after all, only she and her mother had died—but the man had vanished, so he had switched to community history. He scrolls through page after page, paper after paper, and then—

He finds something. The next document on file is a scanned PDF entitled "*Class of 1997.*"

He sits up and forces himself to focus as he scrolls through the pages carefully, reading every single name until—there she is. Alex. Smiling up at him through a low-res school photo. Her eyes crinkle slightly at the corners, and a dimple graces her left cheek. She looks so happy, so carefree. So not like someone who would kill her mother.

This feels huge. If Amber were here, he would bounce ideas off her, but she's out with Jada, shooting more content for Instagram.

The doorbell rings, jerking him out of his focus. He doesn't think much of it until Mom shouts his name. He texts himself a PDF of the yearbook before tearing himself away from the document. Downstairs, Bella is waiting in the doorway.

"Hey," she says. "I just wanted to drop by, you know, to check on things. I know that Cecily still isn't taking visitors at the hospital, but . . ." She looks so hopeful.

"How sweet of you!" Mrs. Cole says. "Come on in. I have to get back to paint swatches, but Rudy, why don't you fill Bella in on how Cecily is doing?"

"Uh, sure," Rudy says, even though part of him is itching to get back to the book, back to Alex.

He leads Bella into the kitchen. "How are things?" she asks. She looks so sad, so concerned for Cecily, that he feels the urgency around the yearbook deflate. After all, it will be online and waiting for him long after Bella leaves. He takes a deep breath.

"It's been . . ." He searches for the word. "Quiet." He doesn't need to fill in the rest of the sentence: *Quiet, since Cecily went to the hospital.* Rudy doesn't know what's harder to believe: that she's been in the hospital for just over a week, or that the Coles have only been in the Tremont Street house for three weeks. To Rudy, it feels like years. "Do you want some, I dunno, Coke or something?"

Bella's brow furrows. "Sure—but, quiet? I was actually expecting you to have a ton of crew around."

Rudy shakes his head and rummages around for the soda. "We decided to let the crew go. Mom and Dad figured that if there was any chance someone on the crew was responsible for . . . what happened . . ." He finds a Coke can and hands it to her, then opens one for himself.

"So it's just you now?" Bella asks, clearly shocked.

"Well, we kept our head carpenter and handyman on," Rudy says. "But aside from him, yeah. Amber and I pitch in as much as possible, too." The Cole parents didn't have much choice other than to trust Joseph. They can't finish the renovation on their own.

"How are you?" Bella asks.

Rudy takes a drink and shakes his head. He thinks about the last several days, about his feverish search for more information, about the picture someone had posted of Cecily in the hospital. He'd had to stop himself from going online and shouting at their fans. He shakes his head. "I'm . . . I don't know." He goes for honesty. "I'm pretty pissed off, I guess."

"And . . . Cecily?"

Rudy swallows. "I know she wants to see you, it's just—" What can he say? His sister wouldn't want him tossing around words like "level-three burn," "plastic surgery," and "trauma therapy." But Bella waves him off.

"I understand. Just tell her that I'm here whenever she needs me, okay?" Bella asks. She hesitates. "You've . . . heard the rumors, right?"

He has. Rumors that the Coles are faking Cecily's injury for attention had spread like wildfire. He nods. "I tried to refute them, at first, but . . ." He shakes his head. "It feels like everyone's turned on us."

Bella nods. "But you're still posting?"

"We need the money," Rudy says. "A lot of our sponsors are taking Amber in Cecily's place. I think she and Jada might actually be out shooting some now."

"Yeah, I've seen some of them," Bella says, taking a drink and scanning the almost-finished kitchen.

"It feels weird to be posting without Cecily," Rudy admits. "But we're doing it for her, so that makes it better. And I think that Amber's . . . really come into her own. I wish it hadn't happened this way, but . . ." Several days before, Rudy and Amber had started with their smallest sponsors, lesser-known beauty products and brands. Rudy had expected Amber to edit them into oblivion, but Amber didn't want to. "I want these to be more *me*," she had said.

"I like them," Bella agrees. "The series she's doing on breaking plus-sized fashion rules? It's pretty cool. I think that a lot of people will really relate to it."

Rudy nods. "Yeah. I think you're right. And it's good for her to get out of the house."

"What about you?" Bella asks. When Rudy looks back at her, she's staring over her Coke can as if she already knows what he's up to. "Have you been getting out of the house?"

"Not exactly," Rudy admits. He gnaws on his lower lip, trying to figure out how much he wants to tell Bella. Maybe it's because of the yearbook he found earlier, or maybe it's because Amber's been gone all morning and he's had no one to talk about it with, but he caves. "I've been researching the house. I think that the follower did this to Cecily." He gives Bella a quick summary of his theories and the research he's been doing. Bella listens from across the table with wide eyes.

"It makes sense," she whispers. "It's . . . terrifying, but . . . you really think it could be someone local?"

"It has to be," Rudy says. "Everything about the follower leads back to Alex, so I've been looking into her—I found this, just before you got here," he adds, pulling up the yearbook photo and sliding his phone across the table.

Bella looks carefully at the image of Alex. "She looks so normal," she says after a few moments. She slides the phone back to Rudy. "I want to help."

"What?"

"Yeah," she says. "I dunno, I feel bad about . . . everything that happened, and if I can't help Cecily in the hospital, I can help you investigate right? I know all the kids in town—I'll keep an eye out for anyone acting suspicious or anything."

Rudy smiles. "Really? That would be—that would be great." He'll definitely make more headway with someone like Bella, who is actually connected to people in Norton. "Maybe you can ask around about Alex. Surely someone in town will know something useful, especially if their parents grew up here, too."

Bella thinks for a minute. "Sure, I can ask some friends. Actually—I was going to meet up with some people after this. Do you want to come? We could see if they know anything about, well, anything."

Rudy thinks for a second. He's needed at home, but Amber is out right now, and Dad's busy collecting a new shipment of siding and won't be back until after dinner . . . "Sure," he says. "Let's go."

Rudy and Bella head into town, to Cityside Coffee, to meet up with some of the kids from the bonfire—Miles, Trent, and Alicia. It doesn't take long for Rudy to figure out that getting any new information from Bella's friends is a dead end. Despite his commitment to sleuthing and his carefully asked questions, none of them reveal any new information about the Tremont house. Even though he'd gone out to collect information on Tremont, Rudy can't stop himself from returning Alicia's banter, arguing about indie bands with Miles, or agreeing to sub in for an injured friend at Trent's Ultimate Frisbee game next week. As easy as it would be to get swept up into the lure of making new friends, Rudy is cautious. After all, any of them could be the person behind the account, behind what happened to Cecily.

He catches Bella's eye from across the table and can tell that she knows exactly how he's feeling.

A little while later, everyone is getting up to go when Bella places a hand on Rudy's arm. "Rudy—I've thought of something. I don't know anything about the town, but I know someone who does. I can't believe I didn't think of it before, but Mr. O'Donnell is part of the historical society. He must know something, right?"

So instead of returning to the Tremont house, Rudy and Bella head to the hardware store. But when Mr. O'Donnell sees them, Rudy can tell he's less than happy.

"The flooring's already in," he says curtly. He has short, cropped hair and what, to Rudy, look like permanent frown lines etched on his forehead.

Bella gives him a small wave. "Hey, Mr. O'Donnell," she says. "We just wanted to ask you a couple of questions." She gives Rudy an encouraging nod. Easy for her to act all optimistic—Rudy has heard that she's a star student at Norton High. But Mr. O'Donnell is looking at him like he's already decided Rudy is just another brainless Instagram model.

"We wanted to ask you about the history of the house my family is renovating," Rudy says. "Who owned it before the Grables? How long has it been around? Can you tell me anything about—"

"It's summer vacation," Mr. O'Donnell says, busying himself with the cash register. "Don't expect any history lessons from me until September."

"But—"

"Why do you want to know?" Mr. O'Donnell asks, looking up at Rudy. "So you can respect the house, or so you can post it all over Instagram? I'm not going to help you exploit that girl's death by telling stories about the people who lived there before she moved in. Besides, I'm not a walking gene-alogy. What I will say is that the Tremont Street home has been there since the eighteen hundreds and would have grown to be a treasured piece of town history if you and your family hadn't hollowed it out for rich yuppies."

"We—"

"I've seen what you've done to the foyer on your Instagram," he says, looking back down. But not before Rudy catches the angry scowl on his face. "Now, are you going to buy anything?"

"Er, no . . . thanks," Rudy mumbles, wondering which part he's thanking the guy for. The part where he insulted his family, or the part where he gave him exactly no useful information?

Rudy says goodbye to Bella and heads home. He'd love to stay out and just be away from the house awhile longer, but he's already been gone for two hours and knows his mom is probably wondering where he is. When he arrives, Amber and his mom are hard at work detailing the kitchen backsplash.

"What can I do to help?" Rudy asks.

"Want to help me take out some tile?" Joseph asks, handing Rudy a pair of safety glasses.

Rudy nods and takes the goggles. He follows Joseph upstairs toward the second-floor bathroom.

"Can you tackle that section there?" Joseph asks, gesturing to a far wall. Rudy eyes the sledgehammer propped in the corner.

"Sure thing," he replies. "I think a little hammering might do me some good."

Rudy hefts the sledgehammer into his palm and swings it at hideous orange-yellow tiling that had to have been put up sometime in the seventies. It cracks, and he feels something in himself give. He swings harder and harder and harder, and suddenly he's not thinking about the renovation— he's thinking about Cecily.

Cecily, burning, crying, melting. The blood on the turret, the rabbit in the sink . . .

He doesn't realize how hard he's hitting until there's a hand on his shoulder.

It's Joseph. "Are you all right?"

Rudy shakes his head. "Yeah. Yeah, I'm sorry. I guess I went a little overboard."

"It's understandable," Joseph says, setting his own sledgehammer down. He removes his safety goggles and gives Rudy a sympathetic smile that makes his guts twist. "If you need to hit hard, hit hard. It's just tile."

Rudy sees the stress lines around Joseph's eyes, sees the signs of sleepless nights and overtime etched across his face. He's been at the Tremont house around the clock ever since the crew had to leave. Rudy realizes that he's been holding eye contact too long, so he breaks it and looks at the floor. He knows that Joseph could be the follower. He wants to be able to suspect Joseph but . . . he can't.

So he just nods and gives the wall a few more hits, sending cracked tile to the floor. They pause for another break, panting from the exertion. Joseph leans against the doorway, glancing down the hallway and through Rudy's open door. He spots the guitar.

"You play?"

Rudy nods. "Sometimes. I'm not good."

Joseph gives him a smile. "Me neither."

"You play?"

His smile widens. "When I was younger. My son and I started taking lessons together when he was in high school. It's been a while since I've played anything, but I can probably still get out Romanza."

Rudy leans against the wall. "Ever do any blues?"

Joseph shakes his head. "Not much. Mostly classical."

"Well, if you ever want to jam . . . ," Rudy offers before he realizes what he's saying. He waits for the awkward excuses, the clumsy denial, but . . .

Joseph nods. "That would be nice. Maybe when the work is all done? Or on a lunch break."

Rudy feels himself grin. He realizes how long it's been since he smiled. "That would be great," he says. "Let's finish this up so we can jam."

"Absolutely," Joseph says. "We should probably get that toilet out of here then, huh? The sooner we can turn the water back on, the better." He gestures toward the toilet, and Rudy walks over to the tank, taking off the cover.

He looks down at the piping and pauses. He sees something. He reaches in and his fingers brush a plastic bag that's wedged inside the tank. He removes it. Inside the plastic bag is a small bottle of pills.

Rudy holds up the bag. Joseph darts over, barely getting out the words, "Maybe you should—" But Rudy is already opening the baggie and letting the bottle tumble into his palm.

Through decaying lettering on the bottle, he reads:

```
. . . Glenarm. Clozaril tablets.
One pill every twenty-four hours
as needed. Prescribed 10-01-96;
Exp 10-01-97.
```

Ninety-seven. The year of the Grable deaths. Rudy makes the connection immediately. Rudy squints at the bottle. He can't make out any of the other lettering. He shakes the bottle; it's full of pills.

"What are those?" Joseph asks.

"Old pills," Rudy says. "Expired decades ago."

"Here—let me dispose of them safely," Joseph says. "And don't worry— odd things turn up during demos all the time. I will say, I've found strange things in walls before, but never medication."

"Do you know what it's for? Clora . . . clozaril, I think." Rudy asks, squinting back down at the label.

Joseph shakes his head. "No. And we need to make sure this is safely thrown out. It could be dangerous."

Rudy nods but clutches the bottle tighter. Is he grasping at straws, or can this be another part of the Alex Grable investigation? "I'll give it to my parents and have them dispose of it properly," he says. When Joseph looks like he's going to protest, Rudy smiles and adds, "Don't worry, I'm not the kind of kid who would try to sell pills or anything like that!"

The tense look on Joseph's face relaxes and he returns Rudy's smile. "I know that, son."

Rudy slips the bottle of pills into his back pocket and returns to work.

But the renovation is the last thing on his mind now.

After so many days of finding nothing, this could be a lead.

Or it could be nothing. There is only one way to find out.

As soon as they take a break, Rudy goes right to the internet, plugging in the name:

Clozaril

A study in medication from the 1990s pops up. Rudy scans it, breathless, and reads: *An antipsychotic, most commonly used in patients with schizophrenia and schizoaffective disorders who do not respond well to other medications. Has been shown to reduce the risk of suicide.*

Rudy sucks in a breath. He hadn't heard anything about Alex Grable being schizophrenic, but what if she'd been on the medications because she was suicidal? He scans the label again to see what else he can look up.

He pulls up a fresh search page.

Glenarm

Nothing.

Glenarm, Norton New York

An article pops up. It's a newspaper article from the late nineties—an obituary.

Bonnie Grable-Glenarm: 1951–1995

Loving wife and mother Bonnie Grable-Glenarm passed away on May 23rd, 1995. She was an artist, a friend to those in need, and a gift to all who knew her. She is survived by her husband, Frank Glenarm, her extended family in Norton, and her young daughter. In lieu of flowers, the family requests that donations be made to support the in-home care of her husband Frank Glenarm, who was injured in the car accident that took Bonnie's life.

Our greatest treasure is the hearts we keep.

Rudy freezes. He doesn't know what this means, but it just feels so . . . important. Bonnie Grable-Glenarm. Why does that name make him feel like he's forgetting something?

Joseph appears over his shoulder. "Ready to get back to it?" Rudy jumps up and snaps his computer shut. He shoves the bottle of pills into his pocket, but Joseph has already seen. "Are those the pills you found before?"

There's no point in lying. Rudy takes the pills out of his pocket and nods.

"Why are you researching them?"

Rudy looks at the pills, then back at Joseph. What if he knows something? "I want to find our internet follower," he admits. "I think they have something to do with the house. I think they have something to do with what happened to Cecily."

Joseph doesn't answer for a second. "Your parents told me about their suspicions when they released the rest of the crew."

Rudy looks at him, trying to gauge his reaction. "What do you think?"

"That you shouldn't be doing this on your own," Joseph says. "And that I don't understand how some medical waste is going to point you in the direction of your internet follower. Do your parents know that you're . . . looking these things up?" Rudy can tell that Joseph already knows the answer to that question.

"They have enough to worry about, with Cecily," Rudy says. "I don't want to, you know, make things worse."

"Do the police know this?" Rudy gives Joseph a sullen nod. "Then maybe you should leave this to the police," Joseph says, a look of genuine concern on his face. "They're good at their jobs. You don't need to take this on yourself."

Rudy gives him a tight smile. "I know." And he knows that Joseph is only trying to look out for him—but he can't let it go.

And then it hits him, out of nowhere: Bonnie Grable, artist. *BG.* He'd found the person who'd painted the mural.

He coughs, trying to hide his excitement. "You're right," he says. He hates lying to Joseph, but he knows that if they keep up this conversation, Joseph will convince him to throw out the pill bottle and tell his parents—or worse, tell them himself. "I'll throw them out. What's next?"

Joseph sets his hands on his hips and glances around the hallway. "Well, we've got to measure new baseboards. . ."

Rudy follows him. "Great," he says, throwing the pill bottle into a white trash bag reserved for demolition debris. Joseph watches him and offers an approving nod. "Ready to get back to work?" Joseph asks.

Rudy nods, measuring tape in hand. They work for another hour or so, until Joseph has seemingly long forgotten the pills. But Rudy hasn't. The minute he hears one of his parents call Joseph downstairs, he runs back to the garbage bag and retrieves the bottle, stowing it in his pocket.

They move on to the next project, and the rest of the afternoon flies by in a haze of hammering and sanding. Then, finally, they are done for the day. Rudy says a hasty goodbye to Joseph and rushes up to his room. He can't wait to tell Amber about the pills.

Amber is in her room, crouched over her laptop when Rudy enters. He tells her about his discovery and hands her the pills. She gives the bottle a thorough examination.

"What about this text here?" she asks, holding the bottle directly under the bright light of her lamp. "Here, check this out."

Rudy hovers over Amber's shoulder as she gestures to faint wording on the bottle that Rudy had been unable to read in the low light of the bathroom. *Doctor Lauren Lenhoff; Upstate Medical Assisted Care Facility.*

And just like that, Rudy has another lead.

Thread on the Cole forum: CECILY COLE'S INJURY: REAL OR FAKE?

XXXXXXXXXXXXXXXXXXXXXXXXXXXXXXX

CHAPTER 19

Cecily

IT TAKES CECILY SEVERAL DAYS TO SURFACE FROM THE ENDLESS blur of stale fluorescent lighting and strong medication. She remembers the last few days in scraps: her mother rubbing her back and saying that things are going to be all right, concerned nurses placing IVs, Rudy and Amber looking distraught.

The nurse that changes her bandages today is delighted to see her so alert. Her name is Monica, and even though Cecily barely manages any answers, she keeps up a distracting stream of chatter as she unravels the gauze from Cecily's face.

But it's not distracting enough. Cecily catches the sight of her marred face in the mirror and freezes. No, not marred. Destroyed. Red, waxy, craterlike melting skin cascades down her brow, a permanent Halloween mask. Monica sees her and pauses halfway through a retelling of her fifth grader's role in the school play. "You're healing up nicely," she says. Cecily almost believes her . . . but she can see the pity in Monica's eyes. "You have one last visitor before bedtime," Monica says as she begins to rewrap Cecily's face. Her voice is a strained kind of forced cheerfulness that Cecily knows all too well. "It's your mom. I'll let you two have a minute."

Monica leaves, and Mrs. Cole rushes in with a wave of motherly affection. "How are you? Is everything okay? Oh, honey, you look great, it's great to see you this awake—Rudy and Amber are coming first thing in the morning, of course, but I wanted to just drop by and say good night."

It's all Cecily can do not to cry as Mom leans in for a hug. She smells like lavender laundry detergent, and Cecily breathes in the scent, as if it could protect her from the sterile medical scent of the hospital. She answers Mom's questions as best as she can: *Yes, the food is fine. Of course I miss you. No, I haven't seen Amber's new posts.*

At her last comment, Mom sits up. "We needed the sponsors, sweetheart—I hope you're not mad, and it won't be long until you're posting, too!"

Cecily forces a smile. "Of course I'm not mad," she says. But how could her mom say that? That it won't be long until she's posting, too, as if things could ever be the same? She tries to calm herself, but as soon as she starts thinking about life outside the hospital, everything spirals. And it isn't the thought about her destroyed career that makes her break down in her mother's arms as much as it is all the small things—like how people will stare at her in coffee shops, how she will never get used to the look of pity from the nursing staff, about how she doesn't know if she'll ever be able to touch makeup again.

Before she can stop it, a sob lurches out of her throat.

Instantly, she's enveloped in another Mom hug. "It's all right," her mom assures her. "Cecily, listen to me—it's going to be all right. You have your sight, and we are so, so grateful for that." Cecily can't stop sobbing. She feels something wet in her hair and realizes that her mom is crying, too. "You are surrounded by people who love you—and that will love you no matter what, you understand? We're putting you in therapy, and—I know it doesn't seem this way right now, but—but things can be okay again."

Cecily nods into her mother's shoulder and tries to stop her sobs. "Thanks, Mom," she says, mustering a smile.

When she finally pulls back, Mrs. Cole wipes away the smallest tear from her perfectly made-up face. "Of course," she says.

"Have you . . . found anything?" Cecily asks. "About . . . how it happened?"

She watches as her mother's face scrunches. "Sweetheart, I don't want you to worry about that right now," she says.

"So, no." Cecily says. She can see her mother weighing what to tell her.

"The . . . the police confirmed that the makeup remover was tampered with," Mrs. Cole finally says. "We've reached out to the manufacturer, and there's a chance that it could still be factory error." Cecily doesn't have it in her to argue with her mom, but she's not sure if she believes that. She's had that product forever, and for it to hurt her only now?

So she lets it go, and the conversation dissolves into renovation updates and small talk. When her mom finally leaves, promising to return with the rest of the family first thing in the morning, it's late enough for Cecily to be exhausted.

But as she closes her eyes to try and sleep, it all comes back to her: the shock, the pain. The terrible, intense pain, And then, the shadow at the edge of her vision. A dark blur at eye level, down the stairs. As if someone was peering around the corner and up into the turret to watch the show that was about to unfold.

So she gives up on sleep. Instead, she sits in her darkened hospital room, leafing through social media, scrolling past pictures of the cursed renovation, pausing on the photos from before. Where she was beautiful, airbrushed, pristine, perfect. Now their feed is full of Amber. Amber, sporting beautiful lip gloss. Amber, with daring makeup looks and bright nails and hashtags like *#NotYourBeautyStandard.*

Cecily knows the sight of her gorgeous sister should make her jealous, mad, or even resentful—but she feels none of this. All she feels is a blank, heavy grief. For a brief, shining period, she had been so close to perfect. So *fucking* close.

She can't stop herself from imagining someone opening her bag, unscrewing the cap, messing with her things. Someone who knew exactly what they were doing, someone who was trying to *blind* her. Her mind reels but she can't cast the thoughts away. She tosses and turns all night, and when she finally does fall asleep, it's only to dream about Rudy's panicked gasps as the makeup burned her skin.

She wakes just in time for visiting hours. Her parents wash over her in a wave of small talk—*How's the food? You feeling okay? Are any of the nurses nice?*—and Cecily is relieved when they finally walk off to talk to the doctor, leaving her alone with her siblings.

Rudy reaches into his pocket and pulls out a small pill bottle. "We think we found something." He hands over the bottle. "I unearthed it from the toilet tank during the renovation. When I googled the Glenarm name, the Grables came up."

"Really?" Cecily asks.

Rudy nods and hands over his phone. "Here's the obituary. The expiration date on the pills is ninety-seven—right around the time of the Grable murder, so he had to be living there at the same time. Our theory is that, if Frank needed in-home care like the obit says, the Grables could have been doing it. And Bonnie Grable-Glenarm—*BG*—matches the initials of the mural artist."

Cecily takes in the obit: Frank Glenarm, his wife, the car crash, their remaining daughter and family in Norton.

Rudy must take her silence as disbelief, because he keeps talking. "We think it all has to be connected," he says. "The follower's been using Alex's name, and whoever they are, they've threatened all of us."

Cecily speaks slowly. "Mom still thinks that it could be a factory issue."

"And you believe that?" Amber asks.

She swallows. "No," she says quietly. "I don't."

Amber swallows. "We also have a theory . . . that Rudy's allergic reaction was intentional, too."

It does make sense.

"The police—" she starts.

"—are already investigating the crew, some of the townies, and the makeup brand about your injury," Amber says. "And besides, we can't prove that Rudy was targeted . . ."

"The turret, me, you, Speckles . . ." Rudy says.

"You can't think that it's a coincidence!" Amber says. Cecily takes in her sister's appearance for the first time that morning. With a jolt, she realizes that Amber looks . . . not better than she always does, but different. She's wearing more makeup, and her shirt and skirt combo are a much . . . sexier look than anything Cecily's seen Amber wear by choice in months. She looks confident. And beautiful. "Alex is the best clue we have. The follower didn't seem to like the idea of us looking into her on the livestream, and now . . . I guess I'm not totally convinced, but I think it's worth a shot."

"Besides," Rudy says. "This has happened before. With the Andrews."

"It was an accident . . . ," Cecily starts, but her conviction wavers.

"Just like my allergy was an accident," Rudy says. He switches gears. "The pills *had* to belong to someone living in the house at the same time as the Grables. I've been trying to find Doctor Lenhoff, but all I've gotten are dead ends. She must have retired a long time ago."

"So we're back to Bonnie," Amber cuts in. "Grable-Glenarm, the one that died in the car crash. The obit says that she left behind her disabled husband, daughter, and relatives in the Norton area. The hyphen means her maiden name must have been Grable, right? I think she was Alex's aunt. If Frank was Alex's uncle, maybe they moved in to take care of him after his wife died? Or were just around a lot."

"Whoever is stalking the house and coming after us is obsessed with Alex Grable," Rudy says. "Think about it, Cecily. Whoever this is chose to use Alex Grable's name. It all traces back to her. I really think Alex is our best shot at finding them."

Cecily nods. It's starting to make sense. Her mind is whirring; she's trying to imagine the shadow she saw as a person, with a face, a name, a history.

"But there's still the Andrews," Rudy continues. "I've been trying to track them down, but I haven't gotten anywhere. My internet research has turned up nothing so I might just start calling numbers from the phone book. It's like looking for a needle in a haystack, but I'm not sure what else to do at this point."

As Rudy talks, Cecily continues to think. Maybe . . . maybe he does have a point. Maybe there is more to the Alex Grable story. And maybe it's worth finding out.

"I know a girl who has some time," Cecily says.

Rudy gives her a worried look. "Are you sure that you should be doing things? We don't want to bother you. We—"

"I can't just sit here!" Cecily says. "I can't just—watch you post things for me, I can't—"

Amber flinches.

"Amber, no, I didn't mean it like—like that," Cecily says. "I mean, I know you're doing this for me, and I appreciate it . . . but I'm worried, that's all. Mom told me you're doing the big hair post." The one that she was supposed to do. Cecily pictures the lovely rose-gold ombré cascading down her own shoulders . . . and then imagines it framing her burned face. She feels sick.

Amber nods. "Yeah. I am."

Cecily forces a smile, and then something hits her with a jolt. If the follower had poisoned her makeup . . . "It's gonna look so incredible on you. But I need you to be careful. Promise me you'll go get all-new stuff. Please. The dye was in the turret . . ."

Amber's eyes go wide. "Definitely."

Cecily gives her sister a tight smile. It really will look gorgeous on Amber. Something about admitting that makes everything click for Cecily. She isn't the perfect Cole sister anymore. She isn't going to be a beauty guru, or a model, or start her own product line. With a face like hers, how can she? She feels tears welling in her eyes.

"I hear you're coming home in a few days," Rudy says.

Cecily nods. "Yeah. That's what they tell me." She croaks out the words.

"You don't seem happy," Amber says sadly.

Cecily shakes her head softly and feels a teardrop escape her unburned eye. She swipes it away, but there's no chance her siblings hadn't noticed. "I'm happy to be out of here, be near you, but . . ." She trails off. What can she say? That it won't be the same? That it will never be the same? That, sometimes, the idea of anyone but her parents and her doctors seeing her face is enough to make her dissolve into an anxiety attack? No one had seen her face aside from her doctors, herself, and her parents. Not even Amber and Rudy. She's not going to be in posts. She's *ruined*. And the thought of being behind the camera as Rudy and Amber create content makes her throat close up.

Amber squeezes her hand. She doesn't say that it's all right, or that she understands. All she says is, "We want you home."

A short time later, Rudy and Amber leave. Cecily feels like her head's going to explode with all the thoughts swirling around inside her brain. She knows she needs to drown out the noise. Focus on something. So she chooses to focus on Rudy's theory about the follower and Alex Grable.

She pulls out her phone, closes Instagram, and starts searching. Hours pass. Doctors and nurses enter and exit, the sound of the hospital carries on around her in a seamless wave of noise. And Cecily searches though internet records and archives until, just as she's finishing the last of her unappealing hospital dinner, she finds something.

A Norton public school directory. And there, under PTA, is Nancy Andrews.

She feels a jolt of excitement as she dials the number, but it's been disconnected.

Three phone calls and several on-hold sessions later, Cecily finds herself dialing a number that's not disconnected. The phone rings and rings into emptiness. Just when she's convinced that she's going to go to voicemail, a shaky voice picks up.

"Hello?"

Cecily tucks the phone to her chin, trying her best to muffle the noises of the hospital around her.

"H-hello? Mrs. Andrews?"

"Who is this?"

"This is—Cecily. Cecily Cole."

The voice on the other end sucks in a breath. Mrs. Andrews knows who she is. Cecily speaks again, fast, before she can hang up on her. "I—I live in the Tremont house. Your old house. Maybe you've seen—maybe you've been on social media—"

"You're on Instagram," Mrs. Andrews cuts her off. "I know. I hope you aren't recording this call."

"No, of course I'm not." She doesn't sound happy, but Cecily has no choice but to continue. "I wanted to ask you about—about Evan—"

"Listen," Mrs. Andrews snaps. "This might all be a joke to you, some fun supernatural story, but my son is dead. I don't want to be part of your—your internet sensationalism."

"No—it's not that. We think that—"

"I ask that you respect the privacy of me and my family in this time," Mrs. Andrews says, her voice suddenly flat. "I do not give you permission to post this online. Do not call this number again."

She hangs up.

Cecily drops the phone into her lap. She sits like that for a long time. She does not move. She does not cry. She only sits in a darkened hospital room as the endless flood of staff and patients swirl around her, replaying the sound of Mrs. Andrews's panicked voice over and over in her head.

Comment on the latest episode of *Tube Talk*:

Daringadvocate: Hey, have you guys heard? Apparently some Cole Patrol member got footage of the house—AND YOU CAN SEE CECILY MOVING AROUND INSIDE. Looks like they're lying about the hospital—what else???

XXXXXXXXXXXXXXXXXXXXXXXXXXXXXX

CHAPTER 20

Amber

AMBER STARES AT THE PHOTO SHE'S ABOUT TO POST. SHE FLICKS her fingers to boot up Photoshop, but she finds herself thinking of Jada. She exits the photo-manipulation software and turns back to the picture. It's of her and Rudy, sitting on the hardwood with their backs against a wall covered in paint swatches.

It'll be the first photo they've posted that has referenced the renovation since Cecily got hurt. Rudy hovers behind her. "Amber, it'll be fine."

The caption reads: *We know things have been tough lately, and we can't thank you enough for your support. Thank you so much for sticking by the Cole family. There's a big surprise coming your way! Hint: These walls aren't the only thing changing color.*

Amber hates the idea of mentioning the renovation again, but they have to tease the hair-color video as well as the upcoming wall color, which are both sponsored. There's so much riding on this post—and so much that could go wrong.

Mrs. Cole had wanted Amber to post the photo as it was: a carbon copy of the post they'd planned for Cecily. But Amber wasn't Cecily. And maybe, for the first time in a long time, she thought that might be a good thing. Amber hadn't posted carbon copies of Cecily's things before, so why start now? She thinks back to their previous sponsored posts and amends the caption.

And today, I'm wearing crop tops. That's right: In this post—and every post I do from now on—I'll be breaking at least one plus-size fashion and beauty rule. Which one should I do next? #LoveEveryBody #NotYourBeautyStandard

She posts the picture.

The likes and comments roll in, but Amber doesn't stay to check the engagement. She shoves her phone into her pocket, afraid of what she might see. Who she might see online. Besides, they have things to do today.

"Ready to head out?"

Rudy nods.

Amber follows him into the Range Rover and they pull off into the hazy summer morning. Rudy had suggested they go out to pick up the hair products today, to take a break from the renovation and get out of the house. But first, they stop to pick up Bella and Jada downtown. They had both jumped at the offer to join her and Rudy on their adventure to Ulta for more hair dye products. Amber finds herself getting nervous as they near Jada's house.

She's been thinking about asking Jada to be her girlfriend, but she worries about what will happen when her family moves. Amber pushes the thoughts aside. Jada is the first person in a long time who she's wanted to date. The first person who is into her for *her*, and not just for her fame.

Then why is she so nervous at the idea of asking her to be her girlfriend?

They pull up to the house and Amber swallows her jitters.

Bella and Jada pile into the car, and before their seat belts are even fastened, Bella starts with the questions.

"How is she? Has she gotten my messages? Did you tell her I've been asking for her?"

Amber turns toward the back and gives Bella a reassuring smile. "She's okay. Nothing new to report, really. She appreciates the support. She just . . . needs some time."

"You guys are so nice," Bella sighs. "If people knew you in real life, they wouldn't say such mean things online."

"Bella," Jada says, a warning tone in her voice.

Rudy and Amber exchange a look. They had made a vow to not do any searches for negative comments about their family and Cecily's accident. They were making a concerted effort to focus on what was really important—making money to finish the renovation and to help Cecily. But what is Bella talking about? Amber feels like she needs to know.

"What things?" she asks, trying to keep her voice even.

"That you're faking for views and sympathy money," Bella says. "There are tons of conspiracy theories out there about how you guys are just doing this for attention. It's really sick."

In the silence that follows, Bella lets out a shaky breath. "You knew about that, right?"

Amber nods. There's no point in making Bella feel bad. "It's all right. We knew." Next to her, Rudy is silent, his focus tight on the road.

Jada leans over from the backseat and whispers in Amber's ear. "Hey, I saw your post. I'm proud of you."

Amber's heart flutters. "Me, too. Want to hang out this week and help me shoot the rest of the breaking-fashion-rules series? I'm thinking body-con dresses, or maybe short skirts, or—"

Jada doesn't hesitate. "Absolutely."

Amber's heart swells.

They plot ideas all the way there—or until Amber looks out the window and realizes they don't seem to be going the right way. She wonders if Rudy is taking another route, but when he misses the exit west that would take them toward Ulta, she realizes her brother is up to something.

"Wasn't that—"

"I know where I'm going . . . ," Rudy says, his voice trailing off.

"We're not going to Ulta, are we?" Amber asks.

"What?" Behind her, the other girls perk up.

Rudy shoots her a look. "Don't worry, we can still go. I just . . . want to make a stop first."

"Where are you driving, Rudy?" Amber demands.

"I found the psychiatric hospital on the pills," he says finally.

Bella and Jada lean forward, and Rudy fills them in on the orange pill bottle he found in the bathroom.

"I talked to Cecily yesterday," he says. "She got in contact with Nancy Andrews—you know, from the family that lived here before we moved in? She said that Nancy wouldn't tell her anything, and—" He cuts himself off. "Right now, this feels like the only lead I have. I just . . . I have to try."

"Why didn't you tell me?" Amber asks.

"Honestly?" Rudy asks. "I wasn't sure I would have the courage to go until we were halfway down the interstate."

"Fair," says Bella, and they all give a nervous laugh. Amber can't blame them.

"If you want to turn around . . . ," Rudy starts. Amber feels everyone's eyes on her.

She shakes her head. "No," she says. "Let's do it."

The medical center is unassuming. It's a dilapidated building with a green awning and a flickering light above it. Not menacing, Amber thinks, just . . . sad. She's not sure if this is better or worse than the creepiness she'd expected.

The lobby is similarly drab and dark. Rudy approaches a bored-looking secretary. He looks up at them without greeting.

"I'm here to ask about Frank Glenarm, " Rudy says. Amber forces herself not to laugh at the deep voice her brother is trying to use.

The secretary raises an eyebrow and types something in his computer. "ID, please?" Amber digs out her ID as the others do the same. It's as if she's on autopilot, handing this guy her ID just because he'd asked for it.

"You here for school or something?" the secretary asks, his voice dry.

"What?" Rudy asks, at the same time that Bella answers.

"Yes. He's our adopt-a-grandparent. We're supposed to be asking him questions about local history," she chirps. Amber flinches; they don't even know if he's alive or not.

But the clerk simply nods and hands them visitors' stickers. "Room 14B. Left hall." He hesitates. "According to our records, this is your first time meeting with Mr. Glenarm?"

"Yes, " Rudy replies.

"And, you're here for some kind of history project?"

" . . . Yes?" Bella answers.

"I'm afraid he's not going to be very responsive. You are aware of his condition? That he suffered severe spinal and neurological damage? He's not exactly our most . . . present patient."

Amber has no idea what to say to that.

Rudy recovers first. "Thank you," he says. Then he heads down the hallway, and Amber and her friends have no choice but to follow him.

Amber catches up to her brother and grabs his arm. "Are you serious right now? What's the plan exactly?"

"I don't know! I didn't think he'd *be* here, I just thought—"

Then they're at the door. They both hesitate.

The door opens. A smiling dark-haired nurse in pink scrubs walks out. Rudy grabs the door before it closes and walks in.

A man is sitting in the bed, staring at the window.

"Mr. Glenarm?" No answer. It strikes Amber how incredibly quiet the room is. The ticking of the clock on the mantle seems to echo through the room. After a second, Rudy continues. "My name's Rudy. I live in your old house. On Tremont Street." He walks farther into the room, and the girls file in behind him. Mr. Glenarm turns to look at them. He's an old man, with a shock of white hair and thick, beige glasses. He smiles at them absently. Amber doesn't think he's understood a word Rudy just said.

"Oh, don't mind him." Amber jumps. The pink-scrubbed nurse is back. She's carrying a cup of water and four little tins of pink pills, which she brings over to the window. "He's not very talkative, but I know he enjoys the company. Isn't that right?"

Mr. Glenarm does not respond.

"The house on Tremont Street," Rudy echoes. "In Norton. I live there now."

Mr. Glenarm begins to speak without looking at them. "No," he whispers. "She still does. She visits me, tells me about the kids, the garden. A whole family is there."

The nurse gives them an apologetic look. "I'm sorry—he's not quite present, sometimes. He's talking about his wife and his daughter. He might be confusing you for someone else."

"I live there now," Rudy says, ignoring the nurse. Amber wants to grab his sleeve and drag him away from this sad room, from this sad old man.

Mr. Glenarm does not acknowledge Rudy. He looks down at the floor, then at the nurse. He takes the pills without question, robotically swallowing them. The nurse gives Amber a look that clearly says that this is all they're going to get out of him.

Amber is just about to tell her brother that they need to leave, that this clearly isn't a good time, when it happens.

Mr. Glenarm speaks.

"I wish she didn't do it," he whispers. Amber freezes. "Ruin our lovely house. Our lovely house. Our lovely house." He repeats it over and over again. Just like—just like the follower had done, Amber realizes. She feels cold. She steps forward to grab Rudy, but her brother isn't going anywhere.

"Our house, our house," he repeats, over and over again.

"Please," the nurse says brusquely. "He's—becoming agitated. Don't worry, this happens all the time . . . it just might be a good idea for us to give you some space, wouldn't it, Frank?"

Mr. Glenarm continues repeating the words "our house" as if on a loop. *Like a broken cassette*, Amber thinks.

"Would you mind returning another time?" the nurse asks. *Translation: Leave now.*

Amber and the others file out of the room. The nurse closes the door behind them, and as she takes off down the hallway, Rudy calls out to her. "Can you—tell us about him?"

The nurse pauses and turns to look at them.

"For a history project," Bella echoes, but she sounds less enthusiastic now. Less enthusiastic and much more scared.

"He was injured in the same car accident that killed his wife, right? Bonnie?" Rudy asks, pushing the words out in a rush. *It's too much*, Amber thinks. *He's pushing it too far. These are not the kind of things kids would ask about for a high school project.*

The nurse looks confused. "I'm sorry. We don't discuss medical history with non-relatives."

"Has he been here since the crash?" Rudy asks. "Please. It's for our project. We don't want to know anything personal. Just how long he's been here."

The nurse shakes her head. "He's been with us since—before I started here. Over fifteen years, now, maybe longer." She begins to turn on her heel.

"And was he somewhere else before that?" Rudy presses.

The nurse shakes her head. "I don't know. Most of our patients were cared for in-home before they began their stay with us; usually when their caretaker is unable to handle the burden anymore. I'm sorry, but I can only reveal medical information to direct family relations."

The nurse looks like she's definitely done talking to them now. Amber sees the desperate look on her brother's face. They did come all this way, after all. And they've made it this far.

"Would he have used—antipsychotics?" Amber blurts out. "Clozaril?"

The nurse furrows her brow and leads them into a small, empty visiting room off to the side. "He's not crazy, if that's what you're asking," the nurse says firmly. "He's a sweet old man, really is—and what did you say your school project was again?"

"Uh . . ."

The nurse sighs. "Look, if you need to see him again, visiting hours are between ten and five." With that, she gestures to the main exit, indicating it's time for them to leave.

Amber looks at her brother, Jada, and Bella. By unspoken agreement, they all beeline past the receptionist, out into the parking lot, and into the Range Rover.

Bella speaks first. "That was so creepy—the way he kept talking about the house, he sounded like . . ."

"Our follower," Amber says. She shuts the door and buckles her seat belt.

"I don't think so," Jada says. "He's too old—no way that guy is on Instagram, much less sabotaging your renovation."

"He has to have some connection to the follower," Bella says. "What if that's who was taking care of him? The nurse said he probably received in-home care before he was sent to Upstate Medical."

Jada shakes her head. "Let me get this straight here. You think the follower has something to do with Alex Grable, and you think Frank had to have known Alex, because . . ."

"Because the pill bottle had his name on it, and it expired the same year that Alex and her mom died," Amber supplies. "We know that Frank's wife was Alex's aunt, so it makes sense that Alex and her mom were taking care of him after the accident."

"Wait," Rudy says slowly. "The pill bottle only said Glenarm. Not Frank. And the nurse said that he wasn't crazy—"

"She also said that she wouldn't tell you about medical records," Jada cuts in.

"But wait," Amber says. "There was also Bonnie, right? And his daughter—"

Bella nods. "The obit didn't say anything besides that she was young . . ."

They speculate all the way to Ulta and back home. Bella and Jada can't remember an old man who could have been Frank Glenarm in any of the Alex Grable legends; Rudy can't stop speculating on what Frank meant by "our house."

Even Jada jumps in, reminding them that Alex Grable had a father who hadn't been home at the time of the incident. Rudy just shakes his head and says, "Believe me, I've tried. He can't be found."

Bella pulls up the obituary on her phone and rereads it. She pauses on the line about Bonnie Grable-Glenarm having extended family in Norton. What if it doesn't mean the Grables, but more Glenarms? They decided that it's a good place to start. Bella and Jada agree to double down on their research and help.

"I'm in," Bella says. "This is . . . getting scary, with Cecily, but . . . if someone hurt her, we need to find out who."

Jada nods. "I'm in, too."

When Jada says she is in, it is all Amber can do not to kiss her again.

They drop off Bella first. After Rudy pulls up outside of Jada's house, Amber steps outside the car with her to say goodbye in private. And to ask her something.

"Thanks for . . . everything. For caring, and for offering to help. It means a lot."

"Of course. I'm here for you," Jada replies. The way she's staring into Amber's eyes makes Amber feel weak in the knees.

Amber leans forward and kisses her. Then, before she can make herself back out, she goes for it: "Can I ask you something?"

"'Sure."

"Willyoubemygirlfriend?" The words come out so much faster than Amber thinks they're going to, and for a second she thinks that Jada has misheard her, that she's going to have to stumble over the words all over again. But then Jada's face breaks into a huge smile.

"Absolutely."

Amber leans forward and kisses her again, leaning into the feel of her lips, her hands on the small of her back—

And then the horn honks.

Amber throws an evil glare at Rudy in the Range Rover. Jada laughs. "I think you have to go. But I'll see you soon." She's smiling from ear to ear.

Amber spends the rest of the ride home feeling like she's floating. She can't stop smiling.

Until she and Rudy turn into the driveway to find their parents waiting on the porch.

"What is it?" Rudy asks, before he's even shut the car door.

"Is Cecily—?" Amber asks.

"Cecily is fine," Mr. Cole says, and when he smiles, it's actually genuine. "She's been cleared to come home on Tuesday."

Amber feels a smile split across her face. Just two days from now. "That's amazing!"

"Now, she'll still be very sick—we'll have to limit her exposure to light, and—"

Amber walks forward and gives her mom a tight hug. "I don't care. I just want to have her back."

"Me, too, sweetheart."

But her parents wouldn't be sitting on the porch waiting for Rudy and Amber if all they had was good news. Amber tenses, waiting for the "but."

"Did the police find anything?" Rudy asks. "Have you talked to them?"

Mr. Cole shifts. "Actually, I called the police today to ask for an update on the case. They confirmed that the makeup brand had no other issues with . . . tainted makeup remover. They say that Cecily's is a . . . targeted incident." Mrs. Cole winces, and Mr. Cole pats her hand before he contin- ues. "I asked if they had any . . . fingerprint matches, or suspects, but . . . they didn't have much to report."

"It's been more than a week!" Amber says. "How can they have nothing?"

Mr. Cole shakes his head. "They said there were too many other prints on the case to make any conclusions. Cecily's, ours, your friends'—they couldn't find any complete prints that belonged to anyone else. It was a dead end."

Or the follower had worn gloves, Amber thinks. Next to her, Mrs. Cole presses her lips together in that way that Amber has come to associate with her trying to hold back Cecily-based tears.

"So the makeup remover was definitely tampered with," Rudy says.

Mrs. Cole nods. "But it was her go bag, so it could have happened around town, at that party you kids went to . . ." Amber and Rudy exchange looks. "Nothing triggered the alarm," Mrs. Cole says. "So we have no reason to believe that we aren't safe in this house."

Next to her, Mr. Cole nods.

All Amber can think about is the shadow.

For a second, the four of them stand in silence.

Mr. Cole breaks the silence. "Hey, some of the furniture came in today—we have a real table! Isn't that exciting?"

The false cheer somehow makes Amber feel even sadder. But she gives her dad the brightest smile she can muster. "Yeah. That's great, Dad."

Amber spends the rest of the day editing posts, but her heart's not in it. She can't get the makeup remover out of her head, can't stop thinking about Cecily or the follower or the shadow. Eventually, she gives up and goes out for a run, but even then she can't get everything out of her head.

When she gets back home, she's starving.

Dinner is pizza again. For some reason, this just makes Amber think of Cecily more. They eat dinner in silence; Amber can sense that there's something else their parents want to talk about. It's not long before her dad confirms her suspicion.

"Your mother and I discussed it, and we're going to move the open house up a week."

A week? They still have so much work do to. And that is so close . . . Amber knows that they need to get out of this house, but at the same time, she can't stop herself from thinking about Jada.

"Can we finish it in time?"

Mr. Cole nods, and Amber watches her mom reach over and squeeze his hand. "I think we can. But we'll have to scrap some of the less critical renovations to the third floor, and we'll have to stick to our plan to leave the attic sealed. Even with those cuts, it will take a lot, from all of us. You kids have been such a great help, and I don't want to overwork you with construction and your online presence, but . . ."

"Cecily is going to need advanced treatment and cosmetic surgeries," Mrs. Cole says. "We'll be looking for a new place, near a good medical center, and we really think that the sooner the better . . ."

Amber nods. "Yeah. Of course."

"We'll help however we can," Rudy echoes.

Mrs. Cole smiles gratefully. "I know you will. Thank you."

After dinner, Amber and Rudy head into the living room to do something that Amber has been dreading. She takes out her phone to begin drafting the open house message and check on their last post. They had scheduled it to go up after they got back; it had been online for a few hours now, but Amber hadn't checked it. *Everything is going to be fine*, she tells herself. *It's just like every other small post we've done.* She tries to summon the same confidence she had when she was talking with Jada earlier that day. Her girlfriend. She feels a smile cross her face.

She opens the post. There she is, smiling, holding a paint roller: *These walls aren't the only thing changing color.*

And there, beneath it. A comment. The comment is boosted to the top, kept afloat by likes and replies from their fanbase. It's a variation on the Alex Grable name to circumvent the block, but it is doubtlessly them.

She gasps, and Rudy is over her shoulder in an instant.

"What the hell is that supposed to mean?" Amber whispers. Rudy doesn't answer. The follower doesn't need to post the message over and over in order to be seen this time. The comment is instantly upvoted, liked, boosted so high that there's no way the Coles won't see it. Amber is paralyzed. Rudy reaches over her shoulder and clicks on the comments.

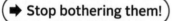

> ➡ Stop bothering them!

> ➡ Leave the Coles alone!

> ➡ Why did you do that to Cecily?

There are also other comments along the lines of what Amber had expected—obvious digs about her weight and the hashtags. But there are a surprising amount of positive comments, too. She reads through them and tries to vanquish the fear with a growing sense of validation. Jada was right. People *do* want to see her on Instagram. And this time, the praise isn't all for Cecily and Rudy—some of it is for *her*.

But of course, all of that is overshadowed by the rest of the comments:

➡ Fake. So obviously fake.

➡ Shame on you! While Cecily's in the hospital?

➡ Cecily's on some private island right now, lmao.

➡ Must not be able to sell the house, must need the PR.

While they read, another comment by the follower pops onto their feed. This one, too, is instantly upvoted to the top:

➡ What great siblings, planning surprises while your sister's in the hospital.

And this time, most of the comments seem to be . . . agreeing.

➡ True!

➡ Poor Cecily. Terrible.

➡ Maybe forgo your second pair of Gucci sliders and take care of your sister—

"They're *agreeing* with him," Amber whispers, in shock.

Rudy shakes his head. "He's trying to mess with us; they're just hopping on the bandwagon." But his voice falters as the comments keep coming in. Their followers don't seem too happy about the Alex Grable comments, or Amber's teaser post.

"Do you think . . . that I should do the next post?" Amber whispers.

Rudy gives her a wide-eyed look. He doesn't answer.

Amber doesn't think she can feel worse until Rudy clicks to view the comment's other replies. Her stomach twists as she reads what the rest of the Cole Patrol has to say.

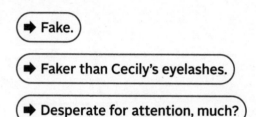

➡ Fake.

➡ Faker than Cecily's eyelashes.

➡ Desperate for attention, much?

And then, the most-liked reply:

➡ Every single one of the Coles deserves to be in that hospital.

Comment on the latest Cole post:

➡ **@ColePat123:** Thoughts and prayers for Cecily! Just donated!

161 Likes   32 Replies

➡ **@Truthtom:** You're deluded kid. They're tricking you for your pity money.

206 Likes   Reply

➡ **@DebbieShalahan:** Profiting off of tragedy. SHAMEFUL.

193 Likes   Reply

Rudy

AFTER A LONG NIGHT OF DELIBERATION, RUDY'S PARENTS DECIDE to make the announcement post anyway, despite the recent follower messages. After all, they can't sell the house if no one knows that it's on the market, can they? The photo is a shot of the exterior of the Tremont house, with Amber and Rudy smiling on the porch. Rudy knows it's a great picture. Amber looks gorgeous. So happy, so perfect. The exact opposite of how they feel. The caption reads:

> ➡ It's been a rough couple of weeks for us here in the Cole family. We want to thank the #ColePatrol for standing by us in these tough times. To address a few rumors: Cecily's health problems are, regrettably, real. While we understand that some find them distasteful, we will be continuing sponsored posts to pay her medical bills. Fans may also donate to our personal SupportMe (link in bio). On a second note, we are aware that a certain follower has been creating alternate accounts to circumvent our block and has been leaving threatening comments. We ask that you do not engage with him.

> ➡ Finally, we have two announcements! First, the amazing people at Miracle Color have sent Amber some hair products, and she's so excited to share a new hair look with you. Second, we are proud to announce that after all our hard work, we will be opening up the Tremont Street home in just one week—Monday, August 15th! We're looking forward to seeing you at our open house, and we want to thank you all once more for your support. Stay tuned for more information.

The post goes live and Rudy waits. Wonders how long until the follower will comment.

He doesn't have to wait very long. The follower comments in less than an hour.

> ➡ Looking forward to it.

Does that mean the follower is planning to come to the open house? Rudy can't get the thought out of his mind. He shows the comment to Amber and, judging from her stricken expression, he knows she's thinking the same thing.

Rudy watches his parents' faces as they read the message. His mom's face grows even paler, and his dad sets his mouth into a firm, angry line.

Together, they decide that they can't back out now.

"I'll contact the police to let them know, and ask them to keep sending patrol cars by," Mrs. Cole says.

"I'll look into the possibility of hiring some extra security for the open house," Mr. Cole replies.

Rudy doesn't ask how he plans to pay for that.

The next day, Cecily comes home from the hospital.

Rudy and Amber wait on the porch as the Range Rover pulls up. Rudy watches Cecily exit the car, guided by their father, a mask of white bandages covering half her face. Rudy and Amber instantly run to her and envelop her in the tightest hug they can muster. As Rudy hugs her, he thinks that she feels smaller and frailer than before. But it feels so good to have her back.

"We missed you," Amber says into Cecily's hair. Rudy nods. Having the three of them together again makes him feel . . . better. Right. Whole.

Their parents lead Cecily inside, and after she dutifully comments on the renovation, Rudy follows Cecily up the stairs and into her room, which Mom has totally transformed to welcome her home.

She spared no comfort for Cecily, but what should look like a glamorous, but still cozy and welcoming bedroom has been totally spoiled by the blackout blinds covering the windows. Cecily's wounds are still sensitive to light, and although the doctors had cleared Cecily for some exposure Mrs. Cole isn't taking any chances. Cecily still has some time before she can be cleared to unbandage her face, and Rudy hates that he is a little glad about that.

He pictures what it would be like to take the bandages off, tries to imagine what Cecily's face would look like now compared to the melted, gory mess he witnessed a couple weeks ago. He knows that she won't be as bad as he remembers, but . . . he can't stop thinking about it. And it's not just the visceral horror of that night. The time in the hospital has hollowed Cecily out; her skin is blotchy and pallid, her posture slumped, her hair dull and lifeless. She smells like medicine. She looks less alive than the sister he knew.

Until Cecily enters her room for the first time and *screams*.

She jumps, yanking him back. He pulls free and darts forward, ready to confront the mysterious shadow, but her room is empty except for one uninvited guest: the doll from their livestream has been placed on Cecily's bed.

He and Amber swear to Cecily that they didn't do it, and she believes them. She's so clearly distressed, but when they insist that they should tell their parents immediately, Cecily refuses.

"Look, I've caused everyone enough stress," Cecily says. Rudy can barely stand how desperate she sounds. "Please, just let it go. I'm sure Mom must have put it there, and she's going to freak out if she finds out it upset me so much. Please . . ."

Rudy and Amber's eyes meet, and he knows they are in agreement. They won't tell their parents about this.

Rudy needs to get the doll out of the house, so while Cecily settles into her room, he puts it on the curb for the garbage pickup. That evening, he goes back to where the doll is sitting on the curb. The sight of it makes him so angry that, without thinking about it, he picks it up and roughly rips its head off, slamming the porcelain orb onto the pavement. He tears the fabric body into several pieces, ripping off each limb and throwing them onto the pavement among the shards of broken porcelain. When he finishes, he stands over the mess he created, panting and frightened by how easy it was to lose control.

This is how Amber finds him when she returns, hot and sweaty and exhausted from one of her runs. They both exchange a wordless look. They have different ways of dealing with stress. Of dealing with what has happened to Cecily.

Rudy tells himself that having her home will help, will fix things. But as he pictures Cecily sitting in her room as the house is constructed around her, he can't shake the heavy, lingering sense of dread.

When he walks back upstairs to his room, Cecily is there. "I saw what you did."

Rudy cringes, imagining Cecily in the window, watching him smash the doll. "Sorry, I just—"

"It freaked me out, too," Cecily says, sitting down on his bed. "But it got me thinking. Have you found anything new, while I was . . . away?"

Rudy sits down in his desk chair and spins to face her. "I was going to wait until later to get you up to speed, but . . . we found Frank Glenarm." He gives her a quick recap of their visit to Upstate Medical. "Other than that, it's only bits and pieces, people that Bella thinks could have *some* kind of connection to all of this."

"Like who?"

Rudy ticks them off on his fingers. "Miles has parents that used to work at Glenarm's assisted living facility. Bella said that people have seen Steve photographing the house. Apparently Alicia said that she overheard Trent bad-mouthing the account. Things like that."

Cecily shakes her head and says what they're both thinking. "None of that is enough to really implicate anyone."

"No," Rudy agrees. "We'll have to keep looking."

Cecily nods, picking at her cuticles. Rudy finds himself fixated on the movement. Her nails used to be so immaculate. Finally, she looks up.

"Have you been online lately?"

Rudy knows what she's talking about, but he dodges the question. "Honestly, no. Mom gave me my admin stuff back, but . . . I haven't really wanted to. Doesn't make sense to talk to our followers when they all think we're making up this nightmare for money." He tries to stop bitterness from tinging the words. He can't. "Besides, I have bigger things to worry about. Research to do," he says, trying to keep his tone light even as he feels urgency rise inside of him. He needs to learn more about the Glenarms, about their daughter. He needs to find the follower before the open house. Before they can do whatever they meant when they posted *Looking forward to it.*

"I meant more . . . about Amber." Cecily says. Rudy tenses. Cecily is staring at her nails. "She's doing really well."

Rudy answers carefully. "She is," he says. "She's really stepped up, and I know it can't have been easy. A lot of sponsors really like the whole body-positive thing she's doing—sure, others don't, but at least we're getting some."

Cecily shoots him a small, sad smile. "I imagine that surprised Mom."

"A little," Rudy admits. His mom had been surprised yet thrilled that Amber may actually be able to replace Cecily—at least, popularity-wise. "But she's been really supportive, which has been nice."

Cecily nods. As the silence stretches on, Rudy finds him grasping for conversation topics, but he can't think of anything except the follower mystery and all the work they've been doing around the clock to prepare the house for exhibition day. The longer the quiet lasts, the more desperate he gets to break it. He's just about to start talking about the progress on the *renovation*, of all things, when Cecily starts speaking again.

"I'm not mad," Cecily says finally with a half laugh. "Like, I'm sad that it can't be me anymore, but I'm not, like, mad at Amber or anything—you guys know that, right?"

Rudy feels himself relax. He hadn't quite known how Cecily would react to Amber's rise in popularity. "I mean, we didn't think—" He stumbles before correcting himself. "I know Amber will be glad to hear that. She's actually kind of got a following of her own now—I haven't seen her this excited about social media in a long time."

"Do you think that excitement is over social media, or Jada?" Cecily laughs, changing the subject. Rudy is relieved to stop talking about the account.

"I caught them making out in the study yesterday," he says, looking pained. "Normally, I'd tease her into the ground, but . . ." He trails off. That wouldn't feel right. "I'm happy for her," he says finally.

Cecily nods. "I'm happy, too," she says, but her voice has a softness to it. It reminds Rudy of something their grandmother used to say about bittersweet things: one part happy, two parts sad. He supposes that's the best he could hope for right now.

The next morning, Rudy wakes up before the beginning of renovation work to do some research. He is revisiting old clues to see if he's missed anything when he comes across the copy of the yearbook where he first saw Alex Grable's picture. And there, on another page, is a second picture. A picture that looks strangely familiar. A smiling African American girl with the name Kendra King. It takes him a second to realize why the photo is so notable, and then it hits him: Those are Jada's eyes. That's Jada's surname.

Is Kendra a relative of hers?

He bounds downstairs and shows the book to Amber. She scrutinizes the photo.

"It has to be someone related to her, right?"

Amber scrunches up her face. "I mean, she does kind of look like Jada . . ."

"Could you ask?" Rudy says. "Please?"

Amber hesitates.

"All I want you to do is ask her," he says. "That can't—it can't hurt anyone, can it?"

Amber doesn't answer.

"Amber, we need to follow every lead we find. What if something happens at the open house? Or after? We need to figure something out. Please. Just . . . just say you'll ask her. If any of her relatives went to school with Alex Grable. Please."

Amber considers for a long while. "All right," she says finally. "But I'm just asking her once. If she says no, that's it. I'm not going to force her . . ."

Rudy nods. "Deal."

Amber's clearly unhappy, but she takes out her phone and snaps a picture of the yearbook, sends it to Jada. A few seconds later, a ping comes in.

"It's Jada's aunt," Amber tells him. "She says she'll ask about it. So I guess now we wait."

They spend the rest of the day painting. Rudy wants to be the one to paint the master bedroom—it doesn't feel right to let his parents do it—but Amber offers to help. He lets her, and together they paint over what he wrote: *This is my house now, bitch.*

They finish quickly and decide to tackle the turret room next.

Rudy lugs the buckets of robin's-egg blue paint up while Amber checks her phone to see if Jada wrote back.

"Nothing yet," Amber reports a moment later.

They crack the lids off the paint and begin working. Rudy thinks that this is going to make him feel good, victorious, even—after all, they're finally destroying something from *this* house. But as he watches the ferns and trees disappear behind *Better Home Magazine's* color of the year, he can't help but feel strangely sad. And then strangely panicked, like he's missing something.

XXX

One evening later that week, after a particularly exhausting day of renovation work, Rudy and Amber catch the strains of a conversation through the dumbwaiter. A familiar name reaches Rudy's ear, and he opens the doors so the sound can echo through. Cecily steps into the hall and moves to join him.

"Listen, Mr. LaRosa, we've run the numbers, and . . . pay you any more than we . . . savings . . . didn't think . . . medical bills . . ."

Cecily looks toward Amber and Rudy. Guilt is strewn all over her face. She buries her one good eye in her hand.

"Oh, Cecily, don't—" Amber starts.

Rudy shushes them, but Joseph's answer has already been muffled.

When Mr. Cole answers, the relief in his voice is palpable. "Thank you, I—"

"It can't be Mr. LaRosa, can it?" Cecily asks.

Rudy shakes his head. "If he did this, why would he help us? Why not just let us crash and burn?"

Amber looks troubled. "We might just crash and burn anyway."

From that night on, she and Rudy start drinking espresso like water and staying up late into the night to screw in baseboards and touch up paintjobs with their parents and Joseph. Slowly but surely, impossibly, the house begins to come together.

And before Rudy realizes that the time has passed, it's the day before the open house. And he and Amber have special plans for the night.

Once the renovation work has ended for the day, Rudy and Amber knock on Cecily's door. Their sister is in bed, staring at her phone in the half-light of the room. "Hey—did something happen?"

"Not exactly," Rudy says. He fumbles for the words. "Uh, we . . ."

"We know that you said you weren't ready to see anyone," Amber says quickly. "But—but that was almost a week ago, and—"

"Amber," Cecily says with a warning tone.

"I invited Jada and Bella over to hang out," Amber blurts out. "Now, we can keep them out of here, they don't have to see you—but—" Her voice breaks. "They really, *really* want to. But only if you're ready."

Cecily freezes. Rudy watches the expression in his sister's one remaining eye transition from nervousness to shock and then, finally, to something he can't place. She swipes a tear away, and when she speaks it's in a whisper. "All right."

"All right?" Amber asks, and in the blink of an eye she's darted over into Cecily's bed and smothers her in a hug. "I'm so excited—we can do movies, and board games, and—"

Over Amber's shoulder, Cecily glances at Rudy.

He mouths the words "thank you," and she gives him an unsure smile back. He wants to share their enthusiasm, but he can't stop thinking about the open house.

Amber pulls away and starts excitedly detailing her plans for the evening. Cecily seems to be warming to the idea of seeing her friends. The girls continue to chat, but he's distracted with his own thoughts. He'd hoped that by now they would have something more on the follower. A way to identify them from the crowd. Rudy wonders if he will somehow recognize them once they're on-site. Would he look into the face that scarred his sister and just *know*?

Looking forward to it, the follower had said.

In his own way, Rudy is looking forward to it, too.

Comment on the latest Cole post:

➡ **@Ccecece123:** OMG. do you think he'll BE THERE? 50 likes and I'll get my mom to take me so we can look for him in the crowd—

299 Likes   Reply

XXXXXXXXXXXXXXXXXXXXXXXXXXXXXXXX

CHAPTER 22

Cecily

IT SEEMS LIKE MERE SECONDS UNTIL HEADLIGHTS STREAK DOWN the driveway, and suddenly Bella and Jada are *here*. Cecily waits for them in the foyer, her one healthy eye done up to perfection, but she still feels so nervous, so scared. If Amber hadn't had that look on her face when she told Cecily they were coming—half-hopeful, half-desperate—Cecily would never have agreed to meet. But seeing how happy it made her sister . . . well, she has to try.

She hears a door shut and light laughter as the two walk up to the porch. She realizes that her hands are shaking. What if they hate her? What if they take one look at her new face and *run*?

The door opens and they're here.

Cecily freezes. So do they.

And then Bella pushes herself into Cecily's arms, and her platinum hair smells like lavender shampoo. Cecily finds herself hugging Bella back as a wave of relief washes over her.

"I've missed you." When Bella pulls away, she's crying. Cecily realizes that she is crying, too.

"Me, too," Cecily says.

Jada hugs her next. "It's good to have you back."

Cecily gives them both a warm, genuine smile, trying to hide how nervous she is. For a moment, she watches as both Bella's and Jada's glances flick to her bandages. She swallows.

"Thanks for having us!" Bella chirps. "It's so cool to see the place—like a sneak peek!" She slings an arm around Cecily, and Cecily feels herself flush. She pushes their wandering eyes out of her mind; she's going to have to get used to people staring at her face. For now, she just wants to bask in the *relief*. They are here. They are with her. After all the horrors of that night, they are still her friends.

"Everyone's obsessed with the house," Jada agrees. "Half the town is going to show up tomorrow, if only because you're so viral."

Bella looks toward Cecily. "Are you going to be there, and, you know . . . see everyone?"

Cecily's face flushes. Bella and Jada are one thing, but—everyone? With their phones and cameras and comments and questions? She runs a hand over the gauze surrounding her eye and whispers, almost to herself. "No. I'll be upstairs. I'm supposed to limit my light exposure, and . . . they don't want to see me, anyway."

Bella immediately jumps in to contradict Cecily. "Hey! Of course everyone wants to see you. Don't talk like that." She softens. "But I understand if you're not ready. It's fine."

"Have you heard anything from your aunt, Jada?" Rudy asks, approaching from behind with Amber at his heels. Cecily shoots him a look of thanks for changing the subject.

"I talked to her," Jada replies. "I was going to ask her to call you, but— she heard about the open house instead. She's going to be here for it tomorrow."

Cecily watches as Jada takes Amber's hand and squeezes it. "Thank you so much," Amber says.

Jada shrugs. "I mean, I don't think she'll know anything but . . ."

"Any little bit could help," Rudy says.

"I can't believe the open house is tomorrow," Amber murmurs. The others shake their heads.

"Hey, want to know what football jocks to watch out for?" Bella asks. "I hear they're all planning on crashing."

And just like that, as they make their way upstairs, the conversation devolves into chatter about high school gossip and Amber's new posts and complaints about Bella's AP chemistry summer work. While Bella swears up and down that it is impossible, Cecily finds herself thinking that if high school is like this, it can't be so bad. At least she'd have a teacher who isn't her mom, and a lab to conduct science experiments in. Either way, it's a welcome change of subject from Amber's posts. Not that Cecily isn't proud of Amber; it's just that talking about their account . . . isn't so easy right now.

Before Cecily knows it, they've gotten through two movies and three bowls of popcorn. As Amber and Jada head downstairs to say goodbye, Bella lingers in Cecily's room.

"Can I talk to you?" she asks. "Alone."

"Sure." Cecily says, sitting back on her bed. She's exhausted and loaded with carbs, but it was totally worth it.

"Have you thought about getting back into makeup?" The question hits Cecily out of nowhere.

"What?" Cecily asks, dumbstruck. Why would Bella even *ask* that?

"You know, Cecily, with your platform . . . this could mean a lot to people," Bella says. "A lot of people have . . . scars, birthmarks, things. Don't they deserve to see someone like themselves online?"

Her eyes—she's so earnest. Cecily opens her mouth then closes it. She so badly wants to tell Bella that, yes, she would do something, that she could go forward with her scarring, that she could be the person that Bella wants her to be . . . but she can't.

"I . . ." She hates how her voice breaks. "I can't." The word is a half sob.

"I'm sorry, I'm sorry," Bella says, but that only makes Cecily feel worse. "It's just—I saw how you looked when Amber was talking about her posts. As if you'd never take another picture of yourself ever again, and—don't you deserve to see yourself online, if that's what you want?"

Cecily averts her gaze, staring at the floor as tears well in her eyes. "I—I don't know," she whispers, and then Bella is hugging her again.

"I know," she says. "I know it's hard, but—I'm here for you. And things will get better, okay?" Cecily nods into her chest.

"Okay." She forces a smile and walks Bella downstairs, where Amber is saying goodbye to Jada. The girls drive off into the night, promising to visit at the open house.

Cecily knows that she needs to rest up for the following day's activities, but the hours tick by and she cannot sleep. She runs her hand over the bandages that cover her face and tries not to think about being back in this house. Every shadow seems deeper than it should be, every noise sounds like a footstep. She can't seem to untense, not even when Rudy and Amber are here. And Bella and Jada . . .

It was in the way that they'd *stared*. Bella kept a peppy smile on her face, assuring Cecily that she would be all right, acting like Cecily was still perfect, like nothing was wrong. And Jada kept glancing between Cecily and Amber, as if searching for tension. When she did look at Cecily, her eyes were sad, as if she was just about to tell her bad news. She knows that they meant well, but . . . it's going to take some getting used to.

Her phone pings. It's the sound of a text from Bella: *Think about what I said, OK?*

She texts back: *I will.*

And it keeps her up all night. Could she really start doing makeup again? She still has most of her products, and Amber could lend her the rest, but . . .

She tosses and turns, and even once, in her exhaustion, almost gets out of bed to go downstairs to stroke Speckles for comfort before she realizes what she's doing. Speckles is gone. Her mind flashes to an image of his poor little body, all ground up, and she has to run to the sink to vomit.

Will life ever be the same again? Can things ever be better?

She can't sleep with thoughts like that, so she lies awake in bed. Her thoughts ricochet between Speckles, Bella, and the open house, and she can't get any of them out of her head. All she wants to do is hide. Hide from her followers, from her friends, from this house and the way that it creaks and groans . . .

And creaks again. And again. In a regular rhythm.

Footsteps.

Cecily closes her eyes and tells herself that she is just being paranoid, that it is nothing—

Another noise.

Not from above, but below.

Cecily feels dread curdle in her stomach. Her family is asleep, out cold from their preparations for the open house tomorrow. They have been for hours. But *someone* is below. The thought rises in her mind: This is the same person who hurt her.

Cecily freezes. She can't move, can't breathe. She needs to tell someone, to do something—she wills her body to move—

But nothing. The minutes pass, and she listens to someone as they walk around downstairs and she still can't move. The terror has her, she can't move, she can't—

Below her, there is silence. Through her panic, Cecily realizes that something is off, wrong, about the quiet. But she can't tell what it is.

A creak cuts through the silence.

And then a solid, heavy *thunk*. As if someone is right underneath her. The kitchen. They're in the kitchen.

Someone is stirring on the second floor. She hears the shifting of covers, and then tiny footsteps as Amber tiptoes past the room. She sticks her head in, sees Cecily there, frozen in terror, and doesn't even have to ask to confirm it: They had both heard someone downstairs.

Then Amber is gone and the footsteps downstairs begin to move fast, and Amber and their parents and now Rudy are in the hallway.

"Cecily! There's someone downstairs!" It's a hissed whisper. As if a spell is broken, Cecily can move again. She scurries to her siblings on the landing. Mom and Dad arrive as she does. She catches Amber's eye, and Amber holds it. Amber knows that she was awake. That she has been awake for some time.

Cecily averts her gaze.

"Cecily—you're awake," Mrs. Cole gives her a tight hug. "It's all right, it's going to—"

Mr. Cole interrupts her. "You four—stay here. Get ready to call the police. I'll go down and investigate."

Before Cecily can fully register what her dad is saying, he's pushing his way past her. As Cecily listens to her father walk downstairs, she realizes what's wrong.

The footsteps she heard below were just footsteps. There were no other sounds—no creaks from the second step on the stairs, groans from older floorboards, confusion or bumbling as someone navigated an unfamiliar landscape. No noises of someone bumping into new furniture or the assorted renovation equipment that had been changed and rearranged every day. Instead, there were just footsteps and perfect quiet. A quiet that would have been impossible for anyone who wasn't intimately familiar with this house.

She's about to explain her rising panic to Amber when they hear Mr. Cole yelling from below: "Marie! Get down here!"

Mrs. Cole and the triplets dart down the stairs. Four sets of feet echo in the stairwell, in the hallway, through the cavernous home, all sense of stealth abandoned. Cecily feels sick; the smell of something sweet in the kitchen reaches out and turns her stomach as she passes through. Their father is a few steps away from the landing.

He turns on the light.

And Mrs. Cole gasps.

There, on the floor of the foyer, in broad, messy strokes, dark and red and bloodlike, are the words:

GET OUT OF MY HOUSE

Beneath those dripping words is the family plaque, neatly broken. Split into five pieces. Cecily wonders if that was the *thunk* she heard.

Mr. Cole darts through the foyer, lights snapping on as he rounds the corner and heads into the kitchen. The others follow him but Cecily stays, staring at the words. She feels dizzy. He was here. Whoever did this was here, had been *here*, could have walked up to her room, could have done anything to anyone . . .

She hears a shout from the other room and runs down the hallway, where her family is standing in the brand-new kitchen. But it doesn't look so brand-new anymore.

The marble countertops have been smeared with the same blood-red paint. The floor has been covered with a strong-smelling liquid that Cecily recognizes immediately: bleach.

Mr. Cole vanishes again. When he reappears a few seconds later, he's out of breath from searching the entire first floor. "There's no one down here. Whatever—whoever—they're gone. It's okay, kids." He surveys the damage in the kitchen and lets out a breath as he takes everything in. "It's going to be okay," he repeats. Cecily can't tell if he's talking to them or to himself. She feels her throat seize up. *Why didn't the house alarm go off?*

Next to Amber, Mrs. Cole has a hand over her mouth. Her mother is trembling, clearly trying not to cry. Amber grabs her mom's shoulder. Finally, she splutters out some words. "Call—the crew, call Joseph, call whoever you can get over here. We need to fix this."

"Marie, it's four a.m. We have an open house in *five hours*. We can't—we can't—"

Mrs. Cole starts to hyperventilate. "This . . . ," she starts. But she doesn't have to say it. Cecily and the others know. They can't show the house like this. They can't sell the house like this. And they need to; they need to sell the house so, so badly . . .

"We have to do something," she stammers. "We can't afford, we can't . . . Cecily . . ."

Cecily feels her face heat. Unconsciously, her hand goes to the covering over her left eye. Her right one is crying, two single tears trickling down her cheek. *Cecily.* Of course her injury is making everything so, so much worse. Her mom can barely keep it together—not because of the break-in, but because of what it means for this family and for her. For *Cecily.*

"We can fix this," Rudy says. "We can clean it up, do something . . ."

"We can't cancel the open house on such short notice," Mrs. Cole says, so quiet that it's barely audible. "People are coming in from . . ."

Mr. Cole gives her a tight squeeze. "I'll see who I can get." The look on her dad's face confirms for Cecily that they both feel the same kind of guilt: her at being the new burden, him at being the older one.

Mr. Cole doesn't gamble anymore, but it seems as if he is *still* willing to bet on this house. So he leaves to make frantic calls for help.

At the other end of the kitchen, Mrs. Cole is also on the phone, trying to reach the police. Cecily and her siblings listen to the half-conversation as she finally connects with Officer Perry. She listens to her mom's voice deescalate from frantic to calm, measured, resigned. Finally, she hangs up. When she turns back to the triplets, Cecily knows that this isn't going to be good.

"I've talked to the officer, and the police will be over . . . but not until after the open house," she says, her voice strained. "We can't have cop cars at our house the morning of the open house—if someone sees—" She cuts herself off. "We need every second between now and the open house to fix . . . everything, anyway," she says, as if she's trying to convince herself that this is the right thing to do. "We can't host an open house mid-investigation. It would destroy any chance we have of making a sale." The triplets nod. Privately, Cecily wonders if they still have one. If they do, her mother is right. The Coles can't afford any more bad press.

Through some miracle, Joseph is able to come. Amber and Cecily watch from the upstairs landing as he walks in, bedraggled and mussed from sleep. But he's here. He looks at Cecily and her siblings and tries to muster a smile.

Cecily almost hugs him for it.

She follows along as her parents and Joseph survey the downstairs. With the lights on, the damage only becomes more obvious. There's paint splattered across the wall, over the floors, on the counter. It extends to the living room, where the cushions of their massive, brand-new sectional have been slashed open. This room had also received the same floor and paint treatment as the kitchen. It's so, so much. Cecily doesn't know how they're going to fix this.

But they are going to try. Together, Cecily's family and Joseph spend the next few hours scrubbing the walls, floors, and counters clean. They get some of it out—but the damage cannot be reversed entirely. They try to cover up some of the destruction by doing things like hanging every photo frame they have to cover the stains on the walls. A happy stock family stares back at Cecily from the one she hangs, as if they're mocking her. Some of the countertops, too, can't be salvaged. They have to resort to an odd assortment of place mats and table runners that look, well, almost as bad as the paint, in Cecily's opinion. She feels dread sink in her stomach like a stone.

The floor is perhaps the hardest thing to fix, or even cover up. In a last fit of desperation, Mrs. Cole and Amber drive a half hour to a carpeting store that opens at seven a.m. and return with a carpet that clashes with everything but covers the unmistakable traces of the follower's lettering in the foyer.

Cecily almost wants to laugh at the absurdity of it all. At least now all aspects of the house look uniformly terrible. No amount of interior-design talk from Mrs. Cole will convince anyone that this was an intentional aesthetic choice.

As the morning sun settles in the sky, Amber and Cecily paint over the kitchen walls as best they can, but there's no hiding the damage. The beautiful marble countertops—which cost more than anyone can stand to think about now—are still stained no matter how hard Rudy scrubs, and the Coles don't have time to really deal with the floor.

As Cecily pauses to look around the kitchen, she imagines that she can feel Amber's eyes on her. Wondering why she didn't wake everyone up when she heard the intruder. Wondering why, if Cecily can't be perfect anymore, she can't at least be *good enough*. Good enough to have at least tried to stop what had just happened . . .

By eight a.m., Cecily's is exhausted and she knows her family is, too. Despite all their hard work, they are going to have to put tarps over some areas of the kitchen and living room. Mr. Cole finally stands up from where he's cleaning and shakes his head.

"We've done everything we can," he says. "This is as good as it's going to get."

Cecily looks around and knows that everything is not nearly good enough, but she doesn't have the energy to disagree with her dad.

Cecily stares at her coffee with a bleary-eyed expression while her parents profusely thank Joseph for his help.

"No problem," he says as he prepares to leave. "Consider it small-town neighborliness. I'm happy to help. I'll be back in the afternoon, after the open house. To help fix up the rest."

Mr. Cole nods. "Wait—in case we're at the station." He reaches into his pocket and presses the spare skeleton key into Joseph's hand. "In case you can't get in. One of us should be here, but just in case . . . feel free to let yourself in. We trust you."

Joseph looks genuinely touched.

The moment Joseph is gone, Cecily watches as her mom takes in a breath, trying to collect herself. She's attempting to salvage something from this disaster, Cecily knows.

Next to Cecily, Amber and Rudy are in similar states of exhaustion and despair. "All right. Damage control," Mom says, trying and failing to snap back into her manager persona. She looks so, so tired. "Amber, I want extraglamorous photos of all the untouched rooms, and a teaser for the open house on Instagram. Then, look your best for the tours down here. Maybe Cecily can help with that," she says, shooting Cecily a smile that manages to be both pained and simultaneously hopeful. "Rudy, same with you. When people ask you about the home—" Her voice falters. "We can't let anyone—*anyone*—know about this. If the sponsors find out, if people start thinking that we can't manage a simple kitchen renovation—" She cuts herself off. Cecily has never seen her mom this out of sorts. "But they won't. We're going to say that we had a problem transporting the countertops and flooring, and that they got damaged in transit, and that there are new pieces in shipment right now—but don't talk about any of that unless they ask. Keep them off topic. Talk about your haunting if you have to."

Cecily doesn't have it in her to argue with her mother. She doubts that Rudy and Amber do, either. Besides, it's not as if she's going to be on the floor during the open house. She'll be hidden away from the public—

because it's one thing for them to see a cracked countertop, but a scarred Cecily Cole? That might truly bring down the whole house of cards.

"Cecily, sweetheart," Mrs. Cole turns to her. "Get some rest, please. You must be so exhausted from the hospital—and you've been up all night—"

"It's okay," Cecily says. "Really." She looks at Rudy and Amber, and realizes that somewhere deep down, she wants to be at the open house with them. She almost says that, but her mom cuts off the thought.

"Lock your door from the inside," her mom says. "We'll be showing off Amber's bedroom as an example, and the master on the third floor, but other than that people should stay out of the upstairs. Hopefully we won't disturb you too much."

Cecily nods. "You won't. It's fine; really." She forces a smile. She watches her mom's gaze stray to her bandages. She tries not to flinch, tries not to think about all the glamorous open houses that she's been a part of. Tries not to think about how she'll spend this one, locked away, disfigured and hiding, while party guests parade through the halls downstairs.

Her room was supposed to be the example one. It always has been. Now that, too, falls on Amber.

Minutes later, she's in the bathroom with her sister, staring at Amber's makeup collection.

"I checked it all," Amber says. "It's . . . safe. I mean, I can do it myself, too, but . . ." But she so clearly wants Cecily to do it. Cecily stares at the makeup, and her fingers tremble.

Then she gazes at Amber. Her sister looks so exhausted. So tired from doing all the posts, from doing everything for Cecily. Slowly, Cecily reaches toward the primer.

A while later—longer than it usually takes, due to Cecily's insistence in triple-checking every product by dabbing it on her forearm before applying it to Amber's face—Amber has the perfect smoky eye for the day, done in shades of brown and taupe, with a healthy-looking glow and a nude lip. Cecily frowns at the work. She can't help thinking that her fear and hesitation show, but at the same time . . . she's proud that she did it. Amber looks flawless.

"You look beautiful," she says, giving Amber a smile. For a brief second, Amber smiles back. Then her face collapses back into exhaustion.

"There's no way that we can't do the sponsored hair post now, is there?" Amber asks. "I mean, I was hoping that maybe, if the sale went okay . . ."

Cecily shakes her head. "I think you're right. Listen, Ambs. About your posting . . ."

Amber bristles. "What about it?"

Cecily tries to smile. "I—I'm glad you're putting your own spin on things; I think that this could have been good for you, but now? With everything?"

"Are you saying I shouldn't post the body-positive hashtags?"

Cecily struggles to find the words. "No, I just think that . . . there's so much pressure on these posts, and then there's the whole . . ." She trails off. She doesn't need to say it. "I just wish . . . you'd be more careful. Not draw attention to yourself. Not do anything extra that could . . ."

"You don't understand," Amber says. "You never had to—" She cuts herself off as Cecily searches for a lip gloss. *Why did Amber stop talking?* Cecily wonders. Is it because she was she going to say something about how she's the perfect one now, and that Cecily's opinion doesn't matter because she's such a mess?

But when she continues speaking, what Amber has to say is even worse than what Cecily had imagined.

"Were you awake last night?" Amber asks, her voice flat as if she's trying hard to keep the emotion out of it.

Cecily freezes, unable to answer.

"Why didn't you call me? Or come and get me?" Amber presses.

Cecily hesitates. Her mind flashes back to the makeup remover, all those weeks ago. To the feeling of her skin melting, the smell of her own burning flesh . . .

She doesn't realize how hard she's trembling until she tries to open the gloss, until she's dropping the wand and hyperventilating. Amber jumps to her feet and calls for Rudy.

The next thing Cecily knows, her sister's worried face is inches from hers, and Rudy is right beside her.

"It's okay, just breathe," Amber says, and Cecily forces herself to take deep, calm breaths. She wonders now, like she'd wondered last night, how long she had frozen up. "The police are on it, remember?"

"And so are we," Rudy adds as he appears in the doorway. He's got his phone in his hands and is typing as he speaks. "We're going to figure it out."

Cecily feels Amber's hand on her shoulder and turns to find her sister holding out a cup of water. She takes it gratefully. When she looks back at her sister, Amber's face is flushed.

Cecily tries to speak. "I'm sorry, I—"

"No, no," Amber cuts her off. "Of course you had a stronger reaction, after everything that happened . . . Cecily, I'm sorry. I really am. That wasn't fair."

Cecily shakes her head. "I wish I'd done something, it's just—I was just so scared, I—"

"So was I," admits Rudy. "I don't think I would have gotten out of bed if Mom and Dad and Amber hadn't been awake first. I was terrified."

Cecily swallows. "It's okay—I'm okay. I am," she says, trying to speak it into existence. She gives her siblings a shaky smile. "Thank you."

When she looks back at Amber, she's surprised to see that Amber is almost crying herself. She watches her sister swipe at her eyes. "Sympathy crier," Amber says, sheepish. "No, no, that's not true. It's just—I'll miss you down there, Cece."

Cecily envelops Amber in a tight hug. "I know you want to figure things out, but I just want to get out of this house as soon as possible. Good luck today—come visit upstairs whenever you want some air. And keep me updated." She feels Amber nod before she pulls back, then gives her sister and brother the best smile she can muster. "You'll be amazing. I know you will."

Cecily takes a teaser photo for the account: Amber and Rudy in the bathroom mirror, all dressed up. They look great. As she stands behind the camera, Cecily can't help but think of how the roles have reversed. But she can't be mad. All she can do is hope that they'll be okay.

She posts the photo before Amber can edit it into oblivion. *We'll miss Cecily at the open house, but we're so excited to welcome everyone to Tremont Street!*

But the comments coming in beneath the post aren't the shouts of support that she'd hoped for.

➡ Looking awfully happy for kids with a half-blind sister.

➡ Where's Cecily?

➡ Fake fake fake

And, all too quickly, there is one from the follower:

➡ I hope you all enjoy what I've done with the place.

And another:

➡ Ask the Coles to show you what those hardwood floors really look like.

Comment on the latest Cole post:

➡️ **@Jules123:** PAY THE OPEN HOUSE A VISIT AND FIND OUT THE TRUTH #WHERESCECILY

185 Likes   Reply

XXXXXXXXXXXXXXXXXXXXXXXXXXXXX

CHAPTER 23

Amber

AMBER DELETES THE COMMENT INSTANTLY, BUT NOT BEFORE several hundred followers see it, screencap it, and scatter it over the internet. At that point, there isn't anything that the Coles can do. Despite Mrs. Cole's initial hesitations, she agrees to call the police, who dispatch officers for the open house. But even the presence of Officer Perry and two of her colleagues doesn't make Amber feel any better, or any safer. She watches Perry walk around the kitchen, examining the new flooring, appliances, and baseboards with the meticulous precision that Amber supposes comes with being an investigative police officer. But still, she thinks bitterly, is small-town officer Perry really capable of taking down the person who attacked her sister with *acid*? What if something happens? What if they get attacked *again*? The vandal had been walking around their house at night—how can she possibly feel safe after that? As much as Rudy wants to solve the mystery, Amber is beginning to think that maybe Cecily is right. Maybe the best thing to do is to sell this house and leave as soon as possible.

But the key to that is, of course, selling the house.

As she gets ready, she can hear her mother laughing. She'd been practicing it all morning, laughing and laughing and laughing into the mirror, searching for the perfect tone and timbre. She'd found it.

So Amber forces a smile on her face and shimmies into the dress she's going to wear for the open house. It's tight and red. She chose it because it usually makes her feel fearless—and it breaks the plus-size fashion "rule" of no bodycon dresses—but all she feels now is fragile. She tries not to think about how an identical one is currently hanging in Cecily's closet. She tries to summon some of her sister's old confidence as she emerges from her room.

When Amber steps into the hallway, Cecily's door is already closed and locked from the inside. Rudy steps out of his room wearing a red bow tie to match her dress. He gives Amber a tight smile. The fact that they are dressed like this only makes Cecily's absence more apparent.

Amber remembers the last time she was "matchy-matchy" with Cecily: at their parents' anniversary party. It feels like a lifetime ago.

Downstairs, they hear the door open and the first of their mom's gales of fake laughter, practiced to perfection.

Footsteps patter into the foyer; appreciative murmurs fill the house. Amber and Rudy take a breath and walk downstairs together.

The open house is *huge*. They have never had this big of a turnout before. The usual realtors are here, of course, but this time they're accompanied by hordes of . . . normal people. Sure, Cole family open houses always get some gawkers, but it seems like half of Norton is here. The locals and the drama chasers are easy to spot. They stare, wide-eyed, at every corner of the house as if they've never been in a multimillion-dollar mansion before. And, above all, they gawk at Amber and Rudy.

Amber tries to summon some of Cecily's old confidence. She works the crowd and she is "on." She smiles, preens, takes selfies, and fields questions about the renovation, the town, their life as Instagram celebrities. She actually gets a few questions about her body-positivity hashtags, which she is more than happy to answer, even when they're really digs about her weight and her health in disguise.

But Amber never forgets her biggest job: steering people away from paying too-close attention to the damage. So in between answering questions, she lies about the countertops and tries to stop people from attempting to lift up the carpets to see the hateful message scrawled beneath them. The follower's post had gone viral; Amber knows that they are playing a losing game. There are too many guests here, and only four of the Coles—five if you count Joseph, who made the last-minute decision to help the family with crowd control.

They need it.

Amber allows herself a moment of rest and tucks herself away in a quiet corner of the hallway. She has a perfect vantage point to observe much of the first floor. She looks around and takes it all in, from Mr. O'Donnell glaring at the new open-concept kitchen to the crowd of high school kids. The historical society stands in a corner, shooting judgmental looks at the new kitchen and the updated flooring that definitely was not installed with historical preservation in mind. The group of high-school-age kids collapse on the living room sectional—its slashes covered with one of Mom's least-favorite throw blankets—and Amber winces at the way they put their feet up.

But her few moments of respite are over quickly because soon she sees Bella arriving with some of the bonfire crowd. While Miles and Trent greet her, Alicia scans the open house.

"Is Cecily here?"

Amber shakes her head. "No. She's still resting."

Alicia gives her a strained smile. "Well, let her know that we're thinking about her. Say hi for us, okay?"

"Absolutely."

The kids eventually peel off to look at other rooms of the house while Amber leads additional tours, steering them all away from the ruined kitchen as much as she can. Amber catches snippets of Rudy's conversation with the boys—promises to start learning lacrosse sometime, an invitation to jam with Trent's garage band—and finds herself wondering if Norton could have actually been *good* if everything hadn't gone so, so wrong.

And then she spots Bella, cornered by Steve. He's leaning against the kitchen wall, arm propped out and effectively blocking Bella's exit. He's wrapping his arm around her shoulder, just as he had attempted to do with Cecily at the bonfire. Bella is clearly uncomfortable. And all of a sudden, Amber just feels herself get so *angry*. Amber catches the words "I don't understand why you don't—" as she approaches them.

She walks up to Bella. "Is he bothering you?"

Steve answers for her. "No, I just—"

"He thinks I know what room Cecily's in," Bella says.

"I just want to visit. Say hi. See her."

"She's not ready to see anyone."

"I'm not just anyone—"

"No." Amber snaps, her voice final. Whoa. She didn't know she could channel her mother like that.

Steve glares at her. "You don't have to be a bitch about it," he huffs, but he stalks off into the crowd.

"Steve—" Bella groans, then turns to Amber. "I'm sorry. Thanks. He can be a bit . . . much."

"I've been called worse," Amber says. As she watches him stalk off, she can't help but think of her sister, locked in that upstairs room. "Hey—want to see Cecily? I'm sure she'd love the company."

Amber escorts Bella up to Cecily's room and is thrilled to hear their chatter start up the moment she closes the door behind her. She pops into the bathroom to check her makeup and then, as she's about to make her way downstairs, she notices a woman trying the locked doors farther down the hallway. Near Cecily's room.

Is she trying to find Cecily? Did Cecily remember to lock her door after she let Bella in?

"What do you think you're doing?" Amber shouts, running as fast as her heels will take her down the hallway.

"What? This is an open house, isn't it?" the woman snaps.

Amber can't tell if this person looks startled or guilty. She decides to try another tack.

"I'm sorry, I just meant to say that the show bedroom is a few doors down. The room with the open door? Here, let me show you . . ."

The woman's huffiness disappears as soon as Amber turns on the charm, but she makes an excuse to head downstairs the first chance she gets.

Is she the follower? Amber wonders as she walks away from the woman. It could be anyone. Anyone on any of the scores of tour groups moving through the house today. She shudders.

Without fail, every tour group Amber leads asks two things: if they can see the turret room and what's wrong with the flooring—what had the follower done? Even when she manages to steer them off that topic, they bombard her with questions about Cecily and the house's other notorious rooms. Amber and Rudy only smile and rehearse their line: that more expansive tours are available to clients with serious interest in purchasing the property.

They're barely an hour into the party when Amber gets a frantic call from Cecily. She doesn't even have time to say hello before she hears her sister's voice: "Someone's at my door—"

Amber sprints upstairs to find a young woman at Cecily's doorknob, rattling it against the lock, calling out for her sister. Amber slows, feels fear choke her throat. Could this be the follower? And then the woman notices her, and her facial expression immediately drops into something so sheepish that Amber discards the idea.

"I was just—trying to see if Cecily was—"

Amber plasters on her fakest smile yet. "Why don't you let me escort you back downstairs, ma'am?" she says, trying to slow her accelerated heartbeat. This is just some other busybody, someone trying to snap another photo of Cecily for the internet fame or whatever reason.

Amber escorts the woman back downstairs, warning Rudy and her father to keep an eye on her. She shakes herself off and tries to put on the same happy smile as she heads to her next tour.

But things just keep getting worse. No sooner have they left the downstairs than a young man in her tour turns on her.

"Amber, I have a question—" She turns, ready to answer, but the expression on his face stops her short. "Where's Cecily?" he asks. Her gaze drops to the phone he's holding, pointed at her, doubtlessly recording her every reaction. "Where's Cecily? If she's really injured, why isn't she down here? That is, if you have nothing to hide?" Amber clenches her fists, so, so tempted to break character—but his cell phone is shoved in her face, recording every move. She can't make a scene. She can't be anything but perfect.

Fortunately, she has years of training on how to blink and smile pretty.

When the tour is finally over, Amber double-checks to make sure that Cecily is undisturbed before heading back downstairs. As she navigates the crowd, she catches snippets of conversation: kids wondering about the follower, snooty adults making comments about how *they* would never let their kids post all over social media like that.

There's one small silver lining: when an adorable little plus-size middle school girl walks up to her with a smile, wearing a crop top. "See?" she asks. "I'm breaking the rules, too."

Amber kneels down and gives the girl a hug. She almost wants to cry.

Then she spots Jada across the room, eating a deviled egg with her mother and a woman that Amber doesn't recognize. Jada makes her way toward Amber, and Amber steps forward and gives Jada a tight hug. Her girlfriend. "I'm so glad you're here." Her hair smells like coconut oil and shea butter, and for a second Amber truly allows herself to relax, to melt in Jada's arms. She explains about the morning in whispers.

"Oh my god," Jada says. "That's terrible. I was wondering about the new carpet—and all the weird stuff, like the photos—"

Amber nods, eyes darting around the crowd. "Just tell people that being kitschy is in this year," she mutters, distracted.

Jada follows her gaze. "What?"

"Sorry," she says. "I guess I just keep thinking that, you know, they could be here."

"You think they're *here?*" Jada asks, her voice hushed. "You really—"

"No. Yes. I don't know. I'm sorry, I'm all over the place right now," Amber says. "And everyone's got their phones out and I—"

"Hey, hey, it's okay." Jada gestures toward the foyer, where some of the bonfire kids are milling around the hors d'oeuvres. "Don't worry. We're all here, nothing is going to happen." From across the hall, Amber gives Alicia, Trent, and Miles a wave. She explains to Jada that Bella is with Cecily.

"Jada! Who is this?" A woman appears over Jada's shoulder. She's tall, with light brown eyes and dreadlocks done up in an immaculate topknot. Amber can clearly see the echoes of the high school yearbook photo.

"This is my girlfriend, Amber," Jada says. "Amber, this is my aunt Kendra."

Girlfriend. She said girlfriend. She hadn't heard Jada say it before. She feels all warm inside; it's good to be official. She catches Jada's eye and feels some of her stress from the horrific morning ebb away. Jada beams at her as she turns to Kendra. "It's nice to meet you."

"My aunt went to high school with Alex Grable," Jada says. "I thought you two might want to talk, but . . ." She trails off.

"Please," Amber says, forcing a smile. "I'd love to learn more about the house, or anything and anyone you remember."

Kendra gives her a pained smile. "Well, I don't know how helpful I can be, but I love what you've done with the place. This house deserves to be a home again. It looks so different than I remember."

"You've been here?" Amber asks.

"Yes, I have," Kendra says, scanning the walls, the windows, the pristine appliances.

"With Alex? What was she like?"

"She was a nice girl," Kendra says. "We ran track together. Good at school, too; got a scholarship and everything. There were a lot of kids who were jealous. She seemed to have it all. And this house, well, it's the largest house in town." She smiles to herself. Her eyes are glassy, and Amber gets the distinct feeling that Kendra is lost in a memory. "Of course, looking after someone full-time isn't easy—but that was her mom, mostly. Alex usually kept to that cool fourth-floor window room, her and her rock-band posters." She chuckles, but there's an edge there. A pain.

"Someone?" Amber asks, breathless.

Kendra nods. "Her uncle. Hurt in a car wreck, poor thing."

Amber nods, taking everything in. Kendra had just confirmed Rudy's theory: that the Grables had been live-in caretakers to Frank Glenarm, after he had been injured in the accident that took Bonnie's life. Bonnie Grable-Glenarm. The hyphen had to indicate that Grable was Bonnie's maiden name, which makes Frank Alex's uncle.

When Kendra looks back at her, Amber is surprised to see tears pricking the woman's eyes. "I guess it just goes to show that no one's life is as perfect as it seems. She was so talented. They called her the shooting star, you know?"

Amber freezes. *Shooting star*. A child's voice comes back to her:

> *Once there was a shooting star*
> *That shot across the sky*

But that meant that the voice on the tape . . .

Kendra continues; she doesn't seem to notice Amber's freeze-up. "Her little cousin loved that nickname—wouldn't stop repeating it. We had so much fun in the nooks and crannies around here," she continues, wistful. "Used to play around in the dumbwaiter, occasionally get forced into babysitting."

"C-cousin?" Amber stutters. *She left behind extended family in Norton and a young daughter. This young daughter. The one they hadn't been able to find any record of . . .*

Kendra nods. "Quiet little girl, but I don't know who wouldn't be a little . . . messed up after what happened to her parents. It was so sad. And Alex, too—it couldn't have been easy. But for Alex to . . ." Her voice trails off; her face is drawn. She gives Jada and Amber a tight smile. "The important thing is that you girls be . . . good to each other, you know? Sometimes I think that if Alex had the support she needed . . ." She doesn't finish her thought. Jada gives her aunt's hand a squeeze, and Kendra shakes herself out of her thoughts. "I'm sorry—I'm sure no one wants to hear these things, especially on a day like today! The house is lovely, Amber. And it was so, so nice to meet you."

Amber nods. She feels . . . numb.

> *But I don't want to see it there;*
> *So that star had to die.*

Amber sees a flash of recognition in Jada's eyes. She gives Kendra a brief goodbye before pushing off through the crowd—she can discuss details with Jada later. Right now, she needs to find Rudy.

Shooting star. And a cousin who couldn't stop repeating the words. Frank Glenarm's surviving daughter had lived with Alex Grable. And Alex and her mother had died after moving into that little girl's house.

Amber's skin prickles. What if Alex hadn't killed her mom? What if Alex hadn't killed *herself*? What if that young cousin is still alive?

She needs to find Rudy.

There's a shriek from the foyer. Amber had been distracted from her post; she hasn't been watching the carpeting—and now there he is. Steve, standing on the hardwood, the end of the carpet in his hands. Yanking it up for all the world to see:

GET OUT OF MY HOUSE

Amber rushes toward him, but it's too late—about a hundred cell phones are pointed at the text, still all too visible, outlined on the floor. She can already feel her phone buzzing with notifications on their account . . .

Amber navigates the crowd, shoving aside gawkers and well-to-do families without notice or apology.

Steve locks gazes with her and stares her down. "Why would you vandalize your own house?" he asks. "Not popular enough on the internet already, huh? What really happened to Cecily? Why are you hiding—"

"Get out of my house!"

Amber flinches at the fury in her dad's voice. He's marching toward Steve, all the exhaustion and pain and stress of the last few weeks igniting, exploding into a shout that sounds more than a little unhinged. Steve jerks his gaze away from Amber and toward her father, staggering backward. He stumbles into the wall, knocking off one of the stock photos. It falls, hits the floor, cracks—and reveals the red, bloodlike smears beneath. All the cell phones photographing the house pivot to him, but Mr. Cole doesn't notice. He hasn't been trained like Amber and her siblings.

"You think you can come in here and trash my home?" he yells, too loud, too angry, too unaware of exactly how terrified Steve has become.

"Dad," Amber starts, finally breaking through the crowd—but it's like she's not even there. "Dad!" Across the room, Officer Perry, too, is pushing toward the disturbance, eyes wide with what must be adrenaline.

"Robert!" Her mother is at his side now, gripping his bicep in a vice, tearing him off Steve and twisting him around so that he can see.

Everyone in the open house has their cameras out, broadcasting the Coles to the world. Amber doesn't even bother asking them not to post it. She can already feel her phone vibrating; it's too late. The video is already up. A livestream. And they have been tagged.

> ➡ LIVE House Party Fight! THIS IS THE REAL
> COLE FAMILY.

Hashtags trending:
#CancelTheColes
#ColesCanceled

XXXXXXXXXXXXXXXXXXXXXXXXXXXXXXX

CHAPTER 24

Rudy

THE VIDEO LOOKS AS BAD AS IT SOUNDS. THE FIRST ONE—THE one that went viral—was shot from a strange angle, so that the viewer can't see why Mr. Cole was suddenly shouting at Steve. All that's apparent is that one second Steve is saying something, and the next Mr. Cole is threatening him in front of the entire party.

Other videos, of course, show off the follower's whole message on the floor.

The aftermath is one of sound: Rudy, Amber, and Cecily sit by the dumbwaiter and listen to Mrs. Cole's footsteps as she paces around the kitchen, finally breaking to shout at their father in a fierce, desperate climax: "You ruin everything! This is all because of *you*!"

Rudy hears his mom's voice crack and then the muffled sounds of sobbing. Even after their mother's breakdown has long faded into the sounds of cleaning up the open house, Amber still can't stop crying. Cecily looks the way Rudy feels: numb.

A short while later, Mrs. Cole comes upstairs.

"I need you and Amber to shoot a video with Dad," she says, her eyes on Rudy. "An apology video."

So they set up the camera. While Rudy and Cecily position key lights and chairs in front of a sad beige wall, he listens to Amber trying to coach their father. "Listen, Dad, just say you're sorry and try to sound . . . sound genuine, okay? Say what happened, and say you're sorry that you scared Steve. Are you sure you don't want a script?"

But their dad shakes his head.

They set him in the frame, seated between Rudy and Amber. Cecily presses Record.

Mr. Cole opens his mouth and closes it. Nothing comes out.

"It's okay, Dad," Amber says. "Whenever you're ready."

But Dad isn't ready. When he finally speaks, it's stiff, canned. "I want to tell our fans that I'm sorry for taking actions to protect my daughter from—some creep—"

"*Dad!*" Amber says, but Rudy can tell that Dad clearly hasn't received the training that they've had.

He tries again, but he's clearly still stressed, exhausted, and angry: "I'm sorry that the stress of the renovation—made me react—I'm sorry he got scared, but after all the internet stuff, well, he shouldn't have tried to lift the rug—"

After three or four more takes that get them absolutely nowhere, Amber throws up her hands. "Dad, it's an *apology video*. You can't blame Steve—"

"Well, it's his fault!" Dad says. He stands up, shoving the chair behind him. "Just—you—I hate having to *lie*. I'm not sorry, I—I need a break." And he storms out, leaving the triplets alone.

Amber swallows and turns to Cecily behind the camera. "Was any of that usable?"

She shakes her head. "I don't think he's coming back," Cecily whispers, moving to turn the camera off. "What are we going to—"

Amber stares at the camera. "Keep filming," she says. Rudy doesn't know what Amber's planning, so he steps out of the shot to stand with Cecily. The camera rolls.

"Hi," Amber begins. "I'm Amber Cole. And here's what's really been happening at the Tremont house."

She spends the next twenty minutes detailing every horrifying incident that had happened leading up to their father's meltdown. The only thing she leaves out are the tapes and the triplets' search for clues. Rudy feels his mouth slowly open as Amber speaks. She appears calm, cool, collected. But this is still absolutely an unapproved video. Amber has never done anything like this before.

When she's done, her eyes are red. She looks at Cecily and Rudy, who are watching in awe.

"Post that one," Amber says. "It's about time someone is honest on this channel." And, just like that, she gets up to follow their father. Rudy and Cecily look at each other. Rudy never in a million years would have thought that Amber could do something like this. He's impressed. He's not sure that even he would have had the stones to pull that off.

They post the video and wait in Amber's room for the fallout to begin.

It doesn't take long for their mom to spot the video, and her reaction is swift and severe.

Rudy realizes that this is Amber's first time being eviscerated by his mom. As the veteran rule-breaker, Rudy has to admit that she takes the verbal lashing well. "After everything, you have to do *this*? I bet Cecily—"

"I had to tell them what happened!"

"You can never tell them what really happens!" Mrs. Cole says, running her hands through her hair. "I thought you would have known that by now! Nothing is real, Amber—come *on!*"

Amber stiffens. "What if I want it to be real?"

"Well, it's not your account then, is it?" she says. "It's ours—and Cecily—"

She cuts herself off, but Rudy knows how his mom would have finished the sentence: *Cecily would never have done this.* Mrs. Cole continues. "We're so lucky that the sponsors agreed to take you. You know I didn't want you on those front-facing posts anyway—"

"Why not, Mom?" Amber yells back, surprising them both. "Why not?"

"I—I thought you wanted to stay in the background . . . I only meant that I didn't want to make you uncomfortable—"

"It never made me uncomfortable! Why would it? Because I'm not skinny?"

Mrs. Cole hesitates. Rudy cringes. "I was just trying to protect you."

Amber rolls her eyes. "Me, or the account? Me, or your stupid brand integrity? Me, or your dumb sponsors? Afraid they'll pull out because of my weight? I don't want a sponsor that would do that, anyway. I thought you wouldn't either."

Rudy watches out of the corner of his eye as Amber's face tightens. But Mrs. Cole . . . she's clearly on the verge of tears. Maybe that's what makes

Amber turn and stalk away. Before Rudy follows her, he catches sight of Cecily, bandaged and huddled on the stairs. He doesn't know how much she'd heard, but, knowing this house, he's willing to guess everything.

Later that afternoon, Sheriff Yang and Officer Perry return to document the break-in. They scan the crime scene, but the open house had obstructed any evidence that might have been left behind—fingerprints, footprints, or otherwise. Rudy sees his mom deflate; he remembers all too quickly that, last night, she had decided to postpone the investigation to focus on having as good an open house as possible. In hopes of making a sale. And now . . .

Officer Perry seems . . . exhausted. Her voice is brusque, clipped. She's probably frustrated with the Coles—well, with Mr. Cole in particular—about the display at the open house. Rudy guesses as much when she opens the conversation with the news that Steve's mother is considering going after Mr. Cole for harassment. Rudy imagines that the Coles hadn't exactly started off the day in Perry's good graces, either, what with being woken up at four a.m. when they called to report the break-in, or the fact that his mother had begged Perry to be present at the open house for security and then return *again* afterward to investigate the break-in.

Rudy is glad that his dad, at least, is being very quiet and respectful as the officers explain that they have no leads on Cecily's injury. Rudy is trying to behave himself, too, but man, it is *difficult* not to interrupt with a thousand questions, suggestions, and theories. But the last thing he wants now is another remark from Perry about how he is "quite the investigator."

Perry continues. "However, we think that there's a high likelihood that this damage was done by the same person—although we're unsure how they could have broken in without the alarm system being triggered."

Rudy imagines that this must be more than the local police usually deal with. Maybe Yang shares his sentiment, because he turns to the Cole parents. "Sir, ma'am, if you feel uncomfortable here, I can recommend several hotels in the area."

Mr. Cole looks at his wife, then back to the sheriff. "No, sir," he says. Rudy sees his father's fist clench and knows that, to him, moving out would be the ultimate sign of defeat. If the Coles are too afraid to spend the renovation period in the Tremont house, how on earth will they be able to convince another family to move here full-time? "We'll stay here. We're hoping to have an offer soon. We don't want to imply that the house is . . . unsafe for residents."

Officer Perry gives an exaggerated sigh. Rudy fights the urge to remind his parents that this police report would be public record.

The sheriff and his deputy nod and file out after taking a few more photographs.

Five p.m. comes and goes. There are no calls. No offers on the house.

There are officers stationed around the house all evening.

Rudy finally has the chance to sit down and check out the responses to Amber's tell-all. He feels his stomach knot up as he reads the top comments. They are even worse than he'd expected them to be.

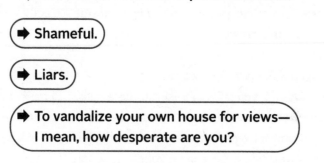

➡ Shameful.

➡ Liars.

➡ To vandalize your own house for views— I mean, how desperate are you?

So little support from the Cole Patrol. Rudy forces himself to keep reading. Maybe there are some supportive comments lower down.

And there are:

➡ You tell 'em, Amber #NotYourBeautyStandard

➡ Fake or not, great to see a curvy girl front and center. #NYBS

Of course, for every positive comment about Amber's body there are ten calling her fat, lazy, and selfish, but Amber doesn't seem to care. Rudy watches his sister light up as she reads, and he finds himself feeling glad that at least *something* positive is coming from this.

Then, Amber freezes.

"What's wrong?" Rudy asks, mind snapping to the follower. But Amber shakes her head.

"We've hit . . . one million," she says in disbelief. Rudy doesn't know how to react. They had anticipated celebrating this moment and all it meant for their account, for their careers, but . . . that doesn't feel right anymore. It just feels so . . . hollow. Then Amber lets out a little squeak, shaking her head, and turns the phone to Rudy.

It's not the follower; just some fan. But that doesn't stop the comment from getting several thousand likes and replies.

➡ One million subscribers! How about a Cecily Cole reveal?

Rudy tightens his jaw. "Don't answer it."

Amber nods. "I won't. I don't want to do a million-subscriber special, either." She sounds so exhausted. "At least the sponsors should be happy about these numbers, right?" It's clear she's anything but excited. Rudy can hear his own weariness echoed in his voice.

"I hope so," he says. "We need it."

Even Mom's reaction is a little subdued. When they tell her, she doesn't cheer like she once would have, but she does seem genuinely pleased. "That's wonderful news! And it'll help so much with engagement, plus we can leverage it to get more sponsors . . ." She trails off. "I know things are bad right now, but you've worked hard for this. You should be proud of yourselves—all of you."

Amber nods and forces a smile. Rudy doesn't answer.

Fortunately, Mom agrees that the timing isn't right to do a million-subscriber special. So Amber posts a generic thank-you message.

The next morning, Rudy and his sisters gather in the bathroom to prepare for the hair dye photo shoot. Rudy sits on the sink and films Amber—

and Cecily from the wrists down—as her hair is divided into careful sections and painted with different colors of dye to achieve an ombré effect.

Cecily sets the timer on her phone for thirty minutes, and Rudy shuts the camera off. Now is a perfect time to take a break from filming and talk to his sisters.

"How did they get in without triggering our alarms?" he asks as he sets the camera aside. "Do you think that Steve—"

"Alex isn't the voice on the tape," Amber says, cutting him off. "Oh my god—with everything happening with Steve, and Dad, I forgot—"

Rudy snaps to her. "What?"

She details what she'd learned from Kendra at the open house: That Alex Grable was the shooting star. That Kendra had confirmed that Alex and her mom were live-in caretakers for Frank Glenarm. That Frank had a small daughter. Alex's young cousin.

Once there was a shooting star
But she won't be here for long—

He'd thought that the voice on the tape was a distorted, messed-up version of a teenage girl's—but what if it wasn't?

Flying and falling and gone

"So the person on the tape . . ."

"Was talking about Alex," Amber confirms. She swallows. "Was talking about . . . killing her."

Rudy locks eyes with his sisters. Something clicks; all the pieces fall into place. After so many weeks of searching, everything suddenly makes *sense*.

"What if—what if the cousin, the daughter—what if she's Reena? The name on the doll?" Cecily asks.

"I hadn't thought of that," Amber says.

Rudy starts to pace. Cecily stares at him, wide-eyed, in the mirror. His mind is moving too fast to keep up with his mouth, but he tries to explain it anyway: "So Reena and her parents live in this house. The car crash happens, and Alex and her family move in. Reena—breaks, or something—and kills Alex and her mom. The people who replaced her parents in this house. Years, years after, Evan moves in here and she kills him, too. And now us . . ."

"Why Evan?" Amber asks. "Why not his parents?"

"Maybe—she didn't want to kill him," Rudy starts slowly, thinking of the follower's messages. "Maybe she just wanted to scare him enough to leave. To get out of the house." He shivers.

Amber thinks. "So you're saying that the antipsychotics . . ."

"Were hers." Rudy says. He swallows. He can picture it: A happy family, living in this house. Together. And then the tragedy that changed everything, leaving Reena behind—motherless, and with a bedbound father. So the Grables came into the Tremont house to take care of Reena and, in the eyes of a young girl, replaced her parents.

And Alex Grable replaced her.

Maybe Reena broke in the aftermath of the accident, or maybe she was already taking the medication for a preexisting condition. Either way, watching her mom die and her father waste away destroyed her. And there was no one to take it out on but the Grables. The shooting star and her family who had invaded the home that Reena loved.

And now the Coles are in her house.

Cecily is silent. She's staring at her hands, marred with pink dye. Pink dye that looks red on her pale skin.

"Cecily?"

Cecily remains quiet. She massages dye into the ends of Amber's hair and presses her lips together in a way that reminds him so, so much of their mom. When she looks back up at her brother, her good eye is crying. "You look—excited," she hisses. "Rudy, this person tried to *blind* me—and two nights ago, they could have—they could have come upstairs and—this is *dangerous*. It's not just some prank, some game—"

Rudy stares at his sister. Does she really believe that he thinks this is a game?

What Cecily doesn't understand is that he's thrown himself into this investigation because he has to know who did this to her. That whoever it is won't get away with what they did to Cecily. To his family.

But as he looks at Cecily's sad, bandaged face, he doesn't think he can explain any of that to her. So he just stops talking.

Two hours later, Amber's hair falls around her shoulders in glossy curls.

She puts on a carefully curated outfit and they head downstairs, searching for an untainted spot for their photo shoot.

"You look amazing, sweetie," Mr. Cole says to Amber, poking his head into their set.

"Very colorful!" Joseph agrees, following him into the kitchen. "I have a niece that would die for that hair." Rudy watches Amber give him a small smile.

It's not hard to settle on a favorite photo; Amber chooses the same one that Rudy also likes best. It's a shot of Amber turning her head to face the camera, curls in motion. She looks absolutely beautiful. Amber comes up with the caption and then Rudy posts it: *It feels great to get some more color in my life! Huge thank you to our sponsor, Miracle Color. Want this look yourself? Watch out for a hair dye video coming soon! The plus-size fashion rule we're breaking this week is bold patterns. Live life boldly! Any interest in fashion hauls or tutorials after we're done with hair dye? Let me know in the comments! #NotYourBeautyStandard #LoveAnyBody #CallItFatshion*

Rudy monitors the comments carefully for the next half hour or so. He's relieved to see that the comments are overwhelmingly pro-Amber.

A little while later, the doorbell rings. Amber explains that Bella is coming over to see her hair in person.

"Is Jada coming, too?" Rudy asks.

"No, her aunt is still visiting, so she's spending time with her," Amber replies.

"Don't worry, I'm sure that Bella will gush enough for both of them about how amazing you look," Cecily says wryly.

As if on cue, Bella bounds into Cecily's room.

"Oh. My. God. It. Looks. Incredible." Bella says, eyes wide as she takes in Amber's hair. Amber grins and flounces it up and down. Rudy can't remember the last time he saw her looking this . . . confident. Happy.

"Can you do mine, too? Pretty please?" Bella squeals.

Amber and Cecily exchange a look.

"We do have plenty of dye left," Cecily says.

"Sure, why not?" Amber shrugs.

"Yes!" Bella says, grinning.

"And I think that's my cue to leave," Rudy says. Witnessing one hair transformation for the day was more than enough.

"You're welcome to stay," Cecily says, and Rudy wonders if that's an olive branch. She hasn't spoken to him much since the episode in the bathroom earlier.

But he has other things he wants to do right now, so he begs off, promising to come back in a little while to check on their progress.

Rudy heads into his room and sits down at his computer. He goes back to investigating the Grables and the Glenarms, redoubling his efforts to find the lost daughter. But despite what he suspects about Reena, he can't find a photograph or mention of her anywhere—not the internet, not the public library archives. He doesn't know where else to look. He even breaks and calls the hardware store, attempting to talk to Mr. O'Donnell again—or, better yet, another member of this budding historic society. But all Rudy gets is the busy signal.

He gives up on his search just in time to watch Cecily rinse the dye out of Bella's hair. To Rudy's surprise, they're talking about the open house. About Steve.

"It's so crazy," Bella says. "Steve is such a jackass. But it's—like—he's not a terrible person, you know? He just wants, I dunno, attention. People to like him. Just like everyone else."

"So he tried to torment us by following the instructions of an internet creep," Amber deadpans.

"When you put it like that . . ." Bella trails off. Then, she hesitates. "You don't think it's . . . him . . . do you?"

The triplets exchange a weighted look. "We don't know what to think," Amber admits.

Rudy gives Bella a brief rundown of their Reena theory. "Of course, we're not ruling anything out about Steve," he adds. "You've known him longer than we have—what do you think?"

"I think he's secretly a fan," Bella says. "All he's been doing is looking at your profile."

"Really?"

"Oh yeah," Bella says. "Just, like, scrolling. I saw him watching some of your vlogs from when you were, like, fifteen at this football team party the other night, it was so weird. But then again, he's just a weird dude."

"Do you think he's . . . dangerous?" Rudy asks, trying and failing to keep the excitement out of his voice. The Reena theory feels so promising, but at the same time he can't help but wonder which vlogs Steve was watching. The peanut allergy one? Cecily's go-bag reveal?

"After almost having his collarbone broken by your dad? No way," Bella says. "Dude is a creep, but he's also a major wimp." Cecily takes out her blow-dryer and starts on Bella's hair.

"So, uh, football party . . . ," Cecily starts, changing the subject. Amber and Rudy exchange a look and wordlessly agree to drop the follower discussion; they'll talk more about Steve as a suspect later.

Bella goes off, yelling over the blow-dryer and giving Cecily all the dirty details on who's crushing on who. "And, of course, they're all dying to see you—"

"All done!" Cecily says, a little bit louder than usual. She holds up a mirror, and Bella is instantly distracted.

"Oh my god," she whispers. "I look just like you. I look just like a *Cole*."

"Uh, you look better than a Cole!" Cecily says. "You look like you."

Bella beams at her then turns to Amber. "Thank you so much. I can't believe we match! We look almost identical. I love it!"

"Here, let me take a photo," Rudy says, but as he prepares to snap a few photos of Bella and Amber, Cecily sidles out of frame. Bella shakes her head and yanks her in. "Come on, these are for me." She sticks her tongue out at his sister. "And you should be celebrating! You've hit one million! When you get to two million, I expect your hair to be even more colorful than this. Instagram would go *crazy*."

Bella gives Cecily another tug, and Cecily . . . actually gets into the frame. Rudy can hardly believe it. The pictures he takes aren't posed, they're not staged—they're just for fun.

"You're pretty good at this," Rudy says as he snaps away.

"Oh please, I am not," Bella replies, but she looks satisfied. "Although, I could become really good at it if my two favorite Insta stars would give me some tips on how to look hot in photos," Bella says with a laugh.

And that's how they launch into an impromptu modeling shoot, complete with lessons and tips from his sisters. They can't seem to stop laughing at one another as they go through their tricks—how to make their legs look longer, how to make their butt pop, how to stand off-balance to accentuate every curve.

Rudy loves every moment of it and happily continues to play photographer for them. Cecily is smiling for the first time in days, and nothing feels more important than this.

He doesn't realize how quickly time has passed until Bella has to go home. They pause on the wraparound porch to hug her goodbye. "Thanks again for the hair," Bella says. "And . . . I know things are awful, but is it bad that part of me is glad you're staying just a little longer?"

Cecily gives her a choked laugh and envelops her in a hug. "I'm glad you're here," she says.

Bella grins. "I'm glad I'm here, too," she says. For a second, her voice goes a little quiet. "Listen, I want to help you figure everything out. Keep me in the loop, okay? And I'll keep my eyes open for clues. I heard one of the lacrosse boys talking about your renovation at the football party the other night. I'll definitely follow up on it."

Rudy gives her a quick hug. "Thank you. Really."

Bella's grin gets even wider as she runs a hand through her hair. "Hey, as long as you guys keep doing my hair this cool and giving me tips on how to feel fabulous, I'll do all the sleuthing you want," She straps on her bike helmet and shakes her hair out behind it. "God, I love the hair. My mom's going to throw a *fit*. Ha!" She mounts her bike and shoots them one last grin. "See you guys soon!"

Rudy and his sisters watch Bella pedal down the long driveway and into the fading light. It would make a pretty picture, Rudy thinks, watching Bella's bright pink hair sway in the wind.

Bella turns a corner, rose-gold hair billowing behind her. And then she is gone.

Comment on the latest Cole post:

➡ **@ColeFanXXX:** Amber looks
AMAZING. #LoveAnyBody

329 Likes   1 Reply

➡ **@ColeFan41:** WHERE IS CECILY?
COLES, IF YOU SEE THIS, WE NEED
TO SEE HER. WE NEED TO SEE
HER FACE!

314 Likes   Reply

XXXXXXXXXXXXXXXXXXXXXXXXXXXXXXXXXX

CHAPTER 25

Cecily

AN HOUR OR SO AFTER BELLA LEAVES, CECILY TRACKS DOWN
Rudy. She finds him in his room, trying to play through a tune on his guitar.
It's been a long time since she's heard him play, and she wants to savor it—
but she can't.

She steps inside. "I need you to know that this is not a game."

Rudy looks up. "What?"

"You, in the bathroom, talking about hunting down the follower—
Rudy, this is real! I get that you're into the mystery, but this person—"

"Hurt you," Rudy says. His voice sounds strange. A little shaky. Cecily
hesitates. "You don't think I know that?" She would have expected him to
be angry, but his voice is almost a whisper. "You don't think I—" He cuts
himself off, shaking his head.

Cecily feels herself falter. "I—"

"I'm not enjoying this investigation in the way you think I am, Cecily,"
Rudy says, standing up. "It's just—someone hurt you, and I need to solve
it. I *need* to, because I can't—I can't—" His eyes meet hers, and she realizes
what he's trying to say. He needs to solve this, because he can't go back
in time and stop it from happening. Because he can't do *anything* else but
solve it.

All the self-righteous anger drains from Cecily. "I just—I don't want
anything to happen to you . . ."

"I know," he says, leaning his guitar against the bedpost.

Cecily gives him a tight smile. "I just want you to be careful." He nods,
and Cecily finds herself thinking that researching a real crime suits him,
somehow. She just wishes that it weren't in their house.

"I will," Rudy says. "Here—why don't we take a break for the night, throw on a movie or something . . ."

Cecily is more than happy to take him up on the offer. He grabs Amber, and they hang out in his room, talking and joking and letting B-grade cartoons run on autoplay. Cecily doesn't realize how late it is until she hears her mom calling from downstairs.

"Kids? Can you come down here?"

Cecily exchanges a look with her siblings as they file downstairs, wondering if they're in trouble *again*. When they reach the kitchen, their mom is clutching her phone, her face tight with worry. "Mrs. DiNatori called—she says that Bella isn't home yet. She left hours ago, right?"

"Yeah," Cecily says, casting a glance at the dark sky outside. "She rode her bike home before dinner."

Mrs. Cole turns back to the phone and relays the information, nodding at whatever Bella's mom is saying on the other end. Cecily can see her mom is worried, and a ball of dread begins to form in her own stomach. How is it that Bella isn't home yet?

"Is there a chance—any chance—that Bella went somewhere else? To another friend's house?" Mrs. Cole asks.

Cecily exchanges glances with Amber and Rudy. "I . . . I don't know," Cecily says. "She didn't say she was going anywhere—I mean, she has lots of friends, but . . . I thought she was going home."

Mrs. Cole speaks back into the phone. Cecily listens to the muffled, worried voice of Bella's mom until Mrs. Cole finally sets down the phone. Something is very, very wrong.

"Bella never made it home," Mrs. Cole says finally. "Her mom is going to go ahead and report her missing—she's never late. I'm—I think I need to go out and look for her—" She cuts herself off. "I'll get your father and take the Range Rover; you kids sit tight."

Cecily feels something tighten in her throat as she watches her parents throw on jackets and shoes. Bella. She feels her breath coming faster and faster as her fear escalates toward panic. She hates that it's Amber and not her who says, "We're coming with you."

"You are staying put," Mrs. Cole says, in a voice that implies there's no arguing. In the hallway, Cecily hears her dad putting on his shoes, preparing to leave. "Please. Just—watch the house, okay?"

And then the door slams and her parents are gone. Just like that. The sound echoes through the foyer, and all of a sudden Cecily can't stop thinking about how large the house is around them, how *alone* they are . . .

How quiet the follower had been.

Cecily opens her mouth. "We . . ."

Rudy stands up. "I'm going to look for her."

Amber nods and begins to shove her feet into her sneakers. Rudy runs into the kitchen. "Where are the flashlights? Where—"

And just like that, Cecily snaps out of it. "Rudy—" Cecily starts. "Guys—"

"Don't stop us."

But Cecily doesn't want to stop them. She wants to join them.

"We can use our phones, " she says. "To text everyone. And also for light."

"Good thinking." Rudy nods.

They set off into the dark.

Halfway up the driveway, Amber's phone pings with a text. "Jada. She hasn't seen her."

"Shit," Rudy utters.

"Relax," Amber says, but she doesn't sound convincing. They turn out of their driveway and start walking toward Bella's neighborhood, scanning the woods with their phone flashlights. Rudy begins to call out.

"Bella!"

"She probably just met up with Miles or something." Amber's voice is small. Scared.

"Bella!" Cecily yells. Her hands start to shake. She shouts her friend's name over and over again until her voice goes hoarse.

The dark is setting in faster now. The light from their phones glints off roadside reflectors, shards of broken beer bottles, the glowing eyes of some wild creature in the brush. Cecily starts to feel cold. What if he is out here, right now?

"Stop," Cecily says. Rudy and Amber freeze. There, on the pavement, caught in her light. A smudge of dirt on a single red shard of glass. It could be part of a bicycle reflector. Rudy's head snaps toward the woods and then steps forward, raking his light across the long grass, shouting for Bella.

The light catches on a brilliant, reflective patch of rose-gold.

Cecily makes a choking, sputtering noise, the sound of someone trying and failing to scream. And just like that, she's frozen.

Amber runs over to Bella, and her scattered light illuminates Bella's broken body.

Cecily feels the panic again, in her throat, in her stomach. It rises, and she starts shivering, her hands shaking—she wants to vomit—

"Call 911!" Amber yells, but Cecily can't; she can only convulse. "Call 911!" she screams, louder this time. Rudy is crouched next to Bella, and he's dialing; Cecily can hear his panicked voice, trying to explain—

And then something in Cecily breaks, and she is finally able to tear through the brush to meet Amber. Thorns catch her hair, her skirt; the skin of her knees cracks open as she falls to them to cradle her friend.

Someone is repeating one word: *No. No no no no no.* Cecily realizes that it's her.

Because the moment she touches Bella, she knows.

"She's not breathing," Amber says. She turns around and scans the forest, searching, searching—there. Bella's bike, thrown a hundred or so yards farther into the forest. Strangely far. Wrongly far.

Rudy stammers into his phone, Amber searches in vain for a pulse, and all Cecily can do is stare at Bella, lying below her, leg and arm crooked, knee bent wrong. Shards of bone poke through the skin, and Cecily can't help but fixate on them—so pale, so blindingly *white*.

She hears the 911 operator on Rudy's phone, staticky and distant: "Can you stay on the phone until help arrives?"

Help. Help will be too late, because Bella is cold. Bella is cold and bleeding from where she's been struck; her legs lie akimbo, clearly broken. As Cecily cradles Bella's head in her lap, she hears her own voice whispering over and over how sorry she is, how sorry . . .

In the distance, she hears the roar of an engine. And then, much, much closer, she hears something else. A softer noise. The buzz of a notification. And then another, and another. A familiar flood that can only mean one thing.

She turns to Amber, face slack with horror. Slowly, Amber lifts her phone and reads. Her face crumples, breaks.

"What is it?" Cecily asks. When she reaches out a hand for her cell phone, she startles. *It's dye*, she tells herself. *It's just hair dye.* But it isn't. She knows that it isn't. Her hands are covered in Bella's blood.

Slowly, Amber starts to cry. "It's the account," she says. "On the hair post. Over and over and over and—oh god, Cecily."

"What?"

Amber shakes her head. She can't say it; she won't. She holds out the phone. With shaking, bloodied hands, Cecily takes it and reads:

> ➡ **Congratulations on hitting one million followers.**

> ➡ **Looks like I hit the wrong rose-gold girl.**

Comment on the latest Cole post:

➡️ **@DramaGramALERT:**
BREAKING: ARE THE COLE FAMILY
MURDERERS?

396 Likes   Reply

Amber

AMBER WATCHES HER PARENTS TALK TO THE POLICE. THEY SEEM so far away. Here, in the station, her parents have the same strange color saturation and solidity of an exceptionally lucid dream or strange Instagram filter. But Amber knows that this is real. Her head is spinning; in the noise of the station, everything feels too loud, too fast, too frenzied in comparison to how Bella had been when they found her. Still. So still. With hair so bright—just like hers.

Every time she thinks she has no tears left, a memory finds her again. She alternates between periods of awful numbness and terrible, rib-shaking sobs. And Cecily? Cecily has barely been able to speak since it happened. She hasn't released their dad, either. She's still at his side, clutching his shirt with a grip that will leave winkles in the fabric once she lets go. Amber's not sure if she ever will.

She watches as Officer Perry questions her mother, who is standing with her arms folded in on themselves and half a fist in her mouth as she nods. Officer Perry's bun has come partly undone. The officer's cuticles are red and bleeding. Her fingertips are ever so slightly stained.

Across the room, Sheriff Yang is consoling Bella's mother. Amber hasn't met the dark-haired woman, but the resemblance is too striking for her to be anyone else. She's keening, wavering back and forth as if drunk. Yang adjusts his glasses—bifocals—and puts a large hand on her shoulder. She sinks into him. He looks surprised at the contact; for a second he is the most flustered Amber has ever seen him.

When she leaves, Mrs. DiNatori passes the triplets and gives them a look of pure *pain* that shakes Amber to her core.

The police take their parents into a separate room for further questioning. The triplets have already told the police everything they know. There is nothing left to do but sit in the front of the station and alternate between numbness and ground-shaking grief.

Bella had been pronounced dead at 10:57 that night.

Bella, who had been at their house just hours before. Who had hugged Amber and said that they matched. That they almost looked identical.

And then the follower. Amber can't stop thinking about them, about someone driving down that road, seeing the bright flash of Bella's hair in the darkness, steering the car toward the girl on the bicycle before they realized that she was too short, too pale, too slight to be Amber—

But by then it was too late.

It makes her feel sick.

The news that Amber, Rudy, and Cecily Cole had found one of their hometown friends dead by the roadside had spread like wildfire. Their follower count skyrocketed; everyone wanted to know what had happened, who did it. One of the bystander videos from the open house with Bella in the background had gone viral; their comment section was being overloaded with speculation and concern. And one other thing: blame.

One of the local high schoolers had found pictures of Bella—first grade, eighth grade, high school—and posted them with the caption, *This is what happens when you hang out with the Coles.* In the photos, Bella is smiling and happy, loved and unbroken. Amber can't look at them. Instead, she spends hours alternating between crying and staring, unblinking, at the grimy police station laminate.

Finally, her parents emerge. "It's time to go."

"What—what did they say?" Amber asks. "What happened?"

Cecily collapses into their father, who wraps an arm around her shoulders. "They don't know for sure," Mr. Cole says. "But they're not ruling out vehicular homicide, or a connection with our . . . incidents. That's all they were able to tell me."

The ride home is still and silent. An email comes in the middle of the night: Miracle Color has dropped the sponsored tutorial video that was meant to follow the hair dye post. Of course they have. How could they not? The Cole family is completely and utterly toxic.

Amber only wishes that she'd canceled it first.

For the first time in a long time, the Coles unanimously agree on what to do with their social media accounts. The next morning, Amber cries and shakes her way through crafting a post.

➡ Bella, there are no words. Rest in peace.

➡ Consider this account suspended until further notice.

Comment on the latest Cole video:

➡ **@xxginastaycion:** You look like a unicorn puked on you. No wonder you have to kill your friends for views. #ColesCanceled

273 Likes   Reply

➡ **@XXRudyXX:** A girl is dead. Your fake follower isn't funny anymore

218 Likes   Reply

➡ **@LunaStarr:** And now they're "Quitting social media?" As if.

104 Likes   Reply

XXXXXXXXXXXXXXXXXXXXXXXXXXXXXXXX

CHAPTER 27

Cecily

BELLA SMILES AT CECILY IN THE MIRROR. CECILY GRINS BACK AND fluffs her hair, turning to look at herself.

"See?" Bella asks, nodding at Cecily's reflection in the mirror. "Nothing to hide at all."

But when Cecily looks back up at her reflection, the mirror isn't there anymore—she's not even in the bathroom anymore. She's in the woods, and she's alone, and she's just about to scream Bella's name when she trips over something. Someone.

Cecily screams and jolts awake.

"Are you all right?" Cecily whirls around, trying to get her bearings, and slowly everything slides into place. It's the middle of the following night. Amber is sitting across from her, laptop open, face scrunched in concern. Cecily is curled up in a chair, where she'd dozed off by accident. Her phone is on the table. Before she'd passed out, she'd been on their account, deleting comments from their Instagram—comments that had been coming in a never-ending flood, ever since Bella—

Bella is dead.

It hits her like a punch to the gut, and Cecily finds herself gasping as it all comes rushing back: Bella's body, in the woods. The police station. How she and Amber had worked for hours to delete hateful comments from their feed before she fell asleep.

And then her dream. Where Bella had been alive again.

Cecily doesn't realize that she's crying until there are tears on the table. Amber appears in front of her and clutches her tightly in a hug. Cecily realizes that her sister is crying, too.

For a long, long moment, they remain like that.

And then there is nothing left to do besides continue deleting comments. Around four in the morning, Cecily removes a nasty comment before she realizes that it's not their stalker but a real account, someone who's been following them for years. It's not the only one:

➡ What happened to that girl? What are you censoring?

➡ Why are you deleting comments if it's not true?

➡ Tell me it's not true. #ColePatrol

➡ I thought you were offline.

They are offline; they're just trying to keep their account from being overrun with posts about the follower, about Alex Grable, about Bella.

Gossip sites keep reposting a photograph they'd somehow gotten from the crime scene: Cecily and Amber, standing in the tall, dark grass with the blue ambulance lights behind them. There is blood on their clothes. Cecily's bandages are in full view.

It makes her sick.

Rudy joins them before dawn, but he doesn't go online. Instead, he pores over the Frank Glenarm newspaper clipping and mutters to himself about the list of suspects. Occasionally, he takes breaks to finger though something on his guitar. *His music is nice*, Cecily thinks. *Nicer than we ever gave him credit for.*

"Rudy, we could really use your help with this," Amber says.

Cecily nods. Amber is right. Even with two of them working at it, they can't keep up with the barrage of nasty comments coming in.

"Who cares?" Rudy shrugs. "They're going to hate us no matter what we do."

Cecily knows he's right. But still she keeps working with Amber to delete the comments.

Eventually, Rudy wanders off to his room to try and get some sleep. An hour later, Amber looks up, bleary-eyed, and tells Cecily that she needs to get some sleep, too.

Cecily agrees and collapses onto her bed. She doesn't want to sleep; she doesn't want to see Bella again. But it's not long until the utter exhaustion takes over.

Later that morning, Cecily is awakened by the muffled sounds of her parents making coffee. There were no dreams of Bella, but the loss is still there. It pulses beneath her skin as she sits up. She can't even look around her room without seeing Bella sitting on the end of her bed, playing with the figurines on her dresser, or lying on the floor next to Rudy, thinking of more follower theories.

Cecily grabs her phone and scans the comments. She's surprised to see that there are no new messages from the follower. She pads over to Amber's room to see if her sister is awake.

She is. "No new follower posts," Cecily tells Amber, who nods. Of course, she probably checked her phone the moment she woke up, too.

Cecily sits in the corner of her sister's bed, exhausted from only a few hours of sleep.

"Did you see all the comments from . . . everyone else?" she asks.

Amber nods. "They're horrible."

Both their phones are on silent, but they still light up with a constant stream of notifications.

Finally, Amber speaks again. "What are we going to do?" she asks. She sounds as tired as Cecily feels.

The "we" hits Cecily wrong; it stings. Without meaning to, she lifts a hand to her face then tries to hide the unconscious gesture—but she's too late. Amber's already seen. "Cecily, I'm sure that—"

Sure that what? Cecily can post online again? Slide right back into her place in the beauty community? Cecily shakes her head. "It's bad, Ambs," she whispers. "I—I can't. People don't want to see this."

For a long second, Amber is quiet. "You know," Amber finally says, "I thought that people didn't want to see me, at first. And then—well, I think I changed my mind." She swallows and looks at Cecily. "Maybe you'll change your mind, too."

Maybe it's the sincere look on Amber's face, or maybe it's her flawless rose-gold waves, or the fact that Cecily notices for the first time that Amber already has makeup on, even though there's no post scheduled for today. Whatever it is, Cecily finally snaps.

"Being fat isn't the same as—as hideous scarring!" Cecily yells. She can feel her face heating, her non–scar tissue going red with rage. "You can go on a diet! But I can't just *lose* my scars, Amber." She sees the hurt in her sister's face and knows that she has gone too far, but she can't stop now—the words are already coming. "You have to be *beautiful* to be a beauty influencer, Amber! My career is ruined, and Bella—"

And just like that, Cecily's anger vanishes, recedes into sadness like water leaking through cupped fingers. On Bella's name, all of her rage splutters out, and suddenly she is sobbing again. "I'm sorry, I—"

She buries her head in her hands and stiffens as she feels her sister's hand on her back. She's ashamed of everything she just said and wonders if her sister will hate her now, too, like all of social media does.

But when Amber speaks, her voice is gentle. Kind. "I'm just saying that . . . there are other people with scars, too, you know? Maybe they'd like to see . . . someone like them, on Instagram."

Cecily lifts her head to meet Amber's eyes. "Maybe I don't want to *be* someone like them."

Amber doesn't respond.

After a few moments of strained silence, Cecily gets up and returns to her room.

Later that afternoon, Cecily and her siblings are summoned to the sheriff's office for another interview, but Cecily can't help but feel like it's the same questions about Bella, the follower, and the hit-and-run all over again. This time, her shaking sobs give way to something worse: complete numbness. She feels like a robot, repeating the words. Faking being human. Even

Perry seems to know that this charade is useless; the deputy spends almost all of Cecily's interview drumming her fingers on the table, as if she's impatient for something to happen. Cecily imagines that she's eager to get back to interviewing real suspects, but when she asks about leads in Bella's case, all Perry says is that she can't disclose case details.

Bella's funeral is the following Tuesday.

And Cecily—Cecily still feels raw. She is dreading it, but somehow the only thing worse than going would be not going. So later that week, she and the rest of her family don their funeral attire. Cecily debates about her bandages for a long, long time, but in the end decides to leave them be. She wears her hair down, but that doesn't help much.

The sight of herself in the mirror almost makes her rethink her decision. She chokes, covers another sob, and prepares for a breakdown, but suddenly Amber is there.

"For Bella," Amber says, putting a hand on her shoulder. Cecily nods, but it's not until her mother offers her a short, black crow's nest veil that she finally feels ready to leave the house. At least, as ready as she will ever be.

The service is beautiful, moving. Tragic. Cecily might have found some comfort in it if she didn't feel like everyone was glaring at her and her family. Kids take sly photographs when they think that no one is looking; adults bow their heads to whisper. Cecily clenches her fists around the funeral program and tries to ignore them. Tries to think about anything other than the fact that these were Bella's friends, family, neighbors. When the service ends, all she wants to do is sprint out of the church, but she forces herself to join her siblings as they walk toward Bella's mother.

Mrs. DiNatori stands at the end of a line of mourners. Somehow, her grief makes her seem large and small at the same time.

They approach. Cecily swallows and tries to say something, anything. "Bella . . . she was such a good friend to me. I was lucky to have her."

Mrs. DiNatori gives Cecily a sharp nod, her lips pressed together tightly—out of rage or the need to keep from crying, Cecily cannot tell.

She supposes that was the best she could have hoped for.

After the funeral, townspeople linger and talk, mourn, reminisce. None of them approach Cecily or her family. Finally, her parents seem to decide they've all had enough and they begin to make their exit—or at least, they try to. They're halfway across the parking lot when someone calls after them.

"Aren't you going to take a picture?" It's one of Bella's high school friends. Cecily tenses. Trent. She'd met him at the bonfire. He'd been so nice before.

"Yeah," another girl says with a sneer. "Take a picture and post it online, I'm sure it'll go viral. I'm sure that her mom won't mind."

"Ignore them," Cecily's mom says.

Don't cry, don't cry, don't cry, Cecily thinks.

"It's your fault!"

The cry rings out through the lot, and Cecily freezes. She knows that voice. When she turns, it's Alicia, whose eyes are streaked with tears, whose chest rises and falls from the effort of shouting. Alicia, Bella's best friend. She glares at Cecily as if she's single-handedly ruined her life. Which she has. Cecily Cole will leave Norton as soon as the house is sold, but Bella DiNatori will be dead forever.

More high school kids detach from the funeral to join the small crowd that's descending fast on Cecily and her family. For a second, the only noise in the lot is the sound of passing cars and the shallow intakes of breath as one of the girls starts to sob.

Then Jada's voice cuts through the crowd. "Bella got hit by a car," she says, her voice emotionless. "Leave it."

"She was my best friend!" Alicia yells. "And then you—" She starts crying and breaking down, with full-on heaving sobs. Miles emerges from the group behind her to grab her arm, but Alicia keeps shouting. "No— they—they're the ones that should be dead. And now they're at her *funeral* looking like it's—fashion week or something—"

Cecily wills herself not to cry, not to break down on the pavement right then and there. She knows better than to try and explain that she doesn't have any nondesigner options, that she only wore the veil so that no one would see her face.

That she, too, loved Bella.

"Alicia—" Miles isn't the only one who is trying to pull Alicia away from Cecily. Some of the other kids are trying to calm her down, but she refuses.

Alicia rips her hand away from Miles. In silence, Alicia raises her phone and snaps a photograph of the Coles.

Alicia finally allows Miles to grab her and steer her away from the Coles. The small crowd of high school kids slowly dissolves behind them.

Only Jada lingers for a moment. She and Amber exchange a few hushed words. Cecily sees the pain in her sister's eyes as she tells Jada she understands, she should go be with her friends now.

Once they finally reach the Range Rover, Cecily notices for the first time just how out of place it looks among the pickups and sedans in the parking lot. Even their car doesn't fit in.

They're about to pile into the vehicle when the police car screams down the street toward the funeral home. Cecily freezes. All eyes snap toward the church as a police car pulls up and Sheriff Yang and Officer Perry get out. Cecily tenses, half-convinced that they're coming for *her*, coming to arrest her because Bella's death is all her fault.

She can't stop herself from panicking. What if—what if the police are going to arrest her parents? Her family? All the high school kids still have their phones out. What are they going to do when photographs of the Coles being forced into a police car go viral?

The police pull farther into the lot, but instead of coming for the Coles, they head into the funeral home. Rudy heads back toward the doors, and after a second, Cecily and Amber follow. They barely get halfway across the lot before Perry and Yang reemerge, holding Steve between them.

Cecily exchanges a look with her siblings, and in unison they dart through the parking lot, stopping across from a crowd of funeral guests that had quickly formed in the doorway. The officers walk Steve to their car and bend him over the hood.

"You are under arrest for the murder of Bella Nicole DiNatori," Sheriff Yang says, snapping cuffs on his wrist.

Steve begins to protest—his eyes are still red from crying; his voice is hoarse as he shouts, "What? I didn't—"

The funeral guests are crammed in the doorway now, watching in stunned silence as the police begin to read him his Miranda rights. They shove Steve in the car, but not before Cecily locks eyes with Steve. Distraught, guilty eyes. But is he distraught because he did it, or distraught because he didn't? She can't tell; she doesn't know. The world is spinning.

Did Steve kill Bella?

Cecily turns to her siblings, only to see her own panic mirrored in their faces.

Cecily tries to picture Steve in the driver's seat of his beater car, yanking the wheel to run Bella off the road, the impact of her body on metal. Realizing that the pink-haired girl wasn't her sister. Then opening his phone to type out the message: *Looks like I hit the wrong rose-gold girl.* Steve, standing over Bella's body, and wishing more than anything that it were her sister.

Ron: And what about the bike?
Vin: The bike?
Ron: I've been reading the police report, and it looks like the girl and the bike were thrown pretty far in the woods. Maybe farther than you'd expect from the car, as if they were trying to make sure she wasn't found.
Vin: What do you mean?
Ron: Well, I'm not saying Cecily Cole murdered her friend for views, but . . .
Vin: Hey, Coles, are you out there? Your fans would love a statement—

Rudy

RUDY PACES HIS ROOM, TRYING TO FIGURE OUT WHERE STEVE FITS in with his theories about Alex Grable. His guitar is lying by his bed, the relic of many brainstorming jam sessions. Cecily and Amber sit next to it. Rudy fingers the cassette as he walks, as if he could read its secrets by touch. He and Cecily have listened to it over and over. He has it memorized by now.

"Do you really think it was Steve?" Cecily asks.

He shakes his head. He wants to believe that it's Steve, wants so badly to feel *safe* now that he's in custody. But somehow . . . he can't. "It . . . it could be. Those high school kids were always talking about ways to sneak into the house, and Steve has been . . . weird to you . . ."

"Bella said he wasn't that bad," Cecily points out. Her voice quivers at Bella's name. "I mean, there's a big difference between hitting on someone and murder."

"But the carpet thing," Amber says from her spot on his bed.

"I don't know," Rudy mutters. It just doesn't feel right.

"You're just mad because it doesn't fit into your Frank-Glenarm's-daughter theory," Amber argues.

"Yeah," Cecily says. "You can't say that Steve . . . doesn't make sense."

Rudy frowns. "I just wish I knew how he was related to Frank—"

"Not everything has to be related to Frank—"

"Kids!" There's a call from downstairs. "Come down. We have some news."

Rudy exchanges a look with his sisters, and then they all fly out of the room.

"Is it Steve? Was he charged?" Cecily asks, breathless.

Mrs. Cole shakes her head. "No. It's . . . about the house. We got a call from a potential buyer."

Rudy can hardly believe it.

"That's amazing!" Amber says, darting forward to give their mom a quick hug. Could it really be true? Could they really be done with this house? If they can leave, they can be *free* . . .

Rudy realizes that he's still holding the tape and recorder. He sets them on the kitchen island. He hadn't been planning on telling his parents about the tapes unless he could find concrete evidence about the follower's identity—and even if he had, there's no way he can do it now. Not when they're so close to a sale. Especially when Steve has just been arrested.

Rudy notices that his mom doesn't look as happy as he'd expected her to.

"Is something wrong?" he asks. "You don't look that excited."

"They're land developers," his mom responds. "They want to . . . tear the house down. Make condos. It'll be a financial loss, and a waste of the renovation . . ." She swallows. "And I know that there are some people in town that really won't like this. But it's better than nothing. They want to meet with us on Wednesday. They'll try to lowball us, so both your father and I need to go. We don't want to leave you here, but if we can sell this house with minimal financial loss . . ."

Rudy doesn't understand what the big deal is with his parents leaving for a few hours until his dad explains that they are going to have to travel into New York City for the meeting.

"We would be gone from late morning until about midnight or so," his dad says. "We don't love the idea of leaving you in light of everything that's happened, but now that the police have someone in custody . . ." He trails off. "I spoke with Officer Perry already. She told me that she can have two squad cars stationed at the end of the driveway, just in case. But of course, we don't want to leave if you're not comfortable." His voice rises as he says the last sentence, as if he's asking them a question.

He is. Rudy exchanges looks with his sisters. Amber is the one who speaks first. "It'll be all right, Dad," she says. "You should go. Get us out of here."

Mr. Cole nods. Rudy can see the relief on his face.

"Officer Perry also mentioned that they want to talk to you again, about Steve this time," their dad continues. "We'll take you in first thing tomorrow morning, then head out after driving you back from the station."

Rudy nods. Next to him, Cecily is trembling. Rudy doesn't really want to be home alone, and he knows that his sisters don't, either. But if being home alone is the risk they have to take to escape Tremont, and if Steve really is the follower . . .

The next morning, Rudy's parents drop him and his sisters off at the station and head out to do some last-minute errands before the big meeting.

Rudy isn't sure what to expect, but this time, the police questions are different. They are totally focused on Steve. *How do you know Steve? Did you ever feel threatened by him? Did he bother your sisters?*

Rudy wants nothing more than to turn the tables on Yang and Perry, to learn what they have on Steve. To ask them the questions—but even he knows that would be a little much. While Yang interviews him, Rudy can't help but notice that when Perry is taking notes, she is pressing into the notepad hard enough that the tip of her pencil breaks not once, but twice. He's willing to bet she's not too thrilled that his mom had asked her to patrol their house while his parents are gone.

Rudy answers the officer's questions and then waits as Yang interviews Amber and Cecily. Finally, Rudy and his sisters stand outside the station, waiting for the familiar sight of the white Range Rover.

But this, Rudy realizes too late, is a mistake, because Cecily is exposed. There are a couple of loitering high school kids across the street, clearly taking photographs of her to post online. Rudy replays the backlash from his father's open house outburst over and over in his head, trying to stop himself from shouting at them.

After a few minutes, a woman exits the station and joins them by the door. She stands with her head in her hands, trembling as she lifts a water bottle to her mouth. She catches sight of the triplets—of Cecily—and Rudy's heart sinks as she instantly beelines toward them. Rudy steps in front of his sisters, but then he realizes this woman is more distraught than confrontational.

"You don't think he did it, did you?" she asks. "My boy."

Steve's mom. It's there in the slope of the eyes, the shape of her jaw. Rudy hesitates. "I—"

"He was such a nice boy—he just wanted all those kids to like him, think he was cool. That's why he pulled up your carpet—" She chokes on a sob. "He can't go to prison. He just can't. He's sixteen—"

"Steve . . . ," Rudy tries to explain. But what can he say?

She is hysterical. All of a sudden, she reminds Rudy way, way too much of his mom with her fist in her mouth, crying in the hospital as they waited for news about Cecily. "He couldn't have done all the things to that girl—he was home gaming all night; he was online, I promise—"

"I'm sorry," Amber stammers. "I don't—"

"It's that house." The woman is openly weeping now, hands trembling as she takes a cigarette out of her purse. "That house, I tell you. It's cursed. Ever since they made that little girl leave."

Rudy freezes. After so many days of unanswered phone calls and fruitless internet searches, he hadn't expected to hear anything about Reena here, of all places.

"Alex Grable?" He feels the disapproval radiate from Cecily and Amber, but Rudy can't stop himself from asking.

Steve's mom shakes her head. "No, no, the other one. The Glenarm girl. She went into the system after the Grable family died and her dad got shipped off—the whole town knew it was wrong, but what could we do? I don't know how Regina does it."

"Regina? How *who* does it?" Rudy asks. He's practically shouting.

"Before you bought it, she was the one who had to keep showing it, to keep trying to sell the place, even after all these years, to all these families that—that—" She shakes her head and rummages around in her purse, pulling out her lighter.

"Regina who?" Rudy presses.

"Armstrong. Your realtor," Steve's mom says, trying to light the cigarette. "She told me once that she didn't even want to sell it. She said she'd buy it, if she could, but she didn't have the money—" She cuts herself off and shakes her head. "She's part of that historical group, you know. The one that wants, well, that wanted you all out of the house."

Rudy freezes. Behind him, the Range Rover pulls up. Cecily tugs at his shirt. He ignores her, because this could be it. This could be *her*.

"Really?" he asks.

"You know, she was really upset when your family bought the house," Steve's mom continues. His parents shout from the car, and Rudy feels Amber's hand on his arm. "You should have heard her, after you bought it. Ran into her at the corner store, she was going on about bad history—I think she was worried for you. Sweetheart, she is."

Or a monster, Rudy thinks. "How do you know her?" he asks.

"We both have family at Upstate Medical—the assisted living place up in Tesford," she says. "We started carpooling. But I couldn't drive today, because—because—" She casts a long look back into the station and starts crying again.

"Rudy!" With a jolt, Rudy realizes that Cecily's been trying to get his attention for some time. He wants to stay, wants to keep Steve's mom talking, but he can't delay his parents. They have to make that meeting. They have to sell the house. So he lets Cecily steer him toward the car.

Rudy's mind is reeling on the ride home. Cecily and Amber are quiet, too, and Rudy is sure they must be thinking about what Steve's mom had said.

As soon as they're home, he ushers Amber and Cecily into his bedroom. "Regina."

"Reena. They so sound similar," Amber agrees. "And she's the right age. She knows her way around the house. It's possible."

"She *sold* the house to us," Cecily protests. "Why would she have sold us the house if she didn't want us to buy it? Think about it—it doesn't make sense!"

"She probably had to," Amber says. "It would be suspicious if she didn't—and remember the tour, how she was going on and on about how we should preserve the integrity of the house?"

In the silence that follows, Rudy can tell that his sisters are turning it all over in their minds just like he is. The only people who had ever talked about preserving the house—besides the follower—were Mrs. Armstrong and Mr. O'Donnell, the leader of the historical society. And if Mrs. Armstrong is a member . . .

The facts are adding up for Rudy. It makes sense in a way that Steve just . . . doesn't.

She knows her way around the house. She had been alive when the murder happened. She is the right age to have been Glenarm's daughter.

"But—how would she get in? We have the alarm system; we've locked it every night," Cecily says.

Rudy doesn't realize that he's drumming guitar fingerings on his desk until Cecily's words make him freeze. She's right. That's the one thing that none of his theories had been able to get around: the alarm system.

"Kids! We're about to head out."

His dad's voice breaks Rudy out of his reverie. He and his sisters run downstairs.

Rudy notices that his parents are dressed in their finest business attire—the same dress and coat from the soiree. Somehow, they look different in it. They stand closer to each other. Rudy knows that none of this meeting will be scripted.

"You guys look nice," Amber tells them.

"Yeah, good luck," Cecily adds. Rudy hears how nervous his sister sounds, but his parents don't seem to notice.

"We're expecting a lowball," his mom says. "So we need to put our best foot forward with the negotiations. It's in the city, so we'll be out until late, probably back around maybe eleven or twelve. Are you sure that's okay with you guys?"

"We'll be fine," Rudy answers for all three of them. This could be their last chance to sell. Last chance to try and salvage something from this nightmare.

Rudy's eyes stray to the tapes, still on the kitchen island where he'd left them yesterday. For one desperate moment he wonders if he should stop his parents from leaving. If he should tell them about Regina. But then he glances at his sisters' faces. Amber looks so hopeful. Cecily looks so nervous. They need this to be over. He can't let a stray remark about their realtor stop his parents from ending this.

"Sit tight, you guys," Mrs. Cole says. "Maybe you can—pack things out of that awful turret room, or clean out the upstairs a bit, get rid of all that junk hiding up there. With any luck, we can start preparing to move soon, and the sooner the better."

The Range Rover purrs out of the driveway.

But something sticks in Rudy's mind. *Junk hiding up there.* Junk. Hiding up there. He walks over to the cassette and turns it in his hand, fingering the delicate spools as he thinks.

And then, a line from the tape that he'd almost forgotten: *one floor, two floor, three floor, four—*

He sets the cassette down. The *clack* of plastic meeting countertop feels so far away.

"The fourth floor," he says.

"What?"

"The fourth floor," he repeats. "What if . . . what if the alarms hadn't gone off because no one was breaking in? What if they were already inside?"

"What are you saying?" Amber asks. "You mean the turret? There's no way someone could hide up there."

But it's Cecily who answers. The bandages cast her face in shadow as she whispers. "The attic. You think someone's been hiding in the attic."

For a long second, no one speaks. It's not the silence of shock, or of incomprehension. Collectively, Rudy and his sisters listen for any noise coming from upstairs, for all the creaks and groans they'd written off as just the house settling.

There is only silence.

"Steve's mom said that Regina was at the old folk's home today," Rudy whispers. "Remember?" She should be gone. The triplets should be alone, if she's away . . .

The early-afternoon sun is streaming through the windows. It is too light out, too nice for them to feel such dread as they walk up the staircase, holding their father's tools. They stand beneath the attic door, looking up at the string.

They all know that it's locked. It's been locked this entire time.

"Maybe there's no one up there," Cecily says. But as much as Rudy wants to believe her, he's convinced that he's right—he has to be. It makes too much sense; it's the only thing that slides all the other pieces of evidence into place . . .

He scans the ceiling, but Amber walks down the hallway, pausing at the dumbwaiter.

"What are you doing?" Rudy asks.

"It's something that Jada's aunt told me," Amber whispers. "That they used to play around in the dumbwaiter . . ."

And just like that it clicks into place. Rudy follows her over and opens the dumbwaiter. It's a thin shaft, for sure, but wide enough . . .

He sticks his head in and looks up. The shaft continues past the third floor. Higher. To the fourth.

"Rudy—"

Rudy ignores Cecily. He takes out his phone light and shines it overhead. And there, in the wall of the dumbwaiter, is a series of holes. One out of every few bricks lining the shaft has been removed to create a sort of make-shift ladder. He reaches upward and feels the indent in the wall, the wide pocket. His blood goes cold.

"We've found her," he whispers. "We've really found her."

Amber and Cecily poke their heads into the shaft and look up at the ladder. For a moment, they are silent.

Rudy decides he needs to be the one to go first. He hands Cecily his phone. Then he sticks his hand into the shaft, trying to ignore the darkness below, trying not to feel the cold wind echoing up from beneath him . . .

One hand on the ladder, then two. And then, for one minute, his legs are free before they catch in a groove just below the entry point for the dumbwaiter.

Rudy takes a deep breath and climbs. The holds are better than he expected them to be. He is reminded in a strange, twisted way of pool ladders carved into concrete.

He hears his sisters start their climbs below him.

And then he arrives at the dumbwaiter door to the fourth floor and pushes it open. In the graying light of a single skylight, a room begins to take shape.

Instantly, he knows that he is wrong.

He is wrong in a way that is so, so much worse than what he'd imagined. Strange shapes emerge from the darkness—shapes that are too orderly, too neat for mere piles of junk.

He turns on the light and steps into the room. Behind him, first Amber and then Cecily poke their heads into the attic and take it in.

"Someone isn't hiding here," Rudy says. "They're *living* here."

Comment on the latest Cole post:

➡ **@BraydenSpeaks:** What, you're dark now? So boring. Unsubscribed.

142 Likes   Reply

Amber

AMBER HAS NO WORDS. HER PULSE PICKS UP AS SHE LOOKS DOWN at the mess before her.

The attic opens up into a space barely high enough for her brother to fully stand up in. The floor is strewn with objects: a mixture of things stolen from the Coles—Mom's Bluetooth headset, a tube of Cecily's foundation—and what has to be *years'* worth of junk. Old toys from past days of the house, mugs, blocks, dolls, and stray pieces of ancient silverware are intermixed with candy wrappers, water bottles, paper, and pencils. There's a small mattress shoved up against the corner on a rickety iron bedframe clearly meant for a child. Amber tries to imagine Mrs. Armstrong on it, curled up in a little ball underneath a threadbare blanket that was once sky-blue.

The Reena doll sits on the end of the bed, in a place of honor. It has been painstakingly reassembled after Rudy destroyed it, pieces of porcelain glued back together with care and precision. More than anything, this is what makes Amber want to scream.

Until she sees the wall. It's covered in small pieces of paper, tacked on one by one over a mural clearly painted by the same hand that did the artwork in the turret room. Castles and horses and trees, all covered in the strange makeshift wallpaper.

Amber takes a step toward it, but her foot hits something. An old composition notebook with a name scrawled across the cover: *Evan Andrews.* The other boy who died. All the paper has been torn out.

The wall is covered in pages from Evan's journal. The handwriting is the same as the writing on the cover of the notebook, so Amber knows the pages belonged to him. But the wall is not only obscured by Evan's pages;

there are other papers, with a different handwriting, interspersed with his. Amber knows what they say before she walks forward. Her breathing accelerates as she goes through letter after letter, reading at a frantic pace:

GET OUT OF MY HOUSE.

How dare you touch my home.

How dare you, how dare you, how dare you—

Amber swallows and reads. The composition notebook's paper has another set of handwriting, not blocky but neat, that grows more and more chaotic as the days progress.

Working today. Thought I heard someone humming. Received a note, not sure if I should go to the police . . .

Notes are faster and faster now. No one believes, not even Mom . . .

Evan had been just like us, Amber thinks with a paralyzing jolt of fear. Evan had been just like them, and . . .

"She killed Evan," Amber whispers. "Alex and her mom, and then Evan. Oh my god, these notes—"

Cecily reads them, too, and Amber notices her sister start to shake. "What are we going to do—"

"We need to call the police, we need to—"

Amber's phone buzzes. It's an all-too-familiar flood of alerts from the Cole Patrol, warning them. The follower has broken their silence, posting on their last message, the one where they went dark. Rudy and Cecily stare at her. "What does it say?"

Amber takes a breath and reads:

➡ **YOU'RE GOING TO REGRET THIS**

Rudy and Cecily whip around, scanning the attic. Amber follows their gazes, half-convinced that Mrs. Armstrong is going to emerge from the shadows, slink out of the woodwork, come for them—

Another series of pings.

➡ **How dare you think that you can sell MY house.**

Ping.

➡ **YOU CAN'T TAKE THIS FROM ME. I WON'T LET YOU.**

Amber forces herself to relax. Tries to get her heartbeat to calm down. "The follower doesn't know that we're here," she says after a few breaths. "She only knows about our parents' meeting . . . But how?"

It's Cecily who figures it out. "The dumbwaiter," she says. "It carries noise, too—like how we've been listening. She hasn't just been using it to sneak around; she's been listening to us. She's heard everything, she knows—"

And then, another message. One that almost makes Amber start to hyperventilate with fear.

➡ **Drive safely.**

Comment on the latest Cole post:

➡ **@BikeMike2019:** THE COLES NEED TO BE STOPPED. #JusticeForBella #BanTheColes #ColesCanceled

336 Likes   Reply

Cecily

CECILY'S MIND HAS GONE BLANK.

"Oh my god," Amber whispers. "It's Mom and Dad—what if she hurts them—"

"We need to distract her," Rudy says. "We need to do something."

Their words fade into a mash of syllables as Cecily's mind hinges on one definite fact: She's been here. The person who did this to her face has been *here. They've been* here this entire time—as she ate, slept, wept, healed. The person who killed Bella has been here. Lives here.

Cecily looks around the room, trying to piece her thoughts together. There are so many things. So many small pieces of the person who killed her bunny and stalked her family. She can't stop herself from staring at the collection of polished rocks on a rickety end table, the small china figurines lined up just right, the meticulous collection of hospital bands . . .

Everything is arranged with a pristine sense of order. Just like her makeup collection had been.

"How can we—"

"We use the room," Cecily whispers. "If we post the room—she'll know we've found her. That we know who she is." She swallows. "If we threaten the room, she'll come."

"She's right," Rudy says. "We can call the police, make a post, lure her here instead of—" He cuts himself off. *Instead of to our parents.*

"We can livestream it," Amber suggests. "Expose her online. That has to distract her. If we call the police first, she should be close enough—right? But . . . are we sure?" Amber asks, her voice small. "I mean, she's crazy. And pretty much a serial killer . . ."

"If we don't expose her, she's going to go after Mom and Dad," Rudy says. "Look, I know this is terrifying, but what choice do we have?" He pauses, and Cecily feels him look at her. Then she feels Amber's eyes on her, too.

Cecily realizes her brother and sister are leaving it up to her.

Cecily grits her teeth. "She—she killed Bella." It's all she has to say.

Amber dials the police station and speaks frantically to Officer Perry while Cecily and Rudy leaf through Evan Andrews's journal. *I think someone is watching me. I think someone is here. Clue?*

There are other trophies up here, too—Alex's track medals, a brooch with an engraved *BG* that must have belonged to Bonnie. Photographs of what can only be Frank Glenarm and his young family.

Amber hangs up the phone. "They're sending officers over."

Rudy nods. "Ready?"

Amber holds up her cell phone, preparing the camera for their livestream. "Get in frame." Rudy joins her to stand in front of the bed, the full wreckage of the attic behind them. But Cecily—she can't move. Amber sees her hesitate.

"Come on, Cecily," Amber says, her voice forceful. "We do this together."

Almost unconsciously, Cecily raises a hand to her bandages.

"For Bella," Amber says.

Cecily steps forward, joining them in the frame.

Amber flicks the camera on. Immediately, their account is flooded with comments.

➡ You're back!

➡ Where are you?

➡ What the hell is that room?

Amber doesn't address any of the questions. "We found you," she says, her voice shaking. "We found your home. The attic. We know who you are. The police know who you are."

Rudy chimes in next. "The police are already on their way to your house."

They wait, as if Cecily is going to say something. She opens her mouth then shuts it. Comments are flying in; her eyes snap to them.

➡ **My god, Cecily!**

➡ **What happened to Cecily's FACE?**

Amber has the final word. "Leave our parents *alone*." She turns off the livestream and takes a breath. "And now we wait."

The echoes of what they've done ring around the room. Cecily can't believe it. Everything feels fake, wrong, like a fever dream. She doesn't want to see the shadow in real life. She doesn't want to know. All she wants to do is escape . . .

"Let's wait downstairs," Rudy says. Cecily agrees. The sooner they get out of this horrible nightmare of a room, the better. Rudy goes first, then Amber, followed by Cecily. They descend the terrible shaft and back into safety. But the house doesn't feel like their house anymore to Cecily. It feels like . . . it belongs to someone else.

They have barely reached the second floor when the pings come in. The Cole Patrol is alerting them to the follower's latest message. A response:

➡ Home Alone.

➡ Home Alone.

➡ Home Alone.

Comment on the Cole livestream:

➡️ **@AvaMaxxx:** THIS is how you come back? A GIRL HAS DIED. SHAMEFUL.

409 Likes   13 Replies

➡️ **@Rextangle:** It should have been them.

381 Likes   13 Replies

Rudy

RUDY SITS NEXT TO CECILY AT THE STAINED KITCHEN ISLAND AND waits, drumming his fingers across the wood and then over the plastic of the cassettes. In the background, Amber is calling their parents, over and over. After they'd gotten down from the attic, she had sprinted to the end of the driveway to see if she could spot one of the police cars that was supposed to be there, or at least patrolling the neighborhood, but she had no luck.

At first, Rudy had wanted to flee the house, but their parents had the Range Rover. Cecily was all too quick to remind him that the follower had no problems running people over.

Rudy bounces the ball of his foot on the ground as he sits with one of his free weights across his knees, ready to use it as a weapon if the need arises.

He wonders what the hell is taking the police so long to get here.

"They're not answering," Amber says, desperation tinting her voice as she redials for the millionth time.

At the kitchen island, Cecily clutches a lacrosse stick, although Rudy doesn't think she'll be able to do much damage with it. She looks terrified, and he doesn't blame her.

But they have a plan. Amber has her phone at the ready. When the follower comes, they're going to livestream Mrs. Armstrong's arrival. They're going to get a confession and stream it out for the world to see, in a last-dich effort to clear their name and Steve's, and to save their parents. After the most recent livestream, their followers are a chaotic mass, asking questions, demanding answers. They want everything from a statement on Bella's death, to an explanation of why the siblings keep exploiting the murder for internet fame, to an opportunity to see Cecily's face—

A car pulls up to the driveway.

The kids freeze. A door opens; feet step onto the porch. Then, someone knocks.

Cecily peers through the window. "It's the police," she whispers, sagging with relief. "Thank god."

She opens the door, and there's Officer Perry, panting, as if she's run here. Rudy waits for her to say something, but for a few seconds she just stands in the open door gasping for breath.

"Uh, thank you for coming," Amber says, ushering her inside. "The follower said they were coming here. That's why we called—"

"We figured out who it is," Rudy adds, trying to shake off the sense of unease that's gnawing at the pit of his stomach. "We think it's Mrs. Armstrong, our realtor, and we think that she's the daughter of someone who used to live here."

Officer Perry cocks her head at him. "Like I said before," she says. "You're quite the investigator."

Perry steps into the foyer, and Cecily locks the door behind her. Perry strides into the house, motioning for Rudy and his sisters to follow her into the kitchen. She is just turning around to speak when another car roars down the driveway.

All at once, this small woman seems fierce, dangerous. "Get behind me."

Rudy steps in front of his sisters as a second pair of footsteps echoes across the porch. Another shadow covers the frosted glass.

The doorknob turns. Sticks. Officer Perry draws her gun.

"It's locked," Cecily says. "It's locked, she can't—"

Ever so slowly, the dead bolt turns. Because they have a key.

The door swings open to reveal Joseph, his face a mask of concern. "Are you kids all right? I saw the livestream, and I saw the police car—"

He spots their terrified stance, the three of them huddling behind Officer Perry. "What's happening?" Joseph asks. He takes several short steps across the room before Perry straightens herself and levels her gun at him.

"Freeze."

"It was Mrs. Armstrong," Rudy says. Why is Officer Perry raising her gun at Joseph? "The realtor—she's been hiding in the attic—"

Officer Perry shoots him a look over her shoulder. "Stop talking."

"But we trust him," Rudy says. "It's not Joseph."

"You can't trust anyone, Rudy. We don't know for sure who is or isn't your follower yet," Perry says. "Can't trust anyone," she repeats, as if to herself. Even though Joseph is unarmed and has his arms raised, as if in surrender, Perry doesn't relax.

"Thank you for coming, Maureen," Joseph says slowly. "I'm glad you're here."

But still Perry doesn't lower her guard. Rudy feels the tension coming off of her in waves, sees the sweat on her forehead. When she speaks again, her voice is less steady. "We believe that these children may . . . may be in danger. I appreciate your concern, but you need to go . . ." She trails off.

Her eyes fall on the cassette tapes on the table, white and shining in the new light. "What are those?"

At first no one answers, so she repeats her question, only louder this time. Frantic.

"We found them in the house," Cecily whispers.

Perry shakes her head, as if she's trying to dislodge a stray thought.

"Joseph, I said—I said go. This is a dangerous situation. Do you want to end up like Alex? Falling and gone? You need to leave, now. It's . . . police business." She's breathing quicker now.

Rudy freezes. Something is very, very wrong.

"No," he says, trying to keep his voice calm. He can't let Joseph leave. "Joseph should stay. Uh, as a witness?"

Perry gives her head one rapid shake. "No."

Rudy slowly backs up toward the kitchen island as an idea begins to form in his mind. Across the room, Joseph has clearly caught on to Rudy's fear, but all his face broadcasts is confusion. Rudy takes another step backward, until he's next to the island. His eyes lock with Officer Perry's. He reaches out his hand and knocks the mixtape to the floor. It hits the ground with a *crack*.

But not before she lunges for it.

As if she knew it. As if it were something precious.

Flying and falling and gone. Just like on the tape.

The cassette hits the floor. Officer Perry freezes midlunge. Slowly, she raises her eyes from the broken tape on the floor to Rudy's face.

Then she stands.

"Mrs. Armstrong isn't coming, is she?" Rudy breathes.

Perry looks at him, and adopts a strange expression. Something almost like . . . relief. She stands up, straight, a far cry from the mousey, note-taking police officer he knew. She gives him a small smile. "It's exhausting, isn't it?" she asks. "Pretending to be someone else. Of course, you three would know a lot about that, wouldn't you?" She takes a step forward, casting wide eyes around the kitchen. "I hope you haven't made a mess. Daddy hates it when you make a mess. This is, after all, his house."

Ron: What do you think about these three exploiting that ghost story? The poor girl's death? What about her surviving family? Friends? How do you think they feel about these three millionaires coming in and profiting from it?

Vin: All I can say is that, if I were a ghost, I'd haunt them.

Amber

AMBER WATCHES THE OFFICER'S EYES SLOWLY TURN ON HER AND her siblings. Her mind tries and fails to wrap around the deception. Perry is Reena?

Reena is Perry.

"Yes," Perry says. "You'd know a lot about pretending. It's how you make a living, isn't it?" She eyes Rudy, still clutching his free weight. "Drop it," she says, gesturing her gun first at Rudy, then at Amber and Cecily. "You, too. No one is going to try anything." Rudy obeys. The free weight seems to echo as it rolls across the floor.

Amber's heart is beating fast—too fast. Next to her, Cecily sways as if she's about to topple over. Amber makes a move to help her sister, and Perry waves the gun at her, letting her know what will happen if she tries.

Perry shakes her head at them. "In thirteen years, no one has ever suspected I was here. Until you. And you. Wouldn't. Leave."

Amber tries to think of something to save them, and then she realizes— their plan. They could still pull off the original plan to livestream Reena, to expose her. Slowly, Amber reaches into her pocket for her phone.

Rudy spots her. Their eyes meet for a brief moment and understanding passes between them.

"You're Frank Glenarm's daughter," he says, drawing Perry's attention. "Reena."

"*Reena*," she corrects, stressing the *Ree*. *Of course*, Amber realizes. Maureen. Reena. It had been a nickname. But now Reena is someone else entirely. "I haven't heard someone call me by that name, well, since I changed it. Right after I aged out of the system."

"Why?" Rudy asks.

Reena raises an eyebrow and brings her gun to eye level, examining it with a detached gaze. "The daughter of Frank Glenarm would have caused ripples when she came back to town. This place had forgotten about me. I saw no need to make it remember. No need to draw attention to the fact that this house has been occupied for the last thirteen years."

Amber unlocks her phone—slowly, slowly . . .

"That was you. Singing. On the tape," Rudy says. Amber's hands are shaking. She fumbles to open Instagram. Cecily sends her a pleading look. Amber wants to tell her this is their only shot.

"You shouldn't have listened," Reena snaps. "If I had known that one of my tapes made it into that box of junk, I would have finished this a long time ago."

"You—how old are you?" Rudy asks.

"You mean how young was I?" Reena asks. "I was twelve. No one suspected a thing."

Joseph takes a few cautious steps closer. "Officer, what is . . ."

"Shut your mouth." Amber finds the harsh edge of her voice almost as terrifying as the gun she's pointing at them.

Amber meets Rudy's eyes and tries to mentally relay that he needs to keep distracting her.

Rudy nods. Message received.

"Alex Grable didn't kill her mother," Rudy says.

Amber sneaks a glance at her phone. There. Instagram. *Livestream.*

She clicks and shoves the phone into her back pocket. It's on. Someone could hear them; someone could come. Someone *needs* to come.

"No," Reena says. "She didn't, did she?" Amber watches as something in her slips, catches—just barely. Reena takes in a shallow, shaky breath. She's almost panting now, breath coming light and fast.

Reena swallows. "They called her the shooting star—but it didn't look like that when she fell. And no one knew but me. That's why it was so much fun, talking to you three. You knew *exactly* who I was. Before, I had to choose—stay unknown and safe, or let everyone know what I had done.

Online, I could have both. I could have *credit* for what I did to you. It makes me wish I'd gone online sooner."

She needs to say her name on camera, Amber realizes. If this has any chance of working . . .

"Maureen. Officer Perry, you don't have to do this. Please—"

"That's not my name," she hisses, her face contorting as she whirls to address Amber. "Perry is a *story,* a make believe—"

Behind her, Joseph looks from Reena toward Rudy's free weight, still on the floor where he'd dropped it. Amber sees Joseph start to tense as he prepares to move. She fights to keep her face straight, but she can't stop the initial flick of her eyes in his direction. He lunges for the weight, and Amber has a crazy moment where she thinks that this is going to work, that he is somehow going to save them . . .

He darts forward. He is impossibly quick.

But Perry's years on the job have made her faster.

She pivots and fires.

Amber's ears ring. Cecily is screaming but Amber barely hears it, barely hears anything but the sound of blood rushing in her ears as Joseph staggers, stumbles, falls. *Someone will have heard the gunshot,* is her first coherent thought. Then she remembers the length of the driveway, the woods surrounding the house. There is no one around to hear.

Joseph is on the ground, and Amber is beside him before she can think better of it. He's crumpled, clutching at his shoulder, where blood has started to soak through his shirt. It is so thick and dark that it almost looks unreal. Fake. As if this is all just a horrible nightmare.

Reena's face is completely blank. As if she'd done nothing.

Amber isn't aware that she's screaming until she stops, until she's raking in a breath to scream again. She tears up the hem of her shirt, trying to apply pressure, trying to stem the flow of blood. Joseph gives her hand a squeeze and mouths the words *"I'll be all right."* She doesn't know whether or not to believe him. Reena's hit his shoulder, but there's so much blood. So, so much blood. On the other side of the kitchen, Cecily is keening a strange, inhuman sound that cuts right into Amber's bones.

"He—he didn't do anything—" Amber chokes out. Reena's expression is unchanged. Amber knows that the police officer, Maureen, is gone now. There is only Reena.

Reena doesn't answer. Instead, she pivots to Rudy, catching him trying to dial 911 as panicked tears stream down his face. She levels the gun at him. "Put the phone down," Reena says. Her voice is light, lilting, rhyming, like a child playing a game. "Put the phone down before I count to three, or I will do something that you don't want to see."

Shaking, Rudy drops it. Amber is all too aware of her phone, still streaming. *Please*, she thinks. *Someone. Anyone. Please come.*

"Good boy," Reena croons. "You know how dangerous those things can be. Social media, and all that. Stranger danger. Bad people on the internet." She looks down at Joseph, bleeding out on the floor. "I have to admit, I didn't plan on you," she says. "But it was quite convenient. And quite tragic. How you were posting all those messages, how you tracked the triplets down. How you forced them to jump from the turret window. And then, how I had to shoot you when you tried to flee the crime scene."

Joseph pants from the floor. "Please."

Reena laughs. "I'm not going to kill you," she says. Her eyes flick to Joseph's wound, to the blood leaving his body. "I don't need to. After all, if I kill you, who is going to kill the Cole triplets?"

"You killed Alex," Rudy says, but he's not confronting her anymore. He's . . . panicking. He's panting, like Cecily, his eyes glassy as they dart from Joseph to Reena. "You killed her—she was taking *care* of you, and—"

"You were a child," Amber whispers, trying to reach Reena, trying to find empathy down there somewhere. But as Reena stares up at her with wide, deranged eyes, Amber realizes that there is no person to reach.

"And when I came back, they said it wasn't my home anymore. They said it was theirs. And then they said it was yours. And then *you* brought her *back* here. She is dead, and—" Rena jerks her gun at the triplets. Amber flinches, but then—

"You hurt me," Cecily whispers. Amber is shocked that her sister has spoken.

"You hurt yourselves," Reena says. Her voice twists again. "There once was a girl with beautiful lies, so I gave her a new set of beautiful eyes . . . Of course, I meant to close them both. Forever." She levels the gun at Cecily. "Mom and I used to sit in the turret and pretend that I was a princess. And then I got my evil stepmother and I knew that it was true." She cocks her head. "But unlike them, I took care of it. And I took care of him. And then you." She turns her gun on Rudy, and Amber has the awful thought that she is eyeing him as if to figure out where a shot will hurt the most.

"Please," Rudy says. "We'll leave, we'll—"

"You missed your chance to leave," Reena says. "Too late! Too bad, oh no, so sad." She looks at them with wide, alert eyes. "There is nothing innocent about this family. I know it. After all, I've been following you."

Comment on the Cole's attic livestream:

➡ **@BeachBess14:** CECILY! What's wrong with her face? What is it? SHOW US!

377 Likes   15 Replies

➡ **@ColeMurder:** I hope it's hideous.

Cecily

REENA GESTURES AT THE TRIPLETS WITH HER GUN. CECILY flinches back, and Reena sneers at her. "Why don't we go up to my bedroom, since you seem to like it so much?"

"Your bedroom?" Amber echoes. "The—the attic?"

"Where I was forced to squat?" Reena asks. "No."

Cecily is quiet. She knows where they are going.

Reena's eyes land on Joseph. "Don't worry," she says. "I'll be back for you, if you're still here. Ruining my kitchen. Rude. Making a mess. Daddy hates it when you make a mess."

Reena levels the gun at Rudy and gestures for the three of them to ascend the stairs. The staircase is covered in stock photos that Mrs. Cole had put up for the renovation—happy, laughing families. Cecily doesn't know how she's moving. It feels like someone else is in her body, walking up flight after flight of stairs, past the bedrooms on the second, then the third floor . . .

Reena pauses near the bedroom that Rudy painted. She shakes her head and locks eyes with Cecily's brother. "This is when I knew I would kill you. And you'd be dead by now, from a fatal allergic reaction, if you hadn't lied on the internet about your weakness."

Reena's voice shifts cadence as they climb, changing, becoming more . . . Reena. Up here, it is more stringy, more shaky, more unhinged. She seems . . . jumpy, as if she's looking for Alex Grable in every shadow. Her face, too, has changed—but it hasn't grown taut with anger or adrenaline or fear as Cecily would have expected it to, for what Reena is about to do. No—Reena's face has softened. She looks almost . . . childlike, in both her control of the triplets and her fear of Alex. She was so young when Alex died. Cecily tries to picture Alex, hanging out the window, looking at her mother, and the small yet powerful hands of Reena on her back . . .

As they climb the flight to the turret, Reena actually starts . . . humming. A lilting tune, the same one they'd heard on the tape. All Cecily can think of are the lyrics:

Flying and falling and gone; flying and falling and gone—

When they reach the turret, Reena's eyes are glued to the blank blue walls. "You erased her," she says. "Mom. You erased all of her."

Her voice has ratcheted up, spiked an octave. She sounds exactly like the tape.

"Father's desk, too. Entitled, entitled."

Reena forces them inside the room and stands in front of the doorway, blocking their exit. This is exactly where they were standing when they'd livestreamed, Cecily thinks. Only this time, there is no audience. Only Reena.

Next to her, Amber is pale and silent. Cecily had seen her sister; she knows that the livestream has to be recording in her pocket—but no one has come.

She is consumed by fear. The weight of Reena's gaze is paralyzing.

"Well?" Reena asks, looking to Cecily. "Did you enjoy my bedroom?"

Her eyes—they're so intense, so frighteningly *blue*. Cold like the sky in winter. Cecily tries to find her words. "It's . . . it's lovely," she stammers.

"Wrong answer," Reena snaps. "It's not for you. It's mine." She pauses. "You're afraid. Alex looked that scared, too. Before she flew."

Reena looks toward the window. "It's time for another game," she says. "Who becomes the first shooting star?"

Amber steps forward and whips her phone out of her pocket. "W-wrong," she says. To Cecily, it sounds like Amber's voice is made of fear. "You're the one with the choice. I've been livestreaming this whole time. Our followers know who you are; they've called the police. It's over. You should run while you can."

Reena reaches for her pocket and checks her own phone for notifications. She keeps the gun leveled at the triplets. And Cecily hates so, so much that she doesn't allow herself to hope, doesn't believe that Amber's idea could possibly work—because it hasn't. No one is here.

"So you have. Smarter than I gave you credit for," Reena says, but when she looks up at Amber, she's smiling. "But let's read the comments, shall we?" She gestures toward Amber's phone with her gun. "Go on. I said *read*. Read them to me."

Amber takes a shaky breath and reads.

"'This is so fake.' 'There's no way.'"

Cecily watches as her sister raises up a hand to cover her mouth. Amber's voice breaks as the last traces of hope drain from her face.

"They deserve—deserve it anyway.

No one would believe this."

A shaky breath. Their followers don't believe them. No one is coming.

"It's just a—just another stunt.

B—bad acting."

Her voice chokes then trails off. Beside her, Cecily hears Rudy's frantic intake of breath. Cecily wants to go to her sister so badly, but Reena is still standing there, gun raised on Amber.

"I'm not worried," Reena says, her voice cool. "How does it feel to be abandoned? It's funny, all those followers and no one seems to care if you live or die."

Amber doesn't answer. Cecily's head is spinning.

Reena turns to Cecily. "But first, I want everyone to know exactly what I've done."

Cecily isn't sure at first what the madwoman is talking about, until she gestures to her own eye. "They've been asking to see it. That beautiful, beautiful eye." She jerks her gun at Amber. "Film it."

Cecily feels her heart pound harder in her chest. The gun is back on her. "Do it. Do it now."

Tears are running down Amber's face as she turns her camera toward

Cecily. Cecily wants to tell her that it's all right, that it's okay, that she doesn't blame her—but Reena interprets this as hesitation.

She turns, points the gun at Rudy, and fires.

Cecily lets out an inhuman shriek; Rudy collapses to the floor, clutching his thigh. He's *bleeding*, crying as he desperately presses on his wound, trying to staunch the flow of blood. Cecily jerks toward him, but Reena waves the gun at Amber and that stops her cold.

It's okay, she tells herself. *It's just his leg. He's still alive, he's still alive.*

"I told you to do it now."

Cecily's hands go to her face. She'll do anything to keep this woman from shooting her brother again. Slowly, she unravels the bandages. She is crying as she peels the last one off.

She knows what she looks like under the bandages. Twisted, hideous scars. Her eyelid sags; warped pockets reveal the places where layer after layer of skin has been burned through to the flesh and bone beneath.

"Get all her good angles," Reena whispers. Cecily catches a glimpse of Rudy as she turns her face to the camera. Her brother is slack and white with pain and, Cecily thinks, shock. She forces her gaze back on Reena, terrified that her attention could make him a target again, terrified that Reena would shoot to kill this time. Slowly, she turns her burned face to the camera as she tucks her hair behind her ear to reveal her ruin. Her eye is still shut. She feels a sob break from her chest as she looks with one eye into the lens of Amber's iPhone.

Reena's face relaxes into a sadistic smile. She turns back to Amber. "And now, for the main event. I'm afraid that your little livestream has cost you the game, Amber. You've lost."

Cecily gasps. Everything is a blur of light and tear streaks across her vision as Amber looks out the window.

The sky is cold and blue—perfect, Cecily thinks, for a picture. She watches Amber walk to the other side of the room as if she were in a dream.

Cecily feels herself backing up. She can't do this, can't watch this.

"Your precious phone," Reena says. "Prop it up, so everyone can see." Amber moves like a robot, following the motions of Reena's gun, standing her phone up on an old wooden chair. The livestream now has a view of the far side of the turret room, the window. "Wonderful," Reena says. "Now they can all watch you die."

Cecily realizes in a strange, detached way, that she is out of frame.

Amber's face hardens, and she is shaking. Her face is white, and in one acute moment Cecily realizes that Amber is going to do it. Amber is going to die, right here, right in front of her.

Out of frame. Cecily is out of frame. And, now that she's turned to focus solely on Amber, Reena has pivoted, ever so slightly, away from Cecily. Ever so slightly, but enough.

Cecily takes a step back. Then another, shaking her head, against the impossibility that this is working, that if she could manage to escape then maybe she could get help, maybe she could do *something.* She takes another step back and then she's standing against her makeup chest.

Her hand brushes across something on the desk.

Amber steps onto the windowsill. She stands, silhouetted against the light. The summer air is languid, thick.

Cecily grits her teeth and swallows. The shadow of an idea forms in her mind. No. She can't do this. She can't do this. She can't do this . . .

She can't do this with only one eye.

Slowly, she forces her burned eye to open.

"Want to say goodbye?" Reena asks Amber. "Your followers are watching. Tell them goodbye. It's rude to leave without saying good-bye, don't you think? Just like it's rude to make messes all over some-one's home."

Cecily's world is a haze of bright, bright light and a small *zing* of pain in the back of her skull. But she can *see.*

On the windowsill, Amber hesitates, shaking, crying. Rudy looks broken and numb, hazy with pain, completely and utterly helpless as he watches his sister prepare to die.

Cecily's world is a mess of streaky light, and her hand—her hand scrabbles across her makeup desk, over the palettes, over her brushes and combs and nail kits . . .

Amber looks at the camera. Her face is a mess; her lips mouth the words but no sound comes out. Finally, she chokes it out. "G—goodbye." Her voice is barely audible. Cecily is shaking her head no even as Amber looks at her, and then at Rudy. She locks eyes with them. Her siblings will be the last things she sees.

Cecily's hands find what she has been searching for. She blinks hard and *focuses*, willing the white-light streaks of the world to snap into place.

Cecily dives.

Reena barely sees her coming before Cecily collides with her, silver shears catching the light in a bright flash. They find the officer's neck and *pierce*—pierce with a sickening sound and an even more sickening scream of anguish as Reena loses her balance and the two topple to the floor.

The gun goes off as they crash to the ground. Somewhere, she hears Amber scream, but Cecily can't see her siblings. She can only feel Reena's weight on top of her as Reena rises, with shears sticking out of her throat. Reena, smiling, teeth clotted with her own blood. She pins Cecily beneath her, and she slams her fist into Cecily's face, bringing it down again and again, breaking Cecily's nose, causing bright white lights to pop across Cecily's vision—

And then the blows stop. Cecily opens her swollen eyes and watches as Reena wrenches the shears from her own neck.

How is she not dead? Cecily wonders. All that blood pouring from her neck.

The shears are above her.

Reena points them down at Cecily, and Cecily feels her pupils dilate from the strain of following the point as Reena orients them at her one remaining eye. Her body is tense, vibrating with adrenaline, but Reena is an immovable weight on top her. The shears inch closer. Closer and closer to her good eye as Reena cackles, delighted at the prospect of blinding her—

And then there is a noise so loud that Cecily doesn't register it as noise, but as the deafness of all other things. A gunshot, right next to her.

And then there is Amber, pulling Reena's body away and clutching desperately for her sister, pulling Cecily upright toward a corner where Rudy is slumped and bleeding, a trail of blood oozing from his leg.

Positioning herself in front of Cecily, Amber turns, gun raised, to where Reena fell. Cecily half expects to see her rise and come lunging for them, but Reena is lying on her back, staring up at them with strange, unfocused eyes as her blood trickles into the hidden compartments beneath the floorboards. She presses her hand to the bullet wound in her side, but it's no use. Her other hand flinches toward her neck, but she doesn't have the strength to press the second wound. Her breath is a soft, quiet gurgle. She reaches for the dropped shears but falters. Her hand falls limply to the ground.

In the background there is the low wail of one siren, then many. Amber's phone on the ground alights with missed calls, all from Jada, Mom, Dad. Someone had seen the livestream. Someone had called the police. They will be right on time to save Rudy and Joseph. The livestream had worked. It just didn't work as expected.

Reena's eyes settle on empty space by the window and lock. The color drains from her face. At first, Cecily thinks that this is because she is dying—because she is, she so clearly is. But then Reena speaks. "Alex."

Cecily gasps. Her eyes snap to the window, but there is nothing—only the thin curtains, swaying in a light wind.

Reena lets out a whimper—from pain or fear, Cecily cannot tell. Reena locks eyes with Cecily. "Don't let her get me." It's a plea, but all Cecily has to offer Reena is a shell-shocked silence as her blood pools on the floor.

Reena's gaze slides away from the window and she darts her eyes around the room. To Cecily, it seems as though she is searching for any kind of solace. Her eyes close then flick open. They rest on the walls, one after one, each in turn. Her wet, gurgling breaths become faint hisses as she seems to seek comfort in something that isn't there. Lost in the new paint, staring at the empty places where her mother's murals used to be.

XXXXXXXXXXXXXXXXXXXXXXXXXXXXXXX

EPILOGUE

Cecily

Cecily runs her fingers over her face, feeling the bumps and ridges of the scarring. The latest round of plastic surgery was a success, but traces of the acid burn will follow her for the rest of her life. Slowly, she is coming to terms with it. She's been seeing a therapist, and bit by bit she can feel the cracked pieces of her starting to pull back together. Still, some days, loving her new face is less than easy. On those days—days like today—she likes to think of Bella. About how much she'd wanted Cecily to have this kind of courage. Cecily smooths out the folds in her peach-colored blouse and gives one final look at her flawless makeup.

Amber appears in her doorway. "You look beautiful," she says. Cecily looks up to find her sister dressed in a sleek black pantsuit.

Cecily gives her a smile. "Thanks."

Rudy joins them. Even though it's been a full nine months since the events at the Tremont house, he still walks with a slight limp. But his physical therapists are optimistic that it will improve even more with time; he's even been approved to play club sports at college in the fall. "Happy birthday to us," Rudy says. "Are you ready to show 'em?"

Their followers hadn't called the police in time to stop Reena, but they had called them in time to save Rudy and Joseph. For that, Cecily will always be grateful.

Cecily casts one last look in the mirror and nods. She will never be the same. None of them will. "Yeah," she says, and her smile is genuine. "I am."

"Excellent. There's cake downstairs, so let's get a move on. Besides, I know that Amber's antsy to see her smokin' hot girlfriend."

Amber elbows him. "Shut *up*."

"It's true . . ."

Together, Cecily and her siblings descend down the stairs and into their party.

The new house is beautiful. And the most beautiful thing about it? It's not a renovation.

The days of flipping houses are a thing of the past for the Cole family, and Cecily could not be more pleased. They're renting a smaller place in west Norton as a kind of all-seasons crash pad. It means that Amber and Jada get to see each other often, and Rudy is able to continue physical therapy with the team that helped him in the aftermath of being shot.

Jada is waiting in the foyer. "You three look great," she says, pulling Amber in for a hug and adding in a whisper, "But, of course, some of you look better than others."

Cecily laughs. Once upon a time, she would have cared, but now she doesn't. They're alive, and that's all that matters.

Reena was wrong—the livestream had saved them. At first, their followers had believed it was all being staged, but once Reena took them up to the turret—and especially after she shot Rudy—thousands of their followers had called it in.

Their parents had even seen it. They made a U-turn and promptly got arrested for reckless driving, but that didn't stop them from calling up everyone they knew, trying to get anyone, *anyone*, to their children.

People had cared about what happened to the Cole triplets.

Cecily saves a slice of birthday cake to take to Joseph tomorrow. He's still recovering from his injuries and unable to come to the party, but Cecily and her siblings visit him often. He's now more like an uncle to them.

In the wake of Reena's visit, hashtags trended all across the internet: #ColeMurder #TheColeTruth #ColePatrol. Their followers came flooding back, and their account exploded. It took Mrs. Cole a while to fully bless their decision to make the account go dark forever, but eventually she did. Even her mother, Cecily knows, is forever changed by the Tremont house.

Months passed without any social media. No makeup, no posts, no comments, no questions. But slowly, Cecily found herself missing her old routine. Missing the comfort and joy that makeup had brought to her. Eventually, she found herself getting back into it. She found herself thinking more and more about what Bella had said, about how maybe having someone like her on the internet could . . . help people.

Cecily wasn't surprised to find that Amber felt the same way about missing some aspects of social media. But not Rudy. He decided to stay dark. Instead of focusing on follower counts or engagement, Rudy said he wanted to focus on himself. Cecily knows that he's been thinking about college. Maybe sociology, maybe criminal justice, maybe journalism— he's not sure. Something to do with investigations. Real investigations, not internet drama. Cecily understands, and she supports him. Rudy had found the follower, after all. She's sure that he'll be good at it. And Cecily will always support her siblings, just like she knows they will always support her.

And so the Cole triplets' account became two separate entities:

@Amber_Cole, a #LoveEveryBody account that focuses on fashion, lifestyle, and navigating social media in a larger world.

@Cecily_Cole, a beauty account that focuses on the chemical analysis of leading makeup brands to find the best solutions for unique or sensitive skin.

Of course, the collaborations are frequent. And all the money they make from joint livestreams goes right into a scholarship: the Bella DiNatori and Alex Grable Memorial Fund for students of the local high school.

A few miles down the road is an empty lot where the Tremont house used to be. It languished for a few months in the property limbo that came with Reena's death. But on a dreary Tuesday last week, most of the town had turned out to watch as it was demolished. The historical society picketed. The local newspaper took photos.

Cecily and her family did not go.

Through a delicate balance of their renewed social media popularity and a deal with the developers, the family finances are hanging on, at least by a thread. In the wake of Reena, their fundraising pages have been flooded with enough donations to keep them afloat. Last week, Cecily caught her parents asleep together on the couch, just holding each other. The fights over money have stopped. It feels like more than enough.

In the kitchen and living room, Mr. and Mrs. Cole entertain adults and hand out business cards, back in their stride and drumming up a new business. They won't be renovating homes this time, but they will be offering their interior design know-how on a consulting basis in addition to selling customized, handmade furniture and decor. At least, until Rudy is done with physical therapy and Cecily with plastic surgery.

Which means that the Cole triplets get to have their birthday party in Norton, surrounded by hometown kids. Their friends. They aren't exactly beloved local celebrities, but the Tremont Street Follower—as news articles call Reena—had at least proven that they aren't money-hungry liars. The whole town is still grieving Bella's death, but most of the local kids have found a way to do so without hating the Cole triplets. The scholarship fund had helped. A lot.

Still, attendance at their birthday party is largely business contacts for their parents. But Jada is here, along with Miles and a few other boys that Rudy had recruited a couple weeks ago for some kind of garage band. Bella's friends are here, as well—a few former classmates who had instantly gotten into Cecily's good graces when they decided to fundraise for Bella's scholarship themselves, expanding the effort from a social media movement and into Bella's hometown. Even Alicia makes a brief appearance to hand them a small card and stammer out an apology and say that she doesn't want to stay. Cecily understands.

Now, Jada snaps a few pictures of Cecily, her sister, and brother laughing, opening presents, and eating their birthday cake. Cecily posts photos without even thinking about editing.

After the party is over, Cecily stays up with her siblings long after the last guest—Jada, of course—has gone home. They open the rest of their presents and read their cards, and each of them devours a second helping of cake.

Outside, the woods are quiet. But it's a good quiet, Cecily thinks. Full of soft, wild noises like insects and small creatures moving through the brush. No sticks crack in the night. No footsteps echo overhead.

Mrs. Cole, who had insisted on tackling all the party cleanup with their dad and no help from them, pops her head into the living room to say good night. "Your father and I are going to hit the hay. We have a long day of touring properties tomorrow." She envelops all three of them in a group hug. "Happy birthday. I love you."

They hug her back.

"Oh," she says. "I guess someone forgot to give you their present! This was on the kitchen table. Good night, sweethearts."

The gift she sets down before them is small, wrapped in the same brown wax paper that Cecily associates with butchers and cuts of meat. She picks it up. Something rattles inside. She hands it to Rudy. "You open it."

"If you insist."

It is tied with a single red ribbon. Rudy unravels it and peels away the wrapping paper to reveal an old, wooden box. Something that looks like it could have belonged in the Tremont house.

Cecily feels her heart rate uptick. She fights it. She breathes in, out, and counts to three in her mind, just as her therapist had told her. Slowly, the fear ebbs away, but she can't shake the feeling of unease. She and Amber draw close to their brother.

Cecily watches Rudy open the box and feels her sense of safety and security dissolve around her. Rudy reaches into the box and pulls out a plain white cassette tape. A mixtape and a note.

Listen closer this time.

XXXXXXXXXXXXXXXXXXXXXXXXXXXXXXXXXX

AcKNOWLEDGMENTS

This book is the result of so much hard work by so many talented people. I would like to extend my heartfelt thanks to Anne Heltzel, Jessica Gotz, Hana Anouk Nakamura, and the entire team at Abrams for all the time and effort they have put into this story.

I would also like to thank my amazing literary agent, Brenna English-Loeb, and all the people at Transatlantic Literary Agency for their help and guidance.

Writing this book would have been impossible without my support network—so to all the friends and family who have bolstered me through this project, thank you. And to anyone out there who is currently enduring the constant "Can you read this?" or "Help! I have a deadline!" from a growing writer, your support means more than you know.

And, of course, here's one for all the creators on social media who provided me with (possibly too many) excuses to take breaks from writing this book in the name of "research."